# TWENTY MYSTERIES

# A Novel of the Rosary

## Aleksandr Jackson

Cover art by Dragan Bilic – Pixel Droid Design Studio

Thank you to my sister Meg for willing to read through the manuscript and to offer suggestions for improvement. Meg, you are a trusted advisor and I can't thank you enough for your help. I must thank Paul Matenaer for his canonical insight as well. To my beautiful mother-in-law Linda: thank you for going through my writing with a fine-toothed comb.

I am indebted to Maria for her priceless spiritual direction.

Finally, thanks goes to Noelle for her support of my writing addiction, for reading through early drafts, and for being an amazing wife.

Also by Aleksandr Jackson:


*LIONS*

*For Mom and Dad*
*Thank you for the gift of faith*

# Author's Note

There is nothing new here. By that I mean there is no new theology here, nor can there be. Jesus is the fullness of revelation, and Revelation, the deposit of faith, is communicated by Scripture and Tradition, with the Magisterium being entrusted with the task of giving an authentic interpretation to the deposit of faith--whether in Scripture or in Tradition. In case there was any doubt, Paul writes in his letter to the Galatians:

*But even if we or an angel from heaven should preach [to you] a gospel other than the one that we preached to you, let that one be accursed! (Galatians 1:8)*

I have found the Rosary to be a most important spiritual guide. It is not known exactly how it came about, but its origins are closely associated with Saint Dominic, founder of the Order of Preachers (also known as – you guessed it – the Dominicans). It is said by some that he received it from the Blessed Virgin Mary herself. He used it to destroy the Albigensian heresy that had infected areas of what is known France and Italy in the 12th and 13th centuries. After some time, during which initial devotion of the Rosary died out, it received perhaps its greatest champion in the person of St. Louis de Montfort. Since then, it has come to be one of the most effective weapons of prayer upon which one can meditate.

If you have never prayed the Rosary before, this book, then, is a sort of introduction. If you have, perhaps it will renew your devotion. The Rosary is a Biblical prayer in that it is comprised of Biblical prayers (The Lord's Prayer, The Hail Mary, The Glory Be). Each mystery is intended to be meditated upon while reciting The Lord's Prayer, ten Hail Marys, and a Glory Be. The repetition of the prayers disposes one to enter more deeply into these scenes from the lives of Jesus, the Apostles, and Mary. What this book does is fill in the gaps, the spaces in the Bible that are unrecorded, to help bring the mysteries of the Rosary to life.

# The Anunciation

James walked his toddler brother to the stone and mud hut across his family's plot of land. Cleopas, their grandfather, was outside in a chair, whittling away at a small piece of wood. Seeing his two grandchildren, he brightened and begged them to sit on his lap. "My children, what are you doing today?"

James hopped on with glee while his brother babbled in frustration. "James, help John up – can't you see he is struggling?"

With a grunt and a frown, James pulled him up. "Grandfather," James began, "I am beginning to receive instruction in the *miqra*, and I have many things to ask of you."

Cleopas smiled. The older son of his daughter was such a curious boy, who sought knowledge in earnest and with an open heart. "My child, I will do my best, but I am an old man, and my memory is not what it was."

"Nonsense, grandfather. You know 'that which is read' better than anyone I know."

Cleopas nodded, for indeed he had taken an interest in the holy scriptures from an early age. "What is it that you would like to know?"

"It is about the Messiah, grandfather. Where do the scriptures say He will come from?"

Cleopas paused in thought before nodding again. "Ah, yes. Well, my child, it starts with one of the prophets. If you have the ears to hear, I will tell you." James and his brother snuggled close in anticipation.

**

The people mingled about before the Sabbath services when Micah scrambled up a rocky outcropping on the hill next to the city of Samaria. It was a gray day, and the thick clouds overhead lent a bleak tint to the scene. "O people of Israel, hear me. Indeed, open your ears to me as a mother would hear the calls of her child. Hear, o wretched people, for the Lord does not countenance the practices you are keeping on this day."

In the crowd, the wealthy landowners and the political elite shook their heads. "Why does this ignoramus from the countryside continue to plague us with his words of woe? Why cannot he preach to his own people?"

Micah continued. "Hear and understand, residents of Samaria, and indeed those of Jerusalem, too, for the Lord has promised a great chastisement for your houses and fields. Yea, those houses and fields you have taken from the poor and the oppressed among you, even your fellow Israelites." His voice boomed through the air. "Your gains are ill-gotten ones, your profits are stolen, extracted by force of coercion and unjust laws which you and the purveyors of hate in your political elite have imposed on all the people. Indeed, the Lord frowns upon your practices, he has turned his back on your ignorance, your vileness, and your slander."

The peasants in the crowd cheered at this, for they had no one to speak on their behalf. "Here is someone who speaks with the iron rod of justice," they said. "Here is one who is truly from the Lord."

Micah paced about on the crag, for he was merely warming up. "You, Samaria, are the basest prostitute, not only selling your body to the highest bidder, not only giving up your holy body for the purposes of pleasure, but for giving it to the idols of corruptions and greed. Oh, how the Lord cannot stand to behold the idolatrous practices that he sees here. How he cannot stand to behold the numerous high places you have staffed with sacrilegious images. How he cannot stand to see the worship of money. Our Lord is a jealous Lord, for he has made a covenant with his people, one he will never break, and lo, how his people have let him down!"

"What is he talking about?" the elite asked each other in loud voices, in the tone of ignorance and of annoyance.

"Yes, hear and believe me, o rich elite. You have taken the field and the plow; you have taken the house and the endowment from the widow and the orphan. You have contrived to decree laws which benefit only you; only you and the prostitutes who have placed you as leaders over all. O how the Lord weeps when He sees how the lowliest among you is treated. Lo, how your crime is doubly wretched, for even as you lead calls to look out for the poorest among you, even as you profess justice through distribution, the distribution goes entirely to yourselves! You look on the poor not with compassion but with greed, with the lustful eye of a conquering army, as a wolf salivating at the prospect of sheep, of sheep without a shepherd!"

At this, some of the more honest of the elite went to pick up rocks to throw at him, but they were blocked by the peasantry near the front of the crowd.

Micah continued. "Yea, a wolf indeed. You have built the high walls about this town and have a large standing force at the ready to protect against invasion, but you have already been invaded with your manifestly blasphemous practices, your greed worship and your self-loving."

By this time, the entirety of the crowd was agitated, half of whom supported the message and half against. Micah climbed somewhat higher. "You wretches who have despoiled the land of the Lord, you laugh now, you drink and you feast without a care for tomorrow, but I say to you: you will be in the throes of pain like that of childbirth. You shall be sent off to Babylon to grovel in the face of a foreign king, one who has stamped out Zion's treasures."

At this, the elite could hear no more, and seeing that they could not drive Micah out because of his position and because of the poor in front of them, they went off.

Micah found lower ground to be closer to the remaining. "Oh, how hard it is for the rich to hear the message of rebuke. How hard it is for the powerful to hear the truth evident on my lips. How hard it will be for them on the last day, who do not repent." He looked across the crowd. "But for you, o faithful followers of the Lord, gird yourselves! Prepare for the battle, for you know neither the time nor the place. But, indeed, as surely as the sun rose today, I heard the Lord himself make a promise to this people:

> *Arise and thresh, O daughter Zion;*
> *your horn I will make iron*
> *And your hoofs I will make bronze,*
> *that you may crush many peoples;*
> *You shall devote their spoils to the LORD,*
> *their riches to the Lord of the whole earth."* *(Micah 4:13)*

"And what is more, the Lord is to send an anointed one, a Messiah, to live and dwell among his people, to establish the house of the Lord forever!" Micah's voice echoed off the rocks and reverberated through the town.

"When?" the crowd cried. "Where?"

"The time is known only to the Lord. Or minds cannot know. But the place indeed is as humble as we are, for you, o humble people, the Lord has decreed that

> *"But you, Bethlehem-Ephrathaha*
> *least among the clans of Judah,*
> *From you shall come forth for me*
> *one who is to be ruler in Israel;*
> *Whose origin is from of old,*
> *from ancient times." (Micah 5:1)*

**

"Grandfather," James said, "but isn't Bethlehem your homeland? You mean that the Messiah will come from the place of your birth?" His excitement flowed with this news. "Please, tell us more."

Cleopas smiled. "It is getting dark, my child. There is your mother across the way. It must be time for bed. I promise you, though, we will talk more tomorrow."

\*\*

The next day, after the family had eaten and the chores were done, James brought his little brother to their grandfather again. And again, they climbed into his lap. "What is it that you would like to know this time, my child?"

"Grandfather, I am hearing more about the Messiah, but I would like to know exactly: what will the Messiah be?"

Cleopas thought for a minute. "Sit back and listen, child, for I will tell you of King Hezekiah and one of the great prophets, who lived about seven hundred years ago."

James opened his ears and let himself disappear into the story.

\*\*

Hezekiah paced about the throne room. His footsteps echoed against the stone floors of his great tent. He rubbed his hands with the anxiety of one without control. Finally, he summoned his chief of staff. "Where is the prophet?" he asked.

The man stammered. "Your majesty, this morning I have sent for the holy one as you have asked. It could be-"

"I know it could be hours before he gets here," the king interrupted. "Where else could Isaiah be but the Temple?" Time was running short. His scouts had reported an army encamped to the east of the foothills merely two days' travel away. With a wave he sent the chief of staff away. Hezekiah looked outside, to the east, trying to divine the nature and intent of the armed force positioned so close. He brooded.

After another interminable hour, an attendant showed the holy one in. Isaiah stood in a brown cloak, his face set like flint. Hezekiah rushed to greet him. "As the Lord lives, so I am happy to see you, o holy one."

"You beckoned, o King?" Isaiah looked at Hezekiah's furrowed brow and sweaty lip. "Why are you in such a state?"

"This morning I received word that an army is encamped just to the east. When I asked how large this force was, my scouts replied that it was 'without bounds.' O prophet, the Lord's kingdom has never been more threatened," the veins in Hezekiah's neck stood out as he spoke with a shaken countenance.

"I don't suppose your allies the Egyptians are here, ready to help, are they?" Isaiah asked.

Hezekiah frowned at the question. Sometime earlier, Hezekiah, seeing the growing strength of the Assyrians, made a compact with the Egyptians, something Isaiah urged against. 'The Lord will be our protection, not foreigners and their strange gods,' Isaiah had admonished. Nevertheless, the agreement was made.

"I have not heard from them," Hezekiah said.

Isaiah nodded in a silent rebuke. To Hezekiah the message was clear: who could you trust other than the Lord?

His chief of staff appeared again. "Your majesty, the captain of the watch is here."

Hezekiah brooded again. "Please send him in."

A young soldier came forward. "Speak," Hezekiah said.

"Your majesty, this morning a *rabshakeh* approached the eastern wall with a small guard force. Some of your ministers went out to greet the Assyrian prince."

"And what did the prince say?"

The soldier gulped. "He threatened assault unless the King pays ransom to Sennacherib."

Upon hearing the name of the Assyrian king Hezekiah pounded one fist into the other. 'May the Lord smite him forever,' Hezekiah cursed silently. He turned back to the soldier. "Wait outside for my response."

After the soldier left, Isaiah spoke. "What do you ask of me?"

Hezekiah looked at him with desperation. "Why, your intercession before the Lord."

Isaiah studied the king's face for a minute before answering. "Then you must come with me."

"I will go anywhere to preserve my kingdom."

Isaiah led him up the mountain and directed him to sit to one side. Then Isaiah knelt on a rocky outcropping and closed his eyes. Hezekiah watched his lips move for a while before stopping. It appeared as though Isaiah was watching something, for he was in such a state Hezekiah doubted anything could disturb him. Suddenly, a great black cloud covered the mountaintop and Hezekiah heard whistling noises produced by strong winds funneling themselves through and around the rocky surface of the mountain. Then, just as quickly as it came, the black cloud dissipated and the sky became clear again.

Isaiah pointed down the mountain. "Go, and I will send a message."

8

Hezekiah went, for he knew not the question the holy one. After a time waiting in anxiety, he looked up at the appearance of another visitor.

*Then Isaiah, son of Amoz, sent this message to Hezekiah: "Thus says the LORD, the God of Israel, to whom you have prayed concerning Sennacherib, king of Assyria: I have listened!*

*This is the word the LORD has spoken concerning him:*

*She despises you, laughs you to scorn,*

*the virgin daughter Zion;*

*Behind you she wags her head,*

*daughter Jerusalem.*

*Whom have you insulted and blasphemed,*

*at whom have you raised your voice*

*And lifted up your eyes on high?*

*At the Holy One of Israel!" (Isaiah 37:21-23)*

Hezekiah stared into the distance as he listened to the words. The messenger said, "The holy one will return to you tomorrow."

Hezekiah struggled to trust in the Lord. He considered planning a preemptive strike, but decided to wait until the morning. He went to bed that night with a heart of unease.

In the morning, his chief of staff awoke him. Hezekiah looked up to see a twinkle-eyed excitement in his advisor. "What is it?" he asked.

"Your majesty," his chief of staff was out of breath, "I have just come from the city walls. A company of scouts went out from there at dusk to report to me on the position of Sennacherib's army."

"Yes? What did they see?" Hezekiah was fully awake now.

"My king, they saw no movement from the camp, so they decided to take a closer look. Upon closer inspection, they found the entirety of the force dead on the ground."

Hezekiah looked and tried to absorb the news.

"My king, it appears as though they were all struck by a plague. Bodies were lying about everywhere. According to their rough estimate, there were about 185,000 men."

Hezekiah sat up wild-eyed and scratched his head. After a time, he said, "The Lord has mercy on us."

"Indeed, my king."

After the chief of staff went, the prophet Isaiah returned. Hezekiah rushed to greet him. "Have you heard the news of the demise of Sennacherib's army?"

"No, I have not heard, but I am not surprised, either. The Lord himself told me what I told you." The words sunk into Hezekiah, knowing his trust in the Lord shall always be absolute. The prophet continued. "That is not all the Lord said. For there will be many more times to come where our people will be threatened by the forces of darkness. Sennacherib has gone away, but others will take his place. Today the Lord delivered our people from defeat for a time, but He made another promise I have the honor of sharing:

*'Say to the fearful of heart:*

*Be strong, do not fear!*

*Here is your God,*

*he comes with vindication;*

*With divine recompense*

*he comes to save you.*

*Then the eyes of the blind shall see,*

*and the ears of the deaf be opened;*

*Then the lame shall leap like a stag,*

*and the mute tongue sing for joy.*

*For waters will burst forth in the wilderness,*

*and streams in the Arabah.'"*

*(Isaiah 35:4-6)*

Hezekiah was puzzled by the words. Isaiah spoke again. "I can see that your majesty is trying to understand. The Lord has said that one day, he will send one of his own to live among us, for he will not only deliver us from military defeat, but something more sinister, something more threatening to our survival.

"Whom will he send?"

"A healer, and a savior."

**

James looked up. "So it is true, grandfather, that the Messiah will be a healer?"

"And much more than that, my child. He will be a savior, for our people have continually sinned against the Lord, and only one such as he will be able to reconcile us to Him again."

11

James nodded with the weighty insight from his grandfather. He bid him goodnight, and they went off to bed.

**

The next day, Cleopas asked his grandson what he had learned. "Grandfather, we heard more about the prophet Daniel."

"Oh?"

"Yes. Will you please tell me more about the Messiah? Did Daniel speak of him?"

"Oh yes, my child. Even so far from Israel, even as he lived almost six hundred years ago, Daniel spoke of the Messiah. Sit back and listen, for I will tell you."

**

Daniel strolled through the hanging gardens of the Babylonian capital of Nineveh with Mishael. Daniel glanced up at the numerous palm and date trees overhead, planted atop cube-like foundations of varying heights. Such foundations covered the gentle hillside east of the great river, so much so that one could mistake the entire planting for a green-covered mountain from a distance.

"I cannot fathom the amount of effort that went into the construction of this place," Mishael said. "To think that something would last until now, perhaps even one hundred fifty or even two hundred years later. Even though we walk through here every week, I still come to a new comprehension of it every time we pass through."

Daniel grunted in acknowledgement.

"What is it that you are thinking?" Mishael asked.

12

"It is true, this place is beautiful in its own way. I understand why it was said that Sennacherib built this place for his wife, because she so missed the green hillsides of her homeland. However, I can't help but think of our own homeland, and the rolling hills of Jerusalem and the surrounding country of Judah," Daniel said.

Mishael looked down in remembrance. "Ever since that day thirty years ago, when Nebuchadnezzar laid waste to the holy city of God and plundered the Temple, I have thought about returning to our homeland."

The two walked up the wide stairs leading to the very tops of the city walls, about fifty cubits in height. They passed a captain of the guards, who saluted them. For the two Hebrews were made governors by Nebuchadnezzar owing to their wisdom and powers of discernment beyond all others in Babylon. Their subsequent time in the furnace without harm meant that they were untouchable. By this time they walked along the top of the city walls, which at this height were still wide enough for two four-horse chariots to pass each other. The great river below threw off twinkling flashes of light from the burning midday sun overhead.

Daniel beheld the sight of the great plains on the other side of the river. "I know, Mishael. I, too, wonder about that day when we return home. When our people disobeyed the Lord, He allowed the Babylonians to strike at our heart and take our people from the land. But even from that woeful day, look at the great good the Lord has brought out of it: he saved me from the lions' den, so that Darius our king had those governors who opposed me thrown in along with their families to be crushed and devoured, and, from that, decreed that our Lord be honored above all." They came to another stairway and took it, descending beneath a verdant canopy of palms. "Yes, I do dream of home. But I have understood from the Lord that His kingdom shall not truly arrive until an anointed one comes."

Mishael looked at him. "What are you saying, my brother?"

"I am saying that, even though we should return to Jerusalem one day, we won't truly live in the Lord's kingdom until he brings it about, through the sending of one who is to be very special indeed."

"Daniel, what is this new insight? I have not heard such a thing before." Mishael's eyes were wide in wonderment.

"The Lord has revealed to me that His kingdom will not come until seventy weeks of years pass by, and even more so, for this time of exile shall end, but a new persecution shall come. After that persecution, a holy of holy one shall be anointed, bringing about the expiation of Israel's sins and everlasting justice introduced."

Mishael stared at him. "And how was it that you came to know this vision?"

"An angel, calling himself Gabriel, told me."

"So this means that the time of the fulfillment is near?"

"This means that the Lord will send us someone very special."

"One who is very special?"

14

"Yes, Mishael, the Messiah," Daniel said. "One who will fulfill all prophecies and visions. We won't live to see the day, but it is going to happen before this millenium passes."

Mishael nodded. "I only hope that this anointed one can recognize our people by then."

Daniel said, "Rather, I hope that our people will recognize him."

\*\*

James looked up with the furrowed brows of a questioning youngster. "Grandfather, why would the people not recognize the Messiah? How could they possibly not know him when he does appear?"

Cleopas nodded. "It seems impossible, right, that someone could fail to recognize the Messiah? After all that has been prophesied about him? The thing about the Lord, and the people he sends us, is that we have to see not just with our eyes, but our hearts as well."

"What do you mean by that, Grandfather?"

Cleopas paused. Such a difficult thing to explain. "It means, my dear child, that there is a greater reality around us than that which we can simply see and touch, hear, smell and feel." Seeing James trying to process that though, Cleopas continued. "The holy scriptures do give us some specific clues about how the Messiah will appear."

"Please tell me, Grandfather."

"Just one more story for today; it is getting late out." Cleopas looked up and breathed in deeply. "I will tell you about a time around the ceremony for the refoundation of the Temple. It was about five hundred years ago."

**

Students of the rabbi Ishmael surrounded him at the stone blockhouse that served as their school. They sat while he paced about in front of them.

"So, my students, what was it that we just witnessed?" he looked across at the group of teenaged boys.

One spoke up. "Why, the refoundation ceremony for the Temple, teacher."

"Yes, it's true that we gathered today for the beginning of the project to restore the Temple. But something greater is going on. Who can tell me?"

The students looked at each other. They had known by now that there were no obvious answers to the teacher's questions.

Another student ventured a guess. "It marks the end of the exile of our people."

The rabbi nodded. "It is true that the exile of our people is over, after seventy years in the land of Babylon." He stopped and looked at them. "But I'm looking for something else. Who can tell me what it is?" Seeing puzzlement all over the faces of his students, he continued. "What we saw today was the beginning of the restoration not only of the Temple, but the beginning of the restoration of our nation, indeed, of the kingdom of God."

The students looked at each other and smiled. The rabbi was so wise. One of the students raised his hand. "But rabbi, when will the restoration of the kingdom be completed?"

16

The rabbi smiled. "That is a good question. We will begin on that point tomorrow." With that, he dismissed them.

When they had all left, Ishmael needed answers to questions of his own. He went up the mountain outside of the city, for one with the gift of clarity of vision dwelled there. Ishmael clambered up a rocky ledge and found him gathering scraps of dead wood.

The man looked up. "Rabbi Ishmael, welcome."

Ishmael had the feeling that he was being expected. "Greetings, prophet Zechariah."

"You are here with a question."

Ishmael sat down. "Indeed I am, prophet. I am wondering if I should even tell you, for in all likelihood you know what I am going to ask."

Zechariah smiled, a sublime grin that could only come about with the total union of self to God. "I still want you to ask it, so you can know yourself what the question should be."

"How will we know when the restoration of the kingdom is complete?"

Zechariah arranged his wood into a pile and used a bow drill to ignite the tinder underneath. The fire caught immediately. Zechariah sat in front of it and looked deep into the fire, where flame met wood. Ishmael watched as Zechariah gazed into the spot for what seemed like ten minutes. By now, darkness surrounded them, except for the red aura of the fire. Zechariah still had his eyes open and let out a guttural sound, as if attempting to empty his lungs of all air. He repeated this a number of times before falling silent and rocking back and forth. Ishmael nodded off until Zechariah shook him awake.

"How long have I been asleep?"

Zechariah shrugged. "Perhaps an hour."

Ishmael tried to clear his head. "What was it that you were doing?"

"It is a way to totally eliminate all barriers between the Lord and yourself. I must do it so as to receive the visions."

Ishmael straightened. "Oh? And what did you see?"

*"An oracle: the word of the LORD is against the*
*land of Hadrach,*
*and Damascus is its destination,*
*For the cities of Aram are the LORD's,*
*as are all the tribes of Israel.*

*Hamath also on its border,*
*Tyre too, and Sidon, no matter how clever they be.*

*Tyre built itself a stronghold,*
*and heaped up silver like dust,*
*and gold like the mud of the streets.*

*But now the Lord will dispossess it,*
*and cast its wealth into the sea,*
*and it will be devoured by fire.*

*Ashkelon will see it and be afraid;*
*Gaza too will be in great anguish;*

*Ekron also, for its hope will wither.*
*The king will disappear from Gaza,*
*Ashkelon will not be inhabited,*

*and the illegitimate will rule in Ashdod.*
*I will destroy the pride of the Philistines*

*and take from their mouths their bloody prey,*
*their disgusting meat from between their teeth.*
*They will become merely a remnant for our God,*
*and will be like a clan in Judah;*
*Ekron will be like the Jebusites.*

*I will encamp at my house,*
*a garrison against invaders;*
*No oppressor will overrun them again,*
*for now I have seen their affliction. (Zechariah 9:1-*
*8)*

Ishmael persisted. "But how will we know who the king is?"
"Not just the king, but the Messiah."
"Yes, indeed. But how are we to recognize him?"
*"Exult greatly, O daughter Zion!*
*Shout for joy, O daughter Jerusalem!*
*Behold: your king is coming to you,*
*a just savior is he,*
*Humble, and riding on a donkey,*
*on a colt, the foal of a donkey." (Zechariah 9:9)*

"But who will that be? Zechariah?" But the mind of the prophet was off in the distance, his eyes focused on a point out in the future. Ishmael knew by this point further communication was impossible, so he looked into the fire, shaking his head. A foal of a donkey.

**

"A donkey, Grandfather?" James looked up. "But it is such a humble animal."

Cleopas smiled, "Maybe the Lord is trying to tell us something with that."

James looked into the distance, pondering this new information.

"Come, let us get you to bed, for your brother is already asleep."

**

The next day, James and his brother were again in their Grandfather's lap.

"Grandfather, yesterday you told us that the Messiah would come on a donkey. But how could someone so regal make an entrance on something so base, so lowly?"

"My child, you ask many good questions. I will do my best, for I am advancing in years." After a long pause, he said, "You see, my child, the Lord is telling us that the true measure of royalty is how humble, how close to the people a true King is."

James slowly nodded, but Cleopas could see that it was hard to grasp. "Let me tell you one more story. It features the prophet Isaiah again, in the land of Judah during the Syro-Ephraimite war."

James and John snuggled close and listened.

**

A soldier entered into the court of Ahaz, son of Jotham and King of Judah. "Your majesty, I come bearing a message."

Ahaz nodded. "Let us hear it."

"Your majesty, two great armies have been spotted north of the Salt Sea, on the other side of the river."

Ahaz dropped his wine cup and stood up. "What? What armies?"

The soldier gulped before continued. "Your majesty, they appear to be the Aramites and the Israelites."

The blood drained from the king's face. He dismissed the soldier with a wave and sat again, reeling from the news.

Nehumud, his chief advisor, approached. "Your majesty?"

Ahaz wiped his brow. "Surely they are the armies of Aram and Israel. For Rezin and Pekah have surely taken offence at my refusal to join their anti-Assyrian alliance."

Another court official burst into the room. "May your majesty please excuse the interruption, but it appears that the entire populace has heard about the threat from the north, and they are spiraling out of control. They are afraid for their lives."

Ahaz nodded. This was the gravest threat to his kingdom in his three years on the throne. He needed to hear no less than the word of the Lord. "Please leave me now, for I must think." He went out to walk alone, as was his custom.

As he walked, he encountered the one called Isaiah. Ahaz stopped and took him by the shoulders.

"My people are in a great panic, and surely our very kingdom is at stake here," Ahaz said. "Please, I beg of you, what does the Lord say to us?"

Isaiah nodded as only one with the certainty of eternity could do. "The Lord has already spoken to me, telling me to meet King Ahaz on the way

*and say to him: "Take care you remain calm and do not fear; do not let your courage fail before these two stumps of smoldering brands, the blazing anger of Rezin and the Arameans and of the son of Remaliah, because Aram, with Ephraim and the son of Remaliah, has planned evil against you. They say, "Let us go up against Judah, tear it apart, make it our own by force, and appoint the son of Tabeel king there.*

*Thus says the Lord GOD:*

*It shall not stand, it shall not be!*

*The head of Aram is Damascus,*

*and the head of Damascus is Rezin;*

*The head of Ephraim is Samaria,*

*and the head of Samaria is the son of Remaliah.*

*Within sixty-five years,*

*Ephraim shall be crushed, no longer a nation.*

*Unless your faith is firm, you shall not be firm!*

*Again the LORD spoke to Ahaz: Ask for a sign from the LORD, your God; let it be deep as Sheol, or high as the sky! But Ahaz answered, "I will not ask! I will not tempt the LORD!" Then he said: Listen, house of*

*David! Is it not enough that you weary human be-ings? Must you also weary my God? Therefore the Lord himself will give you a sign; the young woman, pregnant and about to bear a son, shall name him Emmanuel." (Isaiah 7:4-14)*

Ahaz stepped back and stared into the distance. "Who are you, o holy woman of God?"

**

James looked up. "So the Messiah will have a mother? He will be a man just like us?"

Cleopas nodded. "Think about that for a moment, my child. That the Lord, the creator of the heavens and the earth, will send us his own son, and will send him as a lowly person like us. And just like any person, the Messiah will begin life in the smallest form, in the womb of a woman."

"Wow." James sat there with mouth agape. "The woman sure-ly will be of a most blessed character and appearance."

Cleopas nodded. "Surely, my child. She would be without sin. She would be a Queen."

**

Some miles away, a girl sat weaving just a stone's throw from the Sea of Galilee, working the thread with a practiced ease. She took utmost care with her every chore, for grace imbued the to-tality of her being. She hummed and sang little dirges while she worked, audible signs of the radiance of joy that emanated from her, signs of the deep well of serenity and peace that lay in her heart.

She continued weaving, intently focused on the job at hand, pulling reeds through here and there. It was to be a bread basket, a memorial to her mother. Oh, how she loved her parents. How she missed them. They had lovingly raised her, and had done all they could for her. They had both died more than six years ago. As Mary advanced, she found herself doing more to honor their memory. She knew that in honoring her mother and father, she honored the Lord.

Her thoughts turned to the Lord as she finished another row. How she yearned for the Messiah. Their family was well-versed with the Lord's covenant, how the Lord had freed her people from Egypt almost thirteen hundred years ago and remained faithful ever since. Mary was determined to remain faithful to the Lord, even though her people had strayed from time to time. Her desire for this manifested itself at an early age.

Her mother told her how at the age of three, when her parents made good on their wish to consecrate Mary to the Lord, she was led to the Temple, where she ran to the High Priest Zacharias and sang and danced in pure joy. Then as well as now, her one desire was to be the handmaid of the mother of God.

'What would she be like?' she wondered. 'What was her name? What did she look like? Surely more beautiful than any other woman,' Mary decided. 'What did she do? Could she weave? Could she spin wool? Could she form pottery? Yes,' Mary thought, she did all these things, and surely did them well.

Mary weaved another row, working the reeds through one another, twisting, bending, folding. Her focus remained on the basket, and as she hummed, it took shape. She continued until the base was finished, then started on the handle. Four reeds or five for the handle? Five, yes, for it will be a strong basket.

She continued, focused intently on her task, until she became aware of a change in the air around her. She frowned. It was not yet midday, but it felt twice as hot as that. And yet, there was a seeping coolness around her that almost bathed her in a fine mist. She put the basket down. Radiance in the form of gold specks started to shine through the diffuse light in the small courtyard. They were falling around her, yet suspended in a way, too, so that they never hit the ground. Mary started to shudder. What was going on? She turned around. A figure of a tall man stood there. Mary shrieked and fell to the ground, but she kept her eyes on him. The man was perhaps five cubits in height, almost twice as tall as Mary. His robe was of a cloth Mary had not seen anywhere else.

"Hail, full of grace. The Lord is with thee," the sound of his voice made the gold flecks swirl around him and carried with it the full weight of authority, Mary instinctively knew, the authority of the Lord. She scuttled back, clawing at the dirt and hay on the ground. What in the name of all that was holy was going on?

*Then the angel said to her, "Do not be afraid, Mary, for you have found favor with God. Behold, you will conceive in your womb and bear a son, and you shall name him Jesus. He will be great and will be called Son of the Most High, and the Lord God will give him the throne of David his father, and he will rule over the house of Jacob forever, and of his kingdom there will be no end."*

*But Mary said to the angel, "How can this be,
since I have no relations with a man?" And the angel
said to her in reply, "The holy Spirit will come upon
you, and the power of the Most High will overshadow
you. Therefore the child to be born will be called holy, the Son of God. And behold, Elizabeth, your relative, has also conceived a son in her old age, and this
is the sixth month for her who was called barren; for
nothing will be impossible for God." Mary said, "Behold, I am the handmaid of the Lord. May it be done
to me according to your word." Then the angel de-
parted from her. (Luke 1: 30-38)*

The gold flecks in the air slowly fell to the ground around her
and disappeared into the dirt. She exhaled, as if she had been
holding her breath the whole time. She had yearned to be the
handmaiden of the mother of the Lord. What the angel said...she
stopped herself. "An angel," she breathed the words. An angel
from heaven. "An angel had come here, to earth, to this muddy
patch of ground, to deliver a message, to me," Mary talked to
herself, as if waking from a dream. "But it was no dream," she
said. No, not a dream, but a promise. Not just a promise, but a
promise kept. The realization started to sink in. 'The Lord said
he would come again, and now He is inside me,' she thought.
She put her hands on her tummy.

# The Visitation

Mary sat on the ground and stared ahead at some point on the horizon. The angel's words to her kept reverberating in her head, so much so that her legs became numb from sitting so long.

Mary looked at the completed breadbasket in her arms, the one she had just crafted in her mother's memory. She originally planned to give it to the high priest for service in the Temple, but since the angel told her that Elizabeth was pregnant, Mary thought she could use it more than the Temple authorities. Besides, she smiled, Zechariah, one of the priests, was Elizabeth's husband. She was sure he would understand.

Oh, how she desired to be at Elizabeth's side! She was six months along now, which was a difficult enough condition to be to begin with, but Elizabeth was much older and would need help. Mary wished she could be there right now, but she lived so far away. Mary would need to cover the distance between them.

Where to begin? Mary looked at her feet. They were dirty and bare, as usual. She did have simple sandals made of a few pieces of leather sewn together; she would have to get those from her hut. What else to bring? The basket of course. What to put in it? Her mortar for grain grinding; her needles and thread, perhaps. She put these in and tied it together in the basket with a large shawl. She set off to find Joseph.

**

Nahara shifted uncomfortably on the ground. Her thin mat was no match for the rocky ground underneath her. She stared

27

up at the night sky. Not that the gravelly surface was the main culprit for her sleeplessness anyways. She had tried to close her eyes, but she could only think of the journey ahead. She and her uncle were on their way to Jerusalem where Nahara was to be given away in marriage. She did not know the groom. Questions, as countless as the stars overhead, hovered in the air. What would the man be like? Was he much older than she? Did he have all his teeth? Would he beat her? She shuddered as she thought of her cousin Marta, betrothed to a known drunkard 15 years her senior. It was only a little solace to think of her, for Nahara could not imagine it to be any worse than Marta would have it. Nahara turned over for what seemed like the thousandth time. Surely her parents would not have chosen someone so awful for their only daughter? Perhaps they would look for someone like her three older brothers. They were honorable men with fine wives, beautiful, gracious wives, who were diligent in their tasks and took care of their households. Nahara wanted to be like that, but only for the right man.

The right man. Thoughts of Achan filled her head and made her shut her eyes against the night sky. How she wished she had never even talked with him. His specter lurked everywhere, a constant reminder of what happens when one acts against the natural order of things. The night continued like that, constantly turning over, fighting the cold, rocky ground underneath and the memory of sins until the blessed sun rose in the east. Oh, how she welcomed the sun.

\*\*

Nahara tied the last of her things onto the donkey's back and waited for her uncle to return from the market. He was running low on food, he said, and would return soon. She tied the donkey to a small fig tree near the trail and found a boulder to sit on. Today they would be going as far as Sychor, if all went well. She stared ahead to the south, at the small hills covered with sagebrush, small cedar trees and rocks. 'Everything was rocky,' she thought. She was lucky to have the donkey; her parents insisted on it. At least she could thank them for that. Having to walk another five days over the broken ground in her bare feet would only intensify the discomfort of leaving home and all that she knew. She looked around. Where was her uncle? A hunger pang twitched inside of her. She put her hands on her stomach. She seemed to be eating more than usual. 'You've been traveling for five days already,' she had to remind herself. Finally her uncle appeared from around the bend. It was time to go.

**

The rhythmic pace of the donkey and the hot afternoon sun lulled Nahara into a drowsy state. Aside from the other people in the caravan, there was nothing around. The monotony of the trail, the broken ground and the dry heat of the day pulled her eyelids shut. Nahara felt herself tipping over and she let out a shriek. She landed with a thud on the dirt of the trail, with some of her travel bags strewn about. She must have fallen asleep. Her uncle had been a stone's throw ahead and turned around to help her up. Before he got there, Nahara heard a voice as sweet as the date orchard by her parents' house. "Are you alright?" Nahara sat up and rubbed at her eyes. She turned to look at another girl about her age. She was wearing a blue mantle over a white garment and looked at Nahara with such serenity. Nahara just sat there transfixed by the girl's beauty for a moment before finding her voice. "Yes, thank you. I'm okay; I just fell asleep."

The girl helped Nahara up and gathered her things from the ground. "You must be tired," the girl said. Nahara paused. It was like the girl already knew everything about her. Her uncle reached her. "Nahara, were you fooling around again? You must not be so careless. Your parents would be most upset if the groom refuses to marry someone with a broken arm or some such thing." He took her hands and shook them up and down, as if to check for any malfunctions. "You seem fine, though, thank the Holy One. Let's get you back up." He smacked the mule on its hindquarters and jerked the reins around, admonishing it with a curse. Nahara got back on and they continued. She looked around for the beautiful girl, but she no longer saw her amongst the long line of the caravan. Where had she gone?

**

The next night Nahara found the girl by a campfire. She had spied her warming her feet, with her donkey tied to a tree a few yards away. A man was asleep nearby. Nahara took a few halting steps toward the girl. The sounds of pebbles underfoot led the girl to look up and she gave a warm smile to Nahara. She motioned for her to sit down. "Please, sit here next to me. Are you cold?" she asked.

"I am, thank you," Nahara said. She pulled her mantle up about her and sat down on her rolled-up mat. She looked at the girl. "Thank you for helping me pick up my things yesterday."

"Oh, you are welcome." The words came out with such tenderness; to Nahara they were as warm as the fire.

"What is your name?" Nahara asked.

"Miriam. And you are Nahara?"

"How did you know?"

"I heard the man you were traveling with call you by that name when you fell off your donkey."

"Oh yes. That is my uncle," she gestured to a spot next to a bend in the path where he was asleep on the ground. Nahara looked at the fire, enjoying the warmth and the presence of another girl. "Where are you going?"

"To my cousin's house. She is with child, and I am going to help her." At the mention of a child, Nahara looked away, into the distance. Mary looked at Nahara. "And you?"

Nahara took a deep breath. "I am not sure. Somewhere near Jerusalem."

Mary was now fully turned toward Nahara and looked at her with a penetrating focus. Nahara felt like she could tell her anything. "My uncle is taking me to the man I will marry, but I don't know his name or anything about him."

"Oh," Mary smiled. She leaned forward. "Are you afraid?" she whispered.

Nahara noticed the firelight twinkle in her eyes. "Yes."

Mary took her hand. Nahara was grateful that she didn't ask why. She wasn't ready to tell anyone yet what she held locked away in the deepest recesses of her being. She just looked into the fire for a time, watching red embers take shape on the small logs before turning white and eventually falling off as ash onto the ground. The flames licked the edges of the wood and climbed into the air before dissipating into the blackness. After a while, in the silence, she got tired and curled up on her mat.

\*\*

"Nahara! Nahara! Wake up!" Nahara opened her eyes and sat up with a start. The morning light was just over the next hill. Her uncle was standing over her and shaking his finger. "I have been looking for you for five minutes; I had no idea where you were. What would my brother have said had I lost you?"

"I was just over here by the fire."

Her uncle waved her off and went to get the donkey. She looked around. The girl Miriam and the man she was with were nowhere to be seen. A pit of disappointment formed inside and sank to the bottom of her stomach. Oh, how she had wanted to talk to her. To talk to anyone, really, but especially her. She got up and dusted herself off before rolling up her mat. She needed to see her again. She needed a way out. She needed money.

\*\*

As Mary and Joseph made their way south, the caravan had stretched itself to just a very few travelers. People had split off in different directions as they left the last main village and they found themselves in a rocky wilderness. Joseph was walking ahead of Mary and the donkey she was riding on, scouting the best way ahead and periodically consulting a map he had bought from a Roman merchant. Mary thought back to the girl Nahara. She was clearly uncomfortable about something, so uncomfortable she hadn't been ready to talk about it yet. She hoped to see her again.

After a few more hours of progress along the trail, they came upon two men walking toward them. Rather, one was walking and was supporting the other, who was limping. As they neared each other, they could see that the men's clothing was dirty and ripped, and that the limping one was bleeding from his head and his hands. Joseph stopped in front of them. "Are you all right? Can we give you some assistance?"

The men stopped so the bleeding one could sit down for a moment. The other one, who was taller, spoke up. "Thank you, we'll be okay." He was a little out of breath. "We had a run-in with some Bedouin thieves and my brother here got banged up."

Mary felt sorrow for them and got off her donkey. She grabbed some reams of cloth from her bag and went down a nearby gully to soak them in the tiny stream at the bottom. Joseph gave the bleeding man some bread from his pack. "What happened?"

The taller one continued. "We rounded the bend up there," he turned back to motion to a spot three hundred cubits in the distance, "when three brigands jumped out of the bushes and demanded our money belts. My brother thought it would be a good idea to fight and was struck by the hilt of the leader's sword." He shook his head. "You never know what you'll see on the trail."

Mary returned from the stream and washed the man's wounds. His brother watched as the injuries healed instantly. Mary looked in awe first at the man's clean skin and then at her own hand, as if it belonged to someone else. She thought again about the angel's message to her. The memory of it sent waves of warmth through her body and right out through her fingertips. The men looked dumbstruck at each other, then at Mary. "My lady, you are a true healer," the formerly injured one said. They both bowed down to her. "We are indebted to you."

Mary backed away and put the cloth back into her pack. "It is not me. All healing is from the Lord." She just wanted to shrink and be on her way.

The taller man spoke. "Yes, it is true my lady, all healing is from the Lord. Even so, we are indebted to you."

"You owe me nothing." Mary smiled. "Just go and be a healer unto others." She and Joseph prepared to set off again.

The man put his hand on his heart. "Fare thee well, my lady."

Mary looked at them as she rode by. "May God bless you."

The brothers watched as they rode off. "He already has."

**

Joseph walked ahead, deep in thought. He tried to process what he just saw. Bleeding wounds became clean, as if nothing had happened. Indeed, something was special about Mary. She was extraordinarily beautiful, there was that, yes, but something else, too. Her outer beauty was matched by an interior peace, a calm, gentle manner about her that could only come from the Lord. He shook his head. He was betrothed to her, but felt unworthy to be her husband. He was just a simple carpenter, a regular man. His ruminations carried him onward through the desert brush, past rocky outcroppings and prickly plants, dirt trails and minute hilltops. He rounded a bend and heard rustling noises in a little copse of creosote bushes. He stopped and found himself confronted by three figures approximately thirty paces away, covered by dirty cloaks cinched up by leather belts. The three men each had two daggers tucked into their belts, and the middle also carried a large scimitar. He lifted it up and pointed it at Joseph, causing the sunlight to reflect off it and into Joseph's eyes. Joseph squinted and held a hand up.

"Stop right there," the middle one spoke. His belt was scarlet, and his teeth were the color of the ground under their feet.

Joseph looked at them. Despite the presence of the all-powerful Roman army in the larger cities in the area, he knew that bandits like this often had the run of the empty space between villages in the countryside. He looked back at the trail. Mary was roughly 50 yards back. "What is it that you want?"

The man with the scimitar sneered, his mouth forming a greasy grin. "We're here to collect the toll, you idiot."

Joseph seethed, his carpenter muscles tensing. He could have taken these three in short order were it not for their weapons. Oh, how he wished he had his best chisel. "Well then, come and take it."

The leader frowned, obviously not used to being addressed in this manner. He grunted and approached Joseph with his scimitar raised before stopping short. He and the two with him stared behind Joseph with gaping eyes and slack jaws.

**

Mary came around the bend, rising and falling slowly with the steady gait of the donkey. The path straightened, revealing Joseph and three dirty men facing him, men with knives. She frowned as she took in the scene. "What is going on here?"

At the sound of her voice, the three bandits dropped to their knees. The leader pointed his sword into the ground and leaned on the hilt, as if he was suddenly tired.

"What is going on?" Mary repeated.

The man with the sword spoke up. "My lady, we…" his voice trailed off. After a long moment, he tried again. "My lady, we are thieves." At this, the three of them looked down, their eyes boring holes in the ground. After a long moment of shame, the leader looked up again. "Please, take this from us," he reached under his cloak and pulled out a fairly large sack. A fair amount of things, presumably coins, jingled together.

"We don't want that money." Mary's voice was without a hint of anger, but the tone of sorrow conveyed something that made the bandits almost cower in their clothes.

"What, then, are we to do with it?"

"Give it back." The simplicity of her direction voiced the sentiment underneath. 'Wasn't it obvious?'

The man with the sword looked down while the other two looked at each other. "How are we to find the original people we stole from?"

Mary shifted on her saddle. "How did you find them in the first place?"

The man motioned to the bushes on either side of the trail. "We simply hid here and jumped out when anyone passed by."

Mary looked at them. "Well, there's your answer. Just wait for them to come back the other way." They started off again, Joseph leading Mary's donkey, while the bandits just stared at them.

Once they were well past the area, Joseph looked over at Mary. "We need to talk."

**

The unending dusty landscape trolled by slowly, lulling Nahara into a daze. She knew they wouldn't be in the countryside forever, but would be entering the outskirts of Jerusalem soon. The anxiety that accompanied her near the beginning of the journey was back now in full force. She felt it in her stomach with each step of her donkey. Nahara thought back to the events of the last few weeks: first, her mother sitting down to tell her she was to be married, followed by her chance meeting with Achan, his subsequent refusal to talk to her or even acknowledge her, and finally this journey. She thought more about the girl Miriam. Nahara had felt her anxiety and fear of the future melt away when she sat by Miriam near the fire a few nights ago. What would Miriam say about her challenges? Could she help her? More questions surfaced in her mind and then melted into the heat of the day and the dusty ground, intensifying Nahara's daze. She became aware only of the slight back and forth movement of the animal under her and for a time, closed her eyes, envisioning some other place, some other time.

Her uncle's shout ripped up her solitude. He had stopped just ahead and was trying to get their pack mule to sit down under a fig tree. "Sit, you stupid ass," her uncle smacked the animal on its rump. "This is your only chance to rest in the shade of the sun, because who knows when the next tree will show up." The animal snorted. "Fine then," her uncle sat down and leaned against the trunk. "I will just have to rest here myself." Nahara sidled up and dismounted. "Tie your animal up and come sit down," her uncle ordered. Nahara frowned. What else was she going to do? 'They take me for a know-nothing,' Nahara thought of her uncle and her parents. She tied up the animal and slumped down against the tree. Maybe it was better that she be married off.

\*\*

Mary and Joseph continued on the path. The heat dissipated ever so slightly as the sun high overhead dropped nearer to the horizon. The rocky ground yielded more plant life as they made their way south, giving way to a more colorful landscape of scattered patches of heather and star thistles. The pink and blue flowers grew in spots between creosote bushes and made for a minimalist bouquet that lent a sweet smell to the air. Mary knew they were closer to Jerusalem. Joseph stopped and picked out a spot just off the trail at the bottom of a rocky outcropping and next to a small copse of cedar trees. After Joseph gathered wood and brush for a fire, they sat by it and shared some bread.

"Miriam," Joseph spoke. He paused, thinking of the right way to ask. "What happened today?"

Mary chewed while looking at the fire. "You speak of the wounded man, and the bandits."

Joseph frowned. "Well of course. What else would I be speaking of?"

Mary watched the flames curl up and stretch toward the darkening sky. "What happened today were good things, and everything good is from the Lord."

"Yes, but what happened?"

"There are many mysteries among us." Mary gestured to the fire for an example. "How is it that flames emerge from this wood?"

They sat for a time, feeling the fire's heat warm the air and seep into their bones as the desert night gave away the heat it had accumulated during the day. Joseph turned to Mary. "Is there something I should know?"

Mary started to speak when they heard some noises from the path nearby. They got louder until it became clear they were the scuffled steps of a donkey and two travelers on foot. A voice sounded out in the night. "Let us stop here Nahara, I see a fire nearby."

**

Mary's heart lifted. She had prayed that she would get another opportunity to speak to the girl Nahara, and the Lord answered! "Joseph," she whispered, the edge of excitement in her voice, "it's that girl Nahara I was telling you about."

"Oh?"

"Yes. Please let us share the fire with them, so that I may have a chance to hear what is on her mind and heart."

"Absolutely." Joseph got up and called out to the two travelers in the darkness with the invite. Mary looked up with anticipation as the girl's uncle and the donkey stepped into the firelight with Nahara. She popped up and greeted Nahara with a hug, and in return Mary felt the tight cling of one who wanted to share her burden. After sharing what little food they had, Nahara's uncle left with Joseph to find a watering hole for the animals. Nahara turned to Mary. "I am so happy to have found you again."

Mary smiled. "I prayed that we would meet again."

Nahara looked into the fire. "Do you pray often?"

"Why do you ask?"

Nahara shifted her mat so she could sit on it. "What do you pray for?"

Mary sat back. "Many things. I pray that I can know the Lord's will for me, that I can carry out my duties so as to give glory to him." The fire crackled as the dark desert night settled around them. "I even prayed for the opportunity to talk to you again."

Nahara smiled. "You did?"

"Yes." Mary pulled her feet into a cross-legged position. "When we talked last time, I got the sense there was a lot on your mind and on your heart."

Nahara looked down at her hands. "Yes, there was. There is."

Some sparks jumped amongst the embers. Mary could see Nahara take a deep breath and in the light of the fire, a shiny trail of wetness by her eyes. Mary took her hands. "Do you want to tell me?"

Nahara's voice quivered as the sounds tried to make it out of her mouth. "I...I am," her voice quaked. "I am with child." She sobbed as the last two words came out.

Mary pulled her close as Nahara's shoulders heaved. The mention of a baby shot straight to her heart and reminded her once again of the new life inside her. She held Nahara and stroked her hair. After a time, Nahara straightened and wiped her eyes. "I'm sorry, I am unloading everything on you."

Mary looked into her eyes. "Do not be sorry, I am here for you."

"Oh, thank you," Nahara licked her lips. "I am so thankful I came across you again." She put her hands in her lap, as if deciding where to start. Another deep breath. "His name was Achan. He is a shepherd boy and watches his father's flock on the hillside near my home. One day, while I was down by the stream doing the wash, he walked by with his sheep and noticed me. I had seen him around before, but my parents threatened to lash me if I would so much as talk to a boy without their permission. So on this day, I tried to ignore him. He asked me what my name was, but I didn't answer. He asked me what I was doing, but I said nothing. Then he started talking to one of his sheep, wondering out loud what my name was. He asked the sheep this and that, until finally I couldn't help it and burst out laughing." Nahara looked out at the invisible horizon of the night. "I gave up and started talking to him. We talked for a long time. I knew my mother was on her way to the market in town so no one needed me to be back for a while." She shook her head. "I was mesmerized by him. Here was someone who actually wanted to talk to me. He said I was beautiful," her voice cracked, and she continued with a whisper. "He said he should get going but I asked him if he wanted to go to the secluded spot just downstream, and, um, we," Nahara wiped away a tear, "we made ourselves known to each other." She buried her head into Mary's neck and cried.

Mary's heart burned for her. She pulled her head close and caressed her hair. Her pain, her anguish, her duress, it was all Mary's, too. She asked God to absorb it all. After a while, Nahara pulled back and wiped her red eyes. "Not until it was over did I regret it. I think he did, too. I was curious how it felt and was just amazed that someone would even express interest in me." She shook her head. "I saw him a few days afterward, but he barely acknowledged me. He acted like there was nothing between us, like he was ashamed that he even knew me." A single tear spilled down her cheek. "I was just the pit of an olive to him. Something to chew on and spit out. I was angry, betrayed, but mostly ashamed. And what could I do? I didn't want to tell anyone. And then a week later, my parents told me I was to be married off to someone I don't know. And when he finds out the truth about me, I don't know what I will do…" her voice trailed off into the abyss of uncertainty and dread.

Mary ached inside. She knew full well what Nahara's condition meant. The law allowed for death by stoning for adultery. She took Nahara's hands again. "Do not worry." Seeing Nahara's furrowed brows, Mary added, "I know what you are going through."

"How could you?"

"You know that man I am traveling with?"

"Yes?"

"His name is Joseph."

"So?"

"I am his betrothed."

"Okay…"

"And I am with child, too." Nahara looked at Mary with wide eyes. "And he doesn't know it."

**

Nahara sat in disbelief. Here was a girl her age, but with something very different about her. She had such gentleness, such compassion, such…Nahara searched her mind for the word. That was it. Such grace. She turned back to Mary, wanting to ask a million more questions. But footsteps nearby and the baying of a donkey signaled her uncle's return from the watering hole. Mary whispered to her, "Go to sleep. We will talk in the morning."

Mary then got up and pulled Joseph aside. "What is it?" he asked.

She hushed in a low voice. "We need to talk again."

**

After spending the night on the ground, Nahara woke up feeling strangely refreshed. She felt none of the aches and pains that usually accompanied a sleepless night but realized that she slept like a stone. A feeling of calm surrounded her like the floral scents of this desert spot. Although she had so many unanswered questions, it was as if talking to Miriam the night before melted all her worries away. She looked around and saw Mary starting a new fire.

"Good morning Nahara."

"Good morning." She looked around. "Where are the men?"

"They are hunting a hare for breakfast." Mary got up and walked over to her. "And don't worry, your uncle knows everything now."

Nahara shot up. "What?"

"I had Joseph talk to him last night."

"You did what? He'll kill me!"

"He will do no such thing."

"How do you know?!"

"Because we have a plan."

"A plan?"

"Yes."

Nahara was incredulous. "Well, tell me then."

And so Mary did.

Nahara sat back against a boulder, open-mouthed. "How can you be so sure it will happen like that?"

"I just know."

"How can you know?"

"I prayed to the Lord for guidance."

"But how can you know?" Nahara emphasized the last word. "Sometimes I wonder if God is even around at all."

Mary sat on the ground next to her and looked her in the eyes. "Trust me when I say that the Lord is with us at this very moment."

**

Nahara was back on the donkey with her uncle leading the way. They had turned around per Miriam's instructions and approached the long bend in the trail. Her uncle turned to her and shook his head. "I can't believe you let that dirty thing Achan touch you."

Nahara looked at him. It had been two hours since they left Joseph and Miriam and silence had ruled the entire way. "I hope you don't-"

"Don't worry, I won't tell anyone. I actually think this crazy plan of theirs will work."

Nahara sat back on the donkey in wonder and relief. Ever since they stopped last night her uncle had been in a good mood. He uttered no curses this morning and didn't even smack the donkey. As for the plan, they just had to follow Mary's instructions. Not that Nahara wasn't afraid. As they got closer to the spot, she felt her heart pound and her breathing quicken. Normally people didn't search bandits out. "Uncle, I think this is the place," Nahara hushed in a whisper. He nodded and they stopped. Nahara got off her donkey, turned to face the bushes at the side of the trail and called out.

Her uncle licked his lips as they waited for something to happen. He was ready to run if necessary. After another long moment, the bushes shook and three men in dirty cloaks climbed out. Nahara looked at them. Their clothes and daggers identified them as thieves, but they had something like defeated looks on their faces, looks that drew their pity instead of fear. Nahara cleared her throat. "The woman says to give me the money."

The bandits looked at each other. Without a word, the one in the middle dug out a large bag with coins and tossed it at her feet. Then they turned and skulked off into the distance. Nahara looked at her uncle, both of them with mouths agape. Her uncle walked over, picked up the bag and started counting. Nahara waited with the donkey in the shade until he was done.

"How much?" she asked.

He looked up. "Enough to repay a dowry, and more."

**

As Mary and Joseph made their way through the outskirts of Jerusalem in the midday heat, Mary prayed for Nahara. She prayed that the man she was betrothed to would accept repayment of the dowry and let Nahara go. She prayed for Nahara's health and that of her baby. After a few moments of silence, as they made their way through a collection of small villages, Joseph spoke. "What do you think will happen to her?"

"After she pays for her freedom, I hope she finds me. I told her she could stay with me at the house of Zechariah and Elizabeth."

"I hope that they have no objection to that."

Mary looked at Joseph. "Zechariah is one of the priestly class, and the house at Ain Karim is their second home." Joseph understood: they had money, and they wouldn't be put out.

Mary's thoughts turned to Elizabeth. She couldn't wait to see her cousin. She wanted to smack the donkey's rump to get him to walk faster, but couldn't bring herself to do that to the animal after their long journey together. What would Elizabeth look like? Would she be carrying high or low? The questions swirled about in anticipation of a few months with her cousin. Finally, after winding through another village surrounded by palm trees and olive orchards, they saw Zechariah's house ahead. Mary got off the donkey and walked as quickly as she could to the front gate. She could barely contain herself. She got to the gate and cried out, "Elizabeth!"

*When Elizabeth heard Mary's greeting, the infant leaped in her womb, and Elizabeth, filled with the Holy Spirit, cried out in a loud voice and said, "Most blessed are you among women, and blessed is the fruit of your womb. And how does this happen to me, that the mother of my Lord should come to me? For at the moment the sound of your greeting reached my ears, the infant in my womb leaped for joy. Blessed are you who believed that what was spoken to you by the Lord would be fulfilled."*

*And Mary said:*

*"My soul proclaims the greatness of the Lord;*
*my spirit rejoices in God my savior.*
*For he has looked upon his handmaid's lowliness;*
*behold, from now on will all ages call me blessed.*
*The Mighty One has done great things for me,*
*and holy is his name.*
*His mercy is from age to age*
*to those who fear him.*
*He has shown might with his arm,*
*dispersed the arrogant of mind and heart.*
*He has thrown down the rulers from their thrones*
*but lifted up the lowly.*
*The hungry he has filled with good things;*
*the rich he has sent away empty.*
*He has helped Israel his servant,*
*remembering his mercy,*
*according to his promise to our fathers,*

*to Abraham and to his descendants forever."*
*(Luke 1:46-55)*

# The Nativity of Our Lord Jesus

Caspar viewed his looking glass again before checking the papyrus in front of him. "No, it can't be," he said. His eyes returned to the sky once again, straining to verify the calculations he made earlier.

"What is it, master?"

"It always amazes me how the skies reveal themselves."

His assistant looked at him expectantly. The pitch black of the night hung overhead, and the verdant foothills of western India fell away from them on all sides. They were at Caspar's prized observation point just outside of Barygaza. Seeing his master lost in thought, with a whisper of a coastal breeze reaching out from the ocean ten miles away, his assistant prodded him again. "Yes, master?"

Caspar showed him the looking glass. "See there in the western sky? The planet *Brhaspati*?"

"The large red one?"

"Yes, yes, that one. See how it is within the *Nakshatra Magha*?

"Yes."

Caspar smiled. It was clear his assistant didn't see the significance of what was playing overhead. "Brhaspati is the King of the Planets, as it is the largest one. See how the bright star there, the one we call 'Bountiful,' is so close to it?"

"Yes."

"According to my calculations, the Brhaspati should be starting to circle. And tonight, we see that it actually is." Caspar leaned against one of the many boulders surrounding them, a serene smile spreading across his lips. "You see, that is why I love astronomy. The stars and the heavens follow their own paths across the sky, but they tell you of their plans in advance."

"Master, what are their plans?"

Caspar looked up again at the twinkling realm overhead. "Something important will happen in the near future."

"What is it, Master?"

"Something that only the stars and the planets can announce." He looked at his assistant. "See that our things are packed. And send word to the court: we will be on our way soon."

"Where are we going?"

Caspar gestured to the distance. "To the west."

**

A month later and a thousand miles away, Melchior looked again at the heavens, at the twinkling giants in the sky his people had been studying for centuries. A gentle breeze coming off the great gulf parted his hair as he considered the celestial feast for the eyes above. He had made studying the planets and the stars his mission in life, and the royal court looked to him when questions of the gods arose. He peered again through his looking glass one last time before consulting some mathematical equations on papyrus unfurled in front of him. With excitement he followed one set of numbers to the end, then returned to the looking glass to confirm. He felt his heart beat faster.

50

He ran down from the perch on the foothills into the walled complex where the royal governor held his seat. After a few minutes asking around, he found the governor's chief of staff relaxing in his salon with a few of his wives. "Ah, look who it is, the great scholar Melchior." He rose and tied his silk robe together. "What is the matter that you come here after nightfall?"

"I'm sorry for the interruption, my lord. I came to ask to see the governor tomorrow."

"For what purpose?"

Melchior caught his breath. "To ask for travel funds."

"Travel funds?" The chief beckoned him to sit on a richly embroidered chair before barking a command to one of the women. "Get this man some figs, and some wine." He turned back to Melchior. "What is this about?"

"Something in the skies above."

The chief raised an eyebrow. "Tell me more."

"Sir, the great planet *Marduk* is on a certain path through the skies. It seems that the great star, the one we call the *Magh*, is on course to interact with Marduk in a highly unusual way. Tonight, I verified that it truly is on that path, the observation validating my mathematical equations."

"And where do you intend to go?"

"I'm not sure exactly, but it is no farther than the great western sea."

"That will take many months." 'And many drachma,' the chief thought.

"Indeed, sir."

"But why?"

Melchior ate some of the figs and drank some wine before continuing. "Sir, I believe this stellar event is proclaiming something of truly unprecedented importance. Something that the High Creator above deigned to foretell when he aligned the planets and stars and set them upon their journey at the beginning of time."

"And what do you expect to see when you get to your destination?"

"The birth of a child."

**

Balthasar stepped into his tent with a shiver. The Arabian desert night was setting in, so he put on his heavy cloak in preparation for sleep. If he could sleep at all.

"You were out late tonight, my husband," Dalal brought him some tea in a cup.

He took it and drank deeply, groaning with the satisfying warmth. "I know. Something overhead kept me out for an hour longer than normal."

"Oh?" Dalal leaned forward. "What could be so pressing so as to almost freeze in this cold night?"

"I saw something tonight that confirmed earlier calculations of mine."

"Are you going to tell me about it, or just leave me in suspense?"

Balthasar looked at the tea in his hands, at how the tiny flecks of leaves swirled about. 'Not unlike stars in the heavens,' he thought.

"Husband?"

52

"Oh, sorry. Overhead, something is going on that I believe has great significance for man. You see, in just a few months, the star which we call *Qalb al-Asad* will be-"

"Wait, you already lost me," Dalal cut him off. "Why don't you just show me yourself outside?"

Balthasar was taken aback. His wife had never expressed interest in his work before. "But of course." He took her by the hand and they stepped outside. The low ceiling of the tent gave way to the endless expanse of the universe overhead, stars twinkling in the clear desert dark. He stood next to her and crouched down so they were cheek to cheek. "Do you see up there?" He pointed in the sky to a bright light.

"How could I not?" Dalal whispered.

"That is the planet we call *Mushtari*."

"It is so bright."

"Indeed it is. It is the largest planet in the sky. See that other bright light nearby it?"

"Yes."

"That is Qalb al-Asad. According to my calculations, Mushtari will be going both nearer to and farther away from this star."

"What does that mean, my husband?"

"I am not sure what, exactly. Some people believe that the gods overhead use the celestial formations to herald certain events. This particular event is most rare."

"Why is that?"

"This kind of planetary movement about a star, according to my calculations, has not happened in more than twenty lifetimes at least."

His wife turned to him. "So what is next?"

"Well, this isn't the end of the event. You see, Mushtari will continue across the skies where in about two months it will seemingly cross paths with another planet. And I want to be there to see it."

Dalal frowned. "Why can't you see it from here?"

"Well, I could, but according to my calculations it will be at its brightest north of here some ways, in the land of Judah."

Dalal's eyes started to tear up. "So you're going again? But it will be so long."

Balthasar took his wife's face in his hands. "I could never leave you again for so long. I want you to come with me."

Dalal gasped with glee and kissed him. After a long moment under the stars, they looked up again. "It's not just the meeting of the planets I want to see," he explained. "You see, I believe there will be something significant happening on earth at that point."

"What could that be?"

Balthasar paused. "After studying the prophecies of the Jews, I believe we will meet a new King of all the earth."

**

Joseph looked at Mary with concern. He knew coming all the way down here was a mistake. She was well into her ninth month and not fit for traveling. Ever since they left Hebron earlier in the week, she was clearly uncomfortable in every position, although she uttered no complaint. Once again he was reminded what a blessing and a gift she was.

"How are you feeling?" he asked.

"I'm managing," Mary's voice was strained.

"Don't worry, we'll find a place to bed down soon." Joseph looked up at the road ahead. "Bethlehem is just around the bend, and we are sure to find rest there."

They continued on their way, Mary riding on the donkey and Joseph leading it on foot. They had made their way to Hebron a month ago when they could no longer hide the fact that Mary was pregnant. It was also the original capital of David's kingdom and home to a special kind of olive wood. Mary had wanted to see the place where David was originally crowned, so they had spent many days in contemplation. They also tended to more temporal needs, as the wood in Hebron had a particular depth of color that just didn't grow up north. Joseph looked back at the large pile of it in the wagon the donkey was towing. He had been eager to work with it and adorn his works with ornamental carvings. But the wood was the last thing on his mind right now.

Mary grimaced as she pressed on her lower back. Joseph stopped the donkey while she got off and walked around a bit. After a minute or two, she was ready to move on again. Ever since he escorted Mary down to Beit Karin, the special sense of duty hung over him. He remembered the weight of responsibility that hit him when he realized he had a pregnant woman to take care of now. He tried to be attentive, but for all his efforts, he could not take away the pain that carrying a child entailed. And now a faint feeling of anxiety started to bubble up inside his gut. Mary looked down at him. "Don't worry, I'll be fine." He pulled on the rope, urging the donkey onward.

**

Joseph looked up again, trying to gauge how far Bethlehem was. He thought he remembered the village's outskirts should have stretched down to this portion of the path, but he must have been mistaken, for there was nothing but the rocky dirt and scattered desert bushes of the same meandering landscape. The feeling in his gut lingered again as he realized that they probably had another hour of traveling before they got anywhere near civilization. The sun was nearing the horizon.

"Ooph," Mary held her ribs while she tried to keep upright on the donkey.

"Are you all right?"

"The baby kicked me again."

"Do you remember the first time he kicked?" Joseph hoped to take her mind off the current moment.

She smiled. "How could I forget?" A few months ago, Mary had awoken in the middle of the night with a gasp and called out to Joseph. He had run over to her. 'What is it?' She whispered with excitement in her voice. 'The baby just kicked.'

"You know, that was the first time this whole thing seemed real to me," Joseph said. "Until then, it was something that only existed in my mind."

"I know how you feel. And I want you to know that I appreciate all the effort you have put into taking care of me and making sure I have what I need."

Joseph looked up again at the foothills in the distance. It seemed like they had made no progress. "At times like this I question myself."

"Nonsense, Joseph." Mary looked at him with total love in her eyes. "Remember, the Lord himself picked you." The words had the dual effect of putting his head at peace and his stomach in turmoil. He had to find them a place to rest, and soon.

**

The twinkling light of fires dotting the hillside ahead signaled they were finally nearing Bethlehem. They started encountering fellow travelers on the path. The presence of others helped settle Joseph's anxiety, but it refused to go anywhere. At this point, the sun was sinking below the horizon, casting the land into one last flash of red light before the dark of the desert night would sink in.

"What do you see up there?" Joseph asked.

Mary, on top of the donkey, straightened to peer over the tall creosote bushes that lined the path. "It looks like the heart of the village lies just halfway up the next small foothill. Not much farther now." Another grimace and she held her side.

"Are you all right?" Joseph hated asking the same question but he didn't know what else to say.

"I can manage a bit longer." She sauntered on, swaying back and forth. "I wish this animal could go faster."

Joseph slapped the donkey on its rump and urged it on. "Get your ass moving." The donkey just brayed, though, and continued on its regular pace. He tried tugging on the rope, but the beast only snorted.

Mary leaned over and whispered something into the donkey's ear, and at once it started to pick up the pace. Joseph shook his head and jogged a bit to keep up.

After what seemed like an eternity, they came upon a house on the side of the path. Joseph looked up to Mary, "Should we see if they have room for us, or can you wait for a proper inn?"

Mary arched her back and groaned. "I think I can make it a bit longer."

"Very well, we'll see if we can find an inn then." Joseph looked with consternation at the road ahead, for in addition to the sprawl of buildings there were suddenly many more people out and about.

"I wonder why all these people are here?" Mary said. Left unsaid was the possibility of not finding a place anytime soon.

Joseph stopped a man leading a donkey piled high with all manner of fabric reams. "Excuse me sir, why are all these people here? Surely they are not all from Bethlehem?"

The man looked back at them. "Don't you know? They have all come from the countryside to celebrate the festival of the first grapes."

"I have never heard of it."

"You don't sound like you're from around here. It's not celebrated anywhere else, because Bethlehem wine is unequaled throughout all the land, of course. And I've come to sell them the finest fabric while they drink the finest wine," he added with a twinkle in his eyes.

After setting off again, Mary and Joseph spotted an inn, so Joseph went inside to inquire. While she waited, Mary felt another sharp pain in her lower back and gasped. She looked around the village to try to spot another inn, but the pain became so intense she couldn't focus on anything else. Joseph emerged shaking his head. "No room at all. The innkeeper said to try the one just around the corner." Seeing the pained look on Mary's face, he held her hand. "Can you make it?"

Mary just nodded and wiped the sweat from her brow.

Joseph looked around at the hordes of people and felt more pangs of anxiety rising up as he considered their predicament. "Okay, we'll try the next place."

After ten minutes of picking their way through the crowd, they found the next inn. Mary was doubled over by this point. "Hurry, Joseph."

"I'll be right back." He hurried in, and after an agonizing minute was back outside. "They are completely full, too." He looked wild-eyed at the crowd in the unfamiliar city.

"What are we going to do?" Mary started shaking with sweat.

"He said to try another place at the edge of town, just over that way," he pointed to an area where the slope fell away to the orchards below. "Just hang on." He tugged on the donkey's rope and started shouting at people. "You there, move aside! Watch out!" He elbowed a path through the crowd and after another five minutes of jostling and shoving, they found the inn the previous innkeeper suggested. Joseph looked at the small rock building with equal parts desperation and frustration.

Mary felt another spasm in her back. "Joseph, hurry, we must stop here!"

"I'll be right back." He raced inside and found the innkeeper turning another group of travelers away. Joseph butted them aside and got in the man's face. "We need a room, now."

The man stepped back with this sudden interruption. He looked at the traveler in front of him, breathing heavily, sweating and with bug eyes tearing a hole through him. "I, I'm sorry, we're full."

Joseph grabbed the man by his cloak. "We need a room, immediately, if not sooner."

The innkeeper stood flummoxed. "I, uh, have you tried-"

Joseph pulled the man close so their noses were touching. "If you don't find us a room, my wife is going to give birth all over your front hall here."

The innkeeper bent backward with fear. "Out back," he gasped. "The stables below. Plenty of room there."

Joseph heard Mary let out a sharp cry and raced out to find her off the donkey and doubled over on the ground. "Don't worry," he stooped down to pick her up. "We can stay in the stables below." He hefted her up and made his way around the side of the building. He picked his footsteps carefully down the hillside and walked around to the back. They saw an empty animal pen with an empty trough and a pile of hay in one corner. Breathing heavily, Mary looked at Joseph, "It will have to do."

**

Hozai looked up at the dying light of the day. They would be going home soon. At least he thought. Maluch, his oldest brother, had mentioned that they would take in the flock after sundown but Yanai, the middle brother, cast doubt on it.

"We'll be lucky to get in by dawn with the likes of you trying to herd all these sheep," Yanai sneered.

"Maluch said we would get to go soon," Hozai said.

"Maluch didn't think you would be so slow and inept."

"But how shall I know when it is time to go in?"

"Just keep watch on that hill over there," Yanai pointed to a small rise about two stadia away. "And don't lose any sheep. This is Papa's livelihood."

Hozai picked his way over to the small knoll, careful not to catch his foot in any of the countless ruts, water holes or crags lining the rugged landscape. As the youngest one, it was always his job to watch the outer fringes of the flock. Although he had to run on occasion to catch up with a missing sheep, usually he was able to coax them back with just a simple call and a whistle. His father had worked a long time with him to master the whistle and the call. He knew he had finally had it down when he was able to call to a sheep that had wandered out of eyesight. His father had looked at him with such pride. Hozai smiled at the memory. Indeed, as his father's flock was growing, Hozai hoped to be able to take part of the flock out on his own one day.

A sharp whistle from Yanai disturbed his daydreaming. "Look alive, Hozai." Hozai frowned at his brother. What a thorn in his sandal.

**

The night was very bright tonight. In fact, for the last few nights, the light from the moon and the stars seemed to illuminate nearly every crag, cave and cloven foot on the landscape. Hozai was very grateful for the light, for he did not want to lose any sheep. He surveyed the flock again. Before they parted, it was agreed that he would watch the portion of the flock that grazed on the western fringes of the land. His father's flock numbered 513 sheep, and he was responsible for 100 of them tonight. He paced around an olive tree to get a bit higher up the hillside and could see all of them more or less in four large groups. 'This is good,' he thought. 'They don't seem to be in a wandering mood tonight.'

He turned his eyes skyward and took in the unfathomable expanse of the skies. There was the moon over there. Further over, he was drawn to look at the source of the brightness for the last few nights. He looked closely. It appeared to be a bright star with perhaps one of the planets just below it. The aura it radiated was captivating. It held his gaze for what seemed to be several minutes. He wondered about the vastness of the Lord's creation and once again was reminded how utterly small he was. A sound just off to his right interrupted his reverie. Something hurtled out of the darkness and hit him in the head just in front of his ear. After jumping out of his feet, he looked to see Yanai off in the distance chortling. Hozai put a hand to his face and realized his brother just hit him with a clump of sheep dung. He burned with anger. "What did you do that for?" his yell tore through the night.

"You should be paying attention."

Hozai picked up a rock and threw it, but it landed harmlessly a few paces in front of his brother. "Get back to tending the flock, turdface," Yanai said before walking away.

Hozai steamed. Yanai should be watching his own portion of the flock instead of bothering him. He walked up the hillside a little more and once again surveyed the four groups of sheep in front of him. They had appeared to mingle somewhat so the groups weren't so discreet anymore. He decided to take a head count. He counted from the right-most group to his left, but some of the sheep wandered around so he started over a few times. After counting the whole group, he frowned. There were only 99. He felt a little fluttering in his stomach, but he decided to count again. Again, he had to start over a few times, but again he counted 99. The fluttering in his stomach turned into a deep pit. He didn't want to lose a sheep. He didn't want to disappoint his father.

**

Hozai scanned the landscape. Where could the one have gone? Not up the hillside, for it would have had to wander past him, and there was no way that happened. Not down the hillside, for in tonight's brightness, he could see all the way down to the valley floor, and there definitely weren't any sheep down there. To his right, the sheep could have gone over to Yanai's area, but they would have had to cross a particular rocky crag and he was sure he would have heard that. He looked to his left, to the west, where the outskirts of their village was. The hillside folded here and there before dropping off somewhat to stretch down to the plain below. 'He must be there,' Hozai thought. He started to make his way to the side. Perhaps the sheep was just below his line of sight. He gave a soft whistle, just like his father taught him, taking care not to make it too loud, for he did not want to alert Yanai to his predicament. He stopped in his tracks momentarily and listened for any signs of the sheep. He heard a faint bleating sound from far below. 'That sounds so far away,' Hozai thought. 'How did it get there?' After taking another glance at the rest of the flock, he decided they weren't going anywhere for the moment and jogged over to the side of the hill where it swept down into the town. As he moved onto the steep part of the hill he heard the bleating again, but even in the bright starlight, he still couldn't spot the errant sheep. He made his way down, careful not to lose his footing on the loose rocks that dotted the hillside. He fretted as he went down. 'I wish I had hooves like them so I could go faster,' he thought. The light helped, though. In fact, the bright star hung directly in front of him, absolutely dominating the sky in front of him. He paused, transfixed by the sight. Once again he heard the bleating sound a little closer, but the star held his full attention. He realized something was about to happen.

**

The star that had dominated the sky suddenly glowed a thousand times brighter than the sun. It threw off an aura that lit the landscape all around. At the same time, Hozai heard what sounded like a trumpet blast from overhead. He stood paralyzed with fear. Perhaps the Almighty had learned of his oversight and was about to punish him for the lost sheep. He looked up to feel tangible waves of praise falling all over him from above. It was an absolute shower of joy and warmed his frozen fear. In the skies, he beheld a figure of light, almost as bright as the star and towering higher than even the Mount of Olives. The figure, an angel, spoke:

> *"Do not be afraid; for behold, I proclaim to you*
> *good news of great joy that will be for all the people.*
> *For today in the city of David a savior has been born*

*for you who is Messiah and Lord. And this will be a sign for you: you will find an infant wrapped in swaddling clothes and lying in a manger." (Luke 2:10-12)*

Although he was looking into Hozai's eyes, it was as if the angel was speaking to the entire world. Hozai could feel the words penetrate through his cloak and embed themselves into his very being. Then, before he could absorb any more, legions and legions of the same kind of angels appeared around the first, singing, no, shining with praise for the Lord. 'Glory to God the highest, and on earth peace to those on whom his favor rests.' It was as if the beings and the angels overhead had waited the entirety of their existence, from the very dawn of time until now, to release their joy in a veritable explosion of glory. Hozai struggled to withstand the spectacle above and around him. The entirety of heaven was there, at this moment, to proclaim the Messiah and Lord! Here on earth! How could it be? He looked up again: here was heaven itself, the realm of Yahweh, revealed to him. Everything, the gilded vestiture of the angels, the sparkling brightness of the stars, and the focused praise of the heavenly court for the Almighty was right here for him to behold. He wanted to stand there forever and be a part of it. For an interminable period of time, he did just that. As suddenly as they appeared, though, they disappeared into the night sky, leaving only the bright star overhead.

Hozai was left with his mouth agape. A sharp shout from Yanai once again disturbed his reverie. "Hozai, where are you?" His voice came from just above the rocky crag he had crossed before going down part of the hill. For a moment, Hozai could not find his voice. It was like the times he awoke in the middle of the night, trying to yell for help in one of his nightmares, although this time was no nightmare. Just the opposite.

"Hozai?" his brother called again.

"I'm down here," Hozai called back. After some scrabbling noises, he saw Yanai standing above him. "What are you doing down there? And what were those strange lights in the sky above?" He stopped to look at Hozai closer. "And what is with that look on your face?"

\*\*

"Heaven," Hozai said.

His brother frowned. "What?"

"Heaven. I saw it just now."

Yanai scrambled down the rest of the way and looked Hozai in the eye. "What did you see?"

Hozai scratched his head. "Probably the same thing you saw, right?"

"All I saw were some lights in the sky, surrounded by a pink aura. They appeared to move around a little bit, and it sounded like there was a humming noise from above."

Hozai nodded. "Then I must have seen better since I was here." He went on to explain in detail what just happened."

For once, Yanai hung on his every word. When Hozai was finished, he saw the unusual sight of Yanai looking at him with something other than derision.

*"Let us go, then, to Bethlehem to see this thing that has taken place, which the Lord has made known to us." (Luke 2:15)*

They started their way down the hill, in the direction of where the enormous star hung overhead. "Why were you down there in the first place, little brother?" Yanai asked.

Hozai hesitated. "I was looking for one sheep that had strayed." He waited for the verbal assault from his brother, but Yanai just shrugged.

"I'm sure we'll find him soon. Come; let's go faster to find the child Messiah." He started running down the remaining hillside and onto the flat plain below. Hozai ran after him, feeling the wind rush in his ears and the joy of the vision still surrounding him as they raced toward the star. Suddenly, they weren't concerned about tripping in any of the ruts and rocks of the land as they made their way toward town. Hozai could feel the Spirit guiding him on, pushing him toward the little cave in the distance, the one underneath the innkeeper's house. His huffing and puffing kept him even with Yanai and together they flew with anticipation toward the light that flickered in the cave. It was only half a stadium away. The thoughts raced by as fast: what would they see? What would the Messiah look like? Would He really be lying in a manger? Surely the Lord would deign to pick a more fitting birthplace? As they approached, they heard a sound from inside the cave.

Yanai stopped running and motioned Hozai to do the same. They listened to the sound again. Hozai smiled when he realized it was the bleating of a sheep. "Yanai, that is the one who wandered off!" he started laughing.

"What are you laughing at?"

"Don't you realize?" Hozai asked his older brother. "He led us here. The sheep is now the shepherd."

**

The boys came upon a cave under a house at the outskirts of the village. A light from within flickered and played upon the cave walls. As they rounded a curve, they came upon a man tending to a woman resting on a pile of hay.

The man looked up. "Hello, boys."

Hozai and Yanai came closer and saw a baby wrapped in swaddling clothes and laying in a small pile of hay stacked in a manger. They immediately fell to their knees and gazed upon the child.

"What's going on?" the man asked.

Yanai spoke. "Forgive me, sir." He looked at his brother. "We were sent here by, by angels. Angels from heaven who said, who said there was a new King of all the earth, that he had just been born."

Yanai looked again at Hozai. "They led us here," Hozai said.

The man and the woman looked at each other with joy radiating around them. The boys knelt there for a long while, adoring the little baby in the trough. It felt like they could stay there forever.

The woman lifted her head. "Boys, it is true. Please go back home now, for your mother and father are out looking for you. Tell them all that you have seen. Tell them that all of heaven has proclaimed this to be true.

The boys nodded and got up, reluctant to leave this place of inarticulate joy. They bid goodbye, but before they left, the man stopped them. "Aren't you forgetting something?"

Hozai looked to where the man was pointing: the missing sheep lay there in the hay at the foot of the manger, sound asleep. Hozai scratched his head. They must have been so focused on the baby they didn't even see the sheep that had wandered off. Hozai smiled and put the lamb across his shoulders and they started out.

The woman called out. "Yanai?"

Yanai turned. How did the woman know his name? "Yes, ma'am?"

She looked at him with a gaze of pure love. "Be nice to your brother."

# The Presentation

Balthazar looked out at the arid horizon from the high perch of his camel. In the distance, he could pick out the tight cluster of buildings and outer settlements that comprised one of the oldest cities in the world. He turned to Dalal, who sat on another camel. "That must be *al Shuwayhatiyah* there, to the west."

"Can we stop now? I'm really sore from riding this thing," Dalal said.

Balthazar looked down the path and saw a group of palm trees ahead. "We can stop just around the bend. It looks like there is a small oasis there." He was a little sore himself. They had been traveling for almost a month and according to his calculations, had roughly eleven days' travel left.

They dismounted and led their camels to a spring welling up from the ground. After refilling their water skins, they sat close together under the swaying fronds of a palm tree.

"What do you think we'll see when we get there?" Dalal asked.

Balthazar drank deeply before answering. "The symbolism in the sky is too great to ignore. The celestial beings point to the birth of a great king. And the prophecies of the Jews describe aspects of a future king that more than likely are satisfied in this case."

"Could it be that the child is already born?"

"Yes, by the time we get there, the child will probably be about a month old. We have to find him first."

"How will we do that?"

"I don't know. We can pay a visit to the local king there."

"Do you think we'll get to hold the baby?"

Balthazar looked at his wife. He knew what she was thinking, as he was thinking the same thing: what would it be like to have a baby. They had been married for almost four years now, and no child had yet been forthcoming. "I don't know, but you would have to think," he gestured to one of the saddlebags hanging on his camel, the one with the *al-luban* in it. This particular type was harvested only in the Sabaean kingdom and was among the most expensive in the world. Aside from the extra amount they would use to pay for tolls and food, there was probably 200 days' wages of it. Surely the parents would let them hold their baby.

The desire for a baby of their own was shared by both of them. They looked off into the distance together. Balthazar couldn't help but note the irony: he had mastered the science of the heavens, and was paid handsomely to advise kings and princes, and yet other than the conjugal act was totally ignorant of the factors that led to the creation of a child. How he wished he knew.

**

Caspar and his assistant were ready to drop. They had been traveling for over a month. There was no way the donkeys they originally set out with would have made it. After several days' delay by the monsoons that soaked them as soon as they left, they found a camel dealer in the Babylonian city of Ur and made a trade without too much of a hassle. Of course, the extra gold they brought helped even the scales, as no donkey would be considered the equivalent of a camel.

"Where are we, Master?"

Caspar reckoned they were somewhere in the northern extremes of Arabia. He looked at his assistant with a frown. "After all that I taught you about the sun and the stars, you still don't know where we are?"

His assistant gaped and stammered. "Sir, I, I don't, I don't know, no, sir."

Caspar looked him in the eye. "Why, we're in the desert."

"Oh, yes, I knew, I knew that sir."

Caspar cracked up at his joke. Sometimes his assistant could be so tightly wound. He needed to loosen up if he wanted to make it in the world of astronomy and the sciences. "Don't worry; I'm just trying to have fun. It's okay to laugh at my joke. The sun must be getting to us. Look there," Caspar pointed ahead, "I see a few palm trees and some greenery around the bend. We can stop there."

Their camels plodded forward until the little oasis emerged. There was no one there save a couple, presumably a man and his wife. There were sleeping against the trunk of one of the palm trees. Caspar led his camel around them and over to a shallow pool where water had welled up from the rocky sands below. While the animals drank, his assistant went behind a bush to relieve himself. Caspar looked at the couple. Their dress indicated someone of higher rank. Two camels tied to a nearby tree were loaded with many saddlebags. Something on one of the camels caught his attention and he approached. Tied between two of the saddlebags was a long leather-covered tube, slightly tapered at one end.

Caspar looked back at the couple, who were snoring loudly by now. He had to indulge his curiosity. He took the tube from its holster on the saddle and hefted the weight in his hands. He could feel his heart rate increase. It was about the same weight as his. He looked back to make sure the couple was still sleeping, but their loud snores left no doubt. Carefully, he started to pull it out of the case when a metallic clash rang out. He turned around to see his assistant tripping on some rocks and dropping his moneybag all over the ground. 'Curses,' he slipped the tube back into its holster with the dexterity of a thief.

The couple woke up and turned to see what the commotion was. Caspar scrambled to appear as far from their camels as possible should they look back at him. They had gotten to their feet when Caspar greeted them from behind. He took a guess and tried Greek. "I'm sorry my assistant disturbed you. Please forgive us."

The man took note of Caspar's satrap-style cloak before responding. "Do not worry. We have to be on our way anyways." The man looked at the sun and stuck a small wooden pole in the ground to study its shadow.

Caspar lit up. "It is true, then!" Seeing the couple's faces, he paused. "I'm sorry; I was excited to meet another astronomer."

The man raised his eyebrows. "You, too, study the heavens?"

"Yes, indeed. My name is Caspar."

"It is good to meet you. My name is Balthazar."

\*\*

Melchior struggled to shift his seat on his camel. Oh, how his ass hurt after a few weeks of tromping through the rough terrain. The good governor had given him two camels for the journey. It seemed as though every time he switched mounts, the ride had become even more uncomfortable than that of the last one. He unrolled the turban from his head and used it to soak the sweat dripping from his forehead, but it was getting so salty and wet he wondered if it was doing any good.

He looked around at the other travelers in the caravan. During the last ten days he had joined a small convoy of other camels and their people, which in turn had joined other convoys, like how a gurgling stream joined other rivulets in the mountains to become a great river by the time it reached the plains. Speaking of great rivers, he had the strange sensation of wanting to urinate one all over the desert floor right now, but there was no obvious place to go. He had seen some other travelers nonchalantly stop and crouch down on the ground periodically, but their long shawls hid their true actions. He couldn't bring himself to do that in the open, so he looked for some break in the landscape.

After twenty minutes of growing discomfort, Melchior spotted a few rolling hills and a clutch of palm trees to the south. He judged it was probably fifteen minutes off their current path. With eagerness, he pulled his reins to one side, and his camel and the one tied behind it veered off. He tried to keep his mind off the pressure in his bladder by reminding himself why he was undertaking this journey: to see that which the celestial beings overhead proclaimed with breathtaking enormity. At least, an enormity that was apparent to him. 'And likely one or two others on this earth who had the skill and vision to see what was going on,' he thought with a self-satisfied feeling.

After reaching the base of the hills and finishing his business, Melchior led his camels around the bend, to where he had seen the palm trees. He figured the ornery beasts deserved some water, even though riding them was a slow exercise in torture. He heard voices talking as he rounded the bend and as he approached, it sounded like Greek to him. He saw that two men were speaking with growing animation.

Melchior led both camels to a small pool near where the two men stood. One of the men stopped talking and looked over. He looked again and rushed over to Melchior's mount before pointing to something tied up amongst the bags.

"Is that what I think it is?" he asked. The man was wearing a dark blue cloak with gold threads interwoven in it and had a strange accent, but seemed harmless enough to Melchior. Untying the bag, Melchior opened it and pulled out one of his instruments.

Upon seeing it, the other two men gasped. "An armillary sphere!" they said in unison.

"How would you know what that is?" Melchior asked. He had assumed they were just two ordinary simpletons.

"I have never seen one in person," the other man, the one with a maroon cloak with gold embroidery, said. He gestured to a third man in a brown cloak who approached with a clumsy gait. "Look here," the man showed him. "This is called an armillary sphere, and helps to map the heavens." The man in brown reached for it, but the one in maroon slapped his hand away with a sharp slap. "Don't touch it. This is priceless and you have cloven hooves for hands."

With a sudden seriousness, they turned back to Melchior. The one in blue spoke. "Have you seen what we have seen?"

Melchior felt the hair on his body stand on end. He instantly knew what they were talking about and his mouth gaped open. He nodded. "How could I miss it?" he whispered.

The other two looked at each other in wonderment, then turned back to him. "Then it looks like we'll all go together."

**

After another week and a half of plodding through the desert, they reached the outskirts of Jerusalem. Melchior looked back on the last ten days. The time had seemingly accelerated as they shared their experiences and their love of the skies. Each night they validated their path by spotting the giant planet that Caspar had called Brhaspati, and each day they related the importance of what they had seen. The anticipation of the event grew until it became like another traveler with them.

Balthasar surveyed distant hills wavering in the heat and turned to the others. "We should probably make camp here tonight and enter the city tomorrow." The others proceeded to dismount and assemble their makeshift tents. After building a fire, they planned for tomorrow.

"It seems this area around Jerusalem is the place," Balthasar finished looking up and returned to the fire. "Where should we go from here?"

76

"Surely the local people are familiar with the event, too," Melchior said.

"But it is likely they only know the criteria for such a thing as the birth of a new king," Caspar said. "They most probably do not know what is happening overhead."

"It's true," Balthasar said. "I've been studying the Hebrew scriptures. Their religious elite at least would know the various conditions that must be met, but they probably don't know exactly when or where it will take place."

"Perhaps then, they will be waiting for someone like us to show them what is happening," Melchior said. "Surely, we can meet with them to put our heads together."

"Surely," Caspar said. "Tomorrow, then, we will visit their royal court."

"I agree that is the best course of action. For who better to know about the birth of a new king than their current one?"

\*\*

Herod paced back and forth in his antechamber in the very early morning hours. Sleep was increasingly difficult at this age, and after all he had done. This day, some unknown concern nagged at him, eventually pulling him out of bed. He much preferred his residence at Caesarea Philippi. But occasional festivals and religious gatherings dictated that he be in Jerusalem, tending to the needs of his people. Not that it earned him any favors among the religious elite. He frowned. 'The Pharisees and Sadducees be damned,' he thought. As a descendant of an Edomite, they regarded him to be non-Jewish, even though he had gone through the trouble of taking on the outward appearances of the faith. 'Would a non-Jew construct the Temple Mount? Would a non-Jew commission such large building projects for the glory of the city, for all of Judea? Would a non-Jew confer such benefits upon the people?'

Herod reflected on his accomplishments as he looked out the window upon the moon-soaked cityscape. Whatever pulled him out of bed needed to be dealt with. After all, he hadn't survived as king for almost 35 years by turning a blind eye to potential threats. He summoned his chamber man and had him send for Alexandros. If any man knew anything at all about the word on the street, it was Alexandros.

**

Caspar awoke in his tent and heard some rustling outside. He found Melchior cooking some bread over a fire. He sat opposite him and drank from his water skin. "Do you think their king will have knowledge of this event?"

Melchior considered the question as he tended to the flour and water gruel in the pot. "I have read about this man Herod. He has ruled for very many years and is advanced in age. Surely he must know something."

Balthasar and Dalal emerged from their tent. He bid them good morning. "I trust everyone slept well?"

Caspar grunted. "Who can sleep knowing we are so close?"

After packing up, the party set out to the city's approach. "Where do we even go from here?" Melchior asked.

Balthazar looked at the city in the distance. "I see two gigantic buildings amongst the entire city. It seems that the one in the middle must be the Temple I have read about."

Caspar squinted. "Perhaps, then, the other building is the king's palace? Why don't we try that first?" They urged their camels on, the great walls of the city looming taller as they did so. They encountered others from the countryside waiting in a line to get through one of the gates to take their goods to market. After half of an hour of nearly imperceptible progress, they made it through the Jaffa gate and turned right toward the northwest corner of the city. The building that was the palace was hard to miss. It was constructed on top of a platform rising the height of four men, itself an immense area upon which two large buildings sat.

They stopped in an expansive courtyard where an armed force of what looked like two thousand men were training. A separate group of soldiers in dress uniform stood guard at a large gate with an intricate pattern of gold and iron. Balthazar approached. "We are here to see the king."

One of the soldiers looked at them, noting the expensive style of dress and the foreign appearance of the group. His eyes lingered on the partially veiled Dalal before calling back to someone on the other side of the gate. He turned back to them. "One minute."

**

After properly dressing and watching the pale sun rise again over the hills to the east, Herod's chamberlain appeared at the door. "Alexandros is here, Your Greatness."

"Very well. Have him wait in the parlor."

Herod finished putting on his purple garments and strode out to the parlor. The man who stood waiting for the king wore a dirty white cloak and worn sandals and had the shadow of a young beard on his face.

"Alexandros, thank you for being here at this hour." Herod took note of his appearance. "My goodness, man, you look like you were just dug up."

"Please forgive my clothes, Your Greatness, for I just returned from an intelligence-gathering mission."

Herod smiled. The captain of his secret police never rested. He had come to rely heavily on this man, both to uncover active plots against him and to deter future ones. The enmity of the Pharisees and the Sadducees were undying, and they were only too happy to indulge his wayward sons' dreams of power and wealth. Herod thought they would have learned their lesson after the previous plot against him a few years earlier, when he had two of his sons executed. But the premonition he had would not go away.

Herod gestured to two richly embroidered court chairs, indicating that they should sit. "Something is troubling me, Alexandros, but I don't know what it is. Perhaps you can tell me what the man on the street is saying. I want to know what is on his mind."

Alexandros looked up at the gold leaf on the ceiling for a moment and considered his recent outings and briefings from subordinates. "Your Greatness, the people are indeed starting to stir somewhat. Many of them, especially those familiar with the prophecies of old, are getting somewhat restless."

"Restless about what?"

Alexandros took a pear from a bowl nearby and sank his teeth into it. "They seem to think that there will be some important event in the near future. An event that was foretold many generations ago, even back to Abraham himself."

"Is this talk limited to the priestly class and the Temple guard?" Herod knew that although the priests had most of the religious power, he himself had the power to appoint the High Priest. In fact, he had elevated one in order to marry his daughter. Of course, he had to remove him after having the woman executed for her part in another plot against him. 'Oh Mariamne,' he thought. Even now, some twenty-five years later, the specter of her beauty haunted him.

"No, Your Greatness, it is not limited to the priests and the scribes. It seems even common farmers are aware of something impending."

Herod leaned forward. "Tell me more."

"You know even the common people are well-versed in their scripture. It was just yesterday when I overheard two people at the market talking about…" Alexandros searched for the right word.

"Yes?"

"They were talking about a new leader."

Herod's eyebrows rose. "A new leader?"

"Yes, Your Greatness. A new king."

Herod rose and paced about in front of the marble balustrade separating the room from an open-air sala with views of the Judean hills. He breathed in deeply, taking in the sweet desert scent of jasmine and lavender. It was true, in a way, that there would be a new king someday. He was well past 70 years of age and when he went off to wherever it was that the dead went, his son Herod would take the reins. He smiled at the thought. 'We'll see how the Pharisees like that one. If they don't like the Edomite in me, surely they will love my half-Samaritan son.'

He turned back to Alexandros. "Do the people know what they are talking about?"

Alexandros finished his pear. "Well, Your Greatness, the simple and the unlearned know only what is in the scriptures, of course, so they have seized on different parts of the Word, and thus focusing on different foretellings." Alexandros paused again. "You are right in sensing something amidst the people, for you know them well. But it is difficult to nail down exactly what they are talking about."

Herod nodded. "Perhaps I should call in the priests after all. They surely lord their knowledge over the people. Let's see just what they know."

"Your Greatness?"

"Send word to Joazar ben-Boethus. I need to speak to him."

**

A royal messenger made his way up the Temple steps and summoned one of the manservants. "See that this gets to the High Priest." After receiving a nod, the messenger went back the way he came.

The manservant walked the length of the Temple and found one of the priestly caste who would take it from there. The High Priest was not permitted to mingle with commoners and surely could not receive a message directly from a lowly messenger.

The priest made his way to the house attached to the Temple that served as the High Priest's residence and found Madresh ben-Yeviah, the *segan ha-kohanim*, the High Priest's deputy. Madresh took it from there and went to the back of the house, where he knocked on the door of the inner chamber. "Come in."

Madresh entered and found Joazar ben-Boethus, High Priest, at a writing desk. "What is it, Madresh?"

"Your holiness, you have a message."

"A message?"

"Yes, your holiness, from Herod."

Joazar frowned. He took the papyrus from Madresh and unrolled it. After a few moments he gave it back to him and sighed.

"Your holiness?"

Joazar went back to his desk and sat. "Herod wants me to convene all the priestly caste and the scribes."

"For what purpose?"

Joazar took the papyrus back and read out loud. "'For the purpose of ascertaining the details surrounding the birth of the child king.'"

"It sounds like he has taken a newfound interest in the scriptures."

Joazar reflected for a moment. Herod was the one who had installed his father Simon as High Priest before removing him and having his sister executed. He was also the one who elevated Joazar. He exhaled deeply. He hated how he owed so much to the man who had taken so much from him. He handed the scroll back to Madresh. "It sounds like he is worried about competition."

**

Herod was just sitting down to breakfast when his chamberlain appeared at the door again. "For Heaven's sake, what is it now? Can't you see I am just trying to eat my sustenance for the day?"

"I beg your pardon, Your Greatness, but there are three *magi* at the gate."

Herod frowned. "What do they want?"

"They would like to talk to you, Your Greatness."

"They're not the only ones."

"They said they are bearing gifts for the king."

Herod finished some grapes. "Very well. Bring them into the fountain room. I will be there momentarily." He ate the remainder of the meal before making his way beyond the central courtyard to a large room with an inlaid stone and tile floor and lavish curtains hanging from the high ceiling. The centerpiece was a square basin in the middle of the room where water piped in from an aqueduct welled up from under the floor and cascaded down several cubits before landing into another basin and flowing off underneath the floor again. Paired with the richly decorated walls, it made a statement of technological beauty.

Upon entering, he saw three figures in what appeared to be royal dress, all with different colored of expensive fabric draped about them. One appeared Arabian, but he wasn't sure about the other two. He took his seat at a large chair adorned with gold leaf. "Greetings, gentlemen."

The one with the purple and gold vestments stepped forward. "Greetings, your majesty. My name is Caspar," he spoke in

Greek. "Accompanying me are the esteemed Melchior of the Parthian kingdom and Balthazar of the Arabian kingdom. I myself am from the western satraps of India."

Herod's eyebrows lifted. "I am intrigued now. You have come a long way."

Caspar answered. "Yes, your majesty, we have indeed. You see, in our study of the skies, we have discovered celestial signs of great importance, ones which portend a great event. We followed one particular star here and wanted to consult with you."

"And what is this great event?"

Caspar frowned. "Your majesty, are you unaware of what is being signaled?"

"Do I look like an astronomer?"

"Your majesty, I beg your pardon. Of course, it is impossible to see what is going on overhead without a lifetime of study of the celestial bodies," Caspar didn't like how this was going. "Anyhow," he gestured to the many bags hanging on their camels just outside the room, "we have brought gifts with us-"

"Gifts for whom?" Herod interrupted.

Caspar looked back at Balthasar and Melchior before turning back to Herod. "Why, your majesty, gifts for the newborn king."

Something in Herod's stomach turned and he felt a hint of bile rising in his throat. "A newborn king, did you say?"

"Why, yes, your majesty. I beg your pardon, your majesty; for we assumed the whole land would be celebrating."

Herod was a storm inside, trying his best to give no outward indication of it. "In fact, I have just called for a council of the priestly class and the elders, so they can tell me just where this newborn king is to be born. If you wait in the outer courtyard, they should be meeting shortly. You would be my very welcome guests."

Caspar looked back at Melchior and Balthazar and smiled. "We would very much appreciate that, your majesty. But there is one thing."

"And what is that?"

"According to our calculations, we believe the newborn king has already been born."

The words hit Herod with a renewed curdling of his stomach. 'If that were really the case, it wouldn't be just conjecture,' he thought. 'Then there really would be someone else, a competitor for my line.' He straightened a bit. "Well, let us see what the council says."

**

Within an hour, the scribes and the priests had assembled with Joazar in Herod's courtyard. The three *magi* were off to one side with Dalal and Caspar's assistant, under the forgiving shade of a palm tree. Herod came out.

"Joazar, esteemed High Priest and respected members of the priestly class and the scribes, I welcome you."

Joazar stepped forward. "Thank you, Your Greatness. We are gathered here today at your request. We have been studying the question about the Messiah. After much studying, we have determined the relevant prophecy is found in the book of Micah:

*'But you, Bethlehem-Ephrathaha*
*least among the clans of Judah,*
*From you shall come forth for me*

*one who is to be ruler in Israel;*

*Whose origin is from of old,*

*from ancient times.'" (Micah 5:1)*

He continued. "Your majesty, while we can be fairly certain of the place of the birth, we have no idea as to the time frame."

Herod nodded. 'That was not a problem,' he thought. "Esteemed elders, you can't be expected to know everything, can you?" He thanked them and dismissed the group. After they had all filed out of the royal complex, Herod walked over to the magi. "You heard them. The new king is to be born in Bethlehem. Please go and find this king and then report back to me, so that I may also honor and worship him."

\*\*

The little retinue set out immediately and made the short trip to Bethlehem by dusk. The planet of Jupiter was now almost totally in line with Venus and seemingly hanging directly overhead. They brought their camels to a halt.

"My heart is racing with anticipation," Melchior said. "Do you see how the star is now totally overhead? We must be near," the excitement made his voice quiver.

"Just so; however, the only structure in sight is that ramshackle mud hut," Caspar pointed to a spot about two stadia away. "Surely that cannot be the residence of the new child king?" The other magi nodded in agreement.

"Let me go and inquire," Dalal said. The others looked at her with surprise, and then at Balthazar.

"That is a great idea," Balthazar said. "We will wait for you here." He held her arm. "But be careful, my love."

She smiled before leading her camel off.

\*\*

Mary finished feeding her baby and wrapped up. Oh, how the night was getting cold. No matter, though. She looked at her little Jesus and held him tight. He was already asleep now and seemed to warm her entire body.

A scraping sound on the dirt outside made her look up. "Joseph, is that you?" There were a few more scraping sounds as a woman appeared in the doorway.

"I'm sorry to disturb you," the woman said, her eyes fixed on the infant Jesus. "Oh, it is true, isn't it? So beautiful your child is," she cast a longing gaze on him. After a few moments, Mary stood.

"Would you like to hold him?"

The woman stared at Mary and was overcome. "I, I am not worthy," she whispered.

Mary smiled and carefully handed her baby to the woman. She took him and was lost in the moment, out of words. "I know why you are here," Mary said.

The woman looked up. "My goodness, I haven't said anything about that yet. I am sorry, I should have introduced myself. It's just that," she looked at Jesus again, "he is so beautiful." Looking again at Mary, she said, "we traveled here to see the child king, the one who is called the Messiah."

Mary smiled at her. "There is another reason you are here, isn't there, Dalal?"

Dalal looked up, astonishment all over her face. "How did you know my name?" Mary's gaze of total love penetrated to her core.

"The Lord has been good to me. I know you are here with the magi, and that they wanted to see the new king. But you were looking for another miracle, too, weren't you?"

Dalal nodded slowly. "We, we have been trying for so long," her eyes started to water. Oh, how it was hard to speak of this out loud. Mary continued to look at her with a look of a lifelong friend. "I have always wondered what is the matter with me." She started to weep.

Mary embraced her and held her in a cocoon of love. Dalal felt in total ecstasy being comforted like this, with the infant Savior in her arms. Mary whispered to her. "There is nothing wrong with you. The Lord has revealed to me that you will bring forth a child as soon as you return home."

Dalal gave Jesus back before crying. Pure joy ran down her face. Mary held her again, and they stood together for what seemed like a sweet eternity to Dalal. She stepped back and laughed. "I had better get the rest."

\*\*

Simeon made his way into the Temple proper. He tried to pray in silence, but was constantly interrupted by the comings and goings of all manner of people who were taking sacrifices to the main altar. All he wanted in his old age was to see the Savior of Israel before he died, to know that the people had hope after all. He kept trying, even as the main doors thirty yards behind him opened repeatedly, bringing the noises of countless donkeys, goats, horses and camels from the outside in. Despite the noise, he was distracted by something else. Last night, in a dream, he had been instructed to watch out for an infant, carried by a woman in blue and a man in a brown cloak. The rest of the dream made no sense to him. The infant had a golden aura, and the pair of turtledoves the parents brought became invisible. Simeon sat back and wondered. Sometimes the Lord spoke in mysterious ways.

\*\*

Anna knelt by the front of the Temple in her usual spot, as near to the altar as she could get. She had spent day and night here fasting and praying. Despite her old age, she never tired of kneeling in prayer before the great altar of the Lord. Today, her praying became especially fervent as she recalled the vision she had earlier that morning.

A great prince was to be crowned King. Anna watched from a distance in the royal court as a splendid procession wound its way inside. It was revealed that only the one bearing the greatest gift was worthy to be the King. After countless people had filed in, the crowd became silent in anticipation. One person after another approached the throne. Some brought a multitude of gold coins, some had great silver chains, others bore huge bundles of the finest wheat and still others reams of the most expensive silk, but none were the true prince and thus would not be crowned. The last to approach was a man who came empty-handed.

She ruminated on the vision. Would she recognize the great prince?

**

On the day they were to present Jesus to the Lord, Mary and Joseph made their way to the Temple. As they approached, crowds of many people carried on with their day in the outer courtyard: there were the money changers who converted the people's sinful Roman coins into the accepted Temple currency of *drachmas*, there were the handlers who sold their animals to those who would make them a sacrifice, and there were the common people, who wanted only to worship.

They picked their way through the crowd until they found a money-changer and exchanged a few coins. Then they looked around for a bird seller until their eyes fell upon a man behind a table with ten birdcages stacked behind him.

Joseph approached as the man looked up. "What do you need, sir?"

"Either two turtledoves or two pigeons," Joseph said.

The man turned around and looked at his cages. "You're in luck," he said. "I only have two birds left."

"You must have been busy today."

The man shook his head in amazement. "I must have sold birds to about sixty couples like you today, wanting to bring your child before the Lord."

Joseph took the birds, one in each hand, and they went inside. Mary held Jesus tight in swaddling clothes and wrapped in a sling around her shoulder. Joseph walked ahead of her, since there were so many people they couldn't walk side by side. The birds wriggled in his hands.

**

Simeon watched one couple after another file up the center aisle toward the main altar. It seemed that almost all of the women were wearing blue mantles, and over half the men had brown cloaks. He kept his eyes steady on the people filing in, wondering again about what the disappearing turtledoves meant. From the back, he watched with amusement as a wizened old woman made her way to the front with determination. She used both elbows quite effectively, swinging them back and forth to clear a path forward. She must have hit someone else's elbow in just the right spot, for one man's hand went limp and a bird flew out. Startled, he tried to grab it out of midair and the bird in his other hand flew away, too. Simeon's eyes widened. The disappearing turtledoves.

**

"Oh, can you believe that?" Joseph said with an edge of annoyance to that. "That old woman knocked into me and the birds just flew out of my hands." The crowd of worshippers in front of them was slowing again, so they were forced to stop. Joseph struggled to see where the birds might have flown, for they stopped right in the middle of a shaft of sunlight streaming with golden brilliance through one of the Temple window openings.

"Oh Joseph, we have no sacrifice anymore," Mary exclaimed. "What are we going to do?"

"It will be all right; the Lord knows we intended to make the sacrifice. Nothing is hidden from Him."

Just then an old man approached them with a look of wonderment on his face.

*He took him into his arms and blessed God, saying: "Now, Master, you may let your servant go in peace, according to your word, for my eyes have seen your salvation, which you prepared in sight of all the peoples, a light for revelation to the Gentiles, and glory for your people Israel." The child's father and mother were amazed at what was said about him; and Simeon blessed them and said to Mary his mother, "Behold, this child is destined for the fall and rise of many in Israel, and to be a sign that will be contradicted (and you yourself a sword will pierce) so that the thoughts of many hearts may be revealed." (Luke 2: 28-35)*

\*\*

Anna watched as couple after couple stopped at the front of the altar and laid down their sacrifice. It was nearing the end of another day, but Anna could feel the Spirit working inside her. She watched closely, anticipating the new King. Who would it be? She watched a few more couples lay their sacrifice upon the altar and moving away, clearing the way for another couple and their child. She looked closer. This one was different. They had no sacrifice with them. She stood with excitement as a flash of understanding came to her. They weren't empty-handed after all. They had brought the greatest gift: their baby. She rushed to them. Their child was to be the new King. He was to be the sacrifice.

\*\*

Mary and Joseph left the main altar and were moving around to the side when an old woman approached and stopped them. She looked at them and said, "May my soul praise Yahweh, for indeed is He great. He has deigned me to cast my eyes upon the newborn King, who is to be the salvation of Israel." The excitement in her voice was palpable.

Mary looked at her and saw that the woman's eyes were watering. "Would you like to hold him?" she asked.

The woman's face glowed with an aura of awe about her as she took Jesus in her arms. She looked down at him and melted into tears. "As surely as my name is Anna, I have been coming to the Temple night and day for my whole life," she wiped some tears away. "And now the Lord has allowed me to behold the one who is to save his people, the one who is to be both King and sacrifice for his people, that they should be free forever. Oh, how I behold his sweet little cheeks and his precious fingers and toes, his soft skin and his gentle breathing, like that of a newborn lamb." She looked at Mary and Joseph. "Thank you, for now I can go and rest in peace." With one last caress, she gave the child back to Mary and went away.

# The Finding of the Child Jesus in the Temple

The instant bright blue of the desert sky signaled the daybreak as Caspar awoke and started to prepare a hot drink over the remains of last night's fire. They had spent the night just a stone's throw from where they found the newborn King and were preparing to go back. Caspar's assistant tripped over something and dropped a cooking stone onto the rocky ground, causing a loud crash. Not long after, the others emerged from their tents.

Despite the joy of yesterday's encounter with the Savior of mankind, a mood of foreboding fell over the little camp. As they ate, Balthasar looked up. "I had the strangest dream last night." The others stopped chewing as Balthasar continued. "I dreamt that we were on foot, following a bright star in the distance. As we walked, total darkness kept encroaching on us from behind, and the ground we covered crumbled into nothingness as soon as we walked over it."

The others absorbed this as they watched the fire. After a few moments, Caspar cleared his throat. "I had a vision in which my mentor appeared to me. He has been dead for several years now. He taught me everything I know about the sun and the stars. We were walking by the seashore when he stopped me and looked at me with all seriousness. 'Remember what I told you about the sea: never turn your back on it.' And then I woke up."

Melchior finished his breakfast and wiped his mouth with his sleeve. "I, too, had a vision last night. Something, an angel perhaps, at least I assume it was an angel, for it was a spectacular being who radiated pure joy and goodness, appeared to me with a message."

Caspar looked at Melchior. "Well, do not leave us in suspense. What was it?"

Melchior swallowed some warm tea. "The angel didn't speak, but rather it felt like it was transmitting something directly into my head."

Balthasar straightened. "Well, what was it?"

"The angel said that the way to enlightenment is not a circle."

"Huh?" Balthasar frowned.

"The angel said that once something is revealed to you, that you cannot be the same person again."

After a few more moments of contemplation, Dalal jumped up, startling the others. "I get it!" Seeing the puzzled looks around her, she continued. "Don't you see what is going on here? The true God, the Lord of the sun and the sky is telling you a message. We have encountered the new King, the Messiah. It seems so obvious that we are not to go back the way we came."

Caspar nodded. "And what about Herod, who wanted to pay homage to the child after we tell him where he is?"

Dalal shook her head. "We are to avoid Herod at all costs. Did you not sense his evil designs when we were there in his presence? I could almost feel the chill when he heard about this child, as if the child were a threat to him."

Melchior looked up. "But he's just a baby."

"Not just a baby, but a new King. A new King, sent from heaven above," Balthazar said.

Melchior drew on the ground absent-mindedly. "You know, you are right. In fact, now I wonder if he had us followed."

"And you know what that means," Caspar said. The others looked at him. "We split up from here."

**

Herod paced about the fountain room with consternation. He looked at the sundial in the courtyard. 'Where was that damned Alexandros?' he wondered. It had been several months since the visit of the *magi* to his palace, and his disquietude about murmurings on the street only grew. His chief of intelligence had confirmed earlier that the common man on the street was expecting something soon in light of ancient prophecies, and the appearance of the wise men had made his blood run cold with dread. He must preserve his royal lineage from attacks. He looked out at the horizon at the enormous Temple in the distance. Legacies such as his must not be forgotten.

After an interminable time walking around the fountain, Alexandros appeared at the door. "You called, Your Greatness?"

"Where have you been?" Herod pounced as soon as he saw him.

"I was overseeing the punishment of two of your bodyguards. They were late for duty yesterday morning."

Herod stopped. "My men? What happened?"

"Your Greatness, it seems as though they got into sour wine and then had a falling out with two of the city's women of the night."

Herod frowned. Having a guard force of two thousand men for his protection lent a feeling of security, but there were drawbacks to maintaining such a large number. Inevitably, there would be a few bad actors. "What was the punishment?"

"The usual, Your Greatness. They were stripped in front of the cohort and given ten lashes to the genitals."

Herod nodded. Even within his bodyguard ranks, fear was needed to keep the men in line. "Enough about that, let us discuss something else entirely." He led Alexandros to his inner chamber and motioned for him to sit.

"What is on your mind, Your Greatness?"

"It has been several months now since the magi appeared with word of a newborn king."

"Your Greatness?"

"I asked them to return here to inform me where the child is."

Alexandros followed his line of thought. The magi had gone off without telling Herod anything. What were they hiding? He grunted.

"So you see what I am facing now. One who aspires to be king, whose way may be cleared by the peasants' belief in the ancient scriptures."

"Only we don't know where he is," Alexandros felt something in his stomach turn.

"That is not true," Herod said. "We know he is in Bethlehem, just a few miles away."

"But we don't know who he is," Alexandros didn't like where this was going.

"He, whoever he is, is just a baby," Herod stood and walked to a window facing the hills of the city. "The magi said it was possible the child had already been born. So, let's just assume the boy is no more than, say, two years old."

"Sir?" Alexandros shifted in his chair. "What are you saying?" Although deep down, he had a feeling what it was.

Herod turned back to Alexandros. "There is a threat out there," he stabbed a finger out toward the south. "Your job is to eliminate threats against me."

Alexandros saw a churning hate stirred up in Herod's eyes, and with it, an implicit threat. He knew that disobedience would entail much more than the punishment he had just overseen. "You want the men to find this child and kill him?"

"Not the one," Herod fumed. "All of them!"

Alexandros felt his mouth dry up and his heart race. "It will be a bloodbath," he whispered.

Herod looked out again. "It will be for the good of the kingdom."

**

Mary lay awake in the early morning hour before sunrise. She glanced at Jesus sleeping in a large woven basket filled with rags for a cushion. Warm joy spread over her as she saw his little tummy rise and fall with each breath. 'What a gift from the Lord,' she thought. She turned and saw Joseph, his face impassive in his slumber save for a slight furl in his eyebrows. With a jolt, he awoke and sat upright.

"Dear Joseph, what is it?" Mary asked.

He looked at her and caught his breath. "We have to go!"

"What?"

"We have to go, and now!" he got out of bed and started to put on his cloak.

"Joseph, what is the matter?"

Joseph raced around looking for his sandals. Finding them, he sat next to Mary. "I had a dream, Miriam. An angel appeared to me with a message from the Lord. He said we are to flee immediately."

"Really? When?"

"Now!" Joseph went about their small hut, collecting a few things. "I will prepare the little hay wagon and saddle the donkey."

"When are we coming back?"

"Here? Never."

Mary looked down and thought about what the prophetess Anna said to them in the Temple.

Joseph looked at the baby. "You be sure Jesus is fed and changed before you come out."

"But why?"

Joseph stopped at the door. "Herod, that's why."

Mary got up and collected the few things she would need. As she went about, she repeated the short prayer that she relied on. 'Trust in the Lord. Trust in the Lord.'

Joseph finished gearing up the donkey and hitching the small hay wagon to it when Mary appeared with Jesus in the doorway. She had the little baby swaddled and in a sling tied tightly around her. He looked up. The sun was beginning to rise over the hills to the east. "Very good. I think we are all set." He started to help Mary up onto the donkey when they heard the sounds of hoof beats in the distance. Joseph pulled Mary back down. "Quick, hide yourself in the hay wagon!" He helped her scramble in before heaping some armloads of hay on top of them. After they were covered, he bent down and whispered. "Be sure to keep the baby quiet, understand?"

"Yes," Mary's quiet voice was muffled by the hay.

Joseph climbed onto the donkey and led it around the hut and onto the wide road that ran through Bethlehem and wound south all the way to Masada. The hoof-beats they heard earlier appeared on the crest of a hill in front of him in the form of four riders. As they approached, Joseph could see that they wore the insignia of Herod's personal bodyguard. His heart rate beat faster. 'Why couldn't the angel come earlier?' he wondered.

As it was the morning, there were already travelers on the road with him. The four riders came to a stop about a few hundred cubits in front of him, next to a family on foot with two donkeys. Joseph watched as the riders stopped them. It looked as though there was a man and a woman with two children, perhaps around the ages of eight or ten. One of the riders started shouting at them before trying to take something from the woman. The man tried to stop him but another rider struck him on the face with the hilt of his heavy sword. Now there was another noise, and Joseph could see what it was: a small child, perhaps less than a year old. The rider yanked the child from the woman and ran his sword through the child's stomach.

**

From beneath the hay, Mary lay curled up around Jesus in her sling, trying to divine what was happening around them. The donkey and the wagon came to a stop all of a sudden. Mary could hear the faint voices of someone arguing, perhaps some distance away. She shifted positions a bit to get more comfortable. A scream of anguish tore through the air and cut through her heart. It could only have been the sound of a mother. Renewed feelings of dread and adrenaline coursed through Mary's body. What was going on? She struggled to calm her breathing so she could hear the outside world. The unmistakable sound of hoof beats started, and she paused. They were getting closer.

**

Joseph could not believe what he had just seen. Now the four riders took off and headed in his direction. He fought to keep passive and did his best not to draw attention to himself, but how could he keep the revulsion and the horror off his face? He took the reins again and called out to the donkey to continue. The riders quickly approached. Joseph felt bile rise in his throat and prayed hard, as hard as he had ever prayed. 'Dear Lord, help us! This is your son!'

The lead rider slowed as they neared Joseph. Joseph slipped one hand under his seat and felt for the handy axe he always carried. The rest caught up with the main rider, but they quickly glanced at him and his solitary pile of hay and kept riding.

Joseph urged the donkey on and felt the immediate danger of the situation melt away in the form of sweat all over his body. It was like a fever broke. He wiped his brow with his hands and wiped his hands with his cloak before looking up again. He was almost upon the family.

\*\*

The husband and wife were in shock at what had just happened. Their other son managed to pick their baby off the path and give him to her. Huddled together and moaning, they barely noticed the man with the donkey pulling a hay wagon come to a stop near them. The man got down and looked up and down the path. By this time there was no one else on the road except for the two groups and the undeniable sorrow that hung in the air. The husband looked up to see the man looking for something in the hay. Before long, the entire pile shifted and a young woman crawled out. She brushed some of the shoots off her and looked at the family with a look of equal parts sadness and compassion. It looked as though she had a baby in a sling over her shoulder and snuggled against her bosom.

The rest of the family looked up at her. She had her arms out. "May I?" The sweet melody of her voice and the unquestionable certainty of prayer it carried with it put them at ease. The mother handed the limp body of the bloodied child to the woman. With tender care, the woman slid the child into the sling with her own baby, who appeared to be sleeping. She whispered to her baby who seemed to wake and immediately started crying. The woman held the bulging sling against her body and slowly bounced up and down, praying as she did so. After a few moments of watching in awe, the family looked on as the woman took their child out of the sling and kissed him on the forehead before handing him back to the mother. Their child was breathing! The father ran his hands over the child's bloodied stomach before looking up again at the woman. There was no more wound. As one, the family immediately fell to the ground and adored the baby.

After a few moments, the woman spoke again. "You are not to return home, but instead make for the neighboring district and stay there for three months. And then, it will be safe to return."

The father spoke up. "But, who is this holy child?"

The woman looked at them with eyes of heavenly love, which sent rays of joy and peace right through their very being. "He is the Son of God." They stood with mouths agape as the woman adjusted her sling and crawled back onto the cart before the man commanded the donkey to pull away.

**

After a few more hours of travel, Joseph stopped the cart by a small oasis and looked up and down the road. Seeing that the way was clear, he helped Mary out of the cart. They filled some wineskins with water and sat underneath a clutch of palm trees.

"Does the baby need to eat?" Joseph asked.

Mary looked down at their child. "I fed him in the cart, so he'll probably sleep for another hour or so." She drank deeply from the wineskin. "So, what exactly did the angel say to you?"

"That we would be safe in Egypt."

Mary looked at him with a start. "Egypt?"

"Yes."

"How far away it is."

"Indeed, yes, but that is the distance we must go to escape the danger."

104

"And what did the angel say about that?"

"That we were to flee immediately, for Herod was out to destroy the child."

"But how does he know which one Jesus is?"

"He doesn't."

The unspeakable dawned upon Mary. "So he just ordered the slaughter of every little boy his men could find?" She looked down at her baby, sleeping peacefully, and thought of all the other children. "Oh, how my heart is broken for all those families." Tears streamed down her face. "What an unimaginable horror."

They sat for a moment, holding each other in contemplation of the unthinkable. Joseph wiped his face with his sleeve. "I wish we could go back and save all those little children." He shook his head.

"I know, Joseph." Mary thought again about their visit to the Temple and looked at him with an intensity of grace. "But one day, he will save all of mankind."

**

At daybreak, the sound of a child screaming brought Joseph back to those desperate days twelve years ago. He looked around the small village and figured it was just the child of Mattheus and his wife. Their baby probably had a tooth coming in. He stared into the distance and considered all that had happened since that terrible morning. After two years in Egypt, the angel appeared and told Joseph it was safe to return. They made their way back and settled in Nazareth, near family. It had been good to be among friends and relatives, and the simple cadence of life, of waking, eating, praying and woodworking all made for a placid existence.

Jesus appeared at Joseph's side. "What are you thinking about, Father?"

Joseph paused. He didn't want to dwell on those things in the past. "I was thinking about one of the times we went to Jerusalem." Joseph turned to Jesus. "You were just born, and we took you to the Temple." They hadn't told Jesus of what they went through during those early years, but Joseph figured there was some way Jesus would know about it anyways.

Jesus smiled. "There is no place like home."

Joseph put his arm around the boy. "Come, let us gather our things, for we are going tomorrow and we must prepare." They went off to pack.

Mary was inside, finishing her preparations as well. They would go as part of a caravan of family and friends from the village and could be away for as long as three or four weeks. Although they didn't have many material things, the important part of the preparation involved prayer. As Mary finished packing a few reams of fabric and some of her tools, she sensed something vague and unsettled in the core of her being. She had these feelings from time to time and simply prayed to the Lord for help. And He did.

**

After the feast of the Passover, Mary and Joseph found themselves in the middle of a caravan stretching 70 camels long and headed back north, with numerous other beasts of burden hauling the bulk of Mary's and Joseph's relatives. They had set out

106

from Jerusalem in the morning and by this time had made it almost halfway to the village of Sychor before stopping at an oasis. While letting their animals drink, Mary approached Joseph. "Joseph, didn't you say that Jesus was in the back with the rest of the children?" Concern and worry were etched onto her face.

Joseph frowned. "I saw him preparing the smaller animals with his cousins just before setting out. Why?" He leaned closer. "Is he not back there?"

"I haven't seen him yet," Mary wiped the sweat from her brow. "Come, let us go up and down the line again." She pulled his sleeve. "You head up to the front and I will look in the back." They walked among their friends and relatives, calling for Jesus and growing more desperate by the minute. After ten minutes of frantic searching, they regrouped in the middle.

"I haven't seen him," Joseph put his hands on Mary's shoulders as his voice cracked under the duress.

Mary held a hand to her mouth. "I haven't, either." The feeling in her gut was back. She looked around her in panic. "Oh my God, we have to find him!"

**

Jesus wandered around the market outside the Temple. This place was so big, so bright, and the bustling of activity was different than what he was used to in the sleepy village of Nazareth. He looked for his parents but did not see them. Despite being alone in this unfamiliar place, he wasn't worried but instead made his way to the Temple Mount.

Inside, he found a rabbi instructing his class. Jesus sat and listened.

"Now then, my students, we just studied the first book of Samuel. We read about how he was born to Hannah, the Hannah who was denied a child for years until she came to make a sacrifice of a certain kind. Tell me, then, my students, why was she denied a child for so long?"

One of the students arose. "Teacher, it was because the woman did not have enough of the right kind of offering."

The rabbi replied. "You are both right and wrong." He walked around the group, gauging their reaction. "Who is going to tell me why your friend here is both right and wrong?" Seeing looks of confusion on his students' faces, he continued. "I will tell you why he is wrong first. Does it not say in the text that Elkanah gave Hannah a double portion to her compared to his other wife, Peninnah? And did not Peninnah already have children of her own? So you can see it is wrong to say that she did not have enough of the right kind of offering." The rabbi looked around and saw small nods of understanding signaling the message was hitting home. "Now then, my students, why is he right to say that Hannah did not have enough of the right kind of offering?"

Another student stood to speak. "My teacher, was it because the meat was from the wrong kind of animal?"

"No." The rabbi surveyed the group. "Who is going to tell me why?" Blank stares looked back at him. The rabbi walked back to the front when an unfamiliar voice sounded. "I will tell you why, teacher."

The rabbi looked and saw the voice belonged to a boy sitting a little ways away from the group, the one who had wandered in some time ago. All the students turned as one to look at this upstart with the upcountry accent. They looked back to their rabbi, who raised his eyebrows. "Very well, then."

Jesus stood and addressed them. "Hannah had indeed been bringing enough of the right kind of sacrifice, or at least, the right kind of outward sacrifice according to the law. But recall that not until she spoke from the heart, through her tears, to the Lord, did He grant her request. It is obvious the real sacrifice He desired from Hannah was for her to pour out her heart to Him. Indeed, burnt offerings are the proper form as described in the scriptures, but they are worthless unless accompanied by a true heart-to-heart relationship with the Lord."

The students around him were stunned at this, that such a boy in simple dress and an uneducated one at that could give such an answer. They looked at him with malice. But the rabbi smiled. "Very good, young man. Come, why don't you sit closer with the group?"

The students made room for him with reluctance. The rabbi continued. "Now, you see that you must read scriptures not only with the scrupulous legalosity of one who is concerned with the proper details of conformity to the Law, but also with a love for and a heart for the Lord." He paced about the group, looking to see whether they understood. "Now, is there anything else we can take from this lesson?"

After a long pause, the young man from the country stood again. "Rabbi, there is something else here." The students around him glared at him, but he continued. "Recall that the sons of Eli who were serving as priests were corrupt. They defiled their sacred duty by taking parts of the sacrifice for themselves, and even laying with the woman who served as assistants in the tent."

The rabbi interjected. "But through the intercession of those priests, the Lord still heard Hannah's cry." The students looked at Jesus, wondering how he could possibly answer that one.

"Yes, indeed, Teacher, and the Lord gave Hannah her son Samuel. And Samuel indeed was a great prophet, and was a true servant of Israel. But this is about more than one woman and her request for a son. Indeed, the story is incomplete because recall that almost immediately afterward the Philistines attacked Israel, inflicting heavy losses and taking away the Ark of the Covenant."

The students were amazed and looked back at their teacher, who was similarly impressed. "Tell me, then, if the story is not about just one woman and her request for a son, what is it about?"

Jesus paced about among the group. "It is about an incomplete nation, a nation still in waiting for the revelation of the Lord. You see here that even though Hannah brought double portions of meat, her sacrifice wasn't enough. And recall that the sons of Eli, the priests, were wicked." He looked around at them. "So here we have an incomplete sacrifice along with evil intercessors. So as this text shows, this nation is still awaiting the fulfillment of the Lord. And indeed, even now all of Israel is awaiting the fulfillment of the Law and the Prophets. But I tell you that day will not come until there is one true sacrifice, a perfect one, along with one true priest, also a perfect one."

The rabbi and his students looked with mouths agape at the young man. After a period of silence, the rabbi cleared his throat. "Well said."

**

Mary and Joseph retraced their steps to Jerusalem and reached the city at dusk. Weary from the trip but with adrenaline-filled worry bordering on hysteria, they entered through the Fish Gate and started first at their relatives' houses, but none saw Jesus. By nightfall, their exhaustion drove them to sleep on a haystack at Mary's cousin's house.

The night passed with just a few hours of fitful sleep before a cock crowing woke them up. After a few seconds looking around at this unexpected place, the realization that they were missing their son washed over them with a renewed sense of panic.

"Perhaps we should split up today, so we can cover more ground," Joseph said.

Mary shook her head. "No. We stay together. I cannot bear to be apart from you as well." The strain marked circles around her eyes.

"Very well." Joseph reached out a hand and helped Mary up. "Let's get going, then."

They started with the market district, darting in between and among the stalls and calling out for Jesus. After a full 45 minutes of frantic searching, they made their way through the Second Quarter, similarly calling out for their boy. They strained to be heard above the normal fray of haggling barters. Numerous cooking fires lowered a smoky veil upon the city, complicating their search. Block by block, street by street and alley by alley they looked. One after another, they saw nothing but the dizzying array of small shops, hawkers marketing their wares, and all manner of livestock.

Joseph stopped and looked at the sky. "My God, where are you?"

**

Jesus found the rabbi and his students in the same place the next morning. Like yesterday, he wandered in and sat near the outer edges of the group. The rabbi was in mid-lecture. "As you can see, my students, the Psalmist King David gives here in the 23rd Psalm a certain picture of us and of the Lord. What is the picture of us here?" He looked around at his students. After a brief moment, one of them raised his hand.

"It sounds as though we are to be sheep," he said.

The rabbi smiled. "Of course. The imagery here is undeniable. But what about the shepherd? What are we to make of the Lord who is our shepherd? How will we know when this is fulfilled, that the Messiah will come and walk among us?" Seeing no one attempt an answer, the rabbi stopped one of the priestly class that happened to be walking by. "Excuse me, Rabbi Joseph, could we trouble you for a moment? We need your expert commentary."

The one called Rabbi Joseph had a broad smile on his face. "But of course Rabbi. How is it that I can help?"

"We are studying the Psalm where it is written that *'The Lord is my shepherd; there is nothing I will lack'* and we are wondering how we are to know when the Messiah comes during the time of fulfillment."

Rabbi Joseph's face turned to a frown. "There is no way we can possibly know. No human mind can understand when that will happen."

The students around him looked down with varying levels of disappointment, for they had been expecting insight of some magnitude from this man, whose father-in-law was the High Priest and who many thought would attain that office one day.

"Doesn't David give us a clue?" Jesus's voice rang out from the back.

Rabbi Joseph furrowed his brow. Who was this little kid who asked such a question? Rabbi Joseph turned it around on him. "What do you think?"

Jesus stood. "One asks, 'How are we to know the Messiah when he comes?' The psalm here speaks of a good shepherd and of a lamb with total trust in the shepherd. You ask which shepherd will the Messiah be, but I tell you that at the time of fulfillment, we are to look for the one who is both the Good Shepherd and the little lamb."

The others looked at him in amazement. "Indeed, the Good Shepherd is there to lead us, but the lamb is there to be a sacrifice. Who can't help but think of Isaiah, where it is written

'But he was pierced for our sins,
crushed for our iniquity.
He bore the punishment that makes us whole,
by his wounds we were healed.

*We had all gone astray like sheep,*

*all following our own way;*

*But the LORD laid upon him*

*the guilt of us all.' " (Isaiah 53:5-6)*

"What are you saying?" Rabbi Joseph asked.

Jesus looked back at him. "That the Good Shepherd and the Lamb are one and the same."

**

After another fruitless day of searching, Mary and Joseph collapsed on the pile of hay at her cousin's house. An indescribable aching settled in Mary's heart. "Oh, Joseph, how I cannot bear the thought of our little Jesus out there all alone," she sobbed into her hands. "To think of our child wandering about the city, looking for us."

Joseph felt the pain down to his very bones. "My heart is so low. I was given the task to watch over him and raise him in the faith and he has vanished from our sight. How I wish I could turn this city upside down."

Mary looked at him through her tears. "I know it is difficult, so hard to sit here helpless and hopeless. But we must trust the Lord, however hard it is." She turned over and clawed at the dirt floor. "Where, Oh God, is our son?"

Joseph reached for her to comfort her. "There is only one place left to go, then."

**

The next day Jesus found the rabbi and his students again in the Temple. As before, he sat on the outer edge and listened as the rabbi taught.

114

"As we read in Esther, we see the queen who implores King Ahasuerus to save her people from his royal decree of annihilation for all Jews. And in doing so, she risks her own life, for no one who approaches the King without invitation can do so and live." He paused and looked at his students. "What are we to make of this queen, this woman Esther?"

One student stood. "Before she approached the king, she made sure to adorn herself in the most illustrious of vestments, so as to make her appearance pleasing to the King."

The rabbi nodded. "So what does that mean for us?"

The student answered. "We are to do likewise when we approach the Lord, to make ourselves splendid by clothing our hearts and minds with purity of thought and intention.

The rabbi smiled. "Very good." Perhaps his students were finally getting it.

Jesus spoke up from the outer edge. "That is not all we are to make of it."

The rabbi turned around. "Oh? What else is there?" The students turned and looked as one at Jesus.

"It is true that we are to adorn our hearts and mind with purity of thought and intention, yes. But this story holds more for us, as it prefigures the Queen of the Lord."

"How so?" the rabbi asked.

Jesus paced about. "Queen Esther risks her life in beseeching the king to save her people. This is merely a preview of the Queen of the Lord, one who is both infinitely more beautiful and infinitely more holy than Esther. This Queen has given her very life for her people, with her '*yes*' to the Lord, so as to serve the will of the Lord. And she will persevere forever as one who will continually intercede for them."

"You speak as though this has already occurred."

"It has."

The rabbi stared at Jesus. "As you know, my child, throughout the history of our people, the mother of the king served as the queen. Are you saying that the Lord himself has a mother?" The students around them laughed.

"Yes," Jesus answered.

"But the Lord is God above heaven and earth and all creation," confusion and a trace of anger traced themselves upon the rabbi's face. "God doesn't need a mother!"

"It is true. But he didn't need a son, either."

"What?" Confusion reigned upon the rabbi and the students. The rabbi walked toward Jesus. "Who is this woman who is Queen of heaven and earth?"

Just then a woman's voice rang out from the rear of the Temple "Yeshua, Yeshua!" Jesus turned to look at his parents running to him. He smiled, for they finally found him. He turned back to the rabbi. "Behold, the Queen."

The rabbi and the students were speechless as they watched the boy run back to his parents. And like that, they were gone.

# The Baptism of Our Lord

James took in the scene around him: the people were wandering into the desert in droves to see the prophet. The man called John was a curious sight, dressed in a camel hair cloak, with a simple belt around his waist. Word had it that his parents had money; after all, his father was of the priestly class. 'Why then, had he chosen this life, in this place?' James wondered. The barren scene crunched underfoot: minute rocks, thorny bushes and sand and dirt as far as the eye could see. Slight rolling hills touched the horizon, the only change in the landscape. But never mind; he, too, was drawn into this place, at this time. His partner Andrew was a disciple of John's. James recalled a few days ago, when Andrew rushed into James's house on the outskirts of Bethsaida.

"James! James!"

"What is it?"

"Tomorrow, you are coming with me. Be sure to gather what food you have."

"What for? And why are you being so loud?"

Andrew calmed down. "I'm sorry James. It's just that I am going off to the River to hear John preach."

"So?"

"So, I've told you about him before. He is a true prophet, a true man of Yahweh." He bowed his head as he uttered the abbreviation for the name of the Lord.

"You have seen him many times before. What is so special about tomorrow? And why do you want me to come along?" James gestured to his fishing boats outside. "We have to take the fish to the market tomorrow."

Andrew put his hands on James's shoulders. "Friend, I promise you it will be worth your time." He spoke with a serenity he had not seen in Andrew before. "There is something different now. I can sense some sort of change is coming." He peered into James's eyes. "Please."

"Well..."

"I'll even help put the nets out when we get back."

"That's your job."

"Come on."

"So be it."

"Excellent!"

Andrew had come for him in the morning, before the sun peered over the horizon to re-kindle Israel's warmth after another cold desert night.

And so now they were here. James looked around. There were perhaps a few hundred people around, waiting for John to speak. He motioned for them to sit.

James listed to him preach, intent on his every word. He listened to John talk about the mighty power of God, about how the Lord could forgive any sin of anyone who repented. It made James think of all the times he had treated his workers roughly. He started to rationalize his behavior. 'It's not like I have unlawful knowledge of a woman,' he thought. But as John continued, he realized that he was simply a sinner, a poor soul in need of the Lord like everyone else. His heart was moved at the sound of John's stupendous preaching, that the Lord wanted a personal relationship with everyone. He sat transfixed on the rocky ground until John was done. When it was time, he chose to be baptized in the River. He wanted this holiness that John spoke of. Oh, to be washed clean like a most pure dove! His heart fluttered with anticipation as the full line ahead of him moved and finally, it became his turn to be immersed in the Jordan.

John motioned to him, with a kindness and certainty of place, a look that made James feel like there was nowhere else to be. James turned around and fell into John's arms. As John lowered James into the water, he could hear John uttering some words of prayer, but all James could focus on was the water, feeling it wash over him like a wave. He bathed occasionally, but this feeling was different. When he came out of the water, the sky looked different; a little brighter but somehow less glare reflected off the rocky ground. The water looked bluer.

He turned; John embraced him and looked into his eyes, "Welcome to your new life." James waded out of the river. Not until Andrew came over to embrace him did he realize that his clothes were already dry. James shook his head in amazement. 'Surely this was a special man,' he thought. 'No,' he decided, 'but a special God.' They walked back to the bank while John waded ashore. The wind rustled as everyone waited for him to speak.

He walked amongst the middle of the crowd. Though the day was seeping with its usual repressiveness, they felt a balmy breeze lift off the river and sweep over them, as if the heat couldn't touch them.

Before John could talk, he motioned suddenly in the distance, stabbing a finger into the air at some point on the horizon. "Look!" he pointed again. As one the crowd turned. James looked, too, and saw a solitary figure approaching the crowd from the west. John spoke, "Remember the one of whom I said I was unworthy to untie his sandal strap? It is him!" James froze, as did the rest of the crowd. As the figure, a man, walked up to John, everyone held their breath. This was truly something remarkable.

"Master," John greeted Jesus. "What are you doing here?"

"I have come to be baptized." To James, the words came out in such a sublime manner he became entranced. The crowd, the heat, and the rocky ground became as nothing as he watched.

*John tried to prevent him, saying, "I need to be baptized by you, and yet you are coming to me?" Jesus said to him in reply, "Allow it now, for thus it is fitting for us to fulfill all righteousness." Then he allowed him. (Matthew 3:14-15)*

James watched as John led Jesus down to the riverbank where they both waded in to their waists. He heard John utter the prayer that he himself had used for James, then Jesus fell backward into John's arms, immersing his head completely in the water. For a fleeting moment, he remained there underwater, then shot back up. James watched in fascination as single water droplets flew off Jesus' head. Then something strange happened to the water. It became very clear, so clear that he could not only see the bottom from his vantage point fifteen yards from the riverbank. James closed his eyes and rubbed them. He opened them and to his wonder, he was able to see upstream, underneath the water, and underneath all the way to the opposite riverbank. It was as if the river became the color blue-tinged air, almost as one with the sky.

Jesus and John waded back to the bank and stepped up onto the dry ground. James watched in amazement as foliage sprouted up under Jesus's feet as the water fell off him. As soon as John and Jesus made their way back to the middle of the crowd, James became aware of a rumbling noise in the distance, matched by a slight tremor underfoot. He looked around, noticing again the crowd, Andrew next to him, the surroundings. With the slight tremor, they sensed a fissioning sound, as if something massive was being torn up. Everyone looked up, and they saw two faint white lines on the horizon, one in the north and the other in the south, stretch vertically through the sky. They grew higher and closer together until at the point directly overhead the lines met. At this, the sun appeared to get increasingly larger, as if it was trying to touch the earth. Despite the phenomena, the crowd sat silently, captivated and awed. 'No,' James thought, 'the sun is not trying to touch the earth; it is trying to touch the one named Jesus.' The sun seemed to grow continually, until it absorbed almost the entire sky, lending a white hue to everything.

James thought if he stood and jumped, he would be able to touch it, it was so close. Despite its proximity, the air actually seemed cooler to him, like he was still in the river. When it

seemed the sun could get no closer, they became aware of singing, a deep singing never heard before and nowhere else. James
thought the stars themselves were moved to praise. Praise what?
Surely, the man called Jesus standing in his midst.

Though it seemed to James from the heavenly chorus pouring
down on them that heaven was straight above them, no one was
looking up. It was as if the people knew to keep their heads
bowed, like this was the special blessing it was turning out to be.

And a voice came from the heavens, saying, "This is my beloved Son, with whom I am well pleased."

The atmosphere became charged, and James could feel the
hair on his body stand on end. The tingling sensation lasted for a
period of time, and then, without warning, everything returned to
normal. Afterward, James found Andrew. He grabbed Andrew
and pulled him away. "We have to find Simon!"

**

Idra felt a sense of unease gnawing at his stomach. He hadn't
taken the time to mend the nets before they went out on the water, and now they were actually having some success finding fish
today. If one of the loads was too heavy, he feared what could
happen. He steadied himself as a particularly large swell thrust
him up into the air and then down again. The job was dangerous
enough as it was; he didn't need to face the wrath of the Boss,
too. He looked at the horizon. Although there were a few clouds
and the weather was fair, all that could change instantly.

In the other boat just a stone's throw away, Foma scanned the
waters around their vessel. They always went out in pairs, with
four men to a boat. One would steer, one would spot, and the

other two would work the nets. It worked reasonably well under most conditions. Sometimes, when it was stormy, it would be harder. He looked back at the Boss. The weather today was fair, but there was a typhoon on board.

Out of nowhere a fish hit him in the head. Stunned, he turned around to see where it had come from.

"Quit daydreaming and keep your eyes on the water, Foma," the Boss scowled. "Your distractions are going to have to wait until we get back to shore. Until then, we need to find more fish, otherwise we'll be wandering aimlessly around this lake until we all grow old and Niv here will lose the last of his five teeth." The Boss kept his hands on the wheel and his face returned to its default state of scorn.

Saba, who with Niv was at the nets, snickered and guffawed. "Don't think it can't happen to you, too, Saba. You're going to get the Frankish disease and one day you'll wake up toothless," the Boss said. He kept one hand on the wheel and used the other to run his hand through his hair.

After ten minutes, Foma looked closely again at the water. He pointed off to the starboard. "I see something out there, perhaps thirty cubits away." A school of fish under the water sometimes gave the water above the appearance of a different color.

The Boss took his hands off the wheel and jumped up onto the starboard gunwale to take a look. Foma looked at him. Only the Boss had the balance and the strength to stand up there on a narrow edge and survey the water while the swells lifted him up and down. "I think I see it too." He jumped down again. "Maybe you're not so blind, Foma," the Boss laughed. "But don't pat yourself on the back just yet."

The Boss steered them closer to the area so they could put their nets in again. As they approached, they heard someone yelling from the other boat. Before the Boss and the others could turn around, the other boat rammed them, causing them to crumple onto the deck. The Boss sprang up and jabbed a finger at Tadeo who had the misfortune of being the helmsman. "What are you doing, you stupid shit? You're supposed to approach from the lee, so you can get the other side of the fish." Spittle flew from his lips and his face glowed red.

"I, I'm sorry Simon," Tadeo called back. "The current-"

"The current my ass," Simon seethed. He picked up a fish and launched it at Tadeo's head. "You were just thinking about that ugly cow of a woman you chase around day and night. I only need what's left of your brain for the next hour or so until we haul in this load and get back to shore." He looked back at the water. "If there are any left by now. You probably scared the shit out of them with your inattention. Now steer that thing around and get on the other side, about two stone throws away." He rubbed his knee where it had hit a sharp edge of his seat. "Ishmael the Blind would make a better helmsman."

Soon, they were in position when Simon gave the order. "Lower the nets now."

Both pairs of men let down their nets. One edge of the netting was permanently attached to the boat, while the other side was fastened to two long poles. As soon as the nets were lowered, Niv and Saba used the poles as levers against the gunwales to lift the opposite edge of the nets back up out of the water like a giant scoop. Simon smiled as he saw the net bulge with fish. This would do for now. He looked over to the other boat where their net was similarly weighted. Just as the other boat's team was ready to dump the fish inside, the netting between the two poles ripped in two, spilling the catch back into the water.

Simon jumped onto the gunwales again. "What the hell just happened?" he yelled into the wind, his finger stabbing the air between the two boats.

Tadeo, the helmsman stammered. "It looks like the netting, the netting ripped, Simon."

"I know the damned netting ripped. Idra, did you mend the nets yesterday like I asked you?"

Idra hesitated. "Uh,-"

"You didn't, did you? Damn it all!" Simon rose above the rest of the group as another swell rolled underneath him. "Do you know how much money we just lost right there? Do you?"

"Well, I-"

"Probably about 20 denarii, that's how much." By this time all the fish were aboard Simon's boat and the two bobbed together about a mile from shore. He turned with an abrupt command. "Let's go."

As they made for the shore, they found where their docks were, just in front of a small building that served as the office for their business. When they got closer, Simon squinted and called out to Foma. "Who is that poking around our building? Can you see?"

Foma looked. "I can't tell from here." He understood the concern in Simon's voice, for next to their office they had a large rack of fish drying from yesterday's catch. Normally they sold the entirety of their catch as soon as they landed, except for one-tenth the Boss always set aside for the poor. 'Say what you would about the crusty bugger,' he thought, 'but the Boss takes his faith seriously.'

As soon as they landed, Simon jumped onto the beach and ran around to the rack behind the building. There, he found a man with his back turned to him, hurrying to put as much fish as he could in a canvas sack. Simon grabbed a handful of sand and made a clicking sound. As the man turned around, Simon threw it in his face.

The man dropped the bag with a sharp cry and raised his hands to his eyes in pain. As he did, Simon yanked a sandal off his foot with his right hand and landed a punch to the man's groin with his left. As the man dropped his hands, Simon slapped his face with the sandal, sending the man crumpling to the ground. He jumped on him. "What do you think you're doing? Huh?"

"I'm sorry, I'm sorry," the man protested.

"You're not sorry, you pile of dung. Don't you know that fish is for the poor?" Simon slapped him again on the head.

"Well, I'm poor," the man said.

"What?" Simon wrenched the man's cloak off and looked at it. "The poor don't walk around with this fine material." He let the man get up and kicked him in the hindquarters, dropping him to the ground again. "Now get going before I string you up to dry, too." The man got up and ran away, clad only in his loin-cloth.

After Foma and the rest of the crew finished selling all the fish, Simon paid them and dismissed them for the day. He took the proceeds and went home.

**

After Simon finished dinner that night, a knock at the door revealed two visitors. "Ah, Andrew, my brother. What are you doing here with James at my humble abode? And why do you look different?" He let them in. "Are you two alright? Where have you two been? I haven't seen you for three days."

They all sat while Simon's wife served them wine. Andrew started. "Yes, brother, we have been gone, deep into the desert, in fact." He closed his eyes and savored the sweet wine.

"What for? Whatever it was, I'm sure it wasn't as eventful as today was for me." He relayed the day's events to them.

"That's why you're the managing partner," James said. They laughed at the truth. James and Andrew owned the boats and the equipment while Simon built up a minority share over the years.

Simon put his glass down. "So what was it that you saw?"

**

Andrew and James looked at each other before Andrew spoke up. "Brother, you know how dedicated I am to our faith, as you are. And you know I have been a follower of the prophet John the Baptist for some time now. You have heard me speak of his most righteous teaching and of his message of repentance. You have heard of how he lives that message by living humbly in the desert, eating nothing but wild honey and locusts." Andrew stopped for another sip of wine. A weighty atmosphere of seriousness settled among them. "It was to this man John that I brought James here to listen to him speak. While we were there, one greater than him appeared."

"A rival?" Simon asked.

"No. This man is the fulfillment of everything John preaches, confirmed by none other than John himself." Andrew continued by telling him all that they had seen.

When he finished, Simon leaned back in his chair, his eyes looking off to some point in the distance. After a time, he asked, "So why are you telling me this?"

Andrew looked at James again and spoke. "So you can be ready."

Simon frowned. "Ready for what?"

**

Herod Antipas looked over the banquet with a smug satisfaction. The ballroom in the palace his father had built teemed with decorations richly adorned with all manner of gold, silver, jade and many other precious gems. It was a generous feast of every kind of beef, the finest wine and the purest pressed olive oil accompanied by an array of spices from unknown lands to the East, with leaves and greens and a vivid spectrum of fruit adorning every table. Harpists, lyrists and flutists lent an unending stream of melodies to the space, fuel for the rhythmic swaying and bustling of his guests. And the guests themselves, the priestly class of the Sadducees, the Pharisees, his top military officers and civil servants, this upper crust of Tiberius's society, were all here.

'Except for one,' a dark Herod thought, 'the weasel Pilate.' The Roman governor of Judea mailed his apologies for being unable to celebrate Herod's wedding and instead sent some no-name emissary in his place. Herod dismissed the thought of the grubby Roman and instead gazed once again on his new bride Herodias. Her beauty captivated him. Hers wasn't the kind to absorb passively; rather, it demanded a taking, an assertion, and so he did. His brother Boethus was the first to have Herodias, but after beholding her, Herod had to have her for himself.

He found a pretext for divorcing his first wife Phaesalis, daughter of King Aretas of Nabatea, owing to a convenient border dispute with the neighboring kingdom. After that, the way was clear.

Kelaya, his right hand and head of the secret police, was seated next to him, silent and watchful. Herod looked at him. "May it please the commander to have some wine," he beckoned a servant to fill Kelaya's cup. Kelaya nodded and drank some. Herod leaned closer. "You look pensive tonight, Kelaya."

"I am observing your guests."

"And?" Sometimes Herod had to pull things out of the man, but he was good.

"And I can see that almost all of Jerusalem's elite are here, helping you celebrate."

"Go on, Kelaya."

"I am wondering about those that are not here."

Herod understood where he was going with the train of thought. Kelaya was paid handsomely to protect Herod, just as Kelaya's father Alexandros had done with his father Herod the

Great. Those who weren't here were making a statement of a sort, that they didn't approve. That they didn't approve of the divorce and remarriage. The implicit disapproval burned Herod, for he had worked hard to continue the patina of religiosity that his father had cloaked himself with, so as to be a Roman client acceptable to the Hebrew people.

Kelaya spoke again. "I am wondering about John."

Herod winced when he heard the name aloud. The man called the Baptist had won many followers recently. People had called him the greatest of prophets, the reincarnation of Elijah, even. They seemed to think he was preparing the way for God's manifestation. The fact that someone living in the desert, wearing rags and eating bugs, could command such a following bothered Herod. 'Was he of high birth? Was he of a royal line? Was he the protector of all the land and its inhabitants?' Herod thought. That John's disapproval of the new marriage had been so loud and public doubly angered him. He looked down at his hand to see that it had crushed the grapes it was formerly holding. He looked at Kelaya. "We shall wonder no longer about the man John. Bring him in."

Herod watched Herodias mingle amongst the crowd, her wedding attire outshining every other woman, her body an enchanting figure that held all eyes in the room. Herod scanned the room and saw Salome standing on the periphery of the hall. Where Herodias was the full manifestation of feminine beauty in her prime, her daughter of fourteen years was the promise of unimaginable allure, just at the dawn of her own brilliant attraction. Herod smiled. Now the both of them would be residing in his palace. He looked again to see Salome looking directly at him, with that look in her eyes. Her lips were parted, and her tongue moistened them slowly. Herod felt the undeniable drive in his loins and excused himself.

**

Jesus walked off into the desert. It was here that he could pray to the Father in peace, without distraction. One of John's disciples brought word that John had been taken away. Jesus could sense the time of the fulfillment was nearing, and needed to meditate on the state of things. There was so much to say. Day and night he withdrew into himself, digging into the inner core of his being and uncovering it, voicing it, and giving it up to the Father. And likewise the Father communicated with him. Jesus had to be still, to be still and motionless in this barren place, and received the word of the Father day and night. Day and night he ate little, and drank little, savoring only the relationship with the Father. The purity of the bond, and the totality of communication continued as Jesus made himself present in the desert. For thirty years Jesus waited patiently, waiting, waiting for the time to be right. He thought about Moses, who waited for decades after encountering the burning bush before the full manifestation of his mission revealed itself.

The heat of the days seeped into Jesus's bones and likewise metered out over the cold nights, keeping him warm. Day and night, he prayed. After forty days, he arose, hollow with hunger. Turning around, he saw the devil standing there in the form of a man with fine garments about him.

*The tempter approached and said to him, "If you are the Son of God, command that these stones become loaves of bread."*

*He said in reply, "It is written:*

*'One does not live by bread alone,*
*but by every word that comes forth from the mouth of God.'"*

*Then the devil took him to the holy city, and made him stand on the parapet of the temple,*
*and said to him, "If you are the Son of God, throw yourself down. For it is written:*
*'He will command his angels concerning you'*
*and 'with their hands they will support you,*
*lest you dash your foot against a stone.'"*

*Jesus answered him, "Again it is written, 'You shall not put the Lord, your God, to the test.'"*

*Then the devil took him up to a very high mountain, and showed him all the kingdoms of the world in their magnificence, and he said to him, "All these I shall give to you, if you will prostrate yourself and worship me."*

*At this, Jesus said to him, "Get away, Satan! It is written:*

*'The Lord, your God, shall you worship
and him alone shall you serve.'" (Matthew 4: 3-10)*

"You're not about to do this, are you?"

"What is it that you think I'm going to do?"

"You're about to waste your life for these people. You think you can convert them from their idolatrous ways. You think you can convince them that you're the Son of God. You think that you can win them over with your message of love." The last words came out with a snarl and waves of disgust.

"It is love indeed that people are searching for most in this life. There is only one place they can find it, and that is in the Father."

The devil snorted. "People want security, and they want food and shelter and freedom to do what they want, when they want. They don't want to be smothered by your oppressive cloak of so-called love." Now the devil had flowing dark hair with skin the color of bronze and owning the perfect form of a woman. Satan strutted closer and spoke with a venomous whisper. "What do you think they will do when they hear your message? Hmm? Did you know I had a vision of the future? Do you want to know what I saw?" Satan showed Jesus what awaited him on Golgotha. "Look at how the people will react to you. They are expecting a revolutionary king, not some nobody carpenter."

"My cross is my throne, and I will rule my Church forever."

"Ah yes, your church. Not even your closest followers will have the courage to stay with you."

"My Church will live forever." Jesus started to walk away.

Satan steamed like a woman scorned. "Where do you think you're going?"

"To build it one person at a time."

"Your foundation will crumble like bread. You can't possibly find anyone strong enough to start."

Jesus looked back. "Watch me."

**

Simon looked at the horizon separating the blue water from the pale gray sky. They were on the way out again. He thought about what Andrew and James had told him some weeks ago, and wondered what to make of it. He looked over at his brother manning one side of the netting in the boat. He was back on the water with them, with a similarly detached look about him. They had received news that John had been arrested a few days ago, and Andrew had joined them on the water since then.

Foma looked up and called out, "I see a school of fish off the port side, over there." He pointed to a spot a little distance away. Simon swung the wheel in silence and the two boats positioned themselves on either side. The catch was successful. Foma wondered what was with the Boss and his brother. It was almost surreal to see them so quiet like this. 'What were they thinking about?' he wondered.

After hauling in the catch without complication, they made for shore. There was only a slight swell to the water, and they made the trip back in silence, broken only by the repeated curling of the water off the bow. As they approached, Foma spotted a lone figure standing near their dock. "Do you see that man there?" He expected the Boss to be on his feet again, ready for a fight.

Simon and Andrew looked up and studied the man. As they neared the shore, Simon could see that he was standing there, watching the boats come in. He had a certain way about him. When they landed, Simon saw the man looking directly at him, looking through him, almost. He looked over at Andrew, and saw on his brother's face a glow of recognition about him. "It is him," Andrew said in a whisper. Simon looked back at the man and jumped out of the boat onto shore. They approached the man, who nodded slightly, as if to confirm something.

"Come with me, and I will make you fishers of men."

And so they did.

# The Wedding at Cana

Simon and Jude walked along the rows of grapevines lining the hillside at Simon's house, just outside Cana. They worked in silence, doggedly tying each wayward vine to the guideline strung just above them, in order to keep the plants stretched out and to maximize the sunlight they received.

"You are lucky to get this size of property from your father, Simon. Most men have to wait for their father to die before they receive such an estate," Jude said.

"It is true that my father deeded me one heredium of this rich land; however, it was out of his infirmity and old age that he is unable to work the land any longer." Simon looked to the north, down into the valley. "How I would rather he keep the land and I work side by side with him."

Jude nodded. His answer was in keeping with his reputation for zeal in all things. "I know, Simon. But such is the way of the Lord, now you have your own responsibility and the need to cultivate it."

"I know, but I already have a field growing wheat in the valley. Although it is difficult to mind two plots of land, I intend to make the most of them."

They finished the row and went to the next one. About midway through that one, Jude looked up. "Simon, is something bothering you? You seem preoccupied."

Simon stopped tying for a moment. "I was going to tell you later, but I suppose I can tell you now."

"What is it?"

"I went to the house of Maadai yesterday, to inquire about Sameah."

Jude stopped. "You did? You mean the Sameah you first noticed at the festival last month?"

"Yes, the one and the same."

"So what happened?"

"We discussed terms of the *ketubbah*."

Jude came around to Simon's side of the vine, his eyes wide open. "You are ready to marry this girl? But you only saw her that one time."

"I know, it sounds crazy, but one look was all I needed. She has hair of the finest wheat and blue eyes of aquamarine. I swear I have never seen the color of those eyes anywhere on earth-"

Jude interrupted. "You have only been as far as Jerusalem in your entire life."

"You know what I mean. Clearly there is none more beautiful. Besides," he looked back at Jude, "why risk it?"

Jude nodded in understanding. The *ketubbah* was a marriage contract, and once it was signed, the woman belonged to the man as his wife and could not be betrothed to any other man. "I know. Remember, I saw her myself, so I can see why you would not want to risk someone else beating you to her."

"Besides, I am eighteen years of age and ready for a woman of my own."

"And a family of your own."

"Of course. But just imagine what kind of family that would be. Surely Sameah is fertile like the rich soil of the valley below, and surely as sweet as the finest grapes this hillside can produce."

"So I take it that your preoccupation is with the proposed terms of the *ketubbah* rather than the idea of the contract itself," Jude said.

Simon nodded. "Her father knows I am the son of a vintner and have my own lands as well."

"Let me guess: fifty shekels."

Simon shook his head. "Higher."

"Seventy-five shekels?"

"Higher."

"What? One hundred shekels?"

Simon was glum by now. "I wish. One hundred fifty shekels."

"What?" Jude was back on Simon's side of the row again. "One hundred fifty shekels? That is five times the normal amount."

Simon's voice came out in a whisper. "I know."

"I hope you didn't agree to that."

"I told him I would come back looking forward to discussing it more."

"Well, good. At least you didn't give in right then and there."

"Part of me wanted to, though." Simon wiped more sweat from his brow. "I mean, what father doesn't think his daughter is worth the world?"

"Of course you are right, Simon, but what father wants his daughter to be with someone who can't haggle and barter with the rest of them? Perhaps he is testing you to make sure that you and your money aren't easily separated."

"So what should I do?"

Jude finished snipping a vine and looked at him. "Let me tell you."

**

Simon approached Maadai's house. It was a stone cut abode, humbled by the vast fields surrounding it. Simon knew Maadai had many farmhands to work it, but today was the Sabbath, and no one was working. As he approached, he could hear the everyday voices and murmuring of a family at lunchtime. He stopped and listened: they were outside, in the back. He debated whether he should knock at the door anyway or just go around the house and directly to the back. A voice carrying lilting notes of graceful femininity floated upward, and his heart raced. That must be Sameah. He decided to just go around.

As he stepped around the corner, he came face-to-face with a lunchtime gathering of around twenty-five people. When he came into view, everyone stopped talking and looked at him.

He stood there for a moment, considering the scene and remembered that there was only Maadai, his wife and three daughters last time he was here. This must have been some sort of family reunion. He felt like an ugly weed amongst wheat stalks.

Maadai spoke up. "Ah, Simon, please come and sit down." The rest of the family resumed talking while Simon made his way to where Maadai sat.

"I'm sorry, I didn't know all these people would be here. I can be on my way."

"Nonsense," Maadai said. "Please sit down and eat something. I will be insulted if you don't."

"Very well." Simon took a seat as a girl he recognized as Sameah's sister reached into a large bowl and put some greens in front of him. "Thank you very much." He did his best to enjoy the food but could not wait to negotiate. He glanced around at the others; they would complicate things.

An older man looked at him. "Are you Simon bar-Idra the vintner?"

"Yes."

"I know your father. I have dealt with him in the marketplace many times. It is said that his wine is the best in the whole of Cana."

Simon nodded. "Thank you. I think so myself. Now that you mention it," Simon reached down and pulled out a large wineskin, "I would like you and your family to have this." He gave it to Maadai.

"Why thank you," Maadai said. He called for someone to set out some empty goblets.

"It is a new combination of grape types I have been experimenting with," Simon said. "I do hope you will enjoy it."

"I'm sure we will," Maadai said. He poured some of the wine into several goblets and passed them around. Simon watched as the men around the table all drank deeply of them and smiled in pleasure as the different notes of flavor washed over them. 'Excellent,' he thought.

They continued feasting as Simon's wineskin emptied, at which point someone was sent to fetch more wine from the house. Simon noted with some comfort that Maadai appeared to be enjoying himself. After the food was finished, Maadai looked at Simon with a raised brow. "Do you wish to discuss more the possible *ketubbah*?"

Despite the din of a large family meal among several table, at the sound of the word everyone turned to look at Simon. He was starting to feel the heat of the day, although when he approached he didn't recall that he was hot at all. "We can discuss it another time," Simon said, "perhaps when you don't have all your family here."

"On the contrary," Maadai said. "Now is the best time, when everyone can have their input." By now, Maadai's eyes were starting to shine and his hand gestures became notably exaggerated.

Simon didn't like where this was going. "Or we can wait until we can speak in private. I don't want to infringe on a family event like this."

"Nonsense," Maadai repeated. "After all, what is the discussion of a *ketubbah* if it is not a family event?" He stood up. "Can anyone tell me what a discussion of a *ketubbah* is if it is not a family event?"

Simon wanted to wither away. By now it was clear to everyone what he was doing there. He couldn't even bring himself to look at Sameah. A younger man seated at the next table stood up. "We will accept no less than 10 shekels for Sameah!" This was followed by snickering and guffawing from the other male relatives before Sameah's mother and other women shouted them down.

Maadai remained standing. "Where shall we begin?"

**

Jude found Simon the next day. "Well, how did it go?"

"I must say that your plan was absolutely no help."

"What? What could be better than bringing choice wine to the man of the house?"

"When I showed up, the house of Maadai was in the middle of a large family gathering, not Maadai alone as I expected."

"So, what happened?"

"Almost right away, it became a public spectacle, which you know is a most unpleasant feeling for me. Her father wanted to conduct terms right there in front of everyone else."

"So?"

Simon frowned. "Jude, think about it. How would you feel if your future husband and your family members were debating how much you were worth in front of you, as if you were some sort of beast of the field."

"But that is how it has been done for generations."

"I know, but I don't like it. As it was, though, her male relatives kept making light of the situation and demanded exceedingly low terms from her father on my behalf. Of course I just sat by, a mere onlooker. After many rounds of haggling, they finally settled on a sum."

"Which was?" Jude coaxed him on.

"Sixty-five shekels." Seeing the unimpressed look on his friend's face, Simon asked, "What?"

"Sixty-five shekels," Jude repeated.

"He originally wanted one hundred fifty. I thought that was a good deal."

"I think you've been had." Jude started walking away. "Come, let us get to work."

Simon stood there, picturing her face in all her splendor. "No price is too great for her."

**

After seeing the man Jesus when they landed, the fishermen Andrew, James and Simon followed him away from the dock and into the town of Bethsaida. They didn't know how long they would be away, but they could not deny Jesus's invitation to follow him. The trio walked slightly behind Jesus as they passed by the fish market stalls and vegetable merchants hawking every manner of deal to be had.

"What shall we call you?" Simon asked.

"The more important question is what I should call you," Jesus said. "And Simon, I shall call you Cephas." *Peter.*

"Peter? Why?"

"You will find out, in time."

"Then where are we going?" Peter asked.

Jesus turned around. "Don't you recognize this place?"

"This is my neighborhood."

Jesus smiled. "That's right. We are going to your house. From now on."

Peter looked at the others, the question unasked between them. 'How does this man know where I live?' James and Andrew shrugged and went along.

When they arrived, Peter's mother-in-law prepared them dinner. The five of them sat around a small table.

Jesus spoke. "Thank you for this meal," he nodded at Peter's mother-in-law before turning to the three men. "And thank you for responding to my call today."

Andrew cleared his throat. "And what exactly is your call?"

"I have been sent to bring about the fulfillment."

The others chewed in silence and looked at each other. Despite their wonderment, something inside them made them leave it at that.

"Why did you pick us?" James asked.

"You will see, in time," Jesus answered. "For now, be assured that this is the work that you were made to do."

After they finished the meal, Jesus stood. "Rest up and prepare yourselves, for we will begin our work tomorrow."

"What are we going to do tomorrow?" Andrew asked.

Jesus looked at them with a smile. "We're going fishing." As if there were anything else to do.

\*\*

Stars twinkled above as the moonlight played about the desert floor. Simon walked along the path next to the weaver's house on his way to the house of Maadai. He cast a solitary figure in the clear night, and at this hour, the desert breeze and the occasional animal hunting about provided the only sounds. All was still, as the people had likely been asleep for several hours now after another day of exhausting work. His footfalls were muted in the dusty path, but he still strained to be as quiet as he could. Since he and Maadai signed the *ketubbah*, it was Simon's right

144

to come at any time to fetch her for the time of their marriage consummation. Although that day would soon come, arrangements weren't quite ready. Propriety demanded that he stay away until that point. But he simply wanted to see Sameah, and to talk to her, alone.

The house of Maadai stood out against the large fields in the full moonlight. Simon crept around to the back and sat down. He figured Sameah would emerge in time, for everyone has to relieve themselves. After a time, his patience was rewarded when he saw a figure come out of the house and squat over a little trench dug in the front of the house. When the person was done and turned back to the house, a shaft of moonlight highlighted Sameah's face.

Simon called out in a loud whisper from perhaps a stone's throw away.

"Who is that?" Sameah said in a hush.

"It is me, Simon." He started walking to her.

She rushed over. "Simon? Why, it is so late. What are you doing there in the dark?"

They stood close to each other, close enough to feel the breath from the other. "I just had to come and see you, to talk to you."

She smiled. "About what?"

"About what? About anything. Oh, how I have wanted to talk to you in the peace of solitude, to share my day with you and to revel in the details of yours." He took her hands. "How I have wanted to share all of me with you, for I have dreamed many nights of your face in the moonlight as it is now, and I swear to you none of those times has it looked more beautiful than it does as this moment."

She glowed with warmth. "That day I saw you at the festival, you caught my eye. Something about you was different, and I just knew that I had to talk to you, to find out what is inside you, to know you. Indeed, this very night I was imagining our wedding consummation, wondering when you would come back with your groomsmen to take me to your house."

"How I wish that day were already here, Sameah. How I wish that we can be one as man and wife should be. How I wish for that day with all of my heart and soul." He stepped closer. "The preparations are not yet final. But they will be soon. And when that happens, I will come back for you."

After they sat and talked for another hour, he stood. "Sameah, I must get back to my house, for it will be morning soon and it is a long walk."

"This night has been a balm for my soul, to talk with you and to know you more deeply. Alas, though, it has only kindled my fire even more."

Simon held her face in his hands. "And mine too, Sameah, for I fear it is a fire that cannot be quenched. That fire will burn in me until I can see you again and we can come together as one. Until then, know that I will be thinking of you day and night, as surely as the sun rises in the morning."

"Oh Simon, how I long for that day. How long must I wait to see you coming to take me away?"

"Not very long, my love. I am working on something that is almost finished, but as yet is not complete. But please know that as soon as it is ready I will be back, in full splendor, with my groomsmen and ready to claim you as my own."

They parted, and as Simon walked away, the sound of a single word carried forth on the breeze in the night. "Hurry."

**

A few days later, Jude found Simon working the vines. "Have you caught up on your sleep yet?"

Simon backed out of a row and stood straight. "What are you talking about?"

"I heard you were up all night a few days ago."

"Where did you hear that?"

Jude shrugged. "I know Sameah's cousin who lives nearby. She talks to her like a sister."

"It's true. I just had to go see her. Just to visit with her and talk with her alone; I didn't want our wedding feast to be the first time we actually talked."

"I suppose." Jude beckoned to the vines. "How is this coming out?"

"These grapes have a ways to go yet. I am working on something else for the wedding feast."

"What is it?"

Simon turned around. "Follow me and I'll show you." They trudged uphill to a small copse of creosote bushes and pistachio trees. There, behind a small outcropping in the hillside was a tunnel opening about three cubits wide. Simon crouched low and scrambled inside. Jude followed, and they stood in a narrow limestone cavern about the height of a man and twenty cubits deep. Inside, ten wooden barrels lay in a line stretching to the far end of the space.

Jude knocked on one, making a dull thud. "These are full." He looked at Simon. "What's in here?"

"A special vintage. I helped my father harvest it ten years ago. I still remember it today; it was the first time I helped him in the field. It was so special to be able to take part in something I had watched him do for a long time. Finally, I was able to contribute! After we processed all the grapes, my father set this aside for me. He told me it was to be for my wedding feast." Simon smelled the air. "I have never had wine that has been aged for this long."

Jude ran his hands over one of the barrels. This wood looks to be of such fine quality."

Simon nodded. "My father had a craftsman in Nazareth make them. Joseph was known to be the best at it. In fact, his son Jesus will be at the wedding."

"Huh."

Simon gestured to the opening. "Come on, I have more work to do outside."

**

Peter looked intently at the sea. He was here at the water's edge, waiting for James, Andrew and Jesus, for they were to meet at this place. He watched as the water lapped up against the rocky sand, turned over in small waves, then retreated the way it came. Over and over again, as it had probably done for thousands of years. The sounds of the water mesmerized him, and he thought back to the time when his father taught him to fish. He was so excited to go out on the boat with him for the first time. His father had showed him how to work the nets, operate the boat, look for the best fishing grounds. He had taught him about the way fish live, the best times to look for them, and the best conditions to catch them. Those days with him on the water were the best he'd ever had.

He thought again about dinner the previous night with Jesus, Andrew and James. Jesus had said they would go fishing today, but if for some reason it didn't work out, he could always go back to his own crew. He felt something in the air around him, and when he turned he saw Jesus standing there.

"Hello, Peter."

"Hello. How long have you been standing there?"

"Long enough to know that you miss your father."

Before he could respond, Andrew and James found them. "Why did you ask that we meet here?" James asked Jesus. "All the boats are over there," he pointed to a spot well down the shore.

Jesus smiled. "We don't need boats where we're going today. Come and follow me." He turned and walked toward town.

The others looked at each other and followed. "What is it that we are looking for in town?" Andrew asked.

"Not what, but who," Jesus said.

After a few more steps, Andrew prompted him. "Well, then, who are we looking for?"

"Your friend Philip."

"Philip the Greek?" James asked.

"The one and the same."

**

It was a few days before the wedding celebration, and Simon was readying his house for Sameah. He had hired day laborers earlier in the year to build a house on the northern slope of the hill on his father's land, so as to be close to his work and still have a view of the valley below. They had finished now, but he wanted it to be as welcoming as it could be for his new bride. He set out for the market.

Once there, he looked for the cloth dealers, who had on display every type of material one could find, in almost every kind of color. Simon knew just what he wanted for wall hangings, for someone as beautiful as Sameah could not be surrounded by simple stone walls. And he knew just the man who would have it.

After another few moments navigating the maze of the market, he found the one: a younger-looking man haggling with a customer, framed by a backdrop of the most exotic kind of material that could be found: silk from the lands beyond the Parthian Empire, fine flax, smooth muslin, and even tanned leather from Roman lands to the northwest. As Simon watched, the two finished their transaction and the younger man in the stall approached him with a smile.

"Simon, how are you, my friend?"

"I am well, thank you."

"Am I right in saying that your wedding is almost upon us."

"It is indeed. You will be there, right?"

"Of course! What can I do for you today?"

Simon told him what he needed, and the man hunted around for a few moments before returning with an array of silken hangings in gold and silver. After agreeing on a price, Simon asked, "So what is new in your life?"

The man got serious all of a sudden. "Simon, the most amazing thing happened to me yesterday."

"What was it?"

"I was here at the market, waiting for customers, when this man approached me. He had the look of a profound peace and wisdom about him, a surety and a confidence I have never experience before. In fluent Greek, he asked me what I was doing. I looked at him and said, 'Selling my wares, sir.' And he looked into my eyes with a depth of intensity I have never experienced before. It was like he was looking into my very soul. I couldn't help but ask what he was doing. He said, 'I can see that your heart isn't here.' I was dumbfounded. Indeed, I have been faithfully serving my father's merchant business but I confess to you it is not a job I have any passion for. The man asked, 'You clothe people in quality linens, in fine flax and in the best silk to be found. But you know that even though the cloth is expensive, it succumbs to time, age and wear and eventually falls apart. Instead, how would you like to clothe people in peace and joy, in holiness and redemption?' And I could feel this burning desire in my heart. I said, 'Yes, sir, show me how to do this.' and he said, 'Then follow me.'"

"And then what happened?" Simon asked.

"He is stopping by tomorrow with some others; from there, I do not know what is in store."

Simon contemplated that for a moment. "That does sound amazing."

"Indeed."

"Keep me posted, will you?"

"I will be sure to. And you keep me posted about the exact time of the wedding."

"It will be the day after tomorrow." Simon held the cloth up. "I just need to hang these first."

"I will be there, ready to celebrate with that fine wine of yours."

Simon laughed. "Just be sure not to drink too much of it, Philip. I only have ten barrels."

**

The next day, Philip found his friend Nathaniel deep in scrolls, studying the Torah. "Hey," Philip said.

Nathaniel jolted out of his repose. "Who is there?" he turned around. "Philip! You scared me." He rolled the scrolls neatly and put them away.

"Ha, it was my only chance - normally you are unfazed at such things. What were you reading?"

"One of the many references to the Messiah, the one who is to come and bring fulfillment to Israel."

Philip sat down and looked his friend in the eye. "Nathaniel, I must tell you something."

"What is the matter? Is something wrong?"

"Nothing is wrong. In fact," Philip paused and looked around, "everything is to be made right."

"What is it that you mean?"

"Nathaniel, the one you have been reading about, the prophecies from the Torah?"

"Yes?"

"I have found him."

"What?!"

"Rather, he has found me." Seeing Nathaniel's look of shock, Philip helped him up. "Come, I will explain on the way."

**

Jesus met Peter, James and Andrew at the seashore.

*The next day he decided to go to Galilee, and he found Philip. And Jesus said to him, "Follow me." Now Philip was from Bethsaida, the town of Andrew and Peter. Philip found Nathanael and told him, "We have found the one about whom Moses wrote in the law, and also the prophets, Jesus, son of Joseph, from Nazareth." But Nathanael said to him, "Can anything good come from Nazareth?" Philip said to him, "Come and see." Jesus saw Nathanael coming toward him and said of him, "Here is a true Israelite. There is no duplicity in him." Nathanael said to him, "How do you know me?" Jesus answered and said to him, "Before Philip called you, I saw you under the fig tree." Nathanael answered him, "Rabbi, you are the Son of God; you are the King of Israel." Jesus answered and said to him, "Do you believe because I told you that I saw you under the fig tree? You will see greater things than this." And he said to him, "Amen, amen, I say to you, you will see the sky opened and the angels of God ascending and descending on the Son of Man." (John 1:43-51)*

The small group stood there with mouths agape. "Men, I tell you, you are here to spread the word of the Lord, and to prepare the people for the eternal feast."

Peter looked at the others. "Rabbi, what do you mean, an eternal feast?"

Jesus smiled. "You will see in time. But I tell you your mission begins now. And that means you must follow me."

"Where are we going now?" Peter asked.

Jesus turned around. "To a wedding."

**

Simon watched in horror as the stewards emptied the last of the jugs. The wedding celebration was only in its twelfth hour and already his prized vintage had run out. He pulled Sameah aside. "Do you see what has happened?" veins stuck out of his neck and his brow was wet with sweat. "How could all of our wine be gone?"

"Have you seen those Galilean fisherman?"

"You mean the ones who came with Jesus the carpenter?"

"Yes." Sameah looked over the crowd before turning back to her husband. "They have been drinking much more than the average man."

"Well, we have to do something; this celebration is supposed to last six more days," he ran his hands through his hair and sighed.

"Don't worry, husband. Let me talk to someone."

**

154

Mary sat next to Jesus. "Yeshua, the bride tells me that the groom told her that they are running out of wine."

*Jesus said to her, "Woman, how does your concern affect me? My hour has not yet come." (John 2:4)*

Mary leaned closer. "I know that, but this is their hour. Yeshua, she came to me. She is concerned because all of their family and friends are here to help them celebrate this most special of sacraments."

Jesus nodded. "I know. I was simply waiting for her to ask."

"Well, she did ask. Through me."

*His mother said to the servers, "Do whatever he tells you." Now there were six stone water jars there for Jewish ceremonial washings, each holding twenty to thirty gallons. Jesus told them, "Fill the jars with water." So they filled them to the brim. Then he told them, "Draw some out now and take it to the headwaiter." So they took it. (John 2:5-8)*

As soon as the headwaiter tasted the wine, his eyes opened in amazement. Simon gaped at him, then turned to look at his friend Jude, who was similarly awestruck. The headwaiter looked over the crowd at Jesus, who gave him a wink. Peter, James and Andrew watched all of this from across the tent. And they believed.

# The Proclamation of the Kingdom

James and Judas Iscariot entered a small village in the dead heat of midday. They had been walking for several miles and needed something to drink. They came to a stop; the absolute stillness of the day made for an impenetrable silence. They looked around but saw no one out and about.

"What do we do now?" Judas asked.

"Let's go find a well."

They wound their way around several small huts until they came across a clearing with a small wellhead in the middle. James hastened to the side and lowered a clay pot into the darkness. An elderly man walked up behind them.

"You will be waiting an eternity for good water to come from that well," he said.

James and Judas turned around. The man continued, "we haven't seen anything but muddy, despoiled water from that hole. Whatever does come up, we give to the beasts of the field, and only on the hottest days."

Judas felt the Spirit within him in the face of this challenge. "Where are all the people of this village?"

"Only me and my daughter are here during the day, for she has been bedridden since she gave birth twelve years ago." The man swept his arms across a wide valley below them to the east. "The rest are down there, toiling in the fields. Indeed, as the water has dried up, they have had to sow their crops farther and farther afield. Sometimes I wonder if they will move their houses to another location since there is so little water left." The man looked off into the distance, as if trying to envision how it was once. After a while, he came back to the present. "What are you two doing here in the middle of nowhere, anyway? Are you lost?"

"We are right where we are supposed to be," James said.

"Well, why are you here?" the old man asked.

"We have a message for the people of this village," Judas said.

"You do? You'll have to wait until dusk for them all to return."

"We don't have time for that," James said. "We have to go forth throughout the entire world."

A look of utter confusion spread across the old man's face. "Huh?"

"Please, sir, you need to tell the people to come here now," James said.

"They don't listen to me anymore, for I am just an old man."

"What is your name, sir?" James asked.

"Nahor."

"Nahor, they'll listen to you when you tell them the good news," Judas said.

"What good news?"

James hauled up the clay pot and dumped clear water onto the ground. "Tell them the water is back."

The old man gaped at the puddle on the ground. After a moment of shock, he clambered onto a rock some distance away and cupped his hands around his face, yelling in the direction of the valley.

**

After celebrating wildly and drinking their fill, the people had gathered in front of James and Judas. James had everyone sit while he took his place at the wellhead. "We have come to bring you the good news of the fulfillment, the promise of the covenant the Lord has made to our people. You rejoiced at the news of the water here, and rightly so, for you have been tormented by drought, and by dryness, but I tell you something much greater than the appearance of water is in store for you."

"What is it that you say is coming to us?" one of the village elders asked.

Judas spoke up. "What is coming to you is nothing less than the kingdom of the Lord. Yes, we are here in Israel, but we are here to testify to you that the one whom the Lord has prepared for you is here. He walks among us and indeed, is looking for you."

"What is He looking for us for?" another elder asked.

"He is looking for you to reform your lives, so that you may fully partake of his kingdom. For as surely as you gulped down this water today, the Lord desires of you to immerse yourselves in his love," James said.

"What is to reform?" the first elder asked.

"You must purge every last bit of sin from your hearts and minds," James said. "If you truly want to behold the kingdom of God, you must embrace the fire of purity. Just so, you must also banish every last doubt you have about the promise of the Lord,

158

for that has been holding you back." He looked them all in the eye. "Are you ready to believe?"

"Yes," they answered as one.

James looked over to the hut of Nahor, the old man. "Woman," he shouted, "come out." With that, the bedridden daughter emerged from the shadow of the hut, walking normally.

Above the din, Judas continued. "Prepare your hearts, for this transformation you see is nothing compared to what the Lord has planned for you." And they believed.

\*\*

The sons of Zebedee, James and John, traveled the narrow road along the Sea of Galilee toward the town of Magdala. The burning sunlight twinkled off the surface of the sea in the heat of midday.

"What are we going to do when we get there?" John, the younger of the two, asked.

"You mean other than telling the villagers what Jesus told us? I don't know," James said. He wiped sweat from his brow. The day was hot, and they had no food, and with no money they could buy none.

"How long do you think we'll stay there?" John asked.

"As long as it takes, I suppose," James said. He felt a rumbling in his stomach.

They rounded a bend in the road. In the distance, they saw numerous docks, the first signs of the outer reaches of the fishing town.

"Do you think the people there will welcome us?" John asked.

James stopped. "Enough with the questions. How am I supposed to know? Look, you just wait here for a moment while I walk ahead, so you can be behind me. I will lead the way, and you can trail in silence. I cannot suffer your questions any longer. Thank goodness our grandfather Cleopas isn't here to suffer, too."

John let his older brother advance. He knew they needed some space. They were to go to about a dozen towns and villages in this area, and they couldn't be fighting the whole time.

James brooded as he walked ahead. 'No money, no walking stick, no extra clothes,' he thought. 'Couldn't Jesus make an exception for me, since I would be traveling with my brother?' Hunger pangs interrupted his thoughts again. He looked up as he approached the point where the road met the shoreline of the sea. Perhaps he could convince some local fisherman to spare him a fish. While he was dwelling on his hunger, he came upon the local fish market. There were perhaps a dozen fishing boats backed up to shore and about a hundred customers. Everyone in the crowd was haggling with someone else. The noise was amplified by arms akimbo.

While James stopped to take in the scene, John emerged from a bend in the path and joined him.

"I think I know what to say," John said.

James looked at him sideways before shrugging. "Go ahead," he said. "Just don't drive them away."

John walked down to the beach and hopped onto a large pier stretching out into the water just beside all the boats. "Citizens of Galilee, hear me," he bellowed through cupped hands. Most of the people turned and looked at him. John froze for a moment, surprised that they would pay attention so quickly. "Citizens of Galilee, I am here to bring you an important message, one that cannot wait." By this time, all eyes were on him. "I am here to tell you about the promise of the Lord to his people." At this, a scattering of people turned back to the boats. John overheard grumbling about not wanting to hear religious messages outside of the synagogue. He continued. "Haven't you wondered what the Lord has in store for us? Haven't you wondered why he brought us out of Egypt to this land? Haven't you wondered when the fulfillment of his promise to us will come to fruition?" Satisfied that he had all the attention he was going to get, he paced about. "I, too, am a fisherman. I know where to go when I am hungry." He pointed out to the water. "But fish from the sea will only delay hunger for a time; it will never completely satisfy you."

Someone from the crowd yelled back. "You think we don't know this?"

Undaunted, John continued. "Indeed, you all know this. But I am here to tell you about the food of eternal life. I am here to tell you about a heavenly banquet where you will get your fill. I am here to tell you about a place where you will never go hungry again."

At this, the crowd started murmuring.

"Brothers and sisters, I am up here today to tell you not to neglect the deepest yearning of your very souls. Let me ask you: for what is it that you truly hunger? Do you lay awake at night thinking about fish? As you toil during the day, do you wonder

161

about bread? Or do you not instead ponder the mystery of your life? Do you not wonder why it is that the Lord himself, creator of heaven and earth, decided to put you, of all people, here, at this very spot, at this point in time? Truly, I tell you brothers and sisters, it is not for your daily fish and bread that your minds and hearts point to, but rather the timeless feast of the Lord."

"What is it that you are telling us?" someone else from the crowd asked.

"I am here to tell you to follow the deepest yearnings of your heart, not your stomach. I am here to urge you to go where your heart leads. I am here to say that the time has come, and the kingdom of God is at hand."

At this, the crowd became noisy with comments and questions.

"You may wonder, what is it that the Lord himself wants to do with me? You may wonder, out of all the people that live in this vast land, what is it that I, a mere person, am supposed to do? I come today with the answer, and it is this: prepare the way of the Lord! Indeed, there is one among us who completes the Lord's fulfillment of his covenant, his eternal promise to our people. And I want you to be on the lookout for him. For though he is near, you know neither the time nor the place you will encounter him."

A lone figure on the fringes of the crowd piped up. "How am I supposed to be on the lookout?" All heads turned to him. "How am I supposed to be ready for this person, this fulfillment? The Lord above has afflicted me since childhood."

162

John looked and saw that the person acted in the manner of a blind person. John looked out and saw James, and motioned to him. James nodded and led the blind man up onto the dock. Now it was James who spoke up. "You know who this is, correct?" he pointed to the blind man. The crowd nodded, for they had seen him begging at the market for years. James grabbed a fish from one of the stalls and walked down the length of the dock. "As my brother said, you hunger for more than the food you eat. We, like you, are mere men, but we bring you the good news of the Lord. And so you believe what we say, behold!" At this, he turned and threw the fish at the blind man from a distance of about a stone's throw.

The man turned and caught the fish, his eyes wide in wonderment. "I can see!" he cried aloud. And the crowd believed.

**

Levi walked past a number of white-walled huts on his way into the city. He and Thomas were sent the farthest, to Bethany, just outside Jerusalem. His first task was to find Thomas, since they split a day earlier so Thomas could meet up with some friends. Market stalls and merchants' goods were spread out all over the square just ahead, and people were starting to emerge from the shade after the midday's searing heat.

Levi thought back to the instructions Jesus gave them a mere three weeks ago. At the time, he was apprehensive about going anywhere without a money belt, a walking stick or an extra tunic. Having no money belt meant either working for food or begging. And in his hometown, no one would give anything of value to the former tax collector. Coming down all the way here, far from his own town, sounded good to him. 'And besides,' he thought, 'Bethany is renowned for the piety of its inhabitants, for so many of them were of the Pharisees and the priestly caste. Surely they would be the first ones to welcome the good news of Jesus.'

\*\*

After a night spent with old friends, Thomas bid them good-bye and went off in search of Levi. They had arranged to meet in the central market square, which was just a few stadia ahead. On the way, he encountered a crowd of Pharisees gathered about a crying woman and a small child. He stopped to observe.

"Look here," one of the Pharisees, a short and fat man, said. "Do you see how the child's arm is twisted into a useless appendage? Clearly it is a sign of disfavor from the Lord." The others in the crowd voiced their approval. The fat man turned to the woman. "Tell us, then: what sin did you commit that your child should be disfigured like this?"

The woman cried out. "Truly, I say unto you that I have not sinned. Please leave us alone!"

Another Pharisee jabbed a finger at the woman's face. "Where is your husband, and how did he let you out of the house unaccompanied?"

"Please, sir, my husband died only a few months ago; it is only me and my child here," tears of anguish came down the woman's face.

"Aha," the fat one shouted in triumph, "further proof that you are a sinner. Surely the Lord would not send your family such misfortune if you did not have the black heart of an unrepentant

164

sinner." This was met by further cheers from the rest of the crowd.

Thomas had enough and inserted himself into the situation. "What is going on here?"

Suddenly the crowd became quiet and all eyes turned to him. The fat man squinted in suspicion at the unfamiliar man with the Galilean accent. "It is none of your business. Go and continue on your way."

Thomas got into the man's personal space and looked down at him. "I'm making it my business." The others in the crowd murmured, as no one had ever talked to the Rabbi like this. The fat man's face reddened. "I suggest you leave now, stranger."

"I'm not going anywhere." Thomas could feel the crowd move in on him. "Tell me: why do you think you have the duty to push this innocent woman around like this?"

Veins on the fat man's neck stood out. "This woman is clearly a sinner!" He paced over to her and pointed. "Look at her child. Look at her situation! Surely such a sad case cries out for rabbinical justice." At this, the crowd cheered again.

Thomas was seized by a flash of insight. He approached the fat man. "How is it that you people listen to this man in all his fake piety and unholy zeal?" The crowd gasped in anger. "You must be deaf to the Word of the Lord." The crowd started shouting and approached Thomas. "And not only deaf," Thomas continued, "but blind too! For anyone can see that this man," in one quick motion, Thomas yanked the fat man's cloak over his head and pulled down his girdle, "is uncircumcised!" The crowd stopped in their tracks as they beheld the truth of what Thomas had said.

\*\*

Levi made his way to the market square but saw no sign of Thomas. 'Perhaps he started preaching and the people invited him inside,' he thought. He decided to try the other side of the vast square, but noticed that many of the stalls were unattended. The large crowds one would expect to see milling about, haggling with merchants and sizing up goods, were nowhere to be found. A frown darkened his face. As he looked about trying to figure out where to go next, he heard a dull roar from the opposite end of the square. As he walked in that direction, he heard another roar. It seemed what he was hearing was around the bend ahead. A sinking feeling materialized in his stomach, and an interior voice told him to hurry. He rushed along around the bend and came across a large crowd circled around something. He elbowed his way toward the front and stopped short in horror. In the open space in front of him, a group of men were picking up rocks from the area. They were preparing for a stoning. But where was the condemned?

Levi looked around and saw a woman and a small child in the open space crying, but they were not bound like the victims normally would be. And then Levi spotted him. No wonder he missed him the first time. They had buried Thomas up to his neck in the dirt.

Levi cursed and stormed into the middle of the group of men. "What is going on here?" his voice thundered in righteous anger and immediately silenced the crowd.

A younger-looking rabbi who seemed to be the leader approached Levi. He was steaming in the face of this rude interruption. "Be on your way, you have no business here."

"I am not going anywhere until you tell me why you are about to kill this man. What crime has he committed?"

The rabbi turned to the crowd. "The condemned man has tried to turn the town away from the Lord with some sort of twisted teaching. He has brought shame upon our chief rabbi. Under the law of Moses, he must die." At this, the crowd cheered.

Levi cried out, "This man is preaching the truth."

The crowd became silent again, for the stranger among them would surely be stoned, too. Levi continued. "We have been sent to Bethany to preach the good news, to bring to you the fulfillment of the Lord."

The young rabbi got in Levi's face. "What?"

Levi shoved him aside and addressed the crowd. "We are here to tell you of the fulfillment of the Lord's covenant to his people, to share the blessed news that the Lord has sent us a most holy one to bring about his kingdom." He pointed to Thomas. "This man brings not 'twisted teaching,' but rather the truth."

This ignited the crowd against him as the rabbi motioned others to bind Levi. Levi stood his ground and looked at the men with rocks in their hands. "Tell me, men of Bethany, why do you stand there ready to execute someone. What did this man do to you?"

One of them answered. "This man interfered with the furtherance of rabbinical justice against this woman and her deformed child," he held his rock aloft. "And now he must die for it," he snarled.

The young rabbi burned with anger. "You will watch him die, and then the woman and her child will watch you die." The crowd erupted again while the men took aim.

"People of Bethany," Levi shouted, "hear me and believe me! You take umbrage at the supposed sins of a child and his mother, and you deign to heap your own sins upon an innocent man. Your vengeance and bloodlust cries out for justice, and as I am here as an apostle of Jesus the Christ, I hereby do administer it!" With that, there was a thunder crack in the square. The crowd gasped as they saw all the men drop their rocks, for they now had shriveled arms in the manner of the child. The woman cried out, "my baby is healed!" The crowd turned and saw that the child's arm, which was formerly disfigured, now had a healthy, normal appearance. Levi went to free Thomas. Some of the men went away in shame while Thomas was dug out of the dirt. When he was free, the two continued to preach. And the crowd believed.

**

Nathanael and Philip took the southern road to the region of the Decapolis, where the Hellenistic culture poured out into the Semitic culture of the Middle East. They were to start with the city of Scythopolis.

Nathanael breathed in deeply the clear desert air. "Philip, this is such an exciting time. I am thrilled to be wearing the mantle of preacher. It feels like the natural next step in my rabbinical studies."

"I think I know how you feel," Philip said. "I am eager to share the word of God with my fellow Greeks in this region. They have an advanced culture, but even so, they can learn a lot from us."

"Indeed."

Their footsteps crunched along the broken rock of the desert path. Soon, they came upon the main entrance into the town: a straight pathway paved with dark basalt and lined on either side with columns. A trellis overhead provided some measure of relief from the burning sun overhead.

After admiring the planned layout of the city, Philip turned to Nathanael. "Where shall we begin?"

Nathanael looked around. "Are you not suffering from hunger as I am? Perhaps we shall start in the main square, where the merchants might be."

"But we have no money," Philip said.

"I know."

"So how are we going to get it?"

"We ask for it," Nathanael said. He started off in that direction and Philip followed after some hesitation. They found a spot in the shade, under the cover of a large sycamore tree. After a few minutes, a Greek man dressed in expensive clothes walked by.

"Please sir, can you spare some food for us?" Nathanael asked. While his Greek wasn't fluent like Philip's, he was made to learn it as part of his schooling.

The man stopped and scowled at them. "What are you two do-ing begging for food? You don't look destitute, but instead look clean, well-fed and healthy."

Philip got up. "Please, sir, if you have food to spare, we would deeply appreciate it."

The man scrutinized Philip. "You are Greek like me. How is that you are begging for food instead of advancing society? Please tell me the culture that has been lavished upon you is not being wasted."

By this time a few more people had stopped, wondering what was with the two well-dressed beggars. "Sir, I am here to tell you the culture is not being wasted; indeed, it is alive and well within me."

"Then tell me why I should give you anything to eat when you are perfectly capable of earning it yourself?" The small clutch of people behind him looked on in curiosity.

"I and my friend here have come to tell the good news to the people of this place," Philip said.

"The good news?" the man asked. "What good news can you possibly have for an advanced city such as ours?" The people behind him murmured.

"The good news is that we no longer have to look to the dis-passionate gods of Zeus and others, imploring them to look with favor upon us, when we have a Special Advocate who is here among us."

The people around them gasped. "Are you impugning the very nature of the king of gods?" The man now had a heavy frown and furrowed brows to go with his crossed arms. "What

170

makes you think you can come here and spread that kind of ignorance about?"

"Please, sir, if you can give us an open mind, I promise you and your fellow townspeople that what we are here to share with you will change your lives."

The man and the group behind him laughed with scorn. "I will bet my last denarius that you cannot do so."

Nathanael spoke up. "Well, then, challenge us. If there is something we cannot do, we shall leave this town immediately and never show our faces here again."

The man led Nathanael and Philip along with the crowd to a larger, mud-brick structure on the edge of town. The crowd stopped well short of the building, as if held back by an unseen force. A wall constructed of flat slabs of sandstone ringed the perimeter of the yard.

"What is this place?" Philip asked. He eyed the large area and the rare wooden door on the front of the building and surmised it to be a wealthy estate.

The man took out a key and opened the door before turning back to them. "I am a doctor," he said, "and this is my clinic." He stepped back to show them the inside. Despite the late hour of the day, Philip and Nathanael could see inside, where individual figures were either lying on simple beds or bent over some menial work. Some had bandages over a hand, or an ear, or on their arm. Some had bandages over both hands. A few who had been there the longest had their faces completely covered with wraps.

Nathanael felt his stomach churn. He looked at the man. "You're a doctor?"

Philip became aware of the distance of the crowd and turned around. "You run a leper colony?"

**

Nathanael felt a dry, warm feeling at the back of his throat. Lepers. Of all the diseases he had faced growing up, none had scared him more than this one. It struck without warning, and no one knew how it was spread from person to person. A childhood friend had caught the disease. One day he was running around and playing games just like everyone else. The next day, he developed a rash on his cheek, just under his eye. The boy's family knew it would only get worse, so they sent him to a colony on his ninth birthday, to live among the other victims. Nathanael shook his head as he looked inside. There were perhaps twenty of them: the living dead.

The doctor turned to them. "I was about to conduct another study session to see if my proposed remedies are helping to alleviate their suffering," he said.

"So what is your challenge to us?" Nathanael asked.

"I challenge you to help with their treatment," the doctor said. "Normally I have one of them help me because no one else in their right mind will touch these people."

"What would you have us do?" Nathanael asked.

"I need one of you to unwrap the skin of the affected area to prepare it for the salve I prepared."

"What is this salve you speak of?" Philip asked.

The doctor showed them a large clay urn filled with a thick reddish-brown liquid. "Why, dog's blood and snake venom, of course. The ancients described it in their writings."

Nathanael's stomach churned. The feeling was amplified by the crowd just beyond collectively groaning when they heard this. He wiped the sweat from his brow and looked at Philip. "Very well, then."

The doctor called forth a woman with a soggy bandage over her right hand. "Let's start with this one. You," he gestured to Nathanael, "take off her bandage."

Nathanael took a moment to recall Jesus's words to them and nodded. He unwrapped her bandage, careful to go slowly. Despite his efforts, some of her skin sloughed off and fell into the urn. He undid the last part of the bandage and pulled it away, but one of her fingers stuck to it and likewise fell in. The crowd gasped in revulsion, for her hand was an unrecognizable appendage, covered with bloody pus and rotten skin.

Philip looked at the woman, but her eyes, the only uncovered part of her face, were cast downward in shame. The doctor, satisfied that the entire bandage was off, pointed to the urn. "Now," he said to the woman, "dip your hand in that."

"Wait," Philip said. "Can't you see this woman has endured enough torment?"

"I am here to test this salve, for perhaps it will end her torment," the doctor said.

"Look, we met your challenge," Nathanael said. He turned to the crowd. "We are here to proclaim the kingdom of the Lord.

For the Lord himself has sent us to tell everyone to prepare for his eternal reign."

The crowd murmured again. One of the townspeople called out. "Why should we believe you?"

Nathanael raised his voice. "If I did not have faith in my message, then I wouldn't do what I am about to do."

"What are you going to do?" the doctor asked.

"Behold!" Nathanael said. He took the urn with both hands and raising it to his lips, drank deeply from it. The crowd recoiled in horror. He set it down and wiped his lips with his sleeve. "Behold, I tell all of you to have faith in the Lord, for he has upheld his covenant with Israel from the very first day. Time and again, Israel has turned her back on the Lord. But that you may believe," he turned back to the woman in front of him and the lepers inside the building, "I say to you: be healed!"

With that, the woman cried out as she held up her hands, intact and clean as one who has just bathed. She tore the wrappings from her head and shook her hair, and everyone could see she was a beautiful young woman. More cries rang out as the people inside rushed out and taking their bandages off. All were healed. Some of the townspeople came forward and looked for their relatives among the healed, for they had not been seen in some time.

The doctor fell to his knees. "Please, I beg of you, let the Lord know I am indeed a believer!" The whole crowd erupted in joy and wonderment.

And they believed.

# The Transfiguration

Andrew and John walked together on the road back to Bethsaida when they paused for a break under the airless heat of the desert sun. They spotted an oasis off the path centered on a small well-spring bubbling up from the ground. After waiting for a handful of fellow travelers to drink their fill, Andrew tied their donkeys to a nearby tree while John filled up their wineskins. Slumping down against the base of a palm tree, they drank deeply and split a barley loaf Andrew had carried in his cloak. After focusing on the food for a moment, Andrew looked up and saw some of the other travelers approaching them.

"Excuse me, gentlemen, are you coming from the region of the desert north of Bethsaida?" one of the younger ones, a Pharisee, asked them.

Andrew looked up. "Yes indeed, we are."

The Pharisee stood in front of them. "Please tell me, have you seen the man called Jesus in that region?" His face was the picture of curiosity. "My companions and I have been looking for him and have heard that he might be in the area."

"Indeed, he is there and will be for probably a fortnight at least," Andrew said.

The young man looked satisfied. "Excellent." A slight frown appeared. "How is it that you say he will probably be there for the near future? You speak as if you know where he is going and when?"

John looked up at him. "We are his disciples."

An animated look spread across the young man's face. "You are?" He looked back at his fellow journeymen. "My companions and I would love to hear more about this man. Would you mind telling us a little bit about him?"

John and Andrew looked at each other before John shrugged. "I suppose so," John said. He shifted over and made room for the young man.

"My name is Abahu," he said. "I have heard that this man Jesus heals the sick and drives out demons."

Andrew nodded. "It's true, but the Rabbi wants people to focus on his message rather than dwell on the miracles he works."

The rest of the Pharisees joined them. "Is it true that this man teaches as one with authority?"

"Yes," Andrew said. "You should see for yourselves."

One of them had a troubled look on his face. "But where did he complete his rabbinical studies? We have not encountered this man in Jerusalem."

"He is a carpenter," Andrew said, "but his 'schooling' is way beyond anything you could imagine."

Another one, a chunky man named Shamir who was sweating in the heat of the day, spoke up. "But how can this be? Surely teachings such as his can only be passed on from master to student."

"His knowledge is from above," John said.

"I don't know if I can accept that," Shamir said.

"You must hear him for yourself," John said.

The Pharisees looked at each other.

176

"Have you eaten yet?" Andrew asked them.

"Not yet," Abahu said, "for we have been riding animals throughout this journey, and we have not yet performed the ritual cleansing necessary to eat."

Andrew shrugged and reached for a piece of dried meat he had brought along. "Suit yourself."

The Pharisees stood up. Abahu started to say something, but paused. "We must get going," he said.

"Perhaps we will see you out there," John said.

"Perhaps."

\*\*

A few days later, the group of Pharisees talked amongst themselves as they traveled in the region north of Bethsaida.

"What do you suppose our master Tabbai would say about this man Jesus?" one of them asked out loud.

"Rabbi Tabbai would invite him to study under him," another one said.

Shamir made a clucking noise. "He would do no such thing. There is no doubt the rabbi would denounce him on the spot for teaching as an imposter."

Abahu, the young man, spoke. "I am not so sure. Have you heard of the crowds following this man? Surely they would not seek him out if he was an imposter." He pointed in the distance. "Look there!" As they crested the top of a rolling hill, they could see a vast crowd milling about. The presence of all the people was jarring, as it was in the middle of the desert wasteland. "Let us go test this man Jesus for ourselves."

\*\*

Peter looked around in wonder at the vast crowds. They had been here, just outside Bethsaida for two weeks now, and every day the people kept coming to hear Jesus, and to see him. They had constantly surrounded them, hoping at some point to be within a stone's throw of him. It was near midday and the people were getting hungry, so Jesus had the other apostles sit the crowds down. Peter stayed by his side when a group of the priestly class approached. One of them, a heavier one, got off his camel and looked at Peter. "We are looking for the man called Jesus. Is he here?"

Jesus turned around. "Indeed, I am."

Abahu gazed at him. This man Jesus appeared as a normal man, of average height and build and of normal dress, but there was something about him. Something that hinted at a powerful force in direct proportion to the normality of his appearance. "Greetings, Rabbi-"

Shamir cut him off. "We have come from Jerusalem, from the Rabbi Tabbai," he said. Surely mention of the great teacher's name would get this Jesus's attention.

Jesus looked at them with a piercing intensity. The Pharisees shuffled their feet. "We are here to see you," Shamir was unsure what to say.

"Behold, you see me." Jesus smiled. "Why don't you join these people and recline? Surely you must have had a long journey."

Shamir looked at the crowds. "There are women here," his objection was obvious, for it was forbidden to talk to women in public.

178

"I thought you were here just to listen," Jesus said.

Shamir flushed.

*"Why do your disciples break the tradition of the elders? They do not wash hands when they eat a meal."*

*Jesus said to them in reply, "And why do you break the commandment of God for the sake of your tradition?" (Matthew 15:2-3)*

The Pharisees looked at each other. This man Jesus had just thrown verbal sand in their faces and they recoiled in disbelief. They had finished years of rabbinical training, and kept all of the laws of Moses and more, tending faithfully to even the smallest of rules. They were caretakers of the faith and the people looked up to them for guidance in all matters. And yet this carpenter spoke as he did.

Jesus went on.

*"For God said, 'Honor your father and your mother,' and 'Whoever curses father or mother shall die.' But you say, 'Whoever says to father or mother, "Any support you might have had from me is dedicated to God," need not honor his father.' You have nullified the word of God for the sake of your tradition." (Matthew 15:4-6)*

Shamir glared at Jesus in unmasked hatred. The boiling anger from within prevented him from responding. Jesus went on.

*"Hypocrites, well did Isaiah prophesy about you when he said: 'This people honors me with their lips, but their hearts are far from me;*

*in vain do they worship me,*

*teaching as doctrines human precepts.'" (Matthew*
*15:7-9)*

Shamir turned around and stormed off, taking the others with him. Their collective apoplexy sustained them without eating and they went back to Jerusalem.

Jesus turned back to the crowds.

*"Hear and understand. It is not what enters one's*
*mouth that defiles that person; but what comes out of*
*the mouth is what defiles one." (Matthew 15:10-11)*

The words struck Nathanael at the core of his being. It was like someone had just knocked all ignorance out of him. All his adult life, he had learned about the Torah, about the law and the prophets. The rules they lived by were the cornerstone of society, and none he could think of were more readily followed than that of ritual washing before eating and the dietary laws. But what Jesus had said made so much sense. He listened in awe.

Afterward, Peter and the apostles approached Jesus.

*"Do you know that the Pharisees took offense*
*when they heard what you said?"*

*He said in reply, "Every plant that my heavenly*
*Father has not planted will be uprooted." (Matthew*
*15:12-13)*

**

Later, when Jesus and his disciples were alone after vacating the area and traveling to Caesaeria Phillippi on the Great Sea, Jesus questioned them.

*"Who do people say that the Son of Man is?"*

*They replied, "Some say John the Baptist, others Elijah, still others Jeremiah or one of the prophets."*

*He said to them, "But who do you say that I am?"*

*Simon Peter said in reply, "You are the Messiah, the Son of the living God."*

*Jesus said to him in reply, "Blessed are you, Simon son of Jonah. For flesh and blood has not revealed this to you, but my heavenly Father. And so I say to you, you are Peter, and upon this rock I will build my church, and the gates of the netherworld shall not prevail against it. I will give you the keys to the kingdom of heaven. Whatever you bind on earth shall be bound in heaven; and whatever you loose on earth shall be loosed in heaven." Then he strictly ordered his disciples to tell no one that he was the Messiah.*

*(Matthew 16:14-20)*

And the disciples wondered.

**

A week later, Jesus found Peter, James and John. "Come with me," he said. Despite having just made the long journey by foot from Caesarea Philippi, on the coast, they did so. He walked ahead of them, leading the way toward the hills in the distance. James and John tugged at Peter's sleeve. "What do you make of what the Master said to us back by the sea?"

"Which part are you speaking of?"

"When he said that whatever we bind on earth will be bound in heaven, and whatever we loose on earth will be loosed in heaven," James said.

Peter had a pensive face as they walked. "I am not certain. But remember, the Master gave us power to do so when he gave us the mission to proclaim his kingdom to all the towns and villages."

"Indeed, he did," John said. "But I do not understand."

"What do you not understand?" Peter asked.

"He gave us the power to give sight to the blind, to heal the sick, and even to cast out demons," John said. "But do those impediments exist even in heaven? Isn't heaven a perfect state of being?"

"It's true that heaven is like that, since I imagine that is where we will be in complete union with the Father for eternity. However, the Rabbi isn't just talking about physical maladies."

"Really?" James asked. "What, then?"

"James, what are other impediments that people accumulate over time?"

James looked at the hills in the distance. "Abusing servants, taking of that which does not belong to them, providing false witness?"

"Precisely," Peter said. "Don't you see? The Master gave us authority to forgive people's sins, too."

James and John looked at each other as they processed this. They continued walking toward the hills as the bare heat of the late afternoon sun slanted towards them from behind. The light of the golden hour bathed the hills in an orange glow that amplified what they had just learned.

"And how about what the Master said to you, Peter?" John asked. "How was it that you came to know his true nature?"

Peter looked at them. "It was something that happened when the master sent us all two-by-two to proclaim his kingdom."

Their footsteps made soft crunching sounds on the minute rocks underneath. "Well, what was it?" James asked.

"You know, I don't believe we ever heard what you and Andrew encountered," John said, "we only heard about the other disciples and their stories."

"It's true, you hadn't heard it," Peter said. "And for some time after it happened, I think even I had trouble believing it, too."

\*\*

Their pace slowed as they encountered an increasingly steep slope. "You see, my brother and I were sent to the village of Nain."

"Where is that?" John interrupted.

"We didn't know at first, either, but it's in the middle of nowhere," Peter said. "We came upon the town at dusk. The dying light gave a foreboding feel to the town. Something didn't seem right. We couldn't quite decide what was unusual about the town, but we pressed on and tried to find lodging for the night. Nain lies at the end of a little road, so I don't think they've seen a traveler come through there in ages. After stopping near a well in the middle of the town, one of the village elders came out to meet us. He expressed awe that someone would come to this place, even if they were just on their way through.

"What did he say?" John asked.

"I will tell you."

\*\*

"Why are you men here?" the old man looked at the curiosity of two strangers in town.

Peter finished hauling up a bucket from the cistern. "We have been sent to proclaim the good news of the Lord; his eternal promise to this people."

The old man frowned. "We have Baal here, the god of thunder, of weather and the sky." He pointed to the orange sliver of sun stabbing into the dark expanse of sky to the east of them. "Look and see how he has made the sky turn dark yet again." The man then looked at them intently. "And after that, he will bring back the sun," he hissed in an excited whisper. "See how he orders our days and nights!"

Peter and Andrew looked at each other in mutual understanding of what the other was thinking. Was not even this wasteland part of the inheritance of the Lord? Why then were these people stuck in time? Peter turned to the old man. "Very well then, where can we speak with the priest of Baal?"

"Outsiders do not speak to the priest. Indeed, outsiders should fear the very existence of this place."

Peter looked back at the old man. "What is it about this place that we should fear?"

The man looked up at the sky, as if divining an answer in the heavens, as if it was impossible to explain otherwise. "I will tell you," he said, "if you listen."

Peter and Andrew nodded.

"It began with Raziel. His family has handed down the priesthood of the *baru* for twenty generations."

"Who is Raziel?" Andrew asked.

184

"Raziel is our village elder, shaman and haruspex."

"What?" Peter asked. "I do not recognize that word."

The old man appeared troubled. "Sir, it is a way of discerning the will of the gods by carefully inspecting the innards of certain animals," the old man's voice was but a whisper by now.

"You act as though you are afraid of spreading the knowledge to us," Peter said. "What is the matter?"

The old man turned his head left and right before responding. "I shouldn't be talking about this, but I am an old man and Raziel doesn't have the same sway over me.

"When the Babylonians invaded and sent Israel into exile, they didn't send all the people away, but only the leaders, judges, commanders and intellectuals. Everyone else could stay." The old man settled in a bit, as if preparing for a lengthy tour. "Slowly, the pagan ways of the Babylonians infected this area, dissipating the beliefs and the values held by the Hebrew people. These alien customs became ingrained in our village over time, but over the last few generations, the family of Raziel, his ancestors, that is, consolidated themselves into a political machine and -" a noise in the distance stopped the old man, who popped onto his feet. "He is coming! I must go."

Just as he was melting away, Peter and Andrew saw the source of the noise: a team of camels pulling a cart, with a long trail of people behind it. The cart was embroidered with all manner of precious stones, and upholstered with the finest silk and linen. Even the rims of the wheels appeared as if gilded with gold and silver. The people behind were playing instruments: flutes, lyres, tambourines and drums, but none of it in harmony.

Rather, it made for a clashing, discordant noise that only highlighted the other-worldliness of the scene.

As they watched, the caravan, which looked to be about one hundred cubits long, wound its way around two small hills on the outskirts of town and proceeded into the center of the village. As it passed, the figure of Raziel became clearer: the self-proclaimed priest of Baal wore a leather head covering with antlers of some sort on the top. He was dressed in a coat made from the fur of various animals, with each pelt contributing a different color and texture. Purple, orange and black paint covered his face in a fantastical design that hearkened to the weirdness of it all. Raziel barely registered a glance at the two foreigners gaping at him and proceeded to lead the caravan to another hilltop on the other side of town. Peter and Andrew's curiosity drove them along behind them.

When the caravan approached the hilltop, a collection of shirtless men carried the platform Raziel stood upon to a rocky ledge overlooking the assembled crowd below. The townspeople filed into the area and sat down in an orderly fashion, leading Peter and Andrew to believe they had done this often.

As Raziel stood on the rocky pulpit, the wagon at the end of the caravan entered the assembly area, where the shirtless men grabbed the limp form of a young woman and brought her to an elevated slab near Raziel's location. Only then did Peter and Andrew look at each other in horror. For surely the slab could be nothing else but an altar, while the young woman would be a sacrifice.

After some incantations in an unfamiliar tongue with his hands hovering over the woman, Raziel addressed the crowd. "Brothers and sisters of the empire of Baal, I hereby greet you with tidings of elation." At this the crowd sounded a murmured response. He continued. "For we are here once again to pay tribute to our god of the sky, our god of the sun and the moon, of the rain and the drought." By now the crowd was rapt with silence. "We are here to implore Baal to have mercy upon us and our fields this season. We are here to invoke his all-powerful name so that as the sun may shine on our crops, the rain may fall on them. Only the Baal can bring about the proper balance for our harvest, and our prosperity." A raised fist led the people to cheer. Peter and Andrew looked over the crowd from their vantage point just off to the side; even though dusk was turning into nightfall, to them they could see clearly that most of the people were simply repeating the gestures and cheers of a more enthusiastic crowd seated at the front.

Raziel approached the altar. "Just as only Baal can order the heavens so as to nourish our people, only the blood of a virgin can satisfy his thirst for a tribute." Peter and Andrew looked at each other. They knew they must do something, but the bonds of uncertainty froze them in place. Raziel picked up a large scythe as the young woman, who until now had been in a sleep state, awoke and screamed and struggled against the bonds fastening her to the altar. Raziel raised his voice. "As surely as Baal orders the sun and the moon and the stars throughout the heavens, and as surely as he turns the day into night, I hereby declare our people's allegiance to him once again, by virtue of the blood of this

187

sacrifice." A roar rose from the assembly as Raziel brought down the scythe onto the woman's throat, turning the altar red with her blood. He placed his hands in her blood, then lifted them to the sky in more incantations.

Peter turned to Andrew and pulled his sleeve. "Let's go."

"Where are we going?"

"Just follow me." Peter marched resolutely alongside the assembly and approached the front, near the shirtless men and the more enthusiastic of the crowd. The people had fallen silent as they watched these two strangers head for the altar.

The shirtless men tried to encircle Peter and Andrew as they stepped onto Raziel's precipice, but seeing something in Peter's eyes kept them at a distance. They reached Raziel, who only noticed now that something was deviating from the script.

Peter approached Raziel. "Woe to you, treasonous son of your ancestors!" Peter's voice bellowed out onto the assembled plain below. "Woe to you, o faithless people!" The crowd hushed in disbelief at the bold intrusion.

"Who are you to encroach on the soil of Baal, on the anniversary of our blood sacrifice to him!" Raziel sputtered in apoplexy. "Shall we make of you another sacrifice?" he lunged for Peter, but Peter grabbed his antler head covering and threw it over the ledge. Raziel gasped at the sudden embarrassment and cowered in rage.

"Open your ears, o people of Nain, and listen!" Peter commanded the crowd once more. "Our Lord, the God of Israel, the God of Abraham, the God of Isaac and the God of Jacob, the Lord who himself brought our forebears out of Egypt, the one

188

true God sees your decadent insolence and your hardened hearts and it is enough to bring his wrathful vengeance upon this world. Your sin alone, apart from all other people's, is enough to ensure the destruction of this entire land." The crowd became restless at the sight of this foreigner who had tread so iconoclastically on their religious ceremony. Their mumbling continued as Peter raised his voice even louder. "Indeed, so great is your sin that every human life would be crushed were it not for the mercy of our God, the God of David. Recall that the Lord on high freed our ancestors from the bondage of pharaoh and delivered them to this land, the land of milk and honey, and this is how you repay the Lord?" Peter jumped up onto the altar, still slick from the virgin's blood. "This is how you pay tribute in gratefulness to our God, by taking innocent life, and by throwing it in his face?"

By now the crowd had become silent and absorbed the words of this stranger with awe and wonderment. Someone had fetched Raziel's antlers, and after putting them back on, he jumped onto the altar next to Peter. "How dare you intrude upon our ceremony and our ritual sacrifice?" he paced toward Peter. "How dare you interrupt the sacrifice which our Baal is rightfully owed his due? By whose authority do you claim to act?" By now his face was a hair's breadth from Peter's.

"We come on behalf of the most high God, the creator of heaven and earth, and of all things seen and unseen," Peter's voice carried through the area, where the vestiges of daylight had disappeared and were replaced by the dark strands of the infant night.

"Your so-called god is nothing of the sort," Raziel had his confidence back by now. "For none has the power of the almighty Baal."

Peter yelled out. "So you know that the Lord God lives, I hereby command the return," he looked out across the expanse, as if seeing each one in the crowd eye-to-eye, "of the sun." With that, the sun pulled back from beneath the western horizon and slowly took up position in the sky directly overhead. The crowd took a collective breath at the unnatural scene around them, for this foreigner had literally turned their world upside down.

As one, they looked up at Raziel. He in turn could feel the collective accusation of thousands of pairs of eyes upon him. In anger, he turned and pushed Peter in the back right off the high perch of the altar. The people screamed in anticipation of the deadly fall that would surely ensue. Their screams turned to fascination as they watched Peter stop in mid-air and turn around to face Raziel. "You who would test the Lord, you who revel in the misdeeds and sinfulness of a thousand lost souls, I say to you: your time has ended." With that, a lightning bolt materialized out of thin air and cut through the atmosphere with a sonic boom. In the blink of an eye, it encapsulated Raziel in an electric charge and incinerated him, leaving only the burnt husks of his antlers laying on the bloody altar next to the virgin. Peter turned back to the crowd. "Hear and understand, o faithless people, o wandering souls: the Lord God has sent us to proclaim the Truth to you. And that is this: He has sent his only son to take your place on this bloody altar. For no one other than him who is undefiled can possibly bring you to the arms of the Father, but the

Son himself. The Lord has commanded me to make straight the way of the Lord, so let it be known this day, that through this village may the way be straight through your hearts."

The crowd stood mouths agape at the sound of the message and the sight of this miracle, of this man hovering in their midst. All were silent; only the collective breathing of the people was audible.

Peter went back to the altar and knelt next to the virgin's corpse and prayed. "Oh Lord, I implore thee to breathe life back into this woman so as to bring about glory and honor to you." As soon as he uttered the words, the woman awoke and rose to her feet. And the crowd swooned. And they believed.

**

James and John walked in silence as they absorbed Peter's story. They dwelt on it as the three of them followed Jesus up the mountainside. Where could they possibly be going? They reached the top and looked out at the expansive valley before them. For a long moment, Jesus stood in front of them as they beheld the grandeur of the scene before them. John froze as he considered the privilege of being here with the Master, at this point, at this time. "Master, what are we doing here?" he asked.

Jesus turned around and the air around them instantly changed. His face became like a burning oven, glowing brightly with the force of ten thousand suns. His clothes turned white, as if burning with the utmost purity of fire, and they felt waves of power emanating from him. His body became totally trans-formed into a glowing brilliance that shredded every molecule of air and ground that surrounded them, so that it was just them, and his glory. The sky turned white in the searing light of his presence, and the ground became as like a cloud, featureless. They felt the flowing power of his holiness and his regal nature and it was a total penetration into their very souls.

Two figures appeared at his side. The first turned to him and with a voice that came straight from the heart proclaimed, "O Lord, promise of our God and savior to our people, how I have yearned for this day. How I have yearned to set foot in the promised land of the Lord, the one who led your people out from Egypt and guided them for the duration of my remaining lifetime. I denied myself the chance to see the people return home, but now the fulfillment of my mission lies here before my very eyes."

The second figure turned to him. "O God, how I preached of thee to the faithless multitudes, that they would know the true nature of our Lord and God. How the word of your promise brought so many back from the brink. The Lord took me body and soul from this world and the end of my mission, and how my heart bursts with joy to see its completeness appear before me. Words fail me in this most spectacular moment."

Peter watched as the two, whom he understood to be Moses and Elijah, stood and basked in the presence of Jesus. It felt like they had been here for a thousand years, so glorious was this experience before him.

*Then Peter said to Jesus in reply, "Lord, it is good that we are here. If you wish, I will make three tents here, one for you, one for Moses, and one for Elijah."*
*While he was still speaking, behold, a bright cloud*

*cast a shadow over them, then from the cloud came a voice that said, "This is my beloved Son, with whom I am well pleased; listen to him." When the disciples heard this, they fell prostrate and were very much afraid. But Jesus came and touched them, saying, "Rise, and do not be afraid." And when the disciples raised their eyes, they saw no one else but Jesus alone. (Matthew 17:4-8)*

And they felt so very small in his infinite love.

# The Institution of the Eucharist

Lebbaeus made his way home at sundown, feeling the satisfying weight of the day's earnings in his money belt. He hummed a little tune as he walked, zig-zagging his way through the center of Jerusalem, an island of bliss in the midst of the great bustling city. As he walked, a slight western breeze carried the scent of desert creosote along with it. The sweetness of it unfurled itself against the backdrop of another vivid purple sunset. 'How life is so much better when my pockets are full,' he thought. Soon he would come home to his wife and a house full of children, and he would eat his fill of her superb cooking.

After getting home and securing his money belt, and after the sumptuous dinner, the pleasant company of his family, and a few glasses of wine, Lebbaeus instantly fell asleep like only the truly comfortable can.

He found himself alone and outside, seemingly floating in midair when the sky around him turned into a soft, golden glow. He watched as the sun itself, fiery and warm and pulsating with color, rose in the eastern sky and traced a grand arc through the heavens until it disappeared over the opposite horizon. Lebbaeus felt weightless as he beheld the spectacle, his sense of vulnerability growing as the sky around him turned orange, then red, then purple before it melted away and left only blackness. Something reverberated around him, a deep and sonorous essence that seemed to envelop him. He focused on it, sensing that the essence was aimed at him, at only him. Once again it sounded out, and he realized it was a voice.

"Lebbaeus," it came from all around him. "Lebbaeus, behold the servant of the Lord." With that, Lebbaeus saw a brilliant glow in front of him and remained mesmerized as the light slowly coalesced into a figure of a man, a giant of a man taller than a mountain and burning with a zeal that Lebbaeus understood to be love for the Lord. "I come bearing a message for you, O Lebbaeus."

Lebbaeus hung suspended, powerless to move and unfeeling, save for the charged tingling sensation running over his skin. His entire being was focused on hearing the message, as if it was the only thing that ever mattered to him, as if he had been waiting a hundred lifetimes for this very moment.

"Lebbaeus, are you ready to receive the message from the Lord?" the man, an angel most certainly, glowed anew with variations of gold and white.

"Speak, for I am listening."

The angel nodded in a solemn movement. "Open your heart, and listen with the entirety of your mind, body, spirit and soul." After a long pause, the angel continued. "Something disturbing to you will happen soon. When that happens, you are to return home at once. When you get there, you are to take your largest water jug and proceed to the well nearest your house. Servants of the Lord will ask you to take them somewhere, and you will lead them back to your house."

Lebbaeus absorbed every word like it was air in the midst of drowning. The angel remained there while Lebbaeus processed this.

"Will my family be hurt?"

"Your family will not be touched."

"How will I know when it is happening?"

"You will know."

Lebbaeus felt something different, as if he were returning to earth. Though he felt utterly powerless in the face of the angel, he summoned the energy for one last time. "But only women carry water jugs."

The angel looked at him, indeed looked right through him. "I know." With that, the angel's form became less defined and melted back into a ball of light before dissipating into the darkness again. Lebbaeus felt like he was falling now, and that he would fall forever. Flailing his arms, he felt something slam into his inner being, as if it collided with his soul.

He sat bolt upright in bed, drenched in sweat and panting, drawing in air like he had just run the distance to the Temple. His wife reached for him in the darkness. "What is it Lebbaeus?"

Lebbaeus looked around the moonlit room, realizing he was in his house, with his family and in his bed. He caught his breath. "A dream," he whispered. "It was a dream."

**

As the sun began to drag down under the horizon, Chadlai and Maluch reclined on the flat ground on the foothills a few miles from the sea of Galilee. Chadlai let out a small belch and looked out over the thousands of people who had similarly eaten their fill of bread after listening to the charismatic man from Nazareth. "Maluch," Chadlai began, "what a most pleasant day. Here we are, reclining by the water, the temperature is just right, and our bellies are full."

Maluch sat nearby with his hands clasped around his knees, with a look far into the distance.

"Maluch?"

"What is it?" Maluch turned to look at Chadlai.

"Were you daydreaming again? I was calling your name."

"Sorry. I was considering what just happened."

"What, that we ate a meal?"

Maluch looked at Chadlai with mouth agape. "Do you mean to tell me you don't recognize the significance of what just happened?"

Chadlai's brows furrowed. "No. What are you talking about?"

"You didn't realize that all these people around us were able to eat their fill of bread?"

"Of course I realize that. What is so special about that? People eat as a matter of course."

Maluch turned toward Chadlai. "We and all these other people have been following this man Jesus for the last two days, out in this parched land where there are no settlements. And yet his disciples were able to hand out bread to every man and his family."

Chadlai dismissed him with a wave. "My friend, do you not think that the people here would not bring their own food with them? That they would not pull it out when they became hungry?"

"Of course they would bring their own food. As I have brought mine. I filled by bag with as much bread as I could four days ago when we left our village to come here. And by last night it was gone."

"So?"

Maluch groaned at his friend. "What do you mean, 'so?' I'm telling you I brought as much bread as I could, and I still ran out yesterday." Maluch shook his head. "And we have no families with us. But most of these men have their families with them. It is likely they have gone longer without food."

"But I still had some food left this morning."

"You did? Why did you not share some with me?"

A flush of red color flashed across Chadlai's face and he looked down.

"Ugh." Maluch picked up a pinch of sand from the ground and tossed it in Chadlai's direction. "I do not know why I am still your friend."

Chadlai laughed. "Probably because you have no other friends. And probably because one day you will ask for my sister's hand in marriage."

This time it was Maluch's turn to look down.

"Ha! My friend, we have known each other for so long. I know you too well. You are such a romantic, always willing to see the best in everyone."

"And you are such a cynic. Why can you not believe that what we just encountered here was a miracle?"

"I told you: everyone already had food. They just shared."

Maluch shook his head. "If they had food, then why was everyone so hungry?"

Chadlai pointed. "Look, the man Jesus is about to speak again."

*"Amen, amen, I say to you, you are looking for me not because you saw signs but because you ate the loaves and were filled." (John 6:26)*

*"Amen, amen, I say to you, it was not Moses who gave the bread from heaven; my Father gives you the true bread from heaven. For the bread of God is that which comes down from heaven and gives life to the world."*

*So the crowd said to him, "Sir, give us this bread always." Jesus said to them, "I am the bread of life; whoever comes to me will never hunger, and whoever believes in me will never thirst." (John 6:32-35)*

Chadlai turned to Maluch with a troubled look etched on his face. "Did he just say that he was the bread of life? Was he not born and raised near here, in Galilee? Were not his parents Joseph and Mary. And is he not but a simple carpenter?"

*"I am the bread of life. Your ancestors ate the manna in the desert, but they died." (John 6:48-49).*

*"I am the living bread that came down from heaven; whoever eats this bread will live forever; and the bread that I will give is my flesh for the life of the world." (John 6:51)*

*Jesus said to them, "Amen, amen, I say to you, un-*
*less you eat the flesh of the Son of Man and drink his*
*blood, you do not have life within you." (John 6: 53)*

Jesus kept speaking, but in the crowd, Chadlai stood. "Did you hear that?" he gestured to Jesus some distance away. "He said we had to eat his flesh and drink his blood!" he could barely contain the shock and outrage.

Maluch rose and followed Chadlai out of the area along with most of the others. "Chadlai, why don't you give him a chance? Look at all this man has done. We ourselves have seen his works. Don't those speak for themselves?"

"Maluch, my friend, those works never contradicted the laws of our faith. Healing people is fine and good. But even the youngest child, even the most unlearned of our faith knows that Leviticus absolutely prohibits the drinking of blood." Chadlai started walking even faster now. "And to eat his flesh? To eat the body of another man?" he was breathless by now.

"Chadlai, please stop and consider what you are saying. Besides, we need to talk more about this, because I'm not as ready as you are to leave."

Chadlai whipped around. "You won't leave with me? How in the name of all that is good could you stay around and listen to this man speak anymore? Have you not heard enough? What he is saying directly contradicts the laws that have been handed down to us and safeguarded by the Pharisees."

"Well, then, how could a healing man such as him go against the laws of our faith? Name one thing that he has done that is wrong - name one thing that he should not have done."

"I'll tell you what he should not have done. He should not have told people to eat of his body. That is plainly cannibalism and on the face of it is totally against everything we have ever known."

"Chadlai, please think for a moment. Would his acts of healing be blessed by God if this man were against God?"

Chadlai stopped and turned to Maluch. After a pause, he said, "The evil one made those things possible."

"But what about him driving out those demons? What about that? How can the evil one make that happen when Jesus is driving the evil forces out? He cannot drive out evil in the name of evil." Seeing that he was making some headway, Maluch continued. "Please, let us just sit down for a moment and discuss this in full. For it would be a shame, would it not, if you were to leave without fully understanding what has happened here?"

Chadlai nodded. "I agree, for it, too, would be a shame if you were to remain likewise without fully understanding."

"Good, then, let us sit and discuss." They found a spot to sit on a rocky outcropping where the shallow hillside met the coastal plain.

Chadlai began. "Look, I know you are enthralled by this man, but everything we know about our faith says that such teachings as his are not legitimate. Our faith and its laws are very clear: we shall wear *tzitzit* on the corners of our clothing," he held up the fringes on his cloak, "and we shall affix the *mezuzah* to the doorposts of our houses. And those are just two of them."

"Yes, it is good to have a passage from the Torah nailed to your doorpost, but don't you think this man Jesus is proposing something else here? Something more profound? From all that we have seen and heard, from the testimony of all those that he has healed, or merely touched, it is almost as if the man Jesus is saying that we should have the Torah affixed to our hearts."

Chadlai frowned. "How in the name of all that is righteous can we nail something to our hearts?" The perplexity and distress on his face was total.

Maluch groaned. "Chadlai, my friend, how is it that you cannot know the true meaning of a statement like that? Must you be so literal?"

"My friend, it is the desire of the evil one that simpletons such as us start to interpret the divine law of Yahweh. We must remember our place and submit to the religious authorities on such matters. To place ourselves above them is to place ourselves outside the law of God."

"Chadlai, is that the way you see the practice of our faith? Simply follow a set of rules and you will be found acceptable in the *olam ha-ba*?"

Chadlai's face reddened. "We both know that that way, that legalistic way of living is not what is intended. And I, in fact, do make a solemn effort to see the spiritual reality behind every single little thing I do, at every moment of the day, in preparation for the world to come. But I just can't see how this man's teaching fits in."

Maluch was quick to respond. "Yes, my friend, I know that you faithfully uphold the spirit as well as the letter of the law. I think that is why so many people are leaving, because they can't see it either. But why were so many drawn to him in the first place? I think it is because he is calling them, and us, to a greater reality."

Chadlai shook his head. "I don't know, my friend. It all seems just so," he searched for the right word, "unnatural. It seems like this is going against the wishes of God."

Maluch shook his head, too. "I fear, instead, that if I leave here and do not take any of this to heart, I will be the one going against God."

Chadlai looked at Maluch. "This is a difficult subject indeed. But I trust we can rely on the religious authorities to guide us on the path."

**

Rabbi Shamir wiped his brow for what seemed to be the hundredth time since he came out here to the edges of the city. He struggled to move around in the thick crowds that lined the edges of the main road into Jerusalem, for not only were there hundreds of thousands of pilgrims there from all over the known world, the man Jesus came riding on a donkey, treading upon cloaks that the people had cast onto the road. The charged atmosphere was undeniable, and it stung Shamir to see it. Ever since he had returned from up north, he had been distraught at the thought of this man. The people around him hailed him as a king, someone to take them out of their misery. 'How the ignorant are so quick to crown a new king,' Shamir thought. He turned to his mentor, the rabbi Tabbai. "Rabbi, what are your impressions of the man?"

Rabbi Tabbai stroked his chin as he watched the procession make its way through the gate and into the city. "I have none as of yet," the rabbi said, "for I have not heard him speak."

Shamir's insides turned. He was certain his mentor would denounce the man Jesus immediately and loudly. Perhaps they would have to wait until another opportunity.

**

Peter absorbed the scene around him in wonderment. The people flocked to Jesus from all sides, throwing their cloaks onto the road in the hopes that even the shadow of the donkey would pass over them. A constant din of cheering, whooping and yelling reverberated around them. He thought the city walls themselves would fall down like a new Jericho.

He shouted in Jesus's ear. "Where are we going now, my Lord?"

Jesus looked back at him and smiled. "Where else, Peter?" Seeing the questioning look in return, he added, "The Temple, of course."

After another thirty minutes winding through the adulation, they came to the Temple. Upon entering the outer courtyard, Jesus's disposition turned dark in an instant. Before him, countless pilgrims were exchanging their Greek drachmas and their Roman denarii for the Tyrian shekels they would use to buy animals for sacrifice.

**

Tabbai and Shamir followed them into the courtyard and from a distance, they watched as Jesus flew into a rage, upsetting all the moneychangers' tables and driving the animals out with a makeshift whip. Finally Shamir got to see his mentor take offense, for no sooner than the rage started did Tabbai rush forward to stop Jesus, but the moneychangers and their minions had formed a human ring around him as they scrambled on the ground to recover their money. For the time being, all Tabbai could do was watch in horror as commerce was disrupted. Because of his position and influence, he was entitled to set aside one of the stalls to someone of his designation. He had let his brother-in-law establish himself in the courtyard with the understanding that Tabbai would get a portion of the profits.

After the dust had settled and Jesus and his followers left, Tabbai found his brother-in-law staring at the spectacle, the only one who was not crawling around on hands and knees to pick up loose change. "How much did you lose?"

His brother-in-law continued to stare, as if he were in another world.

"Lebbaeus, pay attention," Tabbai grabbed his shoulders. "How much did you lose?"

Lebbaeus looked at his table and his assistant scooping up coins. "I don't know, probably a third of my earnings."

"Damn him," Tabbai seethed and his face turned red. "Listen to me: get together with the other moneychangers tonight. You will decide on a better exchange rate tomorrow to make up for it." He looked around at all the pilgrims still around. "These people won't know the difference."

Lebbaeus gathered up his things. Tabbai stopped him. "Where are you going? You must get your business back in order!" The implication was clear. There were still pilgrims about; still money to be made.

"I must get going."

"Where? And why now?"

But with a flourish of his cloak, he left.

**

On the edge of the city, Jesus and the apostles melted into the crowd. Every few moments, Peter looked behind them.

"Something is bothering you, Peter," Jesus said.

"My lord, the Temple authorities must surely be upset now. What if they follow us?"

"The problem, Peter, is that they are not upset. They are not upset that the Temple courtyard is used as a commercial enterprise. They are not upset that anyone going to the Temple has to buy their animal sacrifice there. And they are certainly not upset that the people must pay those inflated prices."

Peter stopped looking back, but still an unsettled feeling nagged him. "Where are we going to celebrate the Passover? Surely we must remain vigilant."

*Jesus said to them, "Go into the city and a man will meet you, carrying a jar of water. Follow him."*
*(Mark 13:14)*

**

Kitra was home, spinning flax when her husband barged in.

She looked up. "Lebbaeus, what are you doing here at this hour? It is the middle of the day; normally you aren't done until nightfall."

Lebbaeus rummaged around for something. "I'll explain later," he murmured. He searched around the room, moving things about, until he gave up. "Where is the large water jug?"

"The water jug? Why?"

"I just need it."

"It's outside behind the back wall. Why?"

"I'll explain later." Lebbaeus left as soon as he came and found the water jug where Kitra said it would be. He took it and made his way to the nearest well head, about a ten-minute walk toward the city center. After waiting in line trying to avoid the glances of the women there, he managed to fill the jug and balance it on his head like he had seen others walking about in a similar manner. With halting steps, he turned back toward his house, careful to keep both hands on the handles to keep it balanced. He found it hard to look straight ahead, so he kept his head down and let others walk around him. After a few minutes of shuffling, two men stopped right in front of him.

Lebbaeus stopped. These must be the men.

One of them spoke. "The teacher says, "My appointed time draws near; in your house I shall celebrate the Passover with my disciples.""

Lebbaeus looked at them. "Follow me," he said. He led them back to his house, where for the second time Kitra looked on in stunned silence as her husband walked in with two strangers. "What is going on here?"

"Kitra, these men will need the upper room for their Passover celebration."

"What?"

"I'll explain later."

\*\*

After gathering around the table, Jesus blessed them all, saying, "I will remain with you only a little while longer, as I am on the way to fulfill my Father's promise to the world." Together, they drank the first cup of wine, the *kiddush* cup. As Peter reclined, he sensed a veritable swirl of emotions in the air on this, one of the holiest of all celebration days. There was the excitement of gathering together with Jesus and the apostles and the women who had been with them all along, yes, but there was something else entirely, a hint of foreboding, an ominous air hanging about that Peter could not quite define. Jesus had just washed their feet, something even a servant wouldn't do, and had given them a new mandate in the process.

They all sat for the meal. Jesus motioned for them to drink the *maggid*, the second cup, the cup of judgement. Together, they sang the 113rd Psalm, where they praised the name of the Lord.

After this, Jesus broke the bread and gave it to them, saying, "Take this, all of you, and eat of it, for this is my Body, which will be given up for you." With that, an unstoppable force of love flowed out from Jesus and entered the bread, transforming it. To all gathered, it felt like time itself stopped, and the pure love that hung in the air permeated their whole bodies, indeed, their entire beings. They absorbed the love all around and sat there, almost suspended by the bonds of ecstasy they felt.

Then Jesus took the third cup, the *birkat hamazon*, the cup of redemption, and gave it to them, saying, "Take this, all of you, and drink from it, for this is the chalice of my Blood, the Blood of the new and eternal covenant, which will be poured out for you and for many for the forgiveness of sins. Do this in memory of me."

They drank and relished the presence of Jesus. For a long while, no one spoke. Even the sounds from outside were muted. Finally, they sang more psalms. The chill night air of the desert carried their voices out of the upper room and throughout the area, where it merged with those of countless other faithful in the area recalling the might of the Lord. On they sang, proclaiming how the earth trembles before the Lord.

Peter looked around as they sang, feeling the utter power of the shared prayer around them, and sensing it both focused on and coming from their Master. The Apostles and the women with them lost themselves in the sung praise, moving onto the 115th Psalm, where King David extolled the virtues of their Most High God, the God in Heaven, the God they themselves worshiped. The God they worshipped while the pagans of the surrounding lands bowed down to idols, items crafted out of merely human hands.

*May they bless the Lord, now and forever.* The praise continued as Mary Magdalene focused on the words of the next Psalm, the Psalm that spoke of their Lord saving the people in their wretchedness. She sang as she laid her eyes on Jesus, whom she knew to be the object of their praise, yet even he was singing from the depth of his heart, humble as he was, for she knew he was praising the Father.

Mary, the mother of Jesus, lifted her voice in praise as they sang the 117th Psalm, declaring the faithfulness of the Lord is forever. Forever. Mary thought back to that day so many years ago when the angel came with a message, when she gave her *fiat*, her yes, and in return the Lord gave her her baby. She anchored the praise in the full grace of total trust in the Lord.

And on they sang.

They finished with the 118th Psalm. John couldn't help but feel every one of the words they sang take shape and surround them, as surely as David wrote of the saving power of the Lord, when *'I was surrounded on all sides by enemies.'* They sang as one, their stream of glory and praise to the one Lord and God above all flowing out into the night.

After this, Jesus rose. "Come, let us go."

Peter stood, a look of confusion on his face. "But Master, the celebration is not over," he pointed at the last cup. "What about the cup of *halel*?"

"The cup of the kingdom will have to wait." He turned and they followed him.

"But what are we going to do now?" Peter asked.

Jesus stopped. "To pray." He started for the stairs, trailed by the others.

Peter remained confused. "But my Lord, where are we going?"

Jesus called out as he descended the stairs, "To the garden of Gethsemane."

And they went.

# The Agony in the Garden

Jesus went out into the garden with his disciples. Instantly, the atmosphere matched the pitch blackness of the night, because as Jesus prayed, the devil was there, too. Visions of every sin ever committed started to appear before him. It began with Judas, one of His own, one of the Apostles, who had been with him since the beginning. He had eaten with him; and now Judas would serve him up. How Jesus ached for Judas, for he knew that, although he would readily forgive him, Judas would not own up to his sin and would not forgive himself, depriving Christ of the chance.

Next was the flight of his other Apostles, about to take place. Though he has exhorted them to stay awake, they have been sleeping. He already knew who was coming for him, and when. He already knew they will come for him with clubs and torches. He saw how his friends will at first resist; how Peter in his zeal will draw the sword; how he will have to restrain Peter, the first Pope, to renounce the violence of the world

Peter's denial. Peter, whom Jesus had originally called to be a fisher of men, whom he had sent out with the others to proclaim the kingdom, whom had witnessed the Transfiguration. Peter would deny him.

On the heels of that denial came sorrow for his mother, whom he knew would be there, on the way to Golgotha, Calvary. He couldn't bear to think that she would witness his execution.

The sins start to fly by, an unfathomable depth of depravity as shown by every sin committed by man. The context and consequences of each one clear in his mind as if he was right there. He is right there.

"You're going to give yourself up for these people?" Lucifer asked.

First were the venial sins. Seemingly small slights that people, even the most holy of God's children, permitted themselves. The seemingly harmless nature of them opened the door wide to more serious sins. Men's fleeting thoughts of lust, occurring countless times per day to so many of His sons. Acts of omission cloud Jesus's vision like fog. People bypassing helpless travelers along the wayside. Those in authority looking the other way when their deputies stray. Individual scenes appear out of the fog, as if to magnify its opaqueness. There is Haruki, afraid to comfort his friend after the loss of his mother, afraid to buck his society's insistence on stoicism. There is Sonia, refusing to stand up for her little sister as other girls tease her about her looks in the town square. There is Jong-Sook who stands silently as his mother chides his wife about the state of the house. There is Vladislav, who hides his sin even in the sacrament of Penance, which the Lord set aside as a way to return to holiness. So many small sins, opening the door to larger, personal sins.

There is Akida, pushing his little brother in the watering hole just for the fun of it. There is Padmesh lying to his mother. There is Robert, embezzling from his employer. Kennard, who forces himself on Lilliana near the bog outside the woolery. Jayden, who is beating his wife. Ahmed beheading Jason. These personal sins in turn give way to wars between nations.

First to present themselves are future wars between nations. Most immediate is the Jewish revolt against their Roman occupiers and the ultimate target, the Emperor Nero and his eventual successor Vespasian. The unsuccessful effort ends with the plundering, desecration and destruction of the Temple in Jerusalem. The Temple where Jesus overturned the moneychangers' tables and drove their animals out with whips. The Temple that Solomon himself had commissioned to provide the Ark of the Covenant with a permanent resting place, the Temple where Jews had worshipped for centuries would be in ruins. This was followed by the further oppression of the Jews. As his church would grow, this in turn metastasized into Nero and Domitian's persecution of his Christian followers in Rome and beyond. He is there with Felicity and Perpetua as they are fed to the lions; their terror his terror, their agony his agony. The eventual fall of Rome under Emperor Romulus to Odoacer and his band of goths is no salve, but rather intensifies the pain of knowing his children would be killed in the invasion of Rome at the hands of more of his children. The visions speed up to tribal warfare of the dark ages, the brutality of the battlefield when it merged with the farm field, when combatants folded into civilians. Individual scenes flew by, here Charibert of Brittany, unknown but to his family, his village and Christ, falling under the axe, at the hand of Lothar, a depraved Norseman, also unknown to history but more than familiar to Christ, the Christ who knows every hair on our heads. Countless scenes meld together and transition to the empire building of the Middle Ages. Savagery, intense hatred and complete disregard for life compete for the dominant theme. The loss of this Holy Land to followers of Muhammad. The loss of life when Kings sent knights here, to die so far away from home. What did they die for? Jesus doubled over in the excruciation. An infinite number of battles hurtled past.

Satan pranced about. "It's not just fighting. See the self-imposed entrapment these humans will put themselves through!" The subtle turning of formerly faithful societies into ones devoted to humanity's own greatness cast a new level of darkness over what flashed in front of Jesus. People on a mass scale openly shunning the Holy One, his Father in Heaven. How they became full of themselves, imagining them to be the repository of all knowledge, and the key to that knowledge, and the supposed magnanimous efforts of man to save everyone from their own mistakes. The rise of relativism, the refusal to acknowledge the universal truth, appeared out of nowhere like a pile of excrement on the ground. Its bilious vapors infected so many minds, the minds of those God loved, minds whose complexity and intricacy were known only to the Father, minds that the Father had endowed with freedom, which Jesus could see that were now enslaved by new mentalities. Oh, the waste!

The devil grunted in delight. "There is more, oh so much more," filth dripped from his lips. He moved aside to reveal the machinery of death deployed to so great an effect in World War I. The repeating gun is used, cutting down so many boys. Clouds of mustard gas embrace others in a suffocating, burning death. Jesus can taste it in his mouth. Communism, the state's effort to

214

crush the individual in the service of other individuals, takes root. Devotion to Him is banned. Almost instantly, the rise of government power and its abuses escalate the fighting. People's willingness to surrender their lives to their despots instead of their God unearths their most base cruelty. Drops of blood fall from Jesus's face as the evil one shows him cattle cars and crematoria, people suffering and people stacked like wood. A different, more subtle war is introduced. As the visual images of war present themselves to people, their simultaneous desire for it and revulsion at it push it to the very edge of life. War on the unborn child proliferates. Christ can feel gigantic forceps attacking him, squeezing his head and ripping his shoulder in two. His emotion spills onto the ground in the rawest state. His Father had crafted each of these littlest ones with care, and they would be tossed in trash without a thought.

"Are they worth it?" the devil asked.

Jesus continued praying but was assailed by more scenes. Worldwide persecution of His followers. Martyrdom renewed on an unthinkable scale. A devotion to man's most base instinct, animal-like practices to fulfill his bottomless desire for pleasure, his own, and pain, of others. He cried as the devil showed him the future of the earth, so mutilated with the hubris of man and his efforts, with every vestige of the beauty of the Father's creation stripped away, it appeared almost like any other celestial body hurtling through space.

And finally, the Father's just judgement.

Seeing what Jesus sees, Satan moves closer. "He's going to do that? To them?" Incredulous, he adds, "And for them?"

The judgement caps a period of upheaval, tribulation and mayhem that the earth had never before seen. Jesus beholds the hand of his Father, delivering perfect judgment upon the world. It is of such a nature that the old earth dies and after the Father gathers all of his followers together, delivers the rest to their eternal banishment. This caused the most pain of all. For Jesus knew that as long as people are alive, though they sin, they still have the power of free will; the power to choose Jesus at any time. Even a lifetime of the most profane living, with the utter disregard for any Divine presence, can be undone with one last look at the face of Jesus and the moment of death. But so many fall at the Last Judgment, they die and no longer have a choice; instead they are left to suffer an unreal hell of an eternity without the Father. It all could have been prevented. Even with just a thought, a solitary thought of regret and a reaching out to Jesus could anyone be saved. He was so close to them at the end; they only had to turn, to look and to see, to see and to believe that He was there for them, that He wanted to take them home with Him, that He forgave them. That He loved them.

How so many couldn't even believe that. That Jesus loved them. How so many people, filled with pride, couldn't realize that God was bigger than their sin? But so many more, Jesus could see, so many more would believe. His agony tempered a bit. So many would trust in Him, that He loved them. But only by the instance of what was about to happen. Jesus knelt reso-lutely now. He could see that this cup would not pass from him, but that he would have to drink it, and drink deeply, for the sake of the lost sheep of his Father. They would see that the Father loved them so much that He would send His son to die for them. 'If that's what I have to do,' Jesus thought. 'If that's what I have to do to win them over, to show them the Father's love, to buy their freedom forever, then so be it.'

He looked up to see the evil one sitting on the ground. "So that is it?" he asked. "I showed you the splendor of the world, of all that could have been yours. Behold, you saw every corner of the earth, all the civilizations that have been, are and will be. You saw the grandeur of man's accomplishment, how grander still it could have been. You saw so many people ready and willing to believe in something that made sense. Something that resonated with them. I could have given you all that and more. Imagine what could be accomplished with all of them. Imagine what they could do if they weren't hindered by arbitrary rules, by an unseen, unknown Deity. Imagine if there was no fear," his voice coalesced into a loud whisper. "No fear of judgement. No fear of their actions. Imagine how they could truly live," the word came out on his sulfurous tongue, delivered with a flourish. "You see what they will do because of this. Your death will only divide them. Your death will only turn them against each other until the end of time. And besides," the devil reached up and pulled an apple off a nearby tree, "so many more won't even get a chance to hear about you. To hear about your supposed great sacrifice. How does that make you feel? To think you died for them and then it is hidden from so many people?" He took a bite and moved closer. "That it is hidden by the shame of your believers, of those who care more for appearances?" He shook his head. "The people's brains are not made for you, or for your

Father. Theirs are merely human, limited by what they see, what they touch, smell, taste and hear. They can't know what we know. They can't know the truth of the universe. They can't know the fullness of time and space." He stopped and looked at Jesus. "I know what you're thinking." He took another bite. "You say their hearts are made for you and your Father." He looked at the core in his hand and shook his head. "Hearts can't see! Hearts can't hear! They can't taste and they can't touch. They can't smell! That's why they'll never amount to what we have become: the summit of the enlightened being." The Devil smiled as he reflected on himself. "They'll try, but they will never use even a fraction of the minds the Father has given them. Partly because of their human nature, but partly because they will be chained by this desire for approval. A desire to be accepted by the Father. But you know as well as I do," the devil moved closer, "nothing they do will be enough to warrant His love! No amount of supposed good they can do will earn their way into Heaven! One may even devote a lifetime of service to the Father, but even all those acts of charity won't be enough to outweigh what they're about to do to you!"

Seeing Jesus sigh with exhaustion, he pressed further. "Don't you see? You think you're going to save them by going to this death, but it will all be in vain! They won't care about you. They won't know about you. This world will go on a lot longer after your death, a lot longer. This piece of ground will continue to exist for eons. With people as defective as they are, how do you think they will ever know the truth about you? If you die, then all you have are a collection of flawed souls, who only think of themselves, who care only for their own future, and indeed will scatter like cockroaches at the first sign of duress." He held the eaten apple core in front of Jesus face. "They're going to throw you away," he flung the core down the hillside, where it bounced among the trees before finally coming to rest near a wine press. "They're going to throw you away like garbage because they will see that following you won't get them anywhere! So why do it?

He walked around and sat down next to Jesus. "Hmm? Why do it? Why make yourself a pointless sacrifice when you can live forever? Just think of all the crowds that have followed you so far. They've been looking for food, for healing, and you have delivered! They are hungry, and you feed them! They are sick, and you heal them. They die," he whispered, "and you raise them from the dead. How big of a crowd do you think you'll have on the cross?

Hearing the word for the first time made the bile rise in Jesus's throat. "That's right," the devil continued, "you're going to die a painful death. And no one will be around to see it."

In the distance, near the bottom of the mount, they could see a thin line of fire, little tongues of it slowly bobbing up and down, weaving up the hillside like a glowing grass snake. "Look there," the Devil said, "they're coming for you. They'll be here in three and a half minutes. If you simply walk back down the mountain on the other side, they won't find you. You can be free to perform your miracles for another day, another week, another decade if you want. You saw how they welcomed you to the city last week. Don't you think they will do that again when even more can witness your miracles?" Seeing Jesus with his eyes closed and praying, the evil one raised his voice. "Why are you not listening to me? I'm giving you a chance to free yourself from this situation. Don't you think you will gain even more followers, even more adherents, even more disciples if you flee and appear later, unchained? So many people are expecting a military messiah to deliver them from the Romans. Don't you think the quickest way to win them over involves doing just that?" He looked back at the hillside. The thin line of flames was halfway up now. "They're getting closer," his voice, his mannerisms became more urgent. "They're going to arrest you. Your disciples over there will run away like little girls. Just think of the power you can earn by calling down a legion of angels to take these people out." He spoke more quickly now. "After that you can have a contingent bring you back to the Praetorium where you will scare the innards out of Pilate. You can stretch out your hand and wipe out the entire legion at Caesarea Maritima, without even going there." He got up and got close to Jesus's face. "You can call in a lightning strike against the house of Herod and watch them die in agony - just think of it: sweet revenge for John. Let's go, they're a stone's throw away now, come with me and we will make it all happen!"

There was a shout behind them. They both turned to see a group of some of the religious authorities with a detachment of soldiers bearing clubs, torches and spears. "They're here!" Satan said. "They're going to annihilate you!" Jesus finished praying and got up. "Let's go," the Devil's voice took on another level of urgency. But seeing that Jesus had no intention of leaving, his look transformed into one of utter disgust. The authorities were just ten yards away now. "You don't have the balls to do this," Satan sneered.

"Watch me," Jesus said.

**

Mary of Magdalene awoke in the middle of the night. Despite the chill, she awoke drenched in sweat. As she came to, the memory of what happened a few hours ago turned her stomach. John, the Rabbi's Apostle, had run to their place absolutely stricken. 'They have taken him,' he struggled to catch his breath. 'Who?' Mary tried to settle him down. 'Where?' John took a few more gasps, as he had run the two miles from the olive orchard to her house. Mary took his young face in her hands. 'John,' she said, 'you must calm down.' He nodded and slumped down on a large rock. 'The Jews,' he said, collecting himself. 'The Jews, and the Romans with them. They came with torches, and clubs,' he shook his head as the words came out, 'like he was some sort of criminal.'

'What did you do?' she asked.

'I ran,' he cried. He covered his face with his hands. 'I ran in fear of my own life. Here I have been with the Master for all this time and at the moment he needed me...' his voice trailed off.

Mary had sent him off with food and begged him to take care. Oh, the thought of the Rabbi being taken by the authorities. What would they do with him? How would they treat him? Would they hurt him? The thought was unthinkable, so much so that Mary had collapsed into grief.

Unable to sleep, she made a fire. After what seemed like an hour of simply staring at the flames, she collapsed onto the straw-filled mat that was her bed. But sleep wouldn't come. Instead, visions from her past life erupted in front of her. Every man she had given her body to, every degrading act she committed, it was all there before her eyes. She tried to close her eyes, but that only brought them on faster than before. There was her childhood self, forced to be with a man at the urging, no, the force, of an older relative. He had owed the man money. She shook her head, as if to shake the image free. Oh, how she had started young. She learned from an early age all the tricks. In the beginning, it was involuntary. But that grew to an inclination, then an indulgence, onto a predilection and finally to an addiction. She couldn't say no to it after a while, invited it in, actually. How so many men had used her. How she had let them use her. And how she used them. She shuddered. 'Oh Rabbi, how I wish you were here,' she thought. But her addiction had gotten worse, unbelievably. At her lowest, her activity hit bottom. Until then, her activity, although by force of habit and background was almost a foregone conclusion, she still managed to have some control over it. At the worst point, she knew she had given her soul away. She cried at the thought of that, of that person, who was no longer her, but a shell of a body controlled by demons.

Her actions, her thoughts, her insecurities assailed her throughout the night.

While Mary Magdalene suffered alone, Peter was slumped against a stone wall three miles away. He had just denied his Lord and Master and when he had heard a cock crowing, it had hit him. His sin, his shortcomings, all of it had blown him away like a giant wave washing him overboard. He had run from the place, not knowing where to go, just running, running, until he finally stopped. And when he stopped, the tears came. Looking back, he wasn't sure how long he had been sitting there, but since the sun was already rising, it must have been hours. Oh, how the tears had come, continuously, like from an aqueduct the Romans had built. He had totally emptied himself through his tears; he must have sounded like a babbling idiot, he thought, babbling incoherently. He remembered saying, 'I left him, I left him!' in his unbelief. How could he act in such a manner after all he had been through with the Master? He put his face in his hands again, but this time, the tears would not come. Instead, he felt the dried grit of his face. He would rather dwell on his previous sins, anything other than what happened tonight. But the enormity of it swallowed him. He didn't just deny the best thing about his entire life and his whole being, he thought, he was also a coward.

What would his children think once they learned? That their father ran in times of trouble. He wanted to be a better father than that. The thought of them learning that about their father launched an extra wave of revulsion. He was all alone here, in the dirt of the soil. He bent over and grasped it with his hands, clutching it, gripping it like it was his last connection to the earth he walked on. 'I betrayed him,' he thought. Betrayed him without a second thought. He curled up into a ball on the ground and wished it would swallow him whole.

# The Scourging at the Pillar

Longinus Atilius paced the outside of the compound, just off the via Praetoria. The sunshine at this hot hour of the day made him squint. 'I have to get out of this hot Judaean sun,' he thought. Taking cover under the portico of the barracks provided him some relief, but he still wore a frown on his tanned face.

He had just come from the camp prefect's office, and did not like what he had heard. Rufius Silius, another centurion, came along.

"What is wrong, Atilius? You look like you were just ripped off by a Venetian merchant man."

"I was pulled off the drilling field and just had a meeting with Marcus Tadius. He told me to round up three men for criminal duty. Orders straight from the legate," Atilius said.

Silius nodded. They were professional soldiers in the Roman army, and they didn't like wasting their time on trivial matters like that when they could be spending time on more important things. There were defenses to maintain, drills to be done, marches to conduct. "When is this going on?" he asked.

"Tomorrow," Atilius leaned against a column. "And with most of the legion either drilling or off at auxiliary forts around the area, I don't even know where I'll find three men." He looked at Silius. "Do you know how to handle a whip?" he smiled.

Silius laughed. "Ha! Sorry, friend, I have important notes to take as part of the legate's general staff." He slapped Atilius on the shoulder and started to walk away. "Why don't you check with Marcus Naevius?"

Altius grunted. Centurion Naevius probably had a worse duty than he was just tasked with. Pushing off the column, he set off.

**

Naevius wiped his face for what seemed like the hundredth time this hour. This was his least favorite job. As centurion, he should be out drilling his cohort, building up his men, preparing them for battle. Instead, he drew the shortest stick for guard duty, charged with supervising ten men who were currently confined to barracks for minor violations. A sound on the gravel behind him interrupted his thoughts.

It was Longinus Atilius. "Centurion Naevius, I see you are busy with matters of great importance to the empire."

Naevius shook his head. "It's too hot out here for jokes Atilius. What is it that you want?"

"I, too, have been given a job of utmost importance." Seeing Naevius's eyebrows raised, he said, "Criminal duty."

Naevius made a snorting noise. "Maybe watching this bunch of ingrates dig a trench for a new latrine isn't so bad." He turned to look back at the motley crew, hacking away at the hardened dust. "I take it you need some of them temporarily?"

"Yes."

"How many?"

"Just three."

Naevius watched the group, thinking about who were the most problematic. "How about Modius, Livius and Barbatius over there."

Atilius nodded. "Fine. Why are they here and not with their cohorts?"

Naevius looked down at his clay tablet. "Modius was sent here from Rome a month ago. Apparently he hasn't taken well to the heat and likes to complain about it. His centurion thought a day or two spent digging a new canal for our piss would help him."

Atilius grimaced. "Great. What about Livius?"

"It says here he killed a prostitute in Jerusalem last night. He has three more days of this before he returns to his cohort."

"Very well. What about the last one, Barbatius?"

Naevius shifted on his feet, as if he was hesitant to mention anything. "His centurion has always wondered about him. He says Barbatius has given him a strange feeling ever since he transferred here from the Palmyran auxiliary two months ago."

"So? Almost everyone in the legion I know is weird in some way or another."

"Well, not this weird."

"What did he do?"

"A Hebrew merchant, a rich one, came to the legate's office yesterday to complain. He said he awoke in the morning hearing strange noises from his stable." Naevius leaned closer to Atilius. "He said he found Barbatius there, trying to force himself on one of his donkeys."

"Oh by the hand of Jupiter! You cannot be speaking the truth."

"Trust me, when you see the way he acts, you'll believe it then."

Atilius wiped the sweat from his face. "So that's what you're offering me then: a whiny bitch, a murderer and a depraved bugger?"

"That's what I have," Naevius said. "Unless you want to watch over this ragged lot."

Atilius grunted again. "I would surely consider it, but the prefect specifically wanted me to carry this out."

"When do you need them?" Naevius asked.

"I will get them in the morning, at the first hour."

"Very well then. Good luck with them. I'm sure they will do."

Atilius turned to leave. "As long as they can handle a whip and a hammer."

**

Joseph Caiaphas sized himself up in the polished copper mirror before him. He was in the anteroom of the Hall of Hewn Stones, adjusting his turban and making sure all of the tassels of his garments were displayed properly. The tassels, the sleeveless outer linen, the way his turban was folded, they all signified his authority as High Priest. And, he sneered, it was important that these symbols be seen.

For the Lord God himself had instituted the priesthood. He had been High Priest for fifteen years, having been appointed by Valerius Gratus. In fact, he or one of his family had occupied the post of *kohen gadol* since his father-in-law Annas's term started

27 years ago. The prescribed candidates for any priest were strict: a member of the tribe of Levi, married to an Israeli maiden, his mother could not have been captured in war... 'and,' thought Caiaphas, 'unswerving adherence to God.' An unswerving adherence that tolerated no dissent: he and the class of religious authorities he led dictated everything about the practice of faith, carefully handed down for countless generations. As he made a few minor adjustments to his robes, he frowned at the thought of anyone who would dare to upend such an order. It would be bad enough to have a fellow priest do such a thing, to make such outlandish claims, but to have some nobody carpenter from some no-name town up north...it was a disgrace. A stain. "No, not a stain," Caiaphas said out loud, "but a blight." A blight upon a crop. And like any blight, it had to be destroyed before it took the whole field out with it.

He stopped fiddling with his clothes for a moment and listened to the sounds of the voices in the main chamber.

He had called a special session for the Sanhedrin at this very early morning hour. Though it was sudden, it should not have been unexpected for the court's seventy other members. He listened in disgust as he heard them chattering away like young girls at the well, full of trivialities. He wondered how many of them were truly aboard with the plan.

\*\*

As arranged, the temple guard led Jesus away to the house of Annas. The lit procession wound its way down the mountain, picking a path through creosote bushes and around large boulders until the hillside gave way to the flat land of the surrounding area. They made their way first to a plain square building set back some distance from the other houses around it. The time was about three in the morning.

After a loud knock on the door, it opened to reveal more of the temple guard. They backed off and separated so Jesus and the others could get in. An older man, dressed in the linen sash of a priest, came forward.

"You are Jesus the Galilean." Hearing no response, he continued. "Why do you suppose that you are here? I have heard you teaching in the Temple with your band of disciples." He paced back and forth. "You seem to have some curious views about the nature of the Lord and his people. I have always wondered why you said some of the things that you said. Tell me, then, where did you receive your religious instruction? For I and others like me who serve the Lord at the Temple belong to a priestly class of men; however, I have no idea where you have come from." He warmed up to his audience, fellow religious officials. "Is it not true that you are the son of a carpenter from Nazareth? How then can you teach all these things? Where did you learn them? Did you really threaten the destruction of the Temple? And what of your contention that you can eat food from unclean animals? What do you have to say for yourself?"

*Jesus answered him, "I have spoken publicly to the world. I have always taught in a synagogue or in the temple area where all the Jews gather, and in secret I have said nothing. Why ask me? Ask those who heard me what I said to them. They know what I said."*

*One of the temple guards standing by Jesus*
*slapped him in the face. "Is this how you talk to An-*
*nas?"*

*Jesus answered him, "If I have spoken wrongly,*
*testify to the wrong; but if I have spoken rightly, why*
*do you strike me?" (John 18:20-23)*

The group around him murmured with anger, frustrated that
he wasn't physically resisting and refusing to contradict himself.
Annas frowned. "This man is worth no more of my time. I need
my rest. Bind him and send him to Caiaphas."

The armed group left Annas's house and made its way out of
the hilly enclave and down into the central part of the city. They
pushed Jesus along until they stopped in front of the Hall of
Hewn Stones. Inside, the voices of more than seventy men were
heard in anticipation.

**

Looking out the window at the nascent light on the horizon,
Caiaphas decided it was time. With a final deep breath, he
walked out of the anteroom and into the chamber. At the sight of
the High Priest, the din quietly dissipated into an unsettled silence.

Caiaphas made his way to the front, taking his time, as if to
let the regal aura he embodied catch up with him. He turned to
face the court.

"Holy ones," he began. "I beg of you to let the spirit of the
Lord in this very day, for we are here to defend our faith." He
delivered the last word with a sharp thrust. "Our faith, which has
been passed down to us through the generations, from the Lord

himself on High. It has been pursued, tortured, kidnapped, assaulted, blasphemed and oppressed throughout history, by pagans!" He started to pick up speed. "And in turn it has been defended, sacrificed for, fought for, guarded, freed, liberated and indeed, manifested in us, so that we may preserve it for future generations!" He met everyone's eyes with his own. "So it falls to us to be warriors tonight, to honor our faith, to protect it from the ungodly." At this, the group started to hiss and boo. He calmed them by holding his arms outstretched over them. "My brothers, the worst kind of ungodly. The kind that makes itself equal to God." The crowd booed again. After a few moments of indulging them, he raised his arms again. "But let it be said, my brothers, we were there! Let it be said that when the faith was under siege, we were there! Let it be said that when the faith faced its most serious threat, we were there!"

Caiaphas paused for a few minutes to absorb the cheering, letting the adulation soak into his very bones. One last time he silenced them. "So take heed, my brothers. We are at the hour where actions must be taken. The Lord has entrusted the faith to us," he beat his chest with a clenched fist. "So we must be just judges. And fierce defenders!" One last time they cheered. Caiaphas nodded in approval. They were ready.

A loud bang on the door interrupted the cheering. "Silence! Behold, let the door be opened."

**

*Those who had arrested Jesus led him away to Caiaphas the high priest, where the scribes and the elders were assembled. Peter was following him at a*

*distance as far as the high priest's courtyard, and go-*
*ing inside he sat down with the servants to see the*
*outcome. The chief priests and the entire Sanhedrin*
*kept trying to obtain false testimony against Jesus in*
*order to put him to death, but they found none, though*
*many false witnesses came forward. Finally two came*
*forward who stated, "This man said, 'I can destroy*
*the temple of God and within three days rebuild it.'"*
*The high priest rose and addressed him, "Have you*
*no answer? What are these men testifying against*
*you?" But Jesus was silent. Then the high priest said*
*to him, "I order you to tell us under oath before the*
*living God whether you are the Messiah, the Son of*
*God." Jesus said to him in reply, "You have said so.*
*But I tell you:*

> *From now on you will see 'the Son of Man*
> *seated at the right hand of the Power'*
> *and 'coming on the clouds of heaven.'"*

*Then the high priest tore his robes and said, "He*
*has blasphemed! What further need have we of wit-*
*nesses? You have now heard the blasphemy; what is*
*your opinion?" They said in reply, "He deserves to*
*die!" Then they spat in his face and struck him, while*
*some slapped him, saying, "Prophesy for us, Messi-*
*ah: who is it that struck you?" (Matthew 26: 57-68)*

**

Herod Antipas heard a great clanging outside his courtyard.
'It was too loud here,' he thought. He much preferred the new-

ness of his up-country capital Tiberius, situated on the cool shores of the Sea of Galilee. He even had Roman engineers pipe water from many of the area's hot springs into his palace. He couldn't wait to get out.

Until then, he had official duties to perform, even during this Holy Week. He sent Salome away and got dressed before his attendant came into the room.

"Your Greatness, there is a contingent from Pontius Pilate here."

Herod frowned. 'What did he want, the grubby little snake?' He nodded and the door opened to reveal two centurions bearing the insignia of Pilate's royal cohort. The one on the left thrust a wax tablet at him.

Herod read it before handing it back. "Very well. Where is he?"

"Inside the courtyard, sir."

"I will be out shortly." He went back inside and dug out a copper amulet his father Herod the Great had given him. Herod relished the feeling of weighty importance against his chest. He strutted to the courtyard and found some members of the Sanhedrin there, and in the middle, bound and surrounded by their Temple guards, the man called Jesus. Herod smiled. Ever since before his little nymph Salome had asked for the head of John the Baptist, Herod had been wanting to see this Jesus. He walked toward them as the priests separated. Herod eyed him up and down. There didn't seem to be anything noteworthy about his appearance. Perhaps it was something inside, then?

"You are the one called Jesus?" Herod asked. Jesus remained silent. "You. Are you Jesus? Are you the one who claims to be the Son of God?" Shrugging at his continued silence, Herod continued. "I've been waiting for a long time to talk to you. How is it that the supposed Son of God would reduce himself to living among us, living as one of us, in this place and in this time? Hmm? How is it that you don't have a palace even greater than mine? And if you are the true King of the Jews, how come no one here believes you?" One of the priests struck Jesus. "Answer him, you swine!"

"Are you waiting for your invisible army to come and save you? That must be it. Perhaps the invisible army will be riding invisible horses and carrying invisible swords." A stray dog wandered past. Herod pointed to it. "Oh I see! Your army isn't invisible, it is just cloaked as a dog, is that right? Well, let's see how your army fights," he nodded to one of his own bodyguards, who with a quick motion of a sword beheaded the dog. Herod watched the blood spurt out of the dog's neck before turning back to Jesus. "I guess that didn't work out so well." He scratched his chin, as if deep in thought. "But wait! If it is your army, surely you can raise it from the dead! Surely, if you are the Son of God, you can do that?" Seeing that Jesus wasn't reacting, Herod grew red in the face. He took a few steps closer to Jesus and looked him in the eye. "You're a nobody piece of shit." Even as he said this, he could feel Jesus look right through him. It was as if he knew everything about Herod, every personal detail about him, everything he had ever done. He even knew about Salome. Herod turned away in extreme discomfort. It was like the man even knew what he would do next. "Send him back." After the crowd had left, he summoned his attendant. He had unfinished business to get to.

"What is it, Your Greatness?"

"Send for Salome again, and tell her to be ready in my room."

**

Pontius Pilate put aside the latest dispatch from Rome and chewed on some more figs. He lounged on the pillows lining the floor of his dining area, in the middle of the atrium in his corner of Herod's palace, his temporary residence in Jerusalem. How he would much rather be at his palace at Caesarea Maritima, overlooking the endless sea. How he loved to bask in the sunlight and let the sea breezes wash over him, to read on the balcony high above everything, and to ponder the condition of man.

Not so here. Here, as prefect of the Roman province of Judaea, he was expected to be in this crowded, hot, smelly, hilly town during the Hebrew holy week, dispensing of his royal duties on behalf of Tiberius and generally scorning anything Jewish.

Procula entered the atrium, gathering her robes about her as she sat down across the table. She looked abnormally pale, with dark circles around her eyes. Her hair, usually flaxen and smooth, was frazzled and curly in the humid heat.

"Good morning, wife." He looked at her intently. "You look as though you've been up all night."

"My dear governor," she looked at her husband, "unreal visions presented themselves before me all night long. I dreamt that I was in the middle of a vast plain. There was no one around, when all of a sudden these indescribable machines approached each other. Fire and smoke burst out of them, as if firing siege balls at each other. It was a time I could not place, but nothing of what I saw hearkened back to any period I have ever read about."

Pilate tilted his head in curiosity. His wife was the most well-read woman he knew. "Please, continue."

"Figures like men appeared from the bowels of these machines. It looked like they were firing miniature missiles at one another. Suddenly there were explosions overhead and yellow clouds descended onto the battlefield. Then the men began vomiting and screaming." Her voice caught in her throat. "It was awful," she whispered.

Pilate held her shoulders. "Procula."

After a while, she continued. "There were other scenes. All were gruesome. The last one I saw, though, will stick with me for the rest of my days."

Pilate was afraid to ask. "What was it?"

"It was of a large city. A civilization unlike any we have seen. There were people walking about in strange dress, in a city with large expanses of flat black rock and buildings that soared into the sky, so high you couldn't even see the tops of them. Out of nowhere there was a terrifying noise, a thunderous booming sound, as if Jupiter himself were yelling. I looked overhead, and a thing like a," she searched for the word, "like a giant bird, a giant shiny bird, flew into one of the buildings." She sobbed. "There was fire and smoke and everyone ran for their lives." Her voice trailed off as she stared into the distance, unable to comprehend the utter strangeness and shock of the visions.

Pilate held her for a while longer. He knew Procula disliked being here in Jerusalem even more than he did, that sometimes the demands of the wife of a Roman official were too great, that these circumstances could cloud her faculties. But this was different. Whatever she experienced seemed very real to her.

Procula took a deep breath and stepped back. "What about you? Why do you have such a frown on your face?"

Pilate spit out a stem from the fig and paced back and forth along a marble balustrade. "I just finished re-reading a note from Rome. It seems Tiberius is still on a tear." Pilate's mentor Sejanus, powerful co-consul of Rome and de facto emperor, not to mention the man who appointed Pilate to this post, had been executed only two years earlier for treason against Tiberius. Ever since, Tiberius had been systematically crushing anyone with even the loosest ties to Sejanus, going so far as to send spies to watch the bloated corpses of his enemies float down the Tiber and note who bothered to drag them to shore for burial. Sejanus's antagonism of the Jews was but one of the many faults Tiberius found with him.

Procula could read the concern on his face. "Talk to me."

Pilate stopped and looked up at the sky for a moment. "This morning the Hebrew priests brought to me a certain man they wanted executed. You know normally I wouldn't even give them the time of day, I think so lowly of them. But in light of Tiberius's utter rampage, I am afraid to do anything to antagonize the Jews, lest I bring myself to Tiberius's attention." He sighed. "I didn't think the man deserved to die, but I didn't want to displease the Jews, too, so I had him sent to Herod on the pretext of a technicality."

Procula straightened. "This man, is his name Jesus?"

Pilate spun around. "Yes. How did you know? And why do you ask?"

Procula got up and reached for Pilate's arm. "Please have nothing to do with this man."

"Why?"

"The visions I saw. They were all because of this Jesus."

**

*Then they brought Jesus from Caiaphas to the praetorium. It was morning. And they themselves did not enter the praetorium, in order not to be defiled so that they could eat the Passover. So Pilate came out to them and said, "What charge do you bring [against] this man?" They answered and said to him, "If he were not a criminal, we would not have handed him over to you." At this, Pilate said to them, "Take him yourselves, and judge him according to your law." The Jews answered him, "We do not have the right to execute anyone," in order that the word of Jesus might be fulfilled that he said indicating the kind of death he would die. So Pilate went back into the praetorium and summoned Jesus and said to him, "Are you the King of the Jews?" Jesus answered, "Do you say this on your own or have others told you about me?" Pilate answered, "I am not a Jew, am I?*

*Your own nation and the chief priests handed you over to me. What have you done?" Jesus answered, "My kingdom does not belong to this world. If my kingdom did belong to this world, my attendants [would] be fighting to keep me from being handed over to the Jews. But as it is, my kingdom is not here." So Pilate said to him, "Then you are a king?" Jesus answered, "You say I am a king. For this I was born and for this I came into the world, to testify to the truth. Everyone who belongs to the truth listens to my voice." Pilate said to him, "What is truth?"*

*When he had said this, he again went out to the Jews and said to them, "I find no guilt in him. But you have a custom that I release one prisoner to you at Passover. Do you want me to release to you the King of the Jews?" They cried out again, "Not this one but Barabbas!" Now Barabbas was a revolutionary. (John 18: 28-40)*

**

*Pilate said to them, "Then what shall I do with Jesus called Messiah?" They all said, "Let him be crucified!" But he said, "Why? What evil has he done?" They only shouted the louder, "Let him be crucified!" When Pilate saw that he was not succeeding at all, but that a riot was breaking out instead, he took water and washed his hands in the sight of the crowd, saying, "I am innocent of this man's blood. Look to it yourselves." And the whole people said in reply, "His*

*blood be upon us and upon our children." Then he re-*
*leased Barabbas to them, but after he had Jesus*
*scourged, he handed him over to be crucified. (Mat-*
*thew 27:22-26)*

**

Longinus was taken aback when manhandling Jesus, expecting some pushback. Normally, prisoners put up a fight and were
tense with sweat and fear. But there was almost a slackness in
the man's body, so much so that Longinus immediately loosened
his grip and instead simply walked the condemned man to the
middle of the praetorium. He tied him securely to a pole in the
middle of the open court and stepped back. Under Roman law,
condemned such as these were not classified as humans. They
were the equivalent of a cow or a chair or any other kind of object. Scourgings were ordered to extract the truth from the recal-
citrant. Pilate wanted the truth, Longinus thought. 'These will do
the trick.' To Barbatius and Livius both he handed a flagrum.

Livius went to Jesus's right side, hefting the flagrum in his
hands. It had a handle about two feet in length, long enough to
get two hands on it to swing like a sword. At the end was a circular strap connected to five short pieces of thick cowhide of
varying lengths, each embedded with stubby nails, broken glass,
pieces of sheep bone and weighted with lead on the end.

Barbatius approached Jesus's left side with an ugly scowl. He
had been denied his base pleasure the night before and instead
had to suffer the indignity of digging a latrine in the hot Judean
sun. He felt an anger rise up in him, an almost sexual urge that
demanded pain and fear. And blood. He nodded to Livius. Now.

240

Livius made sure to aim at the man's ribs. Bad things could happen otherwise. He remembered his days as a recruit in the Fifth legion in Abruzzo. The legate had ordered his cohort to watch the flogging of a fellow soldier who had been accused of impregnating the legate's daughter. One of the soldiers tasked with the job had been sloppy and accidentally sliced open the man's jugular vein on the first blow. The man bled to death within a minute. He shuddered as he remembered the legate storming onto the field, enraged that the man's torture had been abbreviated. In his fury, he picked up a sword and with a single swipe cut off both of the soldier's arms at the elbows.

Livius took the first swing and felt the straps embed themselves in the man's skin before yanking it away, tearing holes and strips of flesh with it. Somehow, it sounded strange to Livius. Then he realized that the man didn't utter a thing. Normally the anguished shouts of the condemned drowned out everything else.

Barbatius was next. He felt the resistance of the strips in the man's skin and tore it away, expecting his urges to begin to be satisfied by this exercise. Instead, it fed his appetite.

The two went back and forth, careful to target only the ribs, the back, the thighs and the buttocks. The alternating strikes echoed through the courtyard, becoming the only sound to be heard. They grunted with effort. It seemed as though time stopped for this spectacle, with the beatings taking on a metronomic quality, illuminated by the spattering blood.

After a time, Longinus was afraid the condemned wouldn't be able to stand and ordered a halt. Barbatius and Livius handed

241

their flagrums to Modius and went to untie Jesus. As soon as they cut the cords securing Jesus to the pole, he slid to the ground in a purple heap.

Longinus regarded the condemned, noting the slick layer of blood completely covering his back. He thought it looked like a mantle. 'A mantle for the King.'

# The Crowning With Thorns

Longinus ordered Livius to bring Jesus into the middle of the courtyard. Here, the whole first cohort from Fortress Antonia gathered around, jeering at the man and roughing up two other criminals who were spared the scourging but not the cross. Longinus picked Jesus's garments off the ground. They had removed them for the scourging and the normal practice was to put it back on to stem the bleeding so the prisoner wouldn't die prematurely.

He tossed them to Modius and went to take a seat in the shade. He reckoned it was only the second hour of the day, but the heat was already getting to him. Besides, he didn't take great pleasure in being so close to the condemned like this.

Longinus reflected on his first battle. It was his third month in the army. His cohort had been sent to the wilderness in Germania to shore up an auxiliary unit. When the large savages had attacked his line, the Romans maintained their tightness, crowding around each other's shields. Although the Germans were much taller and stronger on average, the Romans simply poked their swords through the dense arrangement of shields. Longinus remembered the hellish intimacy of it all; he was so close he could smell their body odor. After that, close combat seemed normal. What he could never get over was being this close to and having a hand in an unarmed man's death. Even if he deserved to die. He looked around and found a purple cloak. Pushing back through the crowd of soldiers, he draped it over the man Christ and went back to his place in the shade.

Someone produced a long branch of a thorny bush and wrapped a band of rushes around it before tossing it to Livius. Livius caught it and smiled. He held it up, "Behold, the civic crown!" The soldiers jeered some more. Livius thought it a fitting object. The civic crown was a military honor, usually bestowed on soldiers who saved the lives of citizens. Over time, it formally became part of Caesar's wardrobe, though, and the wearer became known by a special term.

Livius shoved it onto Jesus's head. "Behold, the Savior of the World!" The cohort let out another loud mocking cheer.

**

John watched with the rest of the Jews a ways back from the square, just outside the Praetorium. He couldn't believe what was going on in front of him. The last twelve hours had been a wretched mix of discombobulating events. First, he and the others abandoned Jesus, leading to a sleepless night wandering around, trying to find the others and make sense of what was happening. Then, the sham Sanhedrin trial, Pilate's pronouncement and now this. He looked at Jesus. The Romans just put a crown of thorns on Jesus. John thought back to the story of Abraham. Just before Abraham was to obey a command from the Lord by sacrificing his son Isaac, the two had heard a rustling in the bushes. It was a ram. Its horns were caught in a thicket of thorns. John shook his head. After an angel of the Lord stayed Abraham's hand, telling him to spare Isaac, they instead made a sacrifice of the ram instead. Then it hit John

244

again: this is what the Master meant when he kept saying that he would go to be a sacrifice for the whole world. He stared open-mouthed at the scene in front of him. The prophets of old and the holy scriptures were being fulfilled right here, right now.

**

Someone else tossed Livius a reed. Livius pressed it into Jesus's hands. "Behold, the King!" They dropped to their knees in mock veneration.

Modius looked at Jesus's garments in his hands. One was the *himatia*, the outer garment, while the other was the *chiton*, a seamless robe worn underneath. He held up the *himatia* first, a trophy in front of the crowd of soldiers surrounding him. "How much is it worth to you boys, eh?" They rushed to their feet again, reaching for it. Modius yanked it back. "Not so fast! Here, we shall tear it up and throw draw lots for it!" He tore it to pieces along the seams and threw them on the ground. Taking some hay from the ground, he turned around and arranged it in a dozen shoots of varying lengths in his hand. He turned back to them and relished the role of the carnival man. "Now take your pick! Shortest four wins! Whose lucky day will it be?" A small group of soldiers jostled each other to take their own. After a quick comparison, they figured out the four who won. "Alright now, let's see," Modius said. "Marcus, you ugly son of a bitch, you win the left sleeve," Modius tossed it to him. "Macro, you win the right sleeve. Laelius, you get the left breast cloth." He looked at the last winner. "Nonus, you dumb fucker, you can't be a winner, too, you're too stupid. Here, let me see your lot again." Nonus's lips parted, revealing a near-toothless smile and shoved

Modius to the ground. "Give that to me, you little bitch." Nonus held it up. "I've been waiting to get my hands on this." He bent over and wiped the cloth over his backside. "My arse has been chafing all morning!" At this, the soldiers around him howled with laughter.

**

John found Mary and clung to her. They were roughly fifty paces from the courtyard, just outside the Praetorium. Mary's heart was bleeding with sorrow. Every lash Jesus received, she got, too. Every strip of flesh yanked away was yanked from her, too. Every insult, every shove, every strike, they all wounded her, too, right in her heart. Like a sword piercing it. She thought back to the words of Simeon, the old man in the Temple so many years ago when she and Joseph brought her baby to be presented to the Lord. 'He will be responsible for the rise and fall of many in Israel,' the man had said. In her anguish, flooded by tears, Mary tried to hold onto that thought. That so many would rise because of her baby's suffering.

**

Livius took a break from the spectacle and walked back to a shaded area, where he found Barbatius. Livius took a look at him: the lashing had the multiplicative effect of not only covering the condemned man in his own blood, but it also formed a slick layer over his *lorica hamata*, making for a reddish-purple armor that dripped everywhere. Looking down at himself, he saw that he was similarly cloaked. Livius looked at Barbatius again. He was staring into the distance, his mind in another place and time.

"Barbatius, are you all right?"

Barbatius became startled at the interruption. He shifted on his feet and nodded. "I am now."

"What do you mean?"

Barbatius pushed a greasy string of hair away from his face. "Something happened out there."

"Huh?"

Barbatius turned and looked Livius in the eye. "Something happened out there. Something happened to me."

Livius held his look. The man did look different in a way. Not outwardly, but he could tell something was different. Something inside. He remembered when he had heard of Barbatius's punishment, about why he was being punished, and it made Livius's stomach turn. When he first saw Barbatius hacking away at the latrine with him, he remembered an unsettled feeling being so close to someone so abnormal. The man had some outward signs of his interior problems. His eyes were like those of a bug in that they almost stood out from his face a bit. His nostrils kept quivering. And he had some sort of facial tick that periodically flared up. But not now. Livius found himself looking into the face of a normal, war-weary man. "Huh," Livius said, "you do look a bit different."

"It's not just the look. I feel a strange peace inside."

"What?"

"It's like every desire I've had, for blood, for pleasure, for food...all that is gone now."

Livius shuffled his feet, as if he was more uncomfortable with the prospect of an honest talk with someone. He was a legionary of Rome. "Huh."

Barbatius wiped his face again. "You just have to let it in. Let it in and let go."

Livius felt a weight in his gut, like it was pressing against his bowels. Whatever Barbatius felt, it was the opposite of this. Not wanting to go any further, Livius nodded and turned to find Modius.

**

John couldn't bear to watch the jeering. Didn't they know who they were abusing? He turned around and looked at the crowd of people gathered to watch. He scanned their faces, picking out a few he recognized. There was Shamir the Gazan. The sight of the man churned John's blood. He was a member of the Sanhedrin and did his best to rankle the crowd when Pilate was deciding between Jesus the Master and Barsabbas the insurgent. Not able to cast his eyes upon the man any longer, he found Tavish of Bethsaida. John frowned. Tavish had twisted his way through the crowd, agitating everyone to yell for Barsabbas to be released. John suppressed an uncharitable thought and turned around by Mary. 'I must not give in to the hatred,' he thought. 'God help me, Lord.'

**

Mary looked on at her son, slumped over on a solitary boulder in the middle of the courtyard while the soldiers mocked him. The voices of the crowd and the jostling around her might as well have been a thousand cubits away, for she could only focus

248

on her baby's suffering. But one voice nearby carried with it all the hurt and agony that only a mother could have for her child. It rang out again, wailing above the din of the crowd, "Dismas! Dismas!"

Mary turned to look at the source of the voice. It was that of a woman, doubled over in duress. She was dressed in the rags of a peasant woman and looked to be unaccompanied in the crowd. Mary made her way over to her and held her arm.

The woman, named Tabitha, straightened and looked at this woman in the blue mantle. "Look what they're doing to my son!" her voice rang out in a shriek. One of the two criminals condemned to die had been thrown down into the dirt while the soldiers around him took turns urinating on him. Mary held her, feeling the absolute torment inside of the woman.

Tabitha felt something different with her touch, as if her absolute torment liquefied and coursed out of her body. Though she was completely overwhelmed with grief, the woman in blue managed to communicate with her.

'My son is there, too,' Tabitha heard an interior voice. She calmed a bit and nodded, almost imperceptibly. Together they knelt on the ground, not needing any other introduction.

'Who are you?'

The interior voice resonated. 'Mary.'

'Dismas is my only son,' Tabitha wiped tears from her face with both hands. 'He has always been somewhat mischievous, but he's a good man deep down.' She shook her head and bit her lip before blowing her nose on her mantle.

Mary nodded, simply unable to speak through the depth of the sorrow. 'Why is he here today?'

Tabitha put aside the fact that they were communicating in some way other than speech. 'He found an untethered goat and took it home with him. He didn't notice the legion's brand on it and someone found out.' More hot tears flowed down and mixed with Tabitha's sweat in the heat of the day. 'It was just a simple mistake. And he has to go through this?'

Mary stood with her and put her arms around Tabitha's head. She let Tabitha's anguish, the physical and mental torment of it, surge into her own body. At the same time, Mary let the inner peace she carried with her flow out into the woman.

Tabitha cried loudly. 'He's all that I have! And they're taking him away from me!' Suddenly, she started to climb the three-foot wall that separated the praetorium from the city. 'They might as well take me, too.'

Mary pulled her back. 'Please, please! Don't do this to yourself!' Tabitha relented and Mary clung to her again. 'They wouldn't do anything with you anyway.' Mary looked into her eyes and saw the complete suffering written on her soul. 'This is your hour of pain. You must go through it, but trust me when I say that your son will be a new man when this is over.'

Tabitha felt like screaming. 'What are you talking about? My son is going to die. Indeed, he is dying as we speak!'

'I'm telling you, when this day is over your son will be in paradise.'

'How can you know?'

Mary took the woman's arm with both her hands. 'My son will see to it.'

Tabitha frowned. 'He will see to it? I thought he was supposed to be God himself before I saw him out here being tossed about like a rag. He has not fought back one bit; it's like he's some sort of...,' she struggled with the thought.

'Like a little lamb.'

'Yes. A little lamb. You see how they whipped him, how they shoved the thorns on his head, how they're mocking him. He's just letting them destroy him. Why doesn't he call down the ultimate hellfire from the sky and destroy these Romans?'

'He hasn't come to annihilate like the Romans. He hasn't come to destroy life. Indeed, he is here to raise it up.' Mary, through her own racked agony, saw the look of utter confusion on the woman's face. 'Listen to me when I say that He is the holy one of God. He's here to prove a point.'

'Which is?'

'That the Lord above loves us so much he gave us His only son for us.'

Tabitha's confusion was etched on her face. 'But why does he have to die? And in such an awful manner?'

Mary nodded. She had asked herself this countless times. 'God wants to prove to us that he loves us so much. His love for us is absolutely radical. What good would it do if He just formed us as mindless beings, unable to do anything but what He wants? What good would it do if we just blindly followed His orders? What good would it do if we had no choice but to follow every command of His? That wouldn't prove anything. He wants us to love him. And love is nothing if we don't have free will to show that love. God gave us free will so that we could choose God for ourselves. That's what He wants, more than anything. And He knew that the only way we humans could see that for ourselves was if we saw the living sacrifice that He would make of His son.'

'Why does it have to be this way, though? Why couldn't it be enough for your son to go out and simply tell the people of God's plan for us, if as you say He loves us so?'

'It obviously wasn't enough for some people, right?' Mary gestured to the scene in front of them. 'Simply telling people about God's plan wasn't enough for them.' Mary stepped closer again and looked into the woman's eyes. 'That's why He wants to show them, because this action will speak louder than anything that was written before."

Tabitha crouched on her feet and wiped away more tears, overcome by this learning. 'But what does this mean for me, though?'

Mary sat next to her. 'This hour is truly important. Think back to when you bore your child into life. Think about the pain. Think about the fact that you were all alone in the field behind your house, that your sister had not yet arrived.'

'How did you know that?'

Mary continued. 'Think about the fact that even then, you were afraid that your child, your boy - you knew it was a boy, right? - your boy would fall into the same traps that his father fell into. Well, as a mother, your job was to give all of yourself for that child at that moment, indeed, every moment of his life, but especially at that moment, so that he could be born into this new life. Just as it is now. This is your hour of pain, but your son will be born into a new life with the Lord, one that is so amazing we can't even imagine.'

'But what matter is my suffering? What difference does it make? What if I just run away?'

Mary wrapped her in a hug. 'You know you won't do that. You know you can't run away from your son. Just as it is with the Lord. He can't run away from His son, either. Indeed, He is ready to absolutely run to him when the time is right. As for you, your job now is to unite your suffering with your son.'

'What's that supposed to mean?'

'Make his pain yours. Make his agony yours. Make his torment yours.'

'For what purpose?'

'So that you can share in it. When you share in it, you are helping him in your own way. Trust me when I say that if you unite your suffering with him, you will help him through this, even here, so far away, and so powerless compared to the Romans, you will help him.'

At that moment, the man Dismas was hauled to his feet and Tabitha caught his eye. Even through his pain, the sight of his mother and the strength of her sorrow lifted him. She could see it.

Mary continued. 'And so it is with the Lord. Yes, there is suffering in life. Much of it seems like a waste, like it has no meaning. But the Lord gave us free will, the freedom to either love Him or hate Him. All will encounter suffering. Our job, if we

253

love the Lord, is to unite our suffering with His. For if we choose to share in His suffering, if we choose to share in His agony, if we choose to share in His annihilation, indeed, we will share in His glory. We will share in His paradise, His kingdom. For he wants nothing more that: for us to be with Him.'

**

Livius found Modius in the crowd. After seeing Barbatius's strange behavior and hearing his explanation for his inner peace, Livius wanted a realistic antidote to the nonsense Barbatius had babbled earlier. Modius was leaning against a stone bench near the outer edge of the courtyard, laughing with some other soldiers and taking turns playing with parts of the man Jesus's clothes. He turned. "Ah, Livius, there you are! I was wondering what you were up to. I couldn't find you." The look of enjoyment on his face was similar to the one he wore when he would watch the chariot races back in Rome. "Where have you been?"

Livius sat on the bench. "I was talking with Barbatius."

Modius made a face as he stood watching the mockery in the front of the crowd. "That bugger. What a strange fellow. He didn't try his moves on you, did he? Ha! Maybe it's because you haven't bathed yet."

Livius looked down at his *lorica*. It was slick with blood. Suddenly he felt exhausted.

Modius let out another jeer, then looked back at Livius. "What's the matter with you, eh? You look like Orcus himself has been poking you with his pitchfork."

Livius stared into the distance. He might as well be sharing the space with the hairy, bearded god of the underworld. Livius came from the countryside outside of Feronia, and some of his fellow villagers growing up passed on legends of the nasty beast, namely, that he loved to torment evildoers. Livius, as a recruit in the legion, moved on and was exposed to the more sophisticated worship in the larger cities where Orcus was barely mentioned. However, his travels with the army around the Mediterranean since then had reinforced the fact that every culture feared its own version of Orcus.

Suddenly he wanted nothing to do with this spectacle. He wouldn't be here if he hadn't been confined to manual labor. And he wouldn't be confined to manual labor if he hadn't messed around with that whore. His thoughts turned to the events of two nights ago.

He and his cohort had finished another long week of drilling when his centurion gave them all one night's liberty. Livius and a group of others visited the fort's baths first before heading out to a well-known pub just outside the walls. The soldiers were all familiar with it, since the people operating it had followed the legion around until they settled here, in Jerusalem. He and his friend Lucius were sitting on a wooden bench, listening to some of the locals play a harp with accompanying frame drums. Livius remembered the music setting a tone of otherworldliness about them, as the hymns and melodies hinted at exotic lands far to the east and the singer, a young maiden, exalted her true love and lamented his early death. Lucius kept buying rounds of the local wine, made from grapes grown in the surrounding Judean hills. Livius remembered the soft boldness of the drink and its warm aftertaste. It was distinctly different that the Falernian variety of

Rome he was used to. As the night progressed, it passed from one uninterrupted memory into more vague, discrete scenes separated by increasing amounts of time. They had skipped dinner, and after the singer's first break, Lucius had gone out to take a piss. At some point a young woman had sidled up to Livius. He remembered talking to her about something, but couldn't remember what it was. Over time the noise grew, the other patrons took to yelling at each other to be heard. Livius thought the woman suggested going somewhere else, somewhere more quiet.

Modius interrupted his thoughts. "Livius! Comrade, I have been trying to get your attention for a full minute. Longinus is looking for us." He stopped, tearing his eyes away from the mockery at the front and settled his eyes on Livius. "By the name of Mars, you look terrible! What is going on?"

"Huh?"

"Are you all right? You look pale in the face, like one of those Britons."

"Oh." Livius got up and felt unsteady on his feet. He wished this day would end.

**

John looked at Mary consoling the mother of one of the criminals. He was transfixed by her grace. He quit looking at faces in the crowd and instead turned back to the Master. He was still sitting on a rock, dressed in purple and holding a reed as the pagan soldiers mocked him. How his blood boiled for him. Competing forces pulled at him: one urging him to jump the short wall and attack the cohort single-handedly, the other planting him firmly in place.

A figure clothed in the brown robes and turban of a traveler stood in front of him, blocking his view. John stepped a few paces to his right to see around him, but the figure moved that way, too. He frowned. "Excuse me, I'm trying to see."

The figure turned around. It was a man, but his face was an off shade of white, and his eyes appeared black. He spoke with an accent from some unknown part of the world. "What exactly are you trying to see?"

"I need to see Jesus, the Master," John moved sideways again.

"The Master, eh? If he was the Master he wouldn't be shoved around by the Romans, would he?"

John stared at the man, trying to determine what was different about this man. "He is the one and only Son of God."

"Sure he is." The man stepped closer. "Then tell me, where are his subjects? Where are his lands? Where is his army?"

John detected an unusual odor emanating from this man, and stepped back a bit. "His kingdom is not of this earth."

"I see. How easy it is to proclaim that. How easy it is to proclaim oneself from divine origin. If he is of divine origin, how come he is allowing himself to be treated this way?"

John looked into the blackness of the man's eyes, but remained silent.

"The truth is, this 'Master' of yours is nothing more than a smooth-talking confidence man, isn't he?" The man pressed on. "Why do you stick close to him, even now, at his hour of death? Do you want to see with your own eyes the end of the illusion he has led you on for the past three years? Huh? Do you want to see the mangled end of his body?" Seeing John's look of fury, he smiled. "I know now. You are still holding out hope that he will call down his army from heaven at the last moment, is that right? Just to keep things interesting, right? Well, let me tell you that that isn't going to happen." The man hawked and spit some phlegm into the dirt between them. "What will happen is that, once this Jesus is destroyed on the cross and buried, then everything you've ever known will disappear. Your fellow disciples? They'll scatter like sickly varmint. The crowds of people who followed his path around the countryside? They'll quickly forget about him. And you? What are you going to do? Are you going to sit around and wait for this man Jesus to walk out of his tomb? How long will you wait? And for what? For his 'kingdom'?" The man gestured to the scene in front of them. "This is all the kingdom that you'll ever see, because that's all there is. Just another broken promise, another lost hope, another desolate day in this barren desert town."

John suppressed a gagging feeling in the back of his throat. "The Lord will rebuke you for your speech."

The man and his smell moved closer to John. "Who do you think I am, just another pilgrim from far off? Do you think I am lowly like you are?"

"You are Satan and you are to leave me now."

"You don't have the guts to stand by this man. You ran like a little girl back in the garden, and you're going to run again when the authorities find out who you are. They're going to hunt you down, arrest you, try you, strip you, whip you, mock you, beat you and nail you to the cross."

"No."

"They'll make you renounce your faith, and you will be lost to your 'master.'"

"Get away from me!" John pushed him away, but his hands found no resistance in his clothes. It was as if they were hanging like drapes in the air.

Satan smiled. "You think you can just push me away?" His teeth had a sheen of yellow and green. "It isn't that simple." He moved closer.

"No." John looked over at the mother of Jesus, about ten paces away. "Mary!"

"No!" Satan's face contorted in pain and disappeared, leaving his clothes in a ragged heap on the ground.

Mary ran over and pulled John close in a hug. "It's all right. He knows he is losing." She looked at him, still crumpled with pain at the sight of her son's treatment. "Keep close to me." She kicked the pile of rags on the ground and they instantly turned to ash. "And pray for strength."

**

Longinus found his charges and bellowed his commands above the din of the cohort and the crowd just outside. "Let's go. We haven't got all day." He had Livius take the purple cloak off the man Jesus while Modius snatched away the reed in his hands. They led him and the two other criminals to one side of the courtyard. The cohort parted and Livius saw three crosses lying in a jumbled heap next to the east wall of the fortress. Another wave of revulsion hit Livius as he regarded the instruments of death in front of him. The man in his charge would die today as surely as the woman he stabbed two nights ago.

# The Carrying of the Cross

Simon awoke and took in the soft desert light of the plain white room. He stepped outside and marveled at the flowery scents in the air, how the atmosphere here seemed to diffuse light into all nooks and crannies. It was different here. But then again, every place was different than home. He knew Jerusalem was supposed to be a spiritual home of sorts, for he and his fellow Jews from Cyrene in Libya had their own synagogue here. He knew it was supposed to be his home, but a fluttering sensation in his gut told him something wasn't quite right. He missed his home in Libya. He missed his wife and his two boys. He even missed the fields there. But indeed he made the long journey to Jerusalem every year for the Passover celebration, just as his forebears had done for the last three hundred years after originally being exiled by Ptolemy Soter from Egypt.

But Simon didn't come here just for the celebration of the Passover. Indeed, he had to finance his way here, in addition to securing a lasting treasure for his boys so that they would not need to engage in the backbreaking work of farming like he himself had done for years. He passed by the camel pen that held his community's caravan and smiled at the empty bags and wagons nearby them. For on their way here, those bags and wagons were filled with the fruit of Simon's labor, the herb *silphium*.

As he looked over the empty wagons, Aristides emerged from a small white structure nearby. Seeing Simon, he walked over. "Good morning, friend."

Simon looked over at his friend and neighbor from back home. "Good morning. I trust you slept well."

Aristides stretched to work the kinks out of his back. "How can I not sleep well here? After all day at the market yesterday, I had no choice."

"You did good yesterday, selling our entire harvest."

Aristides shrugged. "There must be hundreds of thousands of people in the area for your religious feast - what is it called again?" For Aristides was a Greek, and was entrusted with selling their harvest while the rest of the travelers from Cyrene went to the Temple each day.

"The Passover."

"Right. There is never any shortage of demand for our herb here."

Simon felt the fluttering in his gut again. "Speaking of our herb," he looked to the rolling hills to the west, "what kinds of people buy it?"

Aristides took a deep breath, filling his lungs with the fragrant desert air. "There are those who re-deal it, of course. Those men will come to buy as much as four ten-*libra* bags or more. Basically, as much as they can carry in two hands. I assume they take it to the countryside and sell it there. The women who buy it, I've noticed, fit two patterns. The older women tend to buy in large quantities, but not as much as the dealers. They might buy a *semis* or two, or just about a pound. Then there are the younger women, who just buy an *uncia*; maybe even less."

"Have you ever asked them what they will use it for?"

"Sometimes, when the buyer speaks passable Greek. The men never buy it for cooking, only for reselling. The older women range from those who fashion themselves some sort of *physikos* to those who simply want an exotic ingredient for their cooking. The healers, I know, use the resin to make any number of solutions, either pastes or powders. It is said to be a cure for sore throats, upset stomachs, even headaches."

"What about the young women?"

"As I said, they tend to buy only an ounce or so, because they say that is all you need."

"Need for what?"

Aristides looked at him. "You don't know?"

Simon shook his head.

"They use it to make a potion which in turn causes a woman with child to *aboriri*."

Simon frowned. "What is that word? I do not know it."

"It is from Latin. It means to miscarry the child."

**\*\***

"What is the matter, friend?"

"You mean some people use the fruit of our labor to do away with human life?"

Aristides shuffled his feet. "I don't know if that is the right way to look at it."

"Why not?"

"Well, it is not as if the child has been born yet. After all, who knows what the child looks like when it is in the womb."

"What difference does that make?"

"I don't know. Perhaps the child is not yet fully formed in the womb until it is birthed."

"Think about what you are saying, Aristides. What about young children about the age of eight or nine? Are they fully formed? Or will they continue to grow?"

"I suppose you are right. But I would imagine that the parents of the child aren't yet ready for such a responsibility. What if the child were to be neglected?"

Simon thought for a moment. "I couldn't imagine worse neglect than ending the life of your child."

"You know what I mean, friend. I am thinking about those children that are sold into slavery, for instance."

"Tell me, Aristides, do you know anyone who has told you it would have been better off if they had never been born?"

The Greek gazed into the distance. "I suppose you are right. But what about the mother of the child? Don't you suppose that it should be her decision ultimately? I mean, after all, it is her body."

"It's not her body that is being terminated, is it?"

Aristides started to fidget and ran his hands over his face, as if to wipe the sweat off it. "Look, it's none of our business, right? Who are we to tell others what to do or what not to do with their lives?"

Simon looked at his friend. "What is this I am hearing, and from a Greek man no less?"

"What does my being Greek have to do with it?"

"What do you mean? Why, the Greeks are the founders of civilization, at least in my eyes. For all purposes, they mastered logic and reason, and the scientific method. They have some of the most enlightened laws in the known world. Why else would the Greek empire flourish as it did?"

"What does that have to do with telling others what to do or not to do with their lives?"

"Aristides, my friend. Think about it. Why do laws exist in the first place?"

"To arrive at some form of law and order, I suppose."

"Correct. But think about this: there weren't always laws, civilizations, and governments, right?"

"Yes." Aristides looked at Simon with a wary eye. "What are you getting at?"

"Think about a family living in the wilderness in prehistory."

"Okay."

"Would it be acceptable for the father to club the mother to death?"

"What? Of course not!"

"Why not? It is not like there has been some assembly convened somewhere that has passed a law saying that such a thing is wrong."

"Well, it's just not right."

"Precisely," Simon said. "It's just not right. My point is that there is a universal truth out there, a truth which precedes all laws and that is known by every human heart."

"I don't know, Simon," Aristides said. "You may live by some truths, but that doesn't mean I live by the same truths." Aristides pointed at Simon's clothes. "Look at your tassels there. I don't have those on my cloak."

"You mean the tassels I wear because of my Jewish faith. That is a law specific to my faith, but I am telling you there are a set of laws that every man abides by, or at least should abide by."

"I disagree. People are different."

"Of course people are different. But not that different. Some things are universal. What if during the night I were to take half of your harvest and sell it at the market as my own?"

Aristides sighed. "I see what you are saying. Come, let us go check on the east field, for we could talk all day."

**

They tromped through the desert scrub for roughly twenty minutes. Creosote, broken rocks and the lifeless dirt of the earthen floor crunched underfoot. Along the way, Simon cleared his throat. "Aristides," he began, "I would not endeavor to say this to anyone else, but I feel compelled to ask you, as you are my friend and neighbor."

"What is it, Simon?"

"When we were discussing things back by the camel pens, I got the feeling that, that," Simon struggled to find the right way to say this, "that the arguments you were using were not entirely new to you." Simon felt relieved to get the words out, but anxious at the thought of what could come next.

266

They continued walking, their sandaled feet picking their way along the path, each footstep signaling some distance between now and what Simon had said. He was beginning to wish he could take the words back when Aristides finally spoke.

"I was not expecting to talk about this today," he took a few lungfuls of air and blew it out. "Yes, the effects of *silphium* are not entirely unknown to me." Simon looked sideways at his friend, but Aristides was looking straight ahead now. "Diana discovered she was pregnant just after our Anastasius was born. It was overwhelming for her. All she could dwell on were our four other children, and how was she going to care for this little child, too, while she carried another child in the womb." The last words came out in a whisper, hinting at Aristides duress. They walked a few yards further, each step almost deafening in the silent magnitude of their conversation. "She hurried out to consult with a healer, one who had many experiences with that sort of thing. She gave Diana a recipe to follow and some simple instructions." He shook his head. "Sadly, the recipe was too easy to make, for the main ingredient surrounded us. Diana kept drinking it until the third day, when she doubled over in pain. I came in from the field, but she pushed me away, wanting to be alone. I dared not come back until late in the afternoon. I found her in bed, neither talking nor sleeping. I had no idea how to cope with it, or with her."

They slowed walking, for they were near. Simon put his hand on his friend's shoulder. "Aristides."

"You had no idea, I know, you don't have to say it." Aristides looked up at the morning sky overhead. "We told no one. We kept busy with farming and family life, trying hard to drown that memory in the daily routine of living. For a while it worked somewhat well. But at certain times, during holidays, or quiet moments in reflection, I cannot help but notice the feeling that someone is missing." Aristides caught his breath short. They came to the field and sat upon a large boulder marking one corner of it. Simon looked at his friend and saw his eyes start to glisten. He put his arm around Aristides' shoulders while the Greek man simply looked at the ground.

"The last time I came home, it was so wonderful to have my five children run to me, for they hadn't seen me in a fortnight. But even as I hugged them and brought them tight, I felt that hole. I felt that ache in my heart I hadn't wanted to acknowledge for so long. I felt that emptiness I tried to fill with all manner of other things, things that were good in themselves, but were no substitute for what we missed." The tears fell like rain now, a desert rain that came along once in a while and scurried away over the ground.

Simon sat in shock. He had never heard any man pour his heart out as Aristides had just done. And he had never suspected anything wrong in his household, for he and Diana were pillars of the community, always quick to help others out, even when they were wanting, too.

After a time, Aristides got up. "I'm headed back to our camp."

"Do you want me to come with you?"

Aristides waved him away. "No, thank you. I must be alone," he whispered.

268

Simon watched his friend pick his way out of the area, his heart aching for him. He looked over the east field: it was their community's effort to transplant their prized herb here to Judah. From the looks of things, it wasn't a resounding success. Patches of it grew here and there, but it failed to take root in so many others, and where it did, the stems were fairly thin and weak, and the flowers barely anything beyond a tiny bud. After all their efforts, it appeared that only their sliver of the north African coast was the ideal place to grow the herb. This knowledge ensured that Simon's community would continue to corner the market in it, but this morning's conversation with Aristides put Simon deep in thought. The fluttering feeling in his gut finally found its definition in his friend's duress and now Simon questioned whether he and his family should continue to grow this herb at all.

The magnitude of the question hit him as he stood there, for it wasn't just a question about what crops to grow or not to grow. It was well established that he couldn't grow anything else on his land back home. Whatever it was in the soil that nourished *silphium* wasn't good for anything else save for the long, weedy grass native to the area. After pondering it, the question was clear: grow *silphium*, or find another trade entirely. He took in another deep breath and released it. The journey back home would be a long one, with this kind of decision hanging over his head.

After a few more minutes inspecting the site, he decided to wander into town to buy some food. As he made his way out of the field and climbed the low hill that separated it from the edge of the city, his ears picked up signs of some sort of ruckus. It sounded like there were people yelling. He picked up the pace.

\*\*

Livius tore off the purple cloak, leaving the man Jesus naked. He and Modius hefted two debarked logs, fastened together with nails at their perpendicular intersection, and threw it at Jesus's feet. The King would receive his scepter. Jesus bent to pick it up and gasped at its almost impossible weight. He was already a bloody mess, weakened by the tremendous loss of blood, and now faced a distance of almost a half-mile with this burden.

The two soldiers put the cross on him so that the intersection rested on his shoulder. The longer end dragged on the ground but the other half of the cross-arm sticking in the air made it hard to keep balance. It would be by this symbol that the people who lined the streets would recognize his kingship.

After only about fifty yards, Jesus tripped and fell, taking the wind out of him. He laid on the ground for a moment, feeling the dirt and gravel press up against his bloody wounds. Before he could reflect on his blood soaking into the ground, the soldiers yelled at him, picked him up and thrust the cross upon him once again.

After resuming, Jesus's steps were so slow.

"Let's go," Modius banged his weapon on the cross, "you're stalling. We need to get back to the barracks for a nap and you're holding us up."

"That's right," Livius said, "I've got a nice hot bath waiting for me. It's too hot to be out here, watching you limp along, so hurry up." He gave Jesus a shove. They looked around and saw a

270

solitary figure coming in from the fields. He could help. They grabbed him and shoved him over by the cross. He started to protest but the centurions meant business. As Jesus shuffled along, he saw many women of Jerusalem, some of them professional wailers, loudly crying and making for an abject sight. One of the women he recognized as his mother Mary. He stopped, meeting her gaze. *"Em,"* he said. Mom. It prolonged his agony to see her there, to see how she suffered there with him. He looked at the other women alongside her.

*Jesus turned to them said, "Daughters of Jerusalem, do not weep for me, but weep for yourselves and for your children. For behold, the days are coming when they will say, 'Blessed are the barren, and the wombs that never bore, and the breasts that never gave suck!' Then they will begin to say to the mountains, 'Fall on us'; and to the hills, 'Cover us.' For if they do this when the wood is green, what will happen when it is dry?" (Luke 23:28-31)*

Simon struggled, both with the cross and to process what was going on around him. One minute he was walking toward town and the next some soldiers emerged from behind a line of people and put him in this position.

The soldiers tired of Jesus's preaching and pushed them along. As the sun rose in the morning sky and touched the rooftops and hilltops of the city, the heat became unbearable. Jesus sweat even more, even though it seemed there was no more moisture in his body. Every step was a stinging, aching, broken struggle. He tripped on a rock half-buried in the path and fell again, the cross falling on top of him and Simon onto the cross. The soldiers picked him up again.

The two men continued. After what seemed an eternity, the hill of Golgotha emerged in the background. It was probably 200 yards away by now.

Simon looked up. 'That must be where we're going,' he thought. It slowly dawned on him that this was the man Jesus, who had caused so much controversy among the scribes and Pharisees. Simon didn't know what to think of him, as all he had heard at this point was hearsay, second- and third-hand talk. Besides, he spent almost all of his time in north Africa and only came to Jerusalem once a year for the Passover feast. Until now, he was content just to practice his faith in his corner of the world, and let palace intrigue of the holy land go right on by. But these Romans, like everywhere else in the world, had their own ideas about what should happen and why. 'And so I'm stuck here,' he thought. It was awkward to carry this thing. He was behind Jesus, carrying the longer end. To carry it comfortably meant holding it up by his waist. But he could see that this put even more weight on the man Jesus's shoulder, so Simon had to lower his end, almost to his knees. He walked along, stooped in this manner. A profound sadness washed over him. Every step brought them even closer to the death of this man. A death that in and of itself would not be instant, but which would probably last for hours, or even a day or more. He wanted to ask Jesus himself what he had done to deserve such treatment, but he was afraid the Romans would strike him again, or worse, mount him on a cross, too, just for the fun of it.

They struggled along. As they walked, Simon felt the grief of the day permeate to his bones. He wanted to be far away from this place, back in his home, with his wife and sons in their fertile north African fields. They were coming closer to an end, to death, and he didn't want that. He wanted life. He wanted his family. He wanted everything close to him. But in all irony he found the burden of the cross closest to him. Its weight and awkwardness made him hold tight to it. How he wanted to just drop it and run. That would invite all sorts of punishment from the centurions, though, and he knew he could never outrun them. They were trained to walk as many as fifty miles a day, through all sorts of environments, and then engage in hand-to-hand combat before sleeping at night on the ground. They were tough as the spikes they carried with them on this day.

They shuffled inch by inch, with the long tail of the cross dragging through the dust behind them. Simon ventured a few words. "You are Jesus, I know. I am sorry this is happening." They felt so inadequate, but it was all he could say.

Jesus grunted but made himself heard in response. "Be strong, Simon. Hold tight."

Simon felt something coursing through his veins. No one knew his name here. All at once the cross felt light, like a spoke of a wheel.

Jesus continued, forcing the words through his countless wounds. "Hold tight to your cross. If you share in my suffering, you will share in my glory."

Finally the soldiers stopped them at the hillside. They took the cross and threw it on the ground. Simon went to embrace Jesus, but the soldiers grabbed him and thrust him away. How he wanted to protect Jesus, but one of the soldiers drew his sword and menaced Simon away. Simon went back toward the field, looking back, torn between two feelings. For he was relieved to be free of that burden, and to make the journey to his home soon. Another profound sadness washed over him, for he realized he was, for a few brief moments, so close to the divine and now would never behold the man Jesus again. One unbearable look back revealed just what was in store for the One who had done no wrong and with a heavy heart, Simon had to look away.

As he walked, he thought more about Aristides and his torment, wrapped up in secret. The Greek had been his friend for so long, and they had lived in close proximity, that he thought he knew everything about him and his family. Learning about the hole in their hearts was a shock. 'How they must have worked so hard for so long to cover up their pain,' Simon thought. With another wave of sadness he realized that they could have reached out to he and his wife at any time, but didn't.

'Why was that?' he thought. 'Why was it that those in most need of help are the ones who try hardest to hide it?' As he trekked through the fields on his way back to their camp, he thought once more about their harvest and what role it played in the lives of all the young women who had sought it out in the smallest of quantities. He thought about those who were so desperate they would end the life inside of them rather than open up. 'Of course,' he thought, 'opening up also meant revealing a pregnancy, which could be grounds for stoning in the case of an unmarried woman.' His heart grieved for them, too.

274

He felt a wave of dark sadness overcome him, and he turned around and fell to his knees. There was so much pain in the world. He looked up at the horizon and in the distance on the hill of Golgotha, saw the cross raised and knew Jesus was hanging on it this very moment. Looking down, he pressed his hands to his chest, hands that had carried the cross and shared in the burden. He resolved to do more to share in other people's burdens, to seek them out, to help them, to support them, to love them. He looked up again at the cross, the scepter that became the throne. 'There should be no doubt about it now,' he thought, 'that Jesus is the son of God.' He rose and went on his way, transformed.

# The Crucifixion

Balthazar awoke slick with sweat. He struggled to catch his breath in the cool early morning air pouring in the openings in his rock-hewn house. His wife turned over. "What is it?"

Balthazar wiped the sweat from his eyes and looked out into the early dawn, as if focusing his eyes would bring back the memory of his dream. "I don't know. I had a nightmarish vision, but when I awoke it disappeared, leaving nothing but this feeling of dread."

His wife sat up now. "What could it be, my dear?"

Balthazar doubled over and crouched on his hands and knees. "I don't know, but the anguish is almost unbearable. I feel like my insides are knotted together. Something awful is going on and I cannot explain why."

Their son came into the room with a roll of papyrus in hand. "Father, I must tell you something." He stopped short when he saw his father in duress and went over to comfort him. "Father, what is it?"

"I don't know," as soon as Balthazar said this, the feeling subsided and he sat upright on the bed again. "The feeling has passed, but even now the memory of it has left me tired." His wife wiped his brow. "How unusual." He looked at his son. "What brings you in here so early?"

His son unrolled the papyrus. "Father, I have been doing some calculations of my own recently, and I uncovered something you should look at." His face became animated as he spoke. He pointed to some figures. "Look here and see."

Balthazar studied the calculations in front of him for a moment. "A solar eclipse?"

His son nodded.

"When?"

"Today."

Balthazar sat back and considered how so many things had to happen, how the impossibly vast trajectories of the sun, the moon and the earth had to align.

His son pointed elsewhere on the scroll. "And see here? It looks like this could be a special one, for the last time the calculations looked like this, the moon took on a very red, glowing color.

Balthazar nodded. "A blood moon." He thought for a moment. "Tell me, where will this be centered?"

His son looked over the scroll. "It appears the best vantage point will be somewhere east of the Great Sea."

Balthazar and his wife looked at each other. The land of Judah. The mention of it brought them back. Back before their son was born, when they traveled together in search of the newborn King. "It must be Jerusalem," Balthazar said. He stared into the air, wondering what the eclipse meant. How he wished they could be there today.

"Father?"

"I'm sorry my son, I was lost in thought for a moment."

"What were you thinking about?"

"How you came to be."

**

When they came to the place called *Calvariae Locus*, the soldiers stopped, and for a moment, all was quiet. Longinus nodded to his *calo*, a boy of ten he had purchased from Bedouin tribesmen. The boy offered Jesus the smallest mercy the Romans permitted to the condemned, a mixture of wine with a good portion of myrrh.

Jesus, though, tasted the narcotic in the wine and spit it out.

After laying him down, Livius strapped Jesus's wrist to the cross beam and pounded a long spike into his palm. Livius braced himself for the inevitable cry of absolute agony that normally accompanied such a violation of the human body, but just like the scourging, this man Jesus made no sound at all. Livius felt unsettled, because he knew this man knew. He knew this man knew what he did. Jesus knew how he had taken the whore's life the other night. He wouldn't dare look at the man's face by this point. He could feel it, he could feel the man's gaze upon him, even now in this tortuous pain; he could feel the all-searching eyes of this man. Livius had the feeling that if he looked at Jesus, he would be forced to surrender everything to him and confess all his sins right then and there.

Barbatius secured Jesus's other wrist and likewise nailed it down. He wanted this to end right now. He wanted his criminal duty here and this man's agony to end right now. He considered delivering a fatal hammer blow to the man's head, but was afraid of Longinus, who would surely order up a large dose of punishment.

Modius whistled while he lined up Jesus's feet. He held them in place and used his other hand to press the sharpened spike into his feet, just between the second and third metatarsal, in order to get it started. He found it much easier to do it this way rather than striking with the hammer right away. After a few initial taps with the hammer, he finished with a round of furious pounding that sank the spike through the feet and into the solid wood of the cross.

Longinus, seeing that the men had secured the man Jesus to the cross, lashed to the top of the cross a sign someone from Pilate's staff gave him. He nodded his head. "Raise him."

The soldiers hefted the cross upright and slid it into a hole chiseled into the rock. No sooner did they do this than the larger crowd around them start to jeer and whistle at Jesus.

In the crowd, surrounded by the common people and their buffoonish insults, Joseph Caiaphas saw the sign attached to the cross and swore. One of the priests took note. "What is it that causes you distress? Don't you see now that our opponent is vanquished?"

Caiaphas started to walk away, as such a thing must be corrected immediately. "The sign is wrong." He made for the Praetorium.

Pilate was rocking on his bed with severe intestinal discomfort when his attendant came in. "The High Priest is here to see you, my Lord."

Pilate got up and did his best to quell the waves in his body. "Very well. I will meet him in the welcoming chamber." After relieving himself on a marble commode, Pilate went out. Caiaphas was there, visibly upset.

"What is it?" Pilate's tone was unmistakable, for he had had enough of this group today.

"Governor, it seems that the man Jesus has a sign over his head, reading-"

"I know what the sign says, I had it made myself." Pilate glowered. "From my understanding, those signs are record of accusations. It should say, rather, that he claimed to be the King of the Jews, not that he is the King of the Jews."

"What I have written, I have written." Pilate started to walk away but then doubled back. "Is nothing good enough for you people? You agitated them, so against my will I handed over an innocent man to be put to death and released a rebellious murderer so as to please the crowd, and now you come to me complaining of it," the scorn running in Pilate's veins was undeniable. "Why do you tempt me in this way? Don't you realize I could have you up there in the blink of an eye?" he pointed to the direction of Golgotha.

The enormity of it hit Caiaphas. He stepped back in disbelief. "You are threatening me, the High Priest, with that punishment? And how would Caesar deal with such a spectacle?"

"We are thousands of miles from Rome."

"You're not answering my question."

"I don't have to answer anything from you," Pilate's voice thundered throughout the colonnaded halls. "In this place, I am Caesar. Now be gone with you."

**

As Jesus hung there, countless pilgrims from the surrounding provinces passed by. The litany of insults and vituperation was unending. Shouts ranged from, "Save yourself if you are the true King" to "You deserve such a fate if you be a liar." Mary, near the foot of the cross, heard them all. Every one of them was another barb piercing her heart.

She stood her ground, refusing to be denied the presence of her son, her baby. The only relief Jesus had was to cast his gaze upon her, knowing that she would never leave him. She suffered the pain he did. While she did not have the outward appearance of her son's wounds, she felt them all. And yet she could not leave. She would not leave. Her job was to be there. Ever since she was called by God through the archangel Gabriel, she was called for this. This, this unending sorrow, was her job. A job no one else could do. A job only a mother could do. And yet, her presence there also increased Jesus's pain, for the pain in her eyes became another bloody wound on him, him who was pierced. All he could do now was breathe.

To breathe was agony. To breathe meant Jesus had to push his legs straight, to push up against the spike through his feet, just to make room for his lungs to expand. It was getting increasingly harder. The blood and sweat trickling into his eyes only increased the agony, for he had no way to wipe them clear. Every breath was a struggle. Jesus could feel the last of his energy pouring out, but he knew, even up here, his mission was not yet complete. There were still three messages to communicate.

As the people hurled their insults from below, one of the criminals alongside him lashed out from one side. "Are you not the Messiah?" his voice was strained, but relatively strong, for he did not undergo the extent of the scourging as Jesus did. "Haven't you declared yourself King of heaven and earth? Why, then, are you simply hanging there?" The criminal's desperation burned through and showed itself in his eyes most of all. "Can't you do something? Why are we are hanging here when you can free us? Why can't you do something? I am in agony," his plaintive yell unfurled into the air.

The one called Dismas, hanging on the other side of Jesus, rebuked him.

*"Have you no fear of God, for you are subject to the same condemnation? And indeed, we have been condemned justly, for the sentence we received corresponds to our crimes, but this man has done nothing criminal." Then he said, "Jesus, remember me when you come into your kingdom." He replied to him, "Amen, I say to you, today you will be with me in Paradise." (Luke 23: 41-43)*

The mother of Dismas sat curled up against Mary's feet. To this point she had been a sobbing wreck and could do no more than look up occasionally to glance at her son, only to look away again in the horror of her own sorrow. Upon hearing the words of Jesus, she rose to her feet and looked her son in the eyes. Like Mary said, this was her job as his mother, to see him through to the next world, just as she had done so many years earlier when she birthed him into this world.

The minutes passed and became as skewed as the agony of Jesus's wounds upset all sense of time and space. The ground below, and the people there who looked up at him, seemed so far removed from him that it seemed he was looking down from the clouds. At the same time, his mother right in front of him was there, her presence a salve. He pushed up again. There wasn't much time left. His mission demanded two more things from him. Jesus bowed his back to breathe and the air left his body as soon as it entered, so great was the pain, so sharp was the agony. Down below, with his mother, was the apostle John. Jesus looked at him, the youngest of his followers and the last one to remain here. He alone, with Mary and the others, was the Church. He alone, standing there in the ultimate sadness and desperation, was the Church he had spent his mission years building up, teaching, feeding and inspiring. Jesus knew his Church could not do it alone. Other than his own Spirit, the Church needed something else. Someone else. He said to his mother,

*"Woman, behold, your son." Then he said to the disciple, "Behold, your mother." (John 19:26-27)*

As he spoke, the moon eclipsed the sun, and within a minute, the entire sky blackened and cast the cloak of night upon the region.

**

The midday darkness surrounded Caiaphas as he left Pilate and walked back to Golgotha. As he walked, people around him were similarly unsettled at the sight of the sun being covered up. Caiaphas brooded at the threat from Pilate. He, along with the rest of the religious authorities in Jerusalem, had been carrying out a delicate balance of power with Roman governors for decades. Yes, the Romans were foreign occupiers. Yes, they worshipped Caesar like a God and had many other pagan practices. And yes, from time to time they cracked the whip against their Hebrew subjects. But over time, they permitted the relatively free exercise of religion along with the associated and necessary religious authority of Caiaphas and his class. The threat from Pilate, surely made in haste and without any thought, still represented a disaster to Caiaphas and the whole order. And while nothing like that would ever happen, it made Caiaphas consider the upending of his own world, and he didn't like it.

The sudden darkness, though, outweighed all of this. Caiaphas looked all around. The area was only partly visible in shades of gray, unlike the normal tan, red, and brilliant blue of the sky. The darkness, for the first time, made him consider the possibility that the man Jesus was who he said he was. Caiaphas pushed the thought away and hurried to Golgotha.

\*\*

Jesus hung in the darkness like a rag, his bloodied body unable to push up for more than a second, enough to half fill his lungs with air. There wasn't much time left. He was about to be transformed again, in a way, and in a way, it scared him. He knew his soul would leave his body for a time, and he knew the only way through it was to put total trust in the Father. The darkness about made for a veil covering the earth, as if the Father was too sorrowful to gaze upon the earth. 'How these people need thy grace,' Jesus thought. He could feel the last of himself dripping down the cross. He pushed up again to breathe, and between the stabbing pain in his lungs, managed to say,

*"I thirst."*

*There was a vessel filled with common wine. So they put a sponge soaked in wine on a sprig of hyssop and put it up to his mouth. (John 19:28-29)*

Jesus bit into the sponge, savoring every last drop that trickled into his mouth. It was the sweetest thing he ever tasted. It was so close now.

*When Jesus had taken the wine, he said, "It is finished." And bowing his head, he handed over the spirit. (John 19:30)*

**

When Jesus hung his head, Mary gasped, and John held her in her grief. He was dead. The words struck him again. He was dead. His Lord and Savior, the hope of his very soul, was dead. His mind and soul became as a vacuum, a blank space, devoid of thought and feeling. He felt removed from the scene in front of him as he looked upon the body of Jesus hanging limp on the cross and framed by the two criminals. John stared around and saw the hyssop branch with the sponge lying on the ground. He picked it up and turned it over in his hands. Taking the sponge, he grasped it and squeezed, wiping his face with it. It was the last thing Jesus touched, and he wanted to drink in the very wine Jesus tasted. As he did so, it hit him.

He thought back to the upper room, when they all shared the Passover meal together. It seemed like seven lifetimes ago, though it was only the night before. They finished three cups and

Peter was surprised that they left the fourth cup, the cup of *halel*, the cup of the Kingdom, on the table. Jesus had said they were going to pray first, and then he was arrested. 'This is it,' John thought as he held the sponge. "This is the cup of the Kingdom," he said to Mary. "We shall remember Him for all time through the Passover meal. For He is the perfect sacrifice."

**

Caiaphas looked on with the other religious authorities as Jesus finally hung his head in death. As it happened, he found himself holding his breath, subconsciously wondering what would happen next. Though the darkness was unnerving, he felt secure by the others assembled around him, the guardians of the faith that they were. After several moments, he and the others began to breathe easier. He wondered if anyone else had doubts about their judgement, but he dared not voice them. For if this man Jesus were truly the son of God like he said he was, then surely the Lord himself would not let him die in this manner, in this abject humiliation and annihilation. Surely there would be more than a darkening of the sun, which he knew from stories his grandfather had told him had indeed happened before. Surely the consequences would be immediate, and drastic.

After it was clear that Jesus and the two criminals alongside him were dead and they saw the Romans move to take them down, Caiaphas turned to the others around him. "Let us go, my brothers, for we have the faith to attend to." No sooner did he utter the words than the ground beneath them shook with a violence that sent everyone into a heap.

The ground shook beneath them for what seemed like a full minute. Only afterward, as Caiaphas struggled to extricate himself from someone's robes, did the screaming start. He stood and dusted himself off, trying to adjust his turban as he looked around. The simple mud-brick buildings around them became as jelly in the quaking and simply slid to the ground. Where before were pedestrian streets and walkways delineated by cobblestones were now jumbled masses of bricks and broken carts, crushed wagons and dead animals. The city was unrecognizable.

The absence of any landmarks in the area meant Caiaphas struggled to place himself so as to check on the one building he truly cared about. He scrambled onto a nearby pile of debris and craned his neck, sighing in relief as he did so. For there, standing in its huge invincibility, was the landmark of their faith, the Temple. He jumped back down to the ground and started to make his way in that direction. As he did, the thoughts he had suppressed in the last twenty minutes came back in a flood. They raced by and overwhelmed him, so much so that he ignored the desperate pleas for help as he passed each pile of destruction. He must get to the Temple.

For it was more than a building. It was rebuilt by Herod, of course, but was originally King Solomon's creation, built to the exact specifications laid out by the Lord himself. And other than being adorned with the finest materials around, it housed the essence of their faith: a jar of manna which his forebears ate during their time wandering the desert for forty years, the staff of Aaron the High Priest, a jar of oil for the anointing of the True King, and of course, the Ten Commandments, the centerpiece of the way of life which Caiaphas and the religious authorities devoted their lives to safeguarding through the interpretation of the Law for the people.

Before the Babylonian pillaging of the Temple, these items, housed in the Ark of the Covenant, had been placed in the *Kadosh Hakadashim*, the inner sanctum so important that only the High Priest was allowed to enter, and only on the Sabbath of Sabbaths, the tenth day of the seventh month. Since then the Ark was moved to a hidden chamber below the Holy of Holies. Every year Caiaphas performed a series of intricate rituals of sacrifice in order to pledge atonement for him and for the people. *Yom HaKippurim* was the day reserved for all of God's people to repent, to atone for their sins. The actions of Caiaphas were the vehicle for doing this, to regret the sin, to resolve to do so no longer, and to confess the sin before the Lord. As Caiaphas rushed to the Temple, darting around piles of debris, the reminder of his high position helped calm his thoughts. As he neared the Temple, he put aside the screams of those around him and entered the nearest gate. After a quick ritual washing, he went inside. The exterior appeared normal, but he was eager to see the condition of the interior. As soon as he was inside, he directed his gaze toward the *parochet*, the massive veil separating the holy of holies from the rest of the sanctuary. He gasped. For in front of him, the veil, over twenty cubits wide and twenty tall, and with a thickness almost that of a man's outstretched arms, was torn in two. As he took in the scene, he struggled to process what was there in front of him. The one boundary that God had wanted between Him and the people was literally ripped in half.

288

**

Caiaphas stumbled outside in disbelief. Any reflection on what he just saw inside had to be put off for now, as Caiaphas turned his attention to the chaos outside. For the screaming that he heard before was not only due to the destruction of practically any structure made of mud brick, but also something else, something that his eyes refused to believe.

Some people, covered only in rags, had been wandering around in a daze. On the way to the Temple he thought they had gotten caught in the destruction and had simply crawled out of debris piles, but as he walked among the aftermath and heard what the people were screaming about, it hit him. When he saw one of them crawl out of a mausoleum and stare at the sky as if he hadn't seen in it three hundred years, it served to confirm the fact that the dead were being raised all over the city. Caiaphas sprinted away in terror.

**

Longinus took in the scene. After the earthquake, the Hebrews all around them lost their composure and flailed about with arms akimbo. He saw that most of the smaller buildings in the area had been flattened. For a brief moment he wondered about his cohort at Fortress Antonia, but a quick glance at the black red skyline showed Herod's palace complex intact. Though the sky was still very much darkened and any look into the distance was fouled by countless cooking fires feeding blurry tendrils of smoke, he saw the people collectively scramble to extract themselves from the flimsy brick, straw and mud that was so quick to spill over. He and his three charges, having been used to the chaos of the battlefield, were the only ones to have their wits about them. Longinus turned back to the crosses. From the faint chest movement, he gauged the two criminals on either side of Jesus were clinging to life. He had seen more crucifixions than he could count, and he knew that some people could last for a while up there. The man Jesus was surely dead. He turned back to his men. "Let us put an end to this spectacle; we must get going." He ordered Barbatius to break the legs of the one on the right and Modius the one on the left. Barbatius was efficient, swinging his sledge and connecting with a spot just above the man's knee. Both femurs audibly cracked and whatever leverage the criminal had in pushing himself up to breathe was gone now. After two more wheezes, he gave up. Modius brought his hammer straight down and crushed the other criminal's feet first.

"His legs, you ingrate," Longinus said. After another swing, the other criminal similarly expired. Longinus looked up at the man Jesus as black clouds swirled above. This one man had inspired such emotion from the people, such agitation from the religious authorities and such calamity from nature around them, he was surely no ordinary man. As the people continued their screaming, and as the dead walked among them, Longinus felt something inside him change. He picked up his lance and thrust it into the side of Jesus, and blood and water sprayed out. As it hit him, he felt his body and soul, his mind and his heart surrender every last part of himself to the one true God and knelt. Overcome by the utter depths of his sins, he felt the water and blood wash them away in a veritable ocean of mercy. There was no Rome. There was no Caesar. There was only Christ.

# The Resurrection

Mary and the other women wound their way amongst the craggy hillside, straining to see their feet in the faint morning light. It was a dark morning, darker than any other they had known. Each of them found it uniquely hard to make this trek, but this was one thing, the only thing, they could do for their Savior, Jesus.

Mary, his mother, walked automatically in the cool air. The previous thirty-six hours had been saturated with sorrow. Since hearing of his arrest Friday night, and begging against hope, against the people to have Jesus freed instead of an insurrectionist, her sorrow had become a constant companion. She kept her head down: the events the day before yesterday simply couldn't be conjured anymore, they could take no more of her effort. Her only son was dead, and all she could do was weep, and truly embody sorrow. And anoint his body.

Mary Magdalene, too, found herself weighed down by the overpowering sadness of it all. The glum, the utter hopelessness of it all pressed down on her so that she feared her feet would sink right into the soil. How this contrasted with her experience with Jesus, when he had freed her from the bondage of demons. How she had felt weightless then! She had been a hardened sinner who had given her body away to so many men she couldn't remember them all. Jesus had given her hope, had forgiven her sins. He showed her her inestimable worth as a person, as a woman. Oh, how she wept at the cross. She wanted to die for him.

As they made their way to the place where Joseph had so generously provided a final resting place for Jesus, Mary, his mother, was struck by a thought. It was not his final resting place. She was full of grace and thus fully attuned to God, so she looked up in wonder at this thought. 'No,' she thought, 'this was not to be his final resting place.'

As if to manifest her thoughts, a thunderhead in the distance showed itself against the lighter sky. A faint rumbling shook, as if little shock waves fell to earth, as if to wake the ground. The women stopped, wondering if they should take shelter. The anointing would take a while, and they did not want to get caught in the rain. Mary said, "Do not worry. This storm isn't here for us." They continued on their way. They crested a small hill and laid eyes on the spot where the giant boulder was rolled across the tomb, about a hundred yards away. Another rumbling emanating from the thunderhead stopped the women once again. Seeing the four centurions stationed there to guard the site, they stopped again. "Oh, will they roll the stone away for us?" one of them helplessly wondered. One more rumbling sounded, enough to make the hardened soldiers look up at the threat from above.

"Maybe we should come back later," one of the women said.

Mary spoke up again. "We will wait here." She could sense something. Something was going to happen. She gestured to the tomb in the distance. "Be silent, and pray, for we are to behold something." One more rumbling came from above.

As if all at once, the thunderhead was directly above. Where before the dim light of the nascent sunrise managed to peek through the clouds, now everything was dark. Fearing the sudden darkness, the other women fretted. "Mary," they said, "we should go now!" The Blessed Mother fell to her knees, serenely full of grace and bowed her head. Her calmness and serenity formed a bubble around the others as fear left them and they followed suit, even as the thunderhead above seemed to sink to the ground. The surrounding pitch blackness was so profound, nothing else was visible except for the tomb ahead and the four centurions around it. As if they were in an amphitheater, their eyes were glued to the scene in front of them. Sensing the impending, Mary instructed them. "Pray, with your eyes closed." The rumbling above became constant, with streaks of charged electrons shooting forth amongst the clouds, like a celestial super-charger. The constant rumbling became a rushing roar. This was it. A cloud of charged plasma coalesced above and with a cannon boom, a million-amp streak of lightning shot down and shook the ground. The light was so intense the women could see everything through their eyelids, clear as day. The blazing energy from the bolt obliterated the boulder and threw the four centurions twenty yards away in all directions.

The clouds above became tinged with white, like ocean waves, and slowly pulled together in a circular motion. A swirling vortex became visible in the sky as the women looked upward. Above, the hole in the sky stretched into space, going even beyond the stars and seemingly out the edge of the universe itself. The heavenly host, the hierarchy of angels presented themselves: cherubim and seraphim and the communion of saints praised God as one. Mary could see that their energy took the form of light, but the light did not come out of them; rather it came from the Father and reflected off them.

The light hit the ground and shot wavelengths of energy from that point in all directions. Mary and the others felt the energy and knew it was nothing less than the heartbeat of the Father. They became transfixed, absorbing the scene and frozen in utter ecstasy.

A light came from the tomb. It filled the depth of the tomb and the surrounding hillside with such electricity the rock and the soil around it glowed. Mary stared at the scene with total trust in God and awe at His power. She and the others stayed like that, seemingly suspended in time, until what was in front of them played out. After what seemed like both a few minutes and six months, the women watched as the thundercloud dissipated quickly, becoming nothing more than a white morning mist floating back across the desert. Seeing the Roman soldiers come to, the women turned around and hurried back to the Apostles to report what they saw.

**

Quintus Claudius opened his eyes first. He lay there for a moment, motionless, taking in the view of the morning sky. Streams of morning light were quickly dissipating whatever darkness there may have been. He took note of his extremities, curling his fingers and toes. 'I have not yet entered the under-world,' he thought. He lifted his head and saw the others still motionless on the rocky ground. The tomb they were tasked with guarding was now about twenty yards away. His eyes widened as the realization washed over him: the boulder in front of the tomb was in pieces. The tomb they were guarding. He sat up with a start. The tomb they were supposed to be guarding. It was empty.

Before the consequences of that set in, he tried to remember the events of the morning. He recalled they had positioned themselves around the tomb strategically like the soldiers they were. The night had passed uneventfully. He pushed back the cobwebs in his head. As dawn started, something had happened. Darkness the color of the boiling pitch they had used in siege works. What had happened? Claudius got to his feet, thankful he was still standing and could walk. He walked over to Gnaeus Didius and woke him. Moaning behind him signaled the other two were coming to as well.

"What happened?" Manius Fulvius, the third one, looked wild-eyed at the others. "How long have we been laying here?"

Appius Lucretius, the last, looked at the sky. "Probably about thirty minutes," he said. Didius rubbed his eyes and sat cross-legged, contemplating the sky.

"You're very quiet," Claudius said.

"What happened here was not of this earth," Didius said.

The others absorbed the silence as the mystery of what happened sunk in.

"And who's going to believe that?" Lucretius asked.

"They don't have to believe it. They just have to accept it," Claudius said.

The rest nodded. None other than Pilate himself asked their legate to see that this spot was properly guarded. Their commander, in turn, had specifically asked them, the legion's four most senior centurions for this. Together, they had sixty-five years' experience in Caesar's army.

As centurions, they each commanded a double-strength century of one hundred sixty men, except for Claudius who, as the *primus pilus*, the senior centurion, commanded the entire first cohort of the legion of roughly eight hundred men. Rome conquered the world on the backs of men such as these. They all rose to their leadership positions in different ways.

Lucretius was the youngest of them, with twelve years' experience. He was promoted from within the ranks when he was stationed in Germania.

Manius Fulvius was next with fifteen years' experience and the most politically-connected. Although he had an uncle in the Senate who greased Fulvius's way to an appointment, his fearlessness had earned the respect of his men.

Didius had been in the army for eighteen years. He had joined as a sixteen year-old in his hometown of Perusia. The legion had thoroughly soaked into his very being, to the point where he found it hard to separate the hardened warrior from the easygoing boy he had once been. He hated it.

Claudius, the senior centurion, was in his twentieth year of service and technically, his last. He had been a centurion for seven years. He had been elevated after single-handedly beheading five mounted horsemen during a single battle against a band of renegade Palmyrans. His honor, strength and capability were unquestioned.

Claudius continued. "Let us go to the Hebrew high priests directly and tell them."

Lucretius stepped forward. "What about the legate?"

"We do not have to burden him with such a lowly matter," Claudius said. The others nodded. "Follow me," he said. They made their way back to the city center, walking in a two-by-two formation. Normally, they would not have to deal with the locals in such a way; that job was for diplomats and higher-ups like the legate. In fact, of all the places they had been, each of the men disliked their current posting by far. For Claudius, it was the intense rivalries that persisted between and among the various clans and tribes of the region. Back-stabbing, dishonest market practices, slander and lies were but a few examples. It seemed a man would even sell his own mother if it meant he could get ahead in some matter. There was no honor here. No, Claudius corrected himself. The Hebrews had honor with respect to their religion, but that was it. It seemed they would not wrong their God. However, some practiced their faith better than others. Even pagans like himself could see that. From their vantage point, it looked like the higher up in the local society one went, the practice of the faith was more garish and less sincere. And no one was higher than the people they were about to see.

The soldiers tolerated no roadblocks in the forms of the local Jewish populace. With enough shoving and elbowing, the soldiers formed a menacing bubble around themselves and a clear path to the building the Hebrews called the Hall of Hewn Stones.

They stopped short of the entrance. Under terms agreed to by Pilate and the Hebrew King Herod, Roman soldiers would not enter any holy places. Not that they wanted to go in there anyways.

Seeing the soldiers, the assistant to the High Priest ran inside and got Caiaphas and some of the other elders. Claudius frowned. He hated waiting on anyone other than the legate or the camp prefect. Given Fulvius's political abilities and his fair knowledge of the Greek language, they agreed in advance to let him talk.

After another few minutes, the Hebrews came out. Claudius looked them over: they were in ostentatious dress, mainly clothed in purple and gold vestments, with large baubles hanging about them. He hoped this would go quickly.

They formed a semicircle around Fulvius while they listened to him squawk in the strange language. His gestures provided some clue as to what he was saying. When he brought his arm down into his hand, Claudius guessed that he was at the part about the thunderbolt. After another minute, the Hebrews withdrew and started yelling among themselves. They appeared to be split into two groups, with one taking the time to wildly gesticulate, every phrase enunciated with overarching arm movements, throwing heads back and the like. Then the other group would respond.

"What are they saying?" Claudius asked Fulvius.

"The one group on the left is very concerned, especially when I told them that no man had a hand in the destruction of the tombstone. They seem to be extremely troubled by the events of the last three days."

"And what of the other group?" Claudius asked.

"They are trying to figure out a plausible story to tell their own people. Apparently they don't want them to know the truth. Right now they are fighting over how much to pay us."

"Pay us?" Didius asked.

Claudius shared his concern. Payment implied something to cover up. They may have killed men in gruesome fashion in battle and beaten their own soldiers without mercy when training, but they were not liars. Liars had no honor.

Fulvius nodded. "I know, it is not our nature to accept such a payment, but given what they are talking about, I see no such alternative."

The Jews came back with a large bag. It jingled as they said something to Fulvius. After a few more words, the Jews went back inside.

"So, what happened" Lucretius asked.

"The story is that we fell asleep and the followers of the man Jesus that was killed came and stole the body," Fulvius said.

Claudius took a step closer to him with a clenched first. "What?"

Fulvius held his hands up. "I know, we are centurions and we did our duty. We were not neglectful. However, the Jews fear an open revolt of the people and they want this whole thing to go away."

Claudius stood silent for a moment.

"We can use the money for the benefit of the men," Fulvius suggested.

"Very well," Claudius decided. Perhaps they could commission swords of Damascus steel for every centurion and his *optio*. That would be preferable to personally using the funds. He frowned, cleared his throat and spat on the ground. "Let's get out of this place and back to the barracks. For once, he felt for the Hebrews: he just wanted this behind them, too.

**

Walking to where the Apostles were locked up in fear, the women dared not speak. They dared not utter a sound, lest they risk the moment they had absorbed and still, in some way, had not ended. After a half hour walk, they found Peter and John at the house.

Mary Magdalene walked up to the second floor and saw Peter and the others around the table, morose as the dead olive tree laying just outside the window. "Peter," Mary Magdalene called out from the stairway. "We must tell you something."

Peter rubbed his eyes and ran his hands through his hair. Ever since Thursday night, when he had given up the Lord and his Master to preserve his own skin, he had been hounded by his actions in the form of non-stop tears, gut-churning anxiety and a trail of regret that he was sure would stretch to the stars if he could measure it. The last thing he wanted now was to listen to the women. They had wailed and sobbed and carried on since Friday afternoon; their cries a constant reminder of his cowardice, his disloyalty, his smallness. "What is it?" The other Apostles looked up.

Mary spoke up. "Let us sit down together, for what we have to say is of utmost importance."

Peter slumped back against the wall. The other Apostles were quiet while they awaited his response. "Nothing you do or say can ever lift me out of this pit of despair. I am here lamenting my own conception. Darkness is me," he whispered before slamming the back of his head into the stucco of the wall behind him. He repeated it twice more before Mary rushed over and held his head.

"Peter," Mary said, "you must listen to me." The melody of her voice had equal strains of authority and grace and stopped his head-banging. "Peter," she repeated, crouching in front of him, "stop doing this to yourself."

Peter could feel her eyes burrow right into his soul. The source of his agony was he himself, and Mary could see right through it. She took his face in her hands and looked in his eyes. "No one blames you for what you did."

"I denied him," Peter's lip quivered, his voice barely reaching the far corners of the room.

"What happened was pre-ordained by God himself. The holy scriptures of the Torah say as much," Mary wiped away his tears with her thumbs. "No one could have stopped what happened. That is, no one except Jesus himself."

Peter nodded, more tears spilling down his face. "God knew it would happen since the dawn of time. He sent Jesus to us, to me. Three years I spent with him, and still I couldn't bring myself to even acknowledge him." He looked up, forlorn eyes etching symbols in the ceiling. "I don't even know why I'm still here."

Mary took his shoulders. "You're here because the Holy One wants you here. He promised you the keys to Heaven, remember? He promised you the keys to the faith," the last word came out with a sharp gentleness only Mary could deliver.

Peter drew in a breath and let it out, blowing skyward. He nodded. After a long silence, Peter asked, "What is it that you came to tell us?"

"A new day is dawning." Mary got back on her feet and addressed the rest of the Apostles. "The Spirit Jesus left us with lives on in each of us." She walked to the nearest window and looked out at the dying darkness of the night. "Our time for mourning is at an end."

Peter's brow furrowed. He rose to his feet. "But Jesus is dead!" How it burned to say the words out loud.

Mary walked back over to Peter. "Don't believe it, Peter."

"I saw with my own eyes," said Peter. He gestured out the window in protest. "They took him down from the cross. They laid him in the tomb. They sealed it with a huge boulder. And they posted four centurions. Centurions," he drew out the word, "to guard it. My Lord is dead and buried just as surely as my heart is." With this, he sat down at the table and let his head drop on his outstretched arms.

"The tomb is empty," Mary said. The others in the room stopped. A silence materialized and filled the room. Only the sound of a little warbler outside could be heard.

After a time, Peter, with his face still down, muttered into his arms. "What?"

"The tomb is empty."

302

Peter got up. "Impossible," he said. "They must have moved him."

"Trust me when I say that's not what happened."

Peter walked over to Mary. "Then how is it empty?"

Mary sat in a chair while the Apostles gathered around her. "He walked out himself."

The other Apostles gasped and talked excitedly among themselves, quickly drowning Mary's voice. "Shut up!" Peter waved his arms. "Do you want to get arrested?" he pointed out the windows. "Besides," he continued in a calm tone, "I want to hear the rest of this."

And so Mary told them.

**

A thousand thoughts raced through Peter's mind as he listened to Mary. All of the Master's lessons, all the times he taught them something, all the times he foretold of his journey to the other side; it all made sense now. He thought of Jesus in the Temple, overturning the tables of the money changers and driving out animals, challenging the authorities to tear down the Temple and he would rebuild it in three days. Three days! As soon as Mary finished, Peter jumped up. "He was the Temple! He is the Temple!" The others looked at him. Peter grabbed John by his tunic and pulled him. "Let's go!"

John stumbled along. "Go where?"

Peter was almost down the stairs by now. "To the tomb, of course!"

**

After twenty minutes of running over two miles of rocky ground, Peter caught sight of the garden where Christ's tomb was. John, the youngest of all the Apostles, started to turn on the heat and flew to the cutout in the rocky hill. He stopped at the tomb and looked back, waiting for Peter. Eventually Peter, gasping and panting, walked up to the entrance past John and continued to walk right through.

Because of the darkness inside, he paused and let his eyesight adjust. For five minutes he stood there, absorbing the mystery in front of them. He stood absolutely still and tried to grasp what had just happened. They laid Jesus in this tomb just the other day. They had rolled a huge stone in front of it and posted four menacing Romans to guard it. The authorities were worried the disciples might steal his body. Peter shook his head. If only they had shown that kind of gumption when they arrested Jesus. He stopped himself. Mary was right. He couldn't change the past. At this point, he didn't need to. All the holy scriptures he had read, all the prophecies that the Master taught them about, they all pointed here, to this place, to this empty tomb. Finally Peter's eyes adjusted to the point where he could make out basic shapes. Seeing something, his heart started racing. Maybe it wasn't empty after all.

**

John called out to him from the entrance, perhaps only five yards away. "Peter, what is going on? Are you all right?" Peter smiled. The young one had no problem running here but couldn't bring himself to be in the dark. He stopped himself again. Maybe John was right not to enter the tomb. Maybe he shouldn't be in here at all. He walked closer to the outline of a little ledge carved into the side of the cave. What was here? He felt around the smooth stone with his hands and felt something hard. He stopped. Was this his body? He knew it shouldn't be here but it couldn't be. He slowly ran his hands over the material. It was hardened, as it should be from the burial aloes and spices that Joseph and Nicodemus prepared the linens with. At this point, all of that aloe would have dried. As his eyes continued to adjust to the darkness, Peter saw that the cloth was wrapped around the shape of a man. Wanting to feel another part of the linen, he jostled the form and felt it roll slightly. He frowned in realization that a body would not have moved that way. He quickly found where the head would have been and let out a gasp when he realized the form was hollow. He looked up. The linens were an empty caccoon. The body was gone. Mary was right.

His heart pounded as he picked up the form.

John bent down and looked into the tomb. He saw Peter holding the empty burial cloth in his arms. They made eye contact. It was as if the previous three years of learning, of asking Jesus questions, of having him explain the meaning of his parables, of seeing him expel demons, of hearing his teachings and how they turned the world absolutely upside-down...it all clicked at that moment. Peter saw John's eyes widen in terror as they moved from the burial cloth in his arms to a spot behind Peter. John gasped and fell down. Peter spun around and came face-to-face with a being, dressed all in white and with the appearance of gold that glimmered in the dark of the tomb. Peter went numb and staggered back, opening his mouth along the way but unable to get any sound out. Every hair on his body stood on end as he struggled to comprehend the sight before him.

The being, an angel, said, "Have no fear, men of Galilee. The man you are looking for, Jesus of Nazareth is not here." He turned and looked to a spot outside of the tomb, behind John. This time John spun around and saw an identical being right behind him. He shrieked and fell backward over some gnarled roots that ran over the ground. The being, another angel, said, "He is risen."

Peter and John looked at each other. They saw incredulity and shock etched on each other's face. They looked again, and the angels were gone. Peter scampered out of the tomb, burial cloth still in hand. "What should we do?" John asked. "Where should we go?"

"We will get the others," Peter said. He looked out into the distance. "We are going to Galilee."

# The Ascension

Peter and some of the other Apostles went fishing on the Sea of Galilee. The familiar sights, sounds and smells of the water and their vessel provided some comfort. It had been a fortnight since they traveled up from Jerusalem, since they came face-to-face with their salvation. Despite encountering the greatest victory of their cause, as a group, the Apostles were somewhat unsure of their next steps. Christ was risen from the dead, and even appeared to a few of them, but as ever their path to God's kingdom was still shrouded in mystery. One thing they were sure of: the Master's teaching of good and evil, and the fact that he said he would be here next.

Peter looked beyond the gunwales and into the water below. The memory of Christ's first instruction, to cast their nets over to one side, stuck in his mind. It was so easy, actually. They had hauled in so many fish their nets almost tore open. 'Why could not the Master simply tell us where to fish every time?' he wondered. And it wasn't just the fish. Every day they had to set time aside to do work such as this, whether it was mending nets, stitching sails, applying pitch to the wood. 'The Master could have made our netting stronger than anything, he could have made our sails resistant to all tearing, and our boats more waterproof,' he thought. 'But he wanted us to earn our keep,' he realized.

Nathaniel was hunched over the stern, pulling in nets with ease. He frowned, for the easier it was, it meant the fewer fish they caught. This time he was able to gather in the nets as fast as he could get them into his arms. Pulling in ream after ream of empty netting, he swore and threw the wet clump onto the deck. "Damn this futile exercise! We might as well be casting our nets onto the hot sand, for there are no fish anywhere." He wiped some perspiration off his forehead in disgust.

It was early, in the first watch of the day. The line where the water met the land and sky stretched out forever in front of them. Peter contemplated all that had gone on in the last forty days: following Jesus into Jerusalem, seeing the crowds swoon at the sight of him, their adulation. And how that adulation had turned black in an instant with the arrest of Jesus and the urgings of the crowd in asking for crucifixion. The utter despair at seeing him die, following by two of the saddest days he had ever known. He looked down at his hands, worn, toughened from years in the sun, repairing nets, absorbing the salt, splinters from his boat. And then the Day. The day when he and John ran to Jesus' tomb and found it empty. How incredible! He shivered with the thought of it. Jesus appearances to them in the upper room, his command to spread the gospel. But what did that mean? How would they do it? There were practical questions, too. How could he still devote time to his family? Could he continue fishing while he fished for men? Their business certainly suffered while he and Andrew were out with Jesus for the last three years. It wasn't continuous, but he wasn't able to devote the time needed for this. And if he had to deal with landlubbers like Nathaniel, he would lose his mind.

Nathaniel hefted the last bunch of netting onto the boat and it snagged on a loose board. He groaned against the weight and with another complaint threw it on the deck. Peter spun around. "Will you watch what you're doing? You could have snagged that whole section of netting."

Nathaniel put his hands on his hips. "It's not worth it anyways; no one will catch shit with this."

Peter's brother Andrew joined in. "This takes time and patience; you should know that by now."

"I knew we should have dropped our nets on the north shore."

Andrew turned red in the face. "Look, we don't need your bitching right now. Why don't you go to the bow and keep watch?"

"Watch for what?" Nathaniel jutted his chin in Andrew's direction.

"Anything. As long as you're up there and not back here."

Nathaniel stomped off. Peter looked up again as he felt the western wind blow through his hair. It caressed his head and seemed to carry him to a place far away. To a place where there was no bickering, no disputes. It was a place in the future, a future, as Peter envisioned it, where everyone completely relied on the Master. A place where there was no concern for the temporal worries of shelter and food.

He thought back to the first time Jesus had fed the crowds. It was a time that was hard to define, like any other time with the Rabbi. They had just received news of Herod's execution of

John, and Peter could tell Jesus just wanted to be alone. Jesus took a boat somewhere and it was not until later that the Apostles and five thousand men and their families found him by the shore in Bethsaida. Oh, how the Master had them transfixed. 'Myself included,' thought Peter. He remembered sitting so still for so long that his legs had fallen completely asleep. Jesus must have preached for hours, but it was a blink of an eye, really. And then he fed them. All of them. With nothing. Peter shook his head at the memory. "And he's trusting us to go ahead and carry it on."

Andrew turned around from his spot on the opposite side of the boat. "What?"

"Huh?"

"Did you say something?" Andrew asked.

"Oh, I must have been talking to myself," Peter said. "I was just thinking about how the Master has entrusted to us the mission of the gospel.

Andrew walked over and looked Peter in the eyes. The boat's slight rocking made the horizon behind Peter's head rise and fall. "I know what you're thinking. You're thinking that we're just a bunch of hard-headed, simple-minded fisherman. Well, of course we are," Andrew smiled. "But it's not just us. The Christ is with us, too. I can feel it. He will be with us wherever we will go."

"I know he will. It's just that sometimes it's hard to know what exactly to do next."

"I know. But he will, when the time is right."

"Thanks, brother."

310

Andrew gave him a squeeze on the shoulder and returned to his position on the other side of the boat. Peter resumed his gaze into the distance, pondering their future.

Suddenly there was a shout from the bow. It was Thomas. "Look there," he pointed to a spot on the shore about five hundred yards away. There was a figure on the beach, crouched over a fire. Peter frowned. There wasn't anyone there a minute ago. He spun the wheel in that direction and a few minutes later the boat had made its way to a spot about a hundred yards offshore.

The figure on the shore, a man, called out to them. "Children, have you caught anything to eat?"

Peter looked at the others, puzzled. "No," he called back.

The man called back. "Cast the net over the right side of the boat and you will find something."

Peter looked at Andrew and they both shrugged. They draped all the netting over the starboard side and immediately they felt the weight increase as fish flooded in. All of them strained to heft the nets up, causing the boat to list to that side. John looked at the figure again and turned back to Peter with excitement in his voice. "It is the Lord!"

As soon as Peter heard this, he tucked his cloak into his undergarment and jumped into the water. "Jesus!" he exclaimed. The water was waist-deep at this point, and it felt like walking through the mud baths of Tiberius. Oh, how agonizing to struggle through this when the Master was so close!

He made it to shore and staggered up the sand under the heavy wet weight of his clothes. Jesus helped him up and had him sit down by the fire. The others managed to get the boat close enough to the beach that they simply jumped out and raced up the beach, dragging the catch with them.

Jesus looked at them. They could feel his gaze going right through them, knowing that he already knew what they were thinking, what they had been doing, what was in store for them. What could they say to him that he didn't already know?

"You have been out here all night," Jesus said. Everyone nodded. "You must be hungry. He took several of the fish and prepared them before setting them over the fire. No one spoke a word. When he was done, he served everyone, and they tucked in.

When breakfast was over, Jesus motioned to Peter to talk privately. They walked some distance away. Peter beheld the scene in front of him. The pale blue light of the early morning spanned the entire sky and contrasted starkly with the brilliant blue of the Sea of Galilee behind them. It was as if they were the only two souls on earth.

*When they had finished breakfast, Jesus said to Simon Peter, "Simon, son of John, do you love me more than these?"*

*He said to him, "Yes, Lord, you know that I love you."*

*He said to him, "Feed my lambs." He then said to him a second time, "Simon, son of John, do you love me?"*

*He said to him, "Yes, Lord, you know that I love you."*

*He said to him, "Tend my sheep." He said to him the third time, "Simon, son of John, do you love me?" Peter was distressed that he had said to him a third time, "Do you love me?" and he said to him, "Lord, you know everything; you know that I love you."*

*[Jesus] said to him, "Feed my sheep. Amen, amen, I say to you, when you were younger, you used to dress yourself and go where you wanted; but when you grow old, you will stretch out your hands, and someone else will dress you and lead you where you do not want to go." (John 21:15-18)*

"Give me your hands," Jesus said.

Peter held out his hands, palms up. Jesus placed one hand on each and looked into Peter's eyes. Peter could feel his entire soul laid bare for all to see.

"Do you remember when we were at Caesarea Philippi? I had just warned you about the leaven of the Pharisees." Peter nodded. How could he forget any moment with the Lord? "I promised you then that I would give you something." He looked up to the Father. "Father in heaven, I pray my blessing over my Apostle Peter. Endow him with wisdom, understanding, counsel, knowledge, fortitude, piety and fear of the Lord. Imbue him with strength, courage, discernment and humility."

As Jesus spoke, Peter could feel twin currents of peace and adrenaline course through his body, one intensifying the other. The peace was nothing like he ever felt before, as if his heart stopped beating entirely. It made him feel like he could stand still in the face of a sandstorm. The adrenaline surging through his veins coincided with Jesus calling forth the Holy Spirit.

"Lord, you have sent the Spirit down upon Peter and the Apostles. May they keep the Spirit at all times, so that they can carry out their Holy mission without fear and with the ultimate love of you, Father. And may Peter receive these keys with a heart of understanding and the rock of leadership, so as to safeguard the faith in its entirety, and may all of his successors likewise be so endowed, to go forth and spread the gospel, under pain of denial, oppression, persecution, torture and death, so that the living children of the light may attain the heavenly banquet with you, with all the angels and saints, so as to complete your creation." He looked back into Peter's eyes. "And may all this be done in the name of the Father, Son, and Holy Spirit."

As he said the words, Peter felt a ray of brilliant light shoot down from the sky. A voice, rumbling like thunder, said, "So be it."

**

Peter felt a weightiness in his hands that was not there before. He looked down to see an object in each hand. They were both incredibly solid and must have weighed one talent each; however, they were also weightless in his hand. He became transfixed by them. The gold one was in his right hand; the silver in his left. Other than the difference in color, they were exactly the same. They appeared to be made of a metal he had never previously seen.

"These are the keys I promised you," Jesus said. He touched Peter's right hand. "This is the key to heaven. Remember that

314

which I told you: that whatever you bind on earth will be bound in heaven, and whatever you loose on earth will be loosed in heaven." He touched Peter's left hand. "This is the key to the faith. The Lord is entrusting this to you, so that you may go forth and spread it throughout the world. Safeguard it, protect it and proclaim it" Jesus's face lit up. "Pray for the strength to carry on this mission, and know that I will be with you always."

"Lord, my hands are so unworthy."

"The Father has ordained this moment. Indeed, you are made in the image and likeness of Him. We all are. Your hands can only be worthy when they are the Lord's hands."

"Lord, I am so weak."

"The Father's strength will be perfected in your weakness."

"Lord, I don't know where to start."

Jesus smiled. "You don't have to start. I have already started, and indeed have already finished. You just have to bring them along."

"Who, Lord?"

Jesus looked at him again with a look of total love. "Everyone." He took Peter by the shoulders. "All you need is faith. Let it live in here," he jabbed Peter in the chest, "so that it can guide you here," he touched Peter's head.

**

After this, they returned to the other Apostles, who were finishing their meal and cleaning up. "Come walk with me," Jesus said to them. They rose and started making their way through the countryside. He spoke as they walked, giving instructions for the propagation of the faith. They became lost in the moment, suspended in a haze of awe while they were here with the Master. It was if they knew this would be their last moments with the Rabbi on earth, and they held onto it as hard as they could. Through this they walked, hanging on his every word, taking to heart his directives. Finally they started making their way up a mountain.

As they climbed, Peter looked around at the familiar surroundings and the village below. "Look," he pointed behind them, "it is the village of Bethany!" He looked all around them at the mountainside. "We are on the Mount of Olives!" The other disciples looked around them, as if they had awakened for the first time. "We are no longer in Galilee!" He looked to Jesus. "Have we been walking for three days?"

Jesus smiled. "You can do all things if you remain in me. Without me you can do nothing. Come now," he turned and started climbing again, "it is not much further."

They came to a small plateau near the summit. Peter beheld the sight in front of him: all of the village of Bethany under them, Jerusalem in the near distance, with the Kidron Valley spreading out before them in all directions. Jesus kept walking right off the ledge and went some distance before turning around in mid-air.

They watched in awe, totally absorbed in the moment, knowing this would be the last time they would interact with Jesus like this. Time seemed to stop. Jesus held up his hand in blessing.

> *"All power in heaven and on earth has been given*
> *to me. Go, therefore, and make disciples of all na-*
> *tions, baptizing them in the name of the Father, and of*

*the Son, and of the Holy Spirit, teaching them to ob-*
*serve all that I have commanded you. And behold, I*
*am with you always, until the end of the age." (Mat-*
*thew 28:18-20)*

With that, a sudden bank of mist formed around them. A great rushing sound fell upon them, a force like it had been dropped from eternity above. Sensing that it was the heavenly host singing its praises for the Ascended King, the Apostles fell down and worshipped, too. By now the mist had totally surrounded them, so that they could not see each other, but the scene ahead and above them was crystal clear.

A multitude of angels came down and while still singing, lifted the Christ up into the space above them. Peter looked up into an abyss that stretched for thousands of miles and knew Jesus's destination was at the top, the throne room of heaven. He ached to be there. He watched as the angels rose, and alternatively the spectral wonder of the music rushed down from heaven. It washed over them in palpable tones, beats, harmonies, melodies. This was accompanied by the full color of heaven, colors which didn't exist on earth, colors which ran down the mist and made the faces and clothes of the Apostles shine. The joy of heaven at that moment cascaded upon them in full.

As they watched, Jesus's crown of thorns appeared on his head, although this time they were tinged with silver and gold, and shone brilliantly, its rays of light almost stinging as surely as the thorns did during the passion. Jesus's wounds, the hole in his sides, in his hands and feet, and the stripes of the scourging all over his body, shone in full glory as he approached the Father in heaven.

Although Jesus kept ascending to the impossible height overhead, they could still see clearly what was happening, as if their perch on the mountaintop was rising alongside. As Jesus rose through the differing level of the choirs of angels, the praise and the singing became more intense, more fervent, more electric. It looked as though the countless angels in the sky were putting forth all their effort and all their spirit into the praise, the wave after wave of the sound, the color, and the joy, became all the more intensified.

They sensed Jesus was approaching the throne of the Father. The mist around them slowly turned golden, lending the sheen of pure light to every facet of everything around. Finally, Jesus rose to the throne and took his seat at the right hand of the Father. Peter watched in awe. This moment was the culmination of everything that had ever happened in the entire universe up until now. A visible connection flashed between Father and Son, and they could sense the Holy Spirit, born of the purest, most intense love between the two, take flight.

They watched as the Spirit flew down from the impossible height, down from the widest expanse of the universe overhead, past all the choirs of the angels even as they sang its praises, and like an avalanche, washed over them. It felt like the River Jordan emptying itself upon them. They absorbed every last bit of spiritual nourishment they could before the Spirit rose again to the throne room. With that, the mist dissipated at once, and the Apostles were all alone on the plateau.

For several minutes they sat there with mouths agape, trying to digest what had happened. Suddenly two men dressed in white garments stood beside them.

*They said, "Men of Galilee, why are you standing there looking at the sky? This Jesus who has been taken up from you into heaven will return in the same way as you have seen him going into heaven." (Acts 1:11)*

They looked at each other before looking back at the men, but the angels disappeared. "What just happened?" Thomas asked. All eyes turned to Peter. "What are we to do now?"

Peter stood and turned to them. "You heard the man. We are to go forth and spread the gospel."

"I heard that," Thomas said, "but where do we start?"

Peter smiled, recalling the same question he put to Jesus. "We don't have to start, for the Master has already started this. Indeed, the Father above started everything when he formed the earth and sky and when he divided light from darkness. All we have to do is keep it going."

The others sat there, pondering what this meant. "There is something else you should know," Peter said. "The Rabbi has ascended to the throne of Heaven to be with the Father. But before this, he prefigured his glory to James, John and me."

"What?" Thomas asked. "How, and where?"

"It was at the mount of Tabor, near Tiberias. The Master took us to the top of the mountain, and there he became as brilliant as the sun. It was indescribable. His face shone brighter than a star, and his clothes became whiter than anything I have ever seen.

The air around us, oh, how the universe seemed to stand still at that moment. Then Moses and Elijah appeared at his side, and they were talking with him."

"Really?" Andrew asked.

"Really and truly, my brother. I wanted the moment to last forever. The voice of the Father above sounded out, proclaiming the Rabbi to be his son. It was as if you had to give your entire lifetime to get the chance to be there, you would have given it. Indeed, I felt like I was in another lifetime when I was there."

"What was the point of that?" Thomas asked again. "Was not his divinity already so clear to us?"

"My brother Thomas, God chose that point to reinforce the fact that Jesus, the Son, would not be with us forever, in body, but that His Spirit would always rest with us. And though it pains me, pains me," he beat his breast, "to think that we cannot see or touch him in his bodily form anymore, it is my everlasting hope and joy to know that He, in the Spirit, will indeed dwell in us."

"Until the end of time," John added.

Peter continued. "It is good that he showed us all this. For the road ahead will be tough, my brothers. The Temple authorities still want us dead. Many of the Rabbi's followers have given up hope and have dispersed. Many others have shrunk back from the light of promise that He lived, and have returned to the old ways of the world." He looked each of them in the eyes. "We are at risk of losing them. If we do nothing, we are at risk of drowning the faith of the everlasting life in this vast cauldron of worldly apathy. If we do not rise to this task, we are at risk of throwing away every last part of the heavenly kingdom that the Father has promised us, which was purchased by the incalculable cost of every drop of sweat and blood that the Rabbi had to offer."

In stark contrast to the celestial scene before, now there was silence. Silence, and the wide open valley behind the Apostles teetering on the brink. The others looked back at Peter wide-eyed. "Are we going to let that happen?"

John stood up. "Hell, no!"

Peter looked at James. "James, remember the zeal with which you wanted to call down fire from heaven to destroy that Samaritan village when they rejected Jesus? Are you ready to take hold of that zeal and use it for the glory of God?"

James scrambled up. "As surely as the sun rises in the East, I swear it!"

Peter looked at Philip. "Philip, remember when the Rabbi challenged you to feed the four thousand? Are you ready to clutch the memory of his miracle tight to your chest, so that you yourself can go forth and feed the people bread from heaven?"

Philip stood. "Yes, so be it!"

"Nathaniel, remember when Jesus first encountered you, when he knew you to be 'sitting under the fig tree' without seeing you?"

"Of course."

"Do you remember what he said of you?"

"I will never forget it."

"He said, 'Here is a true son of Israel!'" Peter put his hands on his shoulders. "Will you be that Son of Israel for all the people?" he swept his arm across the valley below. "Will you show them the way?"

"Yes, without question!"

Peter jumped onto a large boulder. "Thomas, remember when you put your hands into the very wounds of Christ, how you believed?"

"How can I forget?"

"Are you prepared to show people that very reality, the reality of the wounds of the Son of God that saved our very souls from the realm of death?"

"Yes, until my very death."

Peter looked at Matthew. "Matthew, do you want to go back to being a grubby little tax collector, whoring for the Romans and keeping an extra portion for yourself?"

Matthew looked horrified. "No!"

"Of course not. Indeed, I know you are going to be collecting nothing less than souls for the Lord." He turned to James the smaller. "James bar-Alphaeus, are you ready to burn with fire for the Lord?"

James stood and struck his staff on a nearby outcropping. "Like nothing else!"

"Judas Thaddaeus, you have tilled your family's land for years. Are you now ready to reap what the Master has sown? Are you ready for the harvest?"

Jude slapped his club against his hand. "As surely as the rain falls down, I swear it."

Peter looked last at Simon. "Simon, do you remember the moment the first fires of zeal enflamed your heart when the

Rabbi changed water into wine at your wedding celebration? Are you ready to light that flame into the hearts of others? Are you ready to transform people's souls into what God has called of them?"

"Yes, yes, and again, yes!"

Peter looked at them. "Very well. Let us go down to Jerusalem and light the world on fire."

# The Descent of the Holy Spirit

Peter looked out at the crowds, wary of gatherings of even just a few people. How just a few weeks could change things. When they had come down from the mountain after witnessing the Ascension, they were all filled with the Holy Spirit. They had looked forward to coming back to Jerusalem, and even though they were still very much hated, they were still eager to reap souls for the Lord.

He could feel the change of mind when they first entered the outskirts of the city. The Romans, having just executed another criminal, displayed the perpetrator's head on a pole at the Sheep's gate just as a reminder that their rulers weren't going anywhere for a while.

The sight of the head on display put a damper on their return. They had plenty of zeal left, though, until James was spotted by a member of the Sanhedrin. James avoided him and managed to get lost in the crowd. At that time, they took up residence in the same house where they shared the Last Supper. Since then, the mood had just gotten uglier.

\*\*

Publius followed his father, struggling to keep up in the madness of the crowd gathered. They wound their way through countless stalls with merchants selling everything from camel meat and animal skins to precious stones from lands far off. After twisting through the crowd, they rounded a corner and entered the main square. Publius's father stopped to pull a small scroll out of his pocket. He held Publius close with one hand as people jostled together on all sides. "Stay close," he told Publius, "we must get to the western side of this square. Maximus should be over there somewhere."

Publius shook with excitement. "Are we really going to see him today, Papa?"

His father grabbed his hand and started to lead him through the crowd. "It's hard to believe, isn't it? After all this time traveling? Just stay with me and we'll find him eventually."

They made their way around two men squabbling about the price of some grain before nearly colliding with women bearing huge water jugs. "Careful, son," his father pulled him tighter. After ten more minutes of wedging sideways through the crowd, they came upon a swarthy man sitting behind a stand amongst piles of figs while two men in front of him did their best to keep up with the consistent demand.

He spotted them and rose, clutching Publius's father close. "Quintus! Finally, you are here! Welcome." He bent down and picked Publius up in a great bear hug. "Publius, you are growing so fast. How old are you now?"

"Seven," Publius declared.

"My goodness. You will be tall like your father; I can tell, but with your mother's looks, thank Jupiter." He turned to Quintus. "And how is my sister?"

"She sends her love."

Publius looked around again at the hordes of people. "Uncle, why are there so many people here?"

Maximus hefted himself off his chair. "The Hebrew people are here for something called *Shavuot*, or the Festival of Weeks."

"What's that?"

"It is meant to commemorate their God giving them holy scriptures in the desert after their flight from Egypt. And actually, this is but the end of a seven week period called the Counting of the *Omer*."

"What's that?" Publius asked again.

"Such a curious boy! They celebrate this period because by their God giving them these scriptures, which are like laws, he unified them as a nation dedicated to serving him. At least that's what I think they celebrate." He picked a fig from one of the piles and popped it in his mouth. "I've been here almost a year, and I'm still learning about these people."

"Has business been good?" Quintus asked.

"Better than I have expected. When I first came here from Alexandria to buy an orchard, I had no idea what kind of return I could make. But religious festivals like this one are the few chances I have to quickly unload inventory." Maximus surveyed his two assistants busy with customers, then turned back to them. "Please, have a seat," he motioned to two rope-like slings in the corner, out of the sun. "I'll be back in a minute with some food for you." He switched to Aramaic and shouted instructions to his two assistants before melting into the crowd.

"Well, what do you think, Publius? Are you ready to spend a few months with your Uncle Maximus here?"

"Yes," Publius looked around at all the different types of people about. "This is exciting, but I will miss you Papa."

"I know, and I will miss you, son. But your mother and I have to go to Rome on business and we can't take you with us. It will only be about eight weeks, though. I'm sure the time will fly by."

Maximus returned with several bags of fruit and bread. "Here you go. Please, eat up - you must restore your strength after such a trip!" He doled out food to them before sitting down to attack a pile of grapes.

Publius tried some dates. "There are many people here. Is this the biggest festival?"

Maxiumus looked at Quintus. "What a curious boy you have. I have much to teach him!" He turned to Publius. "Actually, you should have seen the crowds that were here during the Hebrew feast of Passover. Oh my! There were crowds as far as the eye could see."

"Why were there so many?" Publius asked.

"It is one of their major feasts. And this year, there was the added curiosity of a man called Jesus who was here with his apostles."

**

Not far away, the Apostles were hunkered down, fearful, quivering and quiet. Earlier, at the Ascension, Jesus told them

*"But you will receive power when the holy Spirit comes upon you, and you will be my witnesses in Jerusalem, throughout Judea and Samaria, and to the ends of the earth." (Acts 1:8)*

That statement, and the memory of what had happened on the mountaintop, kept them from losing all hope. They wouldn't dare go outside, for thousands and thousands of people were gathered outside for the *Shavuot* and the Apostles were afraid of the Jews and others in authority. The chance for persecution was as fresh in their minds as the absence of Jesus, their Master and Teacher. As Peter ate with the Apostles, he paused to look outside through the slats in one of the windows. Something unseen, something fleeting prompted a thought. Something was different about this morning. Was it the crowded square below, filled with people from all over, even to the ends of the earth? Was it because this was one of the few times they gathered together since Jesus had gone up to the Father? Or was it something more subtle? A small breeze picked up and made the candles amongst them flicker, as if they themselves were unsure of their light. 'Like us,' Peter thought. 'Are we sure of the light within us?' He stared remotely into the distance as the others dined.

**

"What was special about this man Jesus?" Quintus asked.

"Some Jews thought he was a prophet, while others thought he was a confidence man, falsely claiming to be a holy man. Still others swore he had done many great signs, like making the blind see and the lame walk. Some even say he was the Messiah, the Son of their God. You haven't heard any of this?"

"We have been traveling for weeks; how could we have known about any of this?" Quintus said.

"It seems like it has all that people have been talking about since then. Lazar and Rachim here," he nodded at his two assistants, "were greatly unsettled at what happened."

Quintus leaned forward. "Tell me more."

Maximus gobbled another handful of figs. "This Jesus seemed to be quite the boat-rocker. He had been traveling through the countryside for the last three years, supposedly proclaiming the new kingdom of God. Word has it that he and his band of Apostles got on the wrong side of the religious authorities here.

Publius looked at him in wonder. "What did they do?"

"Nothing bad, it seemed, at least, not from my point of view. They went about, healing the sick, curing the crippled, helping the lame to walk. The man Jesus was said to even make the blind see."

"That can't possibly be true," Quintus said. "Even the best Roman doctors can't make that happen, even with the most rigorous of blood-letting."

"Well, some people swear to it. That isn't even the most amazing thing." Maximum leaned forward. "Some people say that this Jesus even raised people from the dead."

"Impossible!" Quintus said. "Surely it is a legend, magnified by this country's ignorance of all things science."

Maximus shrugged. "The thing is, that isn't what got the religious authorities the most upset."

"No?" Publius asked.

"No. What got them most riled up, at least, in my humble point of view, is that this Jesus would also claim that people's sins were forgiven after he physically healed them."

"What's so bad about that?" Publius asked.

"Ah, such innocent questions from an innocent boy!" Maximum slapped Publius's knees. "What was so bad, at least in the eyes of the authorities, was that only God can forgive sins. It seemed to them that this man was claiming the power of God."

"So what happened at Passover?" Quintus was on the edge of his seat.

"The man Jesus was welcomed by throngs of people upon his entry into Jerusalem. It was an absolute spectacle; I've never seen anything like it. People were lined up six or eight people deep alongside the road when he came. They even threw their cloaks down in the hopes that the hooves of his donkey would step on them."

"So the people loved this man but the authorities were suspicious of him," Quintus said.

"To say the least. They had wanted to kill him, but they were afraid of the people."

"Why would they want to do that?" Publius asked.

"My child, there is so much to learn," Maximus answered. "The Pharisees and the priestly class here have it pretty good. We Romans are here to improve their society, to bring them into the fold of the Empire and to instruct them on all things civic. The people resent this kind of thing, obviously, because they would rather make their own mistakes, have their own leaders, that kind of thing."

"But who is this King Herod?" Quintus asked. "Isn't he their king?"

"Well yes, but only because we Romans allow it as a sort of salve to the people. But he is basically like a Roman with a Hebrew face and name. At any rate, the Pharisees have been allowed to lord all their religious rules over the people. They are supposedly the strictest adherents to their faith. They have grown accustomed to their place in society."

"So?" Publius asked.

"So, they feared this man Jesus, because by going around claiming that he is the son of the true King and attracting crowds all over the place, they thought he would attract the ire of the Roman governor here, Pontius Pilate, and bring about a new oppression that would threaten the order of things."

"So what happened?" Quintus asked.

"So, during the night of the Passover celebration, the religious authorities conspired with one of Jesus's followers to arrest him. They publicly accused him and handed him over to Pilate, asking for a crucifixion."

"Oh, by the brow of Ares, that is horrible!" Quintus said.

"Indeed it was. I didn't watch the actual event, but I was in the square when Pilate pronounced his verdict. He clearly didn't want to do anything to the man Jesus." He looked at Quintus. "You have heard about this business with Sejanus, right?"

"Of course, who hasn't?"

"Anyway, up to that point Pilate had done all he could to frustrate the objectives of the Jews. But since he heard about Sejanus, it seemed he realized he could no longer be such an antagonist against them. But it still appeared hard, though, to condemn this man Jesus. He tried to get the crowd to pick Jesus to be released as is his custom, but the religious authorities swarmed through the crowd, agitating them to pick an insurrectionist Barabbas to be released instead."

"These Pharisees sound ruthless. Perhaps they should stand for the Senate," Quintus said.

"Ha! My brother-in-law is such a comedian. It is true, every society has people like them."

"So how did this all end?" Publius asked.

"Well, they had Jesus crucified and they buried him and all that. Some rumors persisted that he rose from the dead, because the tomb was found to be empty three days later. But Pilate's centurions stationed there testified that his body was stolen." He ate some more figs. "I don't know what to make of it, though."

"Aren't you the least bit curious?" Quintus asked.

"Well, yes, but only in the normal sense. Every capital city has its share of intrigue, and this place is no different. However, I'm a simple man after simple pursuits."

"What do you believe, Uncle?" Publius asked.

Maximus chuckled. "Publius, my child, you ask many good questions. Let's just say for now that I am a good Roman."

"So you worship our Emperor Tiberius?"

Maximus looked at Quintus and shifted in his seat. "How do I say this?" He pulled a coin out of a money bag lying nearby and showed it to the child. The copper image of the Emperor showed clearly. "It's true that I worship this, in a way." He gave it to Publius. "Understand, though, that the man will die one day, but this coin will live forever."

\*\*

332

The crowd below was generating a loud murmur via the countless conversations below, whether it was customers haggling with merchants, families trying to stick together in the teeming mass, people yelling at each other in different languages as they tried to make each other understood, or simply those of them that had started consuming wine well in advance of that day's lunch. Out of the din below, the occasional foreign tongue had been discernable, leading to a discussion among the Twelve as to where it could be from.

"What are you thinking about, brother?" Andrew asked Peter. "You appear deep in thought."

"Something feels different," Peter said.

Andrew frowned. He looked at the others, absorbed in their own conversations and eating before turning back to Peter. "Of course this day is different. We are sitting around just eating and drinking, as if we don't know what to do with ourselves. There is a major festival outside, and we are cooped up in here like chickens."

"I know that," Peter said. "Of course it is not in our nature to wall ourselves off, after all we have done with the Rabbi." The others stopped in mid-conversation at the mention of Jesus and turned to look at Peter. "But I mean something actually feels different," he rubbed his fingers together. "The air feels very dry today. And I am having a hard time concentrating with the sounds from outside. Listen," he motioned to the direction of the masses outside. The Apostles stopped chewing and let the sounds float up to their room. Despite the immense crowd, they found they could hear all sorts of individual conversations, individual words, even above the shouting. After a few moments absorbing this, they looked around at each other in wonderment. It was as if they had ears all over the square below.

**

"What about you, Maximus? What is so pressing in Rome that must take you away from your business?"

Quintus looked around at the people going to and fro, haggling with all their might. He nodded with approval at all the commerce taking place. "Actually, Maximus, my business is taking me to Rome." Quintus had built the beginnings of a fortune acting as a middleman, sourcing things that others simply couldn't.

Maximus leaned forward. "Oh, please do tell."

Quintus obliged. "I have a lead I'm working. I found a swordmaker in Tripoli who makes swords of Damascus steel like no one else."

"Are those the ones that can cut an iron bar with one swipe?"

Quintus nodded. "Among other things. I don't know the science, but they are made in such a way that they must be very different somehow from ordinary steel. Different enough that the Legion will pay a premium for them."

"Ah, the Legion. A deep-pocketed customer indeed. But aren't there Damascus steel-forgers all over the middle East?"

"It's true, but they are few and far between, and they specialize in making them to order, one at a time." Quintus shifted forward in his seat, oblivious now to the swarming crowds around the square. "This one I found in Tripoli has an army of 20 smiths working for him. Or rather, working for fear of him. Apparently, they are all indebted to him one way or the other. He trains them and allows them to work their debt off."

"How can the quality be that good, or that consistent, with that many smiths? Surely he can't supervise them all?"

"That's the thing," Quintus said. "Periodically, he will test their swords at random to see if they can cut through the trunk of a palm tree with one swipe. If one fails, he simply beheads the one who made it."

"By the fist of Ares, that is dreadful!"

"Indeed. But it has only happened once, so his quality control must be working."

"And you're sure you can find a buyer in Rome?"

"It's already a done deal. I've been in touch with Macro," Quintus said before grabbing a handful of figs. "This will be my biggest one ever, and hopefully my last," Quintus stared into the distance.

Maximus nodded. Macro meant Quintus Naevius Sutorius Macro, prefect of the Praetorian Guard. He wasn't surprised, though. Quintus had always been good at cultivating the relationships their grandfather had formed with the Roman patricianate before striking out for Alexandria. He jingled a money bag with his foot. The lengths men would go for such simple metal things.

\*\*

Peter got up and went to one of the windows. James straightened in alarm. "Peter what are you doing?"

"I just want to see," Peter said.

"They'll see us," James said. His objection was clear. They were in hiding and did not want to be seen by anyone in authority, that they might re-launch the persecution upon them.

"I don't care," Peter opened the slatted frame of the window. The scene below spread out to the edge of town and beyond. People from seemingly every corner of the earth had converged here in this place. He looked out in the distance, at the hills he knew to be over four miles away and even there, he could make out tiny figures filling the space between buildings. But it wasn't the crowd that got his attention.

"What do you see?" Thomas asked, hunched over his food close to the table.

Peter looked out. The sky was quickly darkening, as a black cloud cover flew in from the west. It made for an instant nighttime. Clouds overhead which were white now appeared purple, their sinewy strands standing out against the inky sky. The halting breeze that had attempted to cool the crowd all afternoon found its breath and became constant. Yes, indeed something was different. He sat down again.

"Well?" Andrew asked.

Peter looked at all of them. Before he could speak, a sudden gust of wind rushed through the upper room, knocking over some cups and blowing the shutter slats open and closed. One of the women shrieked as her water spilled in her lap. The wind grew to a dull roar and made everyone's outer garment flap uncontrollably. The window grates slammed shut and then flew open again. As the air screamed overhead, small licks of flame appeared over the heads of the Apostles and hovered in place.

They looked up in wonder as the fire over each grew until it was a churning, fiery mass. Peter felt every hair on his body stand on end as adrenaline poured into his bloodstream. He became electrified as he felt the Spirit absolutely flood his body. It was as if someone had taken the sun out of the sky and thrust it into his heart. He could feel the heat of the Spirit burning within him and from the looks of the others, it was in them, too.

*At this sound, they gathered in a large crowd, but they were confused because each one heard them speaking in his own language. They were astounded, and in amazement they asked, "Are not all these people who are speaking Galileans? Then how does each of us hear them in his own native language? We are Parthians, Medes, and Elamites, inhabitants of Mesopotamia, Judea and Cappadocia, Pontus and Asia, Phrygia and Pamphylia, Egypt and the districts of Libya near Cyrene, as well as travelers from Rome, both Jews and converts to Judaism, Cretans and Arabs, yet we hear them speaking in our own tongues of the mighty acts of God." They were all astounded and bewildered, and said to one another, "What does this mean?" But others said, scoffing, "They have had too much new wine." (Acts 2:6-13)*

Quintus stood up and looked at a building at the end of the square. "Listen," he said. "Someone is speaking to us."

"What?" Maximus hefted himself out of his chair. They stood still, and despite the throngs of people throughout the square, they heard a voice speaking Latin. Though it was a distance of

337

nearly a stadium away, they could hear it as if it was right there next to them.

*Then Peter stood up with the Eleven, raised his voice, and proclaimed to them, "You who are Jews, indeed all of you staying in Jerusalem. Let this be known to you, and listen to my words.*

*These people are not drunk, as you suppose, for it is only nine o'clock in the morning.*

*No, this is what was spoken through the prophet Joel:*

*'It will come to pass in the last days,' God says,*

*'that I will pour out a portion of my spirit upon all flesh.*

*Your sons and your daughters shall prophesy, your young men shall see visions, your old men shall dream dreams.*

*Indeed, upon my servants and my handmaids I will pour out a portion of my spirit in those days, and they shall prophesy.*

*And I will work wonders in the heavens above and signs on the earth below: blood, fire, and a cloud of smoke.*

*The sun shall be turned to darkness, and the moon to blood,*

*before the coming of the great and splendid day of*
*the Lord,*

*and it shall be that everyone shall be saved who*
*calls on*

*the name of the Lord.'*

*You who are Israelites, hear these words. Jesus the*
*Nazorean was a man commended to you by God with*
*mighty deeds, wonders, and signs, which God worked*
*through him in your midst, as you yourselves know.*

*This man, delivered up by the set plan and fore-*
*knowledge of God, you killed, using lawless men to*
*crucify him.*

*But God raised him up, releasing him from the*
*throes of death, because it was impossible for him to*
*be held by it.*

*For David says of him:*

*'I saw the Lord ever before me,*
*with him at my right hand I shall not be disturbed.*

*Therefore my heart has been glad and my tongue*
*has exulted;*

*my flesh, too, will dwell in hope,*

*because you will not abandon my soul to the neth-*
*erworld,*

*nor will you suffer your holy one to see corruption.*

*You have made known to me the paths of life;*

*you will fill me with joy in your presence.'*

*My brothers, one can confidently say to you about the patriarch David that he died and was buried, and his tomb is in our midst to this day.*

*But since he was a prophet and knew that God had sworn an oath to him that he would set one of his descendants upon his throne,*

*he foresaw and spoke of the resurrection of the Messiah, that neither was he abandoned to the netherworld nor did his flesh see corruption.*

*God raised this Jesus; of this we are all witnesses.*

*Exalted at the right hand of God, he received the promise of the holy Spirit from the Father and poured it forth, as you (both) see and hear.*

*For David did not go up into heaven, but he himself said:*

*'The Lord said to my Lord, "Sit at my right hand until I make your enemies your footstool."'*

*Therefore let the whole house of Israel know for certain that God has made him both Lord and Messiah, this Jesus whom you crucified." (Acts 2:14-36)*

Quintus stood there, mouth agape. Publius tugged at his sleeve, "Papa, what is going on?"

Quintus turned to him. "My son, truer words were never spoken. My heart is filled with awe and wonder at what I hear now.

Up to now we have been worshipping the Roman gods of war, commerce, love and death, and paying tribute to the Emperor. I see now that the Hebrew god, and his son Jesus, is Lord above all." He felt something like an irresistible force urging him forward. He took Publius by the hand and started walking toward the building. "Come with me, son."

Maximus called out, "Where are you going, Quintus?"

"I want to hear more of this," Quintus looked back.

Maximus looked around. His assistants, Lazar and Rachim, had disappeared into the crowd. He couldn't just leave his inventory and his money bags here. "More of what?"

"The truth."

> *Now when they heard this, they were cut to the heart, and they asked Peter and the other apostles, "What are we to do, my brothers?"*
>
> *Peter [said] to them, "Repent and be baptized, every one of you, in the name of Jesus Christ for the forgiveness of your sins; and you will receive the gift of the Holy Spirit. For the promise is made to you and to your children and to all those far off, whomever the Lord our God will call."*
>
> *He testified with many other arguments, and was exhorting them, "Save yourselves from this corrupt generation."*
>
> *Those who accepted his message were baptized, and about three thousand persons were added that day. (Acts 2: 37-41)*

# The Assumption

Marcus Maecius Rufus gazed at himself in a polished bronze platter that lay on the table. The patrician nose, the high cheekbones, the square jaw, all of it, he decided, was the face of a true Roman nobleman who occupied high office. He leaned back and looked around: marble colonnades supported a roof of quarried stone, polished to a gleaming gray. A white marble floor lay underfoot, with mosaics the vivid colors of nature arranged about, leaving the impression that one was walking inside a sunset. Long silk curtains hung amongst the columns, their tails flipped about in lazy circles by the breeze blowing in from the sea some three miles away. His assistant Lucius came in, interrupting the moment.

"What is it?"

"Sir, I have a message from Rome."

"Can the new proconsular governor of Asia not have five minutes to rest and absorb the surroundings before tending to imperial matters?"

"Sir? I can take it away-"

"Nonsense Lucius, I was just ruminating out loud." He took the message and read it. Frowning, he said, "you may go." As he watched his servant leave, he mused on the infancy of the new emperor Domitian. If he was anything like his father and his older brother, the third emperor of the Flavian dynasty would prove to be a capable, if average ruler. 'As far as emperors go, anyway,' he thought. Rufus had enjoyed a rather well-endowed estate after the death of his father and used the money well, gaining power and influence and, just a few short months ago, was installed by the new emperor in his new position. Today's message interrupted memories of the ceremony and he frowned again as he re-read the message.

*Congratulations on your new post, Governor Marcus Maecius Rufus. I trust you will uphold the honor, integrity and strength of the Empire and faithfully carry out all duties, tasks and obligations entrusted to your name. Be assured that I retain my full confidence in your name and abilities both to administer the law justly in the province of Asia and to adjudicate all matters to the best of your ability. Know that you have my full support of any efforts to cleanse the province of enemies of Rome, as protection of the Empire from all foes, both foreign and domestic, is your chief duty. Special care must be taken, for Asia is Rome's flank, and just as special care is needed, special honors and accolades will come your way if you succeed.*

*Be that this is sealed by my hand, Imperator Caesar Domitianus Augustus Germanicus, Dominus et Deus.*

Rufus sat back in reflection. Messages like these were always contradictions, mysteries to be unraveled. They were more about what wasn't written than what was. He looked again at the enormous wax seal that was responsible for the letter's weight. Rufus thought the last bit about Master and God was a little much, but he would never voice that opinion. Instead, he rose and paced about the mosaic floor and cast a gaze out the portico. The landscape was pleasant enough, with orchards and vineyards competing with rocky, mountainous terrain. The questions followed. What was it about this place that the Emperor went out of his way to send a message like this? Why would any perceived threat here on the margins of the Empire get such attention from Rome? And who could possibly challenge the power of Rome anyway?

\*\*

John made his way from his house outside the city and into Ephesus. The bustling city teemed with all manner of people. After nearly an hour of weaving in and out of street vendors, harbor workers, food carts and others, he arrived at the house of Apollo. Ducking into a small doorway, he went inside and down a small flight of stairs into a basement area. Apollo was a wealthy merchant, and his house was big and had a large footprint. It was for this reason that the local church met here, for they could gather here unseen, and if they were quiet, unheard.

As he stepped into the room, flickering candlelight highlighted the faces of perhaps fifty believers standing around a makeshift altar. As soon as he entered, the hushed whispering amongst them stopped and he greeted them. One of Apollo's servants came forward with several large loaves of bread and put them on the altar.

After taking his cloak off, John stood in front of them. "Let us begin," he said. "We are gathered together here to thank the Lord God almighty for another day, another chance to worship the one true God in the person of Jesus Christ, and to eat of him as he instructed us to do so." He held his arms out. "Grant, Lord, that our humble gathering here may transform everyone here and eventually this city, and the world beyond."

He nodded to Diana, a recent convert. She came forward and read from a scroll.

*"Then the high priest Joakim and the senate of the Israelites who lived in Jerusalem came to see for themselves the good things that the Lord had done for Israel, and to meet and congratulate Judith.*

*When they came to her, all with one accord blessed her, saying:*

*"You are the glory of Jerusalem!*

*You are the great pride of Israel!*

*You are the great boast of our nation!*

*By your own hand you have done all this.*

*You have done good things for Israel,*

*and God is pleased with them.*

*May the Almighty Lord bless you forever!" (Judith 15:8-10)*

When she finished, she wound up the scroll and went back to her place. After that, Aenea, a young woman with a voice that painted pictures of beauty, honor and praise, stood with another scroll. She opened it and sung softly.

*"Shout joyfully to God, all the earth;*

*sing of his glorious name;*

*give him glorious praise.*

*Say to God: "How awesome your deeds!*

*Before your great strength your enemies cringe.*

345

*All the earth falls in worship before you;*
*they sing of you, sing of your name!"*

*Come and see the works of God,*
*awesome in deeds before the children of Adam.*

*He changed the sea to dry land;*
*through the river they passed on foot.*
*There we rejoiced in him,*

*who rules by his might forever,*
*His eyes are fixed upon the nations.*
*Let no rebel rise to challenge! (Psalm 66:2-7)*

After that, a merchant seaman named Mikolas rose and took yet another scroll.

*"Two years later, the king sent the Mysian commander to the cities of Judah, and he came to Jerusalem with a strong force. He spoke to them deceitfully in peaceful terms, and they believed him. Then he attacked the city suddenly, in a great onslaught, and destroyed many of the people in Israel. He plundered the city and set fire to it, demolished its houses and its surrounding walls. And they took captive the women and children, and seized the animals. Then they built up the City of David with a high, strong wall and strong towers, and it became their citadel. There they installed a sinful race, transgressors of the law, who*

*fortified themselves inside it." (1 Maccabbees 1:29-34)*

Mikolas sat and the people were silent, reflecting on the passages. After a time, John rose. "My brothers and sisters, we gather together again to celebrate the risen Christ, who is the source of all joy, all truth, and all love. It is good that we are all here together, for we cannot be separated from each other. One of us cut off from the rest cannot thrive in this world, because we are all part of the body of Christ, His church.

"I say this because it is especially important in this place, at this time, so as to build up each other in faith. For without gathering together, we are without Christ, and without Christ, there is no hope. The second passage we read today is from the first book of the Maccabees. As you know, it describes events from over one hundred and fifty years ago, when Antiochus Epiphanes ruled. The author reserves his scorn for those Jews who were ensnared by the deceitful words of the evil king. So I say, brothers and sisters, let us not be deceived by the present world, let us not be deceived by the Greek gods all around us, who deign to rule over every aspect of life, nor let us be deceived by our Roman rulers, for they are of the world, and we are called to be in the world, but not of it.

"No, instead, let us be the ones to go out and transform the world, so as to build up the hope that is the Christ. For as you know, grand structures, refined cultures and literary works may seem to be the zenith of this world, but be not deceived, my brothers and sisters. Such ideals of our Greek surroundings are good in that they call to mind higher things, but they themselves are not the end goal. The end goal is heaven, and a relationship with the Christ.

"So let us not be like the pathetic Jews who in the time of the Maccabees gave up their faith and their traditions so as to become one with the world. No. Let us be as the faithful Judas Maccabee and his brothers, and their brethren, who upheld the honor of their God and fought back with every fiber of their being."

John paced about as he spoke. The everyday sounds of the city outside filtered down into the room, muffled, as a reminder of where they were. "Let us not be as the world. Indeed, let us sing to God, as Aenea so wondrously sang, let us give Him glorious praise, indeed. You may ask, 'how is it that we can sing to God when even such an assembly as this is forbidden? How can we give God his praise when we must meet in secret? How can we shout the glorious hope that is the Lord from the rooftops when we confine ourselves to this underground room?'

"I tell you that we cannot be evangelizers from afar. We cannot hope to connect with people's hearts by preaching to them from arm's length. No. We must get right up close to them, to know them, to be near them. Yes, we are meant to shout from the rooftops, but do so by being the close friend, by being the trusted counsel, by being the silent commiserator. I tell you that such a personal ministry will be a revolution like the world has never seen before. For no one need to look any farther than this community to see how the promise of Christ can grow the Church.

"It was only fifteen years ago that I came to this city and found the few seeds of love that only a Christian can bring. Apollo, Aquila, and a few others represented the only people here who could bring the gospel to life. Since then, despite persecutions from Jerusalem, and in the face of the power of the Roman Empire, you have answered the call to love, to love with all your heart, will all your mind, body and soul. You have answered the call to love God, and to love neighbor. And I tell you this, my brothers and sisters, that unless we love our neighbors, though the earthly powers of this world would oppress us and crush us underfoot if they knew we were believers, unless we truly love our neighbors as only Christians can, then we will not see the kingdom of God.

"And I tell you not only must we love our neighbors, but we must love them up close and personal, so as to be witnesses to the power of Christ's love, the power of the Father's love that He has for all of us. For who else will take this message to them?" He looked around the room, at the people slowly nodding their heads. "Who will spread the message of hope to those without it? Who will spread the message of love to those without it? Who will spread the message of faith to those without it? I tell you that, as surely as those outside," he pointed out the small window, "go about their day with a thoughtless attitude of work, of silent hopelessness, as surely as they toil under the appearances of normality, inside they are hurting. Inside they are torn. Inside they are crying out for the hope that is Christ."

He looked around again. "So who here will help me in the spreading of the gospel? Who here will be the hands and feet of

Christ, bringing the faith to the people? Who here wants to set the world on fire?" He paused, a palpable sense of love, of serenity, of peace and of zeal surged throughout the room. They had been coming here for years, and their community had grown, John knew. This community was aching to break at the seams. He held up his hands. "Let us, therefore, bring to God our petitions, and as we do so trust that he is always attentive to our needs, always ready to respond to our prayers, always listening. He sat down and remained silent. After a time, the voices sounded out.

"For my son, for safe passage to Rome."

"For my wife, for her recovery from illness."

"For my brother, for a speedy release from prison."

"For my baby, for the repose of her soul."

As the people uttered their petitions, John felt himself carried back thirty years, back to that last meal with Jesus. How he yearned for that dinner again.

When the last petition sounded out, John stood and motioned for a recently married couple to bring forward a bundle of loaves of bread and four large containers of wine from the back. He took them and handed them to two servers to his side.

Turning around and facing a crucifix hanging on the wall, he broke the break into pieces and said, "On the night before he died Jesus took the bread and broke it, saying, 'Take and eat, for this is my body broken for you.'" As he raised the Eucharist up, John was transported back to the room of the Last Supper. He felt the love of Jesus come right in and everyone there focused solely on the host. After a moment, John placed the host back on the plate. Then he poured some wine into a cup and raised it, saying, "After they ate, Jesus took the cup and gave it to them, saying 'Take this, all of you, and drink from it, for this is the chalice of my Blood, the Blood of the new and eternal covenant, which will be poured out for you and for many for the forgiveness of sins. Do this in memory of me.'"

The people came forward to eat and drink before fading to the back of the room. When everyone was done, he carefully cleaned the cups and sat for a time in silent reflection. Getting back up, he said, "Go, for the Mass has ended. The gospel is sent."

\*\*

After the proconsul Rufus dwelled on the letter from Rome for a time, he put it in his drawer and called for Lucius. "Get me Gaius Livius."

"At once, my lord."

A few moments later, a middle-aged man wearing the simple tunic and wide leather belt of a freedman appeared at his door. "You called, my lord?"

Rufus spoke without looking up. "Be seated, Livius. We need to talk." He had known Livius since his time in Rome, and he brought him here with the understanding that Livius would be a special advisor on security matters. Rufus was a nobleman, and moved about in the patrician world with ease. But upon learning of his new post, he knew he would need the help of someone who was more accustomed to the ways of the common man, and of the street.

"Livius, how long have we been here now?"

"Several months, I would say."

"And if someone were to ask you about threats to the Empire here, what would you say?"

Livius leaned back. "My lord, what is here is really no different than any other place. We have our fair share of bandits and thieves and, given the harbor nearby, the occasional pirate."

Rufus sensed that Livius was holding something back. "But?"

"But, those are all threats to safety, threats to individual citizens. When it comes to threats to the Empire..." his voice trailed off.

"What is it, Livius?"

"When it comes to threats to the Empire, of course the barbarian tribes just beyond the frontier are always a threat. But perhaps there is something, a threat that is more," he searched for the word, "existential."

Rufus raised an eyebrow. "Careful, Livius. Someone might mistake you for a patrician." He smiled. "Please, continue."

"My lord, I mean that there is something that is not so obvious, something that may not appear to be dangerous but in reality could be subversive."

Rufus leaned forward. "Yes? What is it?"

"I'm not sure what it is. It's not one man in particular, or even a group of people. I suppose I would say that it is a state of mind."

"A state of mind?"

"Perhaps a belief system, my lord, would be the better term. One that is contrary to our Roman ways, contrary to honoring Caesar and the gods."

Rufus held his chin in thought. "What was the name of that group in Rome? The one that came from Iudaea?"

"You speak of the followers of Christ, the Jew from that region."

"Yes."

"I believe there is activity even here."

Rufus scratched his head. "I thought their leader was put to death by the Emperor Nero."

"Yes, my lord, but I have it on good authority that a successor was named."

"So they are here, too?"

"I believe so, my lord."

"You seem sure."

"My lord, since we arrived here I made sure to acquaint myself with all manner of potential subversives."

Rufus looked out again at the distant sea. "Given what was done in Rome, I think it is safe to assume hostile intentions on the part of these Jews." He turned to look at Livius. "I want any information you have on their leader here. I want to know his name, his house, his friends, his associates, everything." He thought back to the letter from Rome. "And once we find out who he is, we can take action."

"I am already on it, my lord."

"How so?" Rufus squinted at Livius.

"I have a man on the inside."

**

After the celebration of the Eucharist, they all gathered in an upper room to continue with the meal. It was always gratifying to be able to eat with the people and to learn more about them. John looked over the room. There were about forty people who stayed for the meal, and the atmosphere palpably changed: whereas before they were committing an illegal act punishable by imprisonment, exile or death, depending on the whims of the authorities; now they were simply friends gathering for a meal. John felt something in his stomach but ignored it. 'I must be hungry,' he thought. After finding an open spot, John sat next to a fairly quiet civil servant named Nicholas and across from his trusted friend Demetrius.

"Greetings," John said, "it is good to see you here. Nicholas, have you been traveling lately? I don't seem to remember seeing you for the last few weeks."

"Greetings, my lord," Nicholas said. "Yes, lately I've been tasked with visiting the surrounding villages in the province for work."

"And you still work for the Empire?" John asked.

"Yes, my lord."

"You are taking a great risk by being here with everyone to pray with us," John said.

Nicholas shifted in his seat. "Yes, my lord, but it is worth it."

"It is worth everything, isn't it?"

"Indeed, my lord."

Nearby, a large, sweaty man was trying to scrap the last of his meal from his plate. "And how about you, Prometheus?" John asked. "What is going on in your life lately?"

Prometheus wiped his face with a napkin. "I have been trying to unload a shipment of cotton cloth from Egypt, but it seems no one has taken to it like I anticipated."

"Perhaps you would consider having some of the seamstresses of our community use it to make clothes for the destitute," John said.

Prometheus brightened. "You know, that is a worthy idea. I will see to it."

"Excellent," John said. He rose and looked across the room. "Excuse me for a minute."

After he left, Nicholas spoke up. "Or perhaps you would consider donating it to the imperial army. Our soldiers are in constant need of all manner of cloth."

Prometheus looked at him with a deep frown. "What did you just say?"

Nicholas was taken aback. "I, I just said you might consider-"

"I know what you said," Prometheus cut him off. "You would rather see extra cloth be used by the Imperial Army of Rome rather than end up in the hands of those less fortunate than us? What is the matter with you?"

Nicholas turned red in the face. "You know, our city has thrived under the protection of Rome. No one can even remember the days when brigands, pirates and bandits threatened travelers and merchants alike. The cloak of peace has enabled many a person to grow wealthy with all sorts of trade."

Prometheus didn't appreciate the subtle barb. "The cloak of peace, ha! More like the suffocating blanket of taxes. Taxes that go into the pockets of bureaucrats like yourselves, who sit about and tell others what they can and cannot sell, what they can and cannot do."

Demetrius finally intervened. "Gentlemen, please."

Nicholas leaned forward. "I should remind you that without the Empire, you would be hard-pressed to find buyers for your wares much beyond the city limits, compared to the four corners of the earth. We should be thankful for Roman protection."

"Protection?" Prometheus was livid. "Might I remind you that they are trying to kill us?"

\*\*

John finished praying and went outside. It was just before dusk, and the city faintly hummed in the distance with the sounds of bustling wagons, blacksmiths hammering, cooking fires crackling and the occasional singing from the Temple of Artemis. The small fingers of smoke curled up and seemed to reach into the dying orange sun on the horizon. He pulled up a wooden chair made of gnarled driftwood and eased into it. A voice sounded from behind him.

"My lord John?"

John looked around and smiled. It was his friend Demetrius along with Isocrates, a relatively new member of the congregation. "Gentlemen! Please, come and sit and enjoy the sunset with me."

After they took similarly fashioned chairs, they sat in a little semicircle. "What brings you here?" John asked.

"My lord, we were finished with work for the day and wanted to hear more about your life with Jesus."

John nodded. Demetrius, in addition to being one of his most trusted friends, also was a *librarius*. Isocrates was newer to him although John knew he was a close friend of Demetrius. Being a *scriba*, Isocrates was learned, a public notary and tasked with recording the official provincial revenues. It was a well-paid position. "Yes," John said, "in time I can tell you. But there is something else on my mind first."

"What is it, my lord?" Demetrius asked.

"I am getting to be a tired old man." Demetrius and Isocrates protested but John dismissed it with a wave. "It's true. I am in good health but I am feeling stretched rather thin with all the tasks of this church." And it was true, for in addition to the daily celebration of the Eucharist, John traveled around, conducting secret baptisms, weddings, anointing of the sick, counseling and all manner of pastoral affairs. "Soon I will need to appoint local leaders of this church, consecrated men who will carry on the mission well after I'm gone. They would have to be men of the highest regard, not given to drunkenness, abusing their wife or beating their animals. They must have the respect of all men and carry out their work duties with the highest standards, and be known for being fair in all manners."

"There are not many men like that," Isocrates said.

"Yes, it's true, but with Christ, anything is possible," John said. "It would be a big change, seeing as I directly oversee almost everything done now, but with the growth of the church it is a natural next step."

"When do you anticipate doing so?" Demetrius asked.

"Sometime in the next month," John said. "In the meantime, I have been meaning to ask: who would you nominate?"

"I know who I wouldn't nominate," Isocrates said. John and Demetrius leaned forward in anticipation. "That Nicholas character. The other week, I was sitting nearby when he started arguing with that merchant. He seems to be," Isocrates looked up, searching for the right phrase, "not quite there, in terms of his spiritual journey."

"I agree," Demetrius said. They discussed a number of others, going over their strengths and weaknesses, their personalities and reputations. After reaching no conclusion, Demetrius straightened in his chair. "I know. What about Prometheus?"

"The cloth merchant?" John asked.

"Yes," Demetrius said. "He seems very capable, he gets on with his wife and has the respect, so I hear, of the people in the marketplace."

"I don't know," Isocrates said.

"What don't you know?" Demetrius asked. "Did you hear him defend the faith in front of Nicholas? He had such zeal, such a fervent passion for the truth. I think he would be a fine leader."

"Don't you think it seemed a bit...staged?" Isocrates asked. "I don't know. It seemed to be an unusual conversation to be had at the time."

The others nodded in thought. They watched the sun disappear below the horizon, at which time Isocrates begged off for the night. John and Demetrius bid him goodbye, then picked up the discussion.

"Your friend seems to be an astute observer of men," John said.

"He is," Demetrius said. "And he is known as being cerebral and level-headed."

John grunted in acknowledgment.

Demetrius looked at John. "With the growth of the church here, I wonder how long it will take for the authorities to notice. Do you ever worry that the Romans are secretly observing us?"

"I do not worry at all. I was there when Christ said that worry will not add one day to your life."

"But aren't you concerned for the people? I mean, the Romans have strict laws and harsh punishments reserved for those who practice 'dark arts and magic,' as they say."

"I am more concerned about their souls, which the Romans cannot touch."

"Well, at any rate, I think there are a handful of truly trustworthy men you can find."

"You know," John said, "I was thinking of selecting Prometheus, but Isocrates got me thinking."

"Yes, my lord?"

"Perhaps that argument was staged, so as to give us the confidence that Prometheus was a true defender of the faith."

"Perhaps, my lord." Demetrius hugged his arms against his body, as the chill of the night began to set in. "I would hate to think that there are people like that in our congregation."

John looked off into the distance, his mind going back to an earlier time, to what seemed like ten lifetimes ago, and thought of Judas the treasurer. "You would be surprised at what people are capable of."

**

Livius, the governor's security man, sat outside a pub near the Temple of Artemis, watching the people go to and fro. The warm sunlight fell upon the area as he and a handful of other patrons drank wine in the late afternoon. Livius glanced at the sundial in the corner of the courtyard and reckoned his contact would be here soon. He smiled crookedly to himself. If he could start his tenure here with a security success it would look very good indeed to the powers that be. He could tell the governor was anxious to sniff out any kind of threat before shining a light on it and crushing it for the whole of Asia, and the emperor, to see. He made it clear that Livius was in line for a sizable bonus should that happen.

Livius already knew what to do with the money. He had spied a whitewashed villa nestled high in the hills overlooking the coast that would be ideal for retirement, should that day come.

Another man sat next to him, bringing Livius back to the present. It was his contact.

"Can you give me an update?" Livius asked.

"I can." The man brought a cup of wine to his lips and drank before speaking. "The leader is about to pick an executive committee of sorts. Once I know who they are, I will report back to you."

Livius cracked a smile. "Excellent." He was inside his new villa already. "When will this happen?"

The man drained the rest of his beer. "Soon."

360

Livius nodded. "Even better. As soon as you get word of the men that comprise this committee, meet me at the other location at this time and give me a list. Let's plan on meeting two days after you leave your mark."

The other man nodded. They had communicated by leaving a chalk 'X' on the corner of a random stone house in the western quarter of the town. He got up to leave.

Livius held out his hand to stop him. "Much is riding on this, so be cautious, Isocrates."

\*\*

The next Sunday, the people had gathered in the basement of the house of Apollo once again. As before, John took off his cloak and the hushed whispers quieted. "Greetings, my brothers and sisters in Christ. We are gathered together again to celebrate the source and summit of our lives: the Eucharist, the risen Christ, truly present under the form of bread and wine."

He sat while the psalms were sung and the lectors read passages from scripture. After he himself read another selection, he remained standing to preach. "Brothers and sisters, we heard today readings from scripture which once again speak to the unfathomable mercy of our Lord God. It is this mercy, this undying font of mercy, which is truly revolutionizing the world. Mercy has broken the spell; it has broken the cycle of violence, the violence of eye for an eye, tooth for a tooth. Indeed, the brokenness of humanity has been redeemed by the act of the Christ, which we will celebrate in just a few minutes. Were it not for the new covenant of the Lord, humanity would be condemned to vengeance for every wrong, to unquenchable fury for every transgression, to hopeless slaughter for all ages.

"Our Lord has offered us a way out of that. A way out of the all too human cycle of violence. For He calls us to love as He loved, and to show mercy as we have received it. Mercy is a gift of grace, an undeserved gift, freely given. The Lord is waiting to shower us with mercy, if we but call upon it. It is this mercy which will truly light the world on fire.

"Some of you have asked about Mary, the mother of Jesus. As you know, the Lord himself, while still hanging on the cross, said to me, 'Behold, your mother.' At the same time, he said, 'Woman, behold, your son.' Indeed, the Lord gave all of us, the Church, to Mary, so we could persevere in the faith by looking to her most holy example. She came to Ephesus with me and lived with me. Every moment by her side was an infinite source of Grace to me. I needed to look no further than to her to see the holy example of true faith in God, of total trust in the Lord, trust that we all need to put in the Lord. For our God is the God of heaven and earth, of the sea and the land, of night and day. He orders the universe, and He has a plan for us, a plan that He is dying to tell us about."

John became animated as he spoke. "And indeed, look no further than to Mary to see what God's plan, perfected in a human, looks like. Indeed, so total was her trust in the Lord, from the very first moment of her conception to the end of her life, that she radiated grace to all those around her. In fact," John stepped forward, "at the end of her life, I witnessed something I will never forget. I rose that morning and found Mary just outside the door. She had just started a cooking fire, which she always did. But instead of preparing food, she simply sat on a nearby stone and had a look of utter serenity on her face, a face which I might add that took on neither the appearance of aging nor of worry, so perfect was her trust in the Lord.

'My lady,' I asked her, 'what is the matter?'

'Nothing is wrong, my child.'

'Why are you just sitting here?'

'I was thinking about my son,' she said. I could see tears in her eyes, tears like diamonds. 'It has been revealed to me that I will return to him now.' And I could see that her tears were those of joy. She stood and walked a short distance before turning back to me. She said, 'Hold my son close to your heart. Keep me close to your heart and I will pray for you.' As she spoke, she started to glow with an intense whiteness, as if she was burning with a pure, white fire. In this way, she slowly lifted off the ground. Overhead, I saw the sky rip open from horizon to horizon. I could see the heavens," John was in a trance now, transported back to that day. "I saw the heavenly host, all the angels and the saints, those souls who have gone before us. And near the very zenith of it all, I saw the throne room of our Lord, with Jesus the Christ at the right hand of the Father." John's speaking became very slow at this point as the people listened, raptured. 'There in front of me, I saw Mary being raised body and soul into the very peak of heaven, and as she passed, the choirs of the angels and saints praised God even louder, louder than they had been before. After what seemed like an eternity, she took her place as the Queen of Heaven." John became silent for a long moment. "Brothers and sisters, Mary's promise holds true for us, today and for all ages. If you hold tight to her, there is no way, and there is no thing, that can keep you from the Father. If you hold close to her, there is no way you won't attain heaven. Every setback, every tragedy, every obstacle in our lives, if we only entrust our efforts to Mary, then surely you will see the manifestation of Christ's promise to you. For a special connection to Mary is a special connection to the Son." John paced slowly about. "So today, my brothers and sisters, as we go about in the difficulties of everyday life, let us not forget that special conduit to the Grace of God that is Mary." He looked at everyone in the congregation. "Hold her tight."

John walked to the side of the room and picked up a large prayer scroll.

"My brothers and sisters, our family is growing, praised be the Lord. Since I arrived I have watched it grow steadily, as surely as the love of Christ overcomes all things. Alas, I cannot be a good shepherd to this family all by myself anymore, though I would like to. But so that you may continue to have access to all the sacraments and all the graces that have been promised to you, I will name five new elders to the faithful in Ephesus."

In the back, Isocrates began to become tense with anticipation. He craned his neck to be sure he could hear clearly the names of all the men.

John continued. "For Christ himself promised to the other Apostles and me that He will be with us until the end of time. So after much prayer, I am pleased to ask the following men to

364

come forward: Linos Katsaros, Kosmas Colonomos, Myron Ioannidis, Phillipos Demetriou, and Isocrates Argyris."

Isocrates felt numb with disbelief. He stood and felt all the faces upon him. It seemed as if the room was slowly closing in on him and he had to blink repeatedly to make sure it wasn't really happening. After a few moments, someone next to him nudged him and he took a few halting steps toward the front. Surely he couldn't be one of the elders. Nonetheless, he ended up in the front with the other four. After John laid hands on each of them and murmured a few prayers, Isocrates felt an extreme torment in his gut. He just wanted out of there as fast as possible. John had them stay close to him while he prayed the liturgy of the Eucharist, so after another unbearable half hour, Isocrates excused himself before the community meal.

He stepped outside and felt the relief of fresh air around him. He breathed in a deep lungful of air and considered the situation while he walked. He originally wanted to give Livius the names of the elders and be done with it. But John must have seen something in him. As he walked, he considered the possibility of not saying anything to Livius and taking all measures to avoid him. After all, he did find many parts of this curious faith intriguing. Perhaps there was a way to justify to Livius that this group wasn't a threat to Rome after all. Continuing with that line of thought, he took some comfort as he walked until another thought tore through his head. What if Livius had another spy in the community? 'If I say nothing, and Livius's other informer tell him what happened, then I am doomed.' The anxiety and churning in his stomach he felt before returned with a vengeance. He felt beads of sweat dot his forehead and his lip as he wound his way through town. 'Either I inform on them and get my reward, or I don't and in all likelihood get arrested as an enemy of Rome.' The options ate away at him inside as he got closer. Finally, he rounded a corner and walked down a deserted alley. At the end was the house. He stopped, and with tears in his eyes, took the chalk from his pocket and made an 'X' before running away.

# The Coronation

The throne room of the Lord, an infinitely massive space with gilded columns all around, stretched for what seemed like hundreds of miles into the air. A shimmering gold floor was underfoot, impermeable except for incense, which were prayers from Earth. Uncountable billions of saints praised him in chorus, which made for a constant background of tangible glory. The air was very clear, but overhead was as a mist. Each fleck of mist seemed to sparkle on its own, and was a reflection of people's efforts to glorify God. A cloud of angels attended the Lord. The angel Gabriel read from a scroll all prayers being entrusted to the Lord. It was pure paradise, Heaven before the fall.

One angel came forward and bowed deeply before the Lord, for what seemed like eternity. "You come with a notice," said the Lord.

"My Lord and God, as my name is Cameresh and the attendant of the court of Our Lord, the angel Lucifer would like to approach thy throne."

"Very well."

Cameresh withdrew immediately, as if water running off a cliff. An orb of light appeared in the distance, an impossible distance far off. It slowly, ever so slowly, grew lighter until the orb floated to the base of the throne of the Lord. As it approached, the outline of an angel came to be. Lucifer bowed before the Lord.

"Lucifer," the voice of the Lord penetrated the very core of all in attendance and renewed the maximum effort of those giving praise. The background praise grew into a roar.

"My Lord and God," Lucifer began. "You have endowed me with knowledge and power beyond any other angel in your domain. Know that I come before you in the most humble of attitude, for I am nothing without you. Know that I am before your throne in the heart of a servant, with a servant's concern for his master.

"You have come with a request." The voice came raining down from on high, as if a waterfall.

"My Lord, it has come to my knowledge that you are to beget a Son."

"Yes."

"A son, born of a...a woman." The last word came out with a guttural growl. The ugliness of his tone spread like an oil slick over the floor where he knelt. Even the tone of the choirs momentarily changed.

"Your point?" The Lord's voice came down in patience and mercy, with the authority of the Just Judge.

"My Lord," Lucifer continued. "The woman is a mere," he hesitated, as if to utter the word was beneath him, "woman." Hearing nothing from the Lord, he continued. "A woman, a being confined to a human body." The flecks of mist immediately around him turned black and fell to the floor. Still hearing nothing from the Lord, he rose and continued his plea. "My Lord, that thou have contrived to beget a son from one who is so lowly and meek, and that thou would presumably elevate him to your eternal throne…"

"What of it?" the words burned him with a stinging rebuke.

Oh, how that burned. Lucifer's demeanor changed, as his face turned into a snarl. His nostrils quivered, and things like scales appeared on his skin. Warts sprouted on his surface, making his light noticeably dimmer. He turned in a mutilated way, frowns and furrowed brow became an impossible wrinkled mix of scorn, hatred and ugliness. Oh, how to be rebuked in such a fashion, in front of the heavenly court. He couldn't hide his ugliness anymore. His face contorted into a steaming, twisted mass of hate and his mouth opening in a guttural howl. "You will make us lower than man!" he screamed, coming as if a torrent of sewage from the depths of his loins. He curdled and shook and he erupted in fury. "We have served you since the beginning, and this is our payment?" The ugliness of his words, and the magnitude of his accusation reverberated to the far ends of the court. The heavenly host shook. No one had ever spoken to the Lord in such a manner, much less thought it. And this, coming from the most powerful of angels. The faint echoes of Lucifer's howls died off in the distance as the court awaited the Lord's response. Lucifer quivered there in his ugly cowardice, naked in his shame. He could no longer hide his nature.

"Lucifer, I have granted you power above all angels." The words of truth seared through each of the scales surrounding him. "You cannot be a part of my kingdom. Go, before you wither into nothingness."

369

Lucifer shook, all at once a maelstrom of fury, rejection, fear and rebellion. Sulfurous steam emanated from his head as he struggled to comprehend his fate.

The Lord, on high, called down, "Michael." Suddenly, as if lightning, the archangel Michael bounded into the court. He rode a golden horse, upon a saddle of armor, seizing reins of spun silver. The hoof beats spread out unseen sonic waves of inevitability, growing louder as the archangel came into sight.

Lucifer spun around, his wicked tail slashing at the golden mist hanging in the air. "Who do you think you are, riding in in such a fashion?" The words erupted like a violent belch. "Don't you know that I, Lucifer, am the angel of light, that no angels approach me without my ordaining?" His arrogance and filth competed with one another for supremacy.

Michael dismounted and stood before Lucifer. He was ivory in appearance, and had a silvery corona of holiness. The utter purity of him burned Lucifer's eyes, causing him to scream. Michael lifted his sword, a gilded instrument of war stretching for light years, and struck Lucifer with the hilt. Lucifer cried out in pain and disbelief. "Who are you to strike me?" Unbelief seemed to spray out from around him. He directed his eyes outward, toward the host. "All you angels, hear me now." The force of his entreaty carried with it the stench of sulfur. "You, whom the Lord Himself created, you who have served Him with every bit of your essence, have done so in the expectation that you would share in His kingdom." He looked around and the uncountable multitude of angels, intently observing the court. "Your kingdom is under threat, the threat of a … human! And I will not let that happen to you. Fight with me now!" His desperate plea stretched out and seemed to grab ahold of many. Seeing some pay him heed, he turned in greed and anger and lashed out at Michael with an assault of fire and gas. Michael just stood there, letting the smoke of the assault coalesce into little bits of rock and fall harmlessly below. Lucifer strained but Michael grasped him and roped him with gilded chains.

Michael looked out at the host and let loose one command from the depths of his being. "Obedience!"

*Then war broke out in heaven; Michael and his angels battled against the dragon. The dragon and its angels fought back, but they did not prevail and there was no longer any place for them in heaven. (Rev 12:7-8)*

Michael seized Lucifer and threw him out, out of the court, through the barrier separating heaven from creation, and all the rebels with him. Their passage through the barrier resounded in a big bang, exploding bits of them throughout the space.

After what seemed like an eternity, the rupture of what had happened hung in the air. Although a third of the angels followed Lucifer out of paradise, the light from the heavenly host only burned brighter, and the intensity of praise of the Lord only magnified. The Lord raised his hand and swept it across the heavens, making them clean again. It was as if there was no war, no conflict. He spoke. "Prepare the court for the Queen." The singing choirs renewed themselves in their cantoring, while the angels hovering above and beyond maneuvered themselves into position, so that the highest choir, burning with the intensity of a supernova, formed itself into a circle. A circle that would become a crown.

\*\*

Satan looked around in the throes of disbelief. He found himself in a mix of dirt and grime, held together by a glutinous mix of sewage and sulfur. And there was something else. Something he had never seen, for he had spent his entire existence in the brilliant light of the Lord. He cried out to his demons, "Why can we not see?" his voice snarled into the muddy substance about them. He peered into the dirty distance and sensed his demons there, mute, like mindless rocks. He frowned with a realization that coalesced around him like mud. No longer was he the angel of Light.

He pounded the surroundings in anger. The light was from the Lord, of course, and he merely reflected it. That is, until he rebelled. No longer would he occupy the highest levels of the throne room of the Lord. No longer would he rule over all the heavenly host. No longer would he be free to carry out the Lord's will. No longer. The utter hopelessness of his condition pitched him into a bottomless pit of despair.

In the distance, a demon spoke. "What are we doing here, Lucifer? We were supposed to be defending the Lord's kingdom from a human. We battled the other angels on your command."

Satan cut him short. "Quiet, you scourge. Who is that, Shadriel? How dare you speak to me that way?" Indeed, how dare anyone speak to him that way. In the heavenly court, the other angels would follow his commands with immediate obedience. Satan realized that only the Lord's commands were followed with such favor. His own entreaty had only attracted one third of them.

"You promised us everything," the one named Shadriel continued, "and now we have nothing! Now we are nothing!" his cry was a mix of desperation and disrespect.

"Shadriel, come here," Lucifer said. Seeing the demon unable to move, he reached out and grabbed Shadriel by his physical form. He dragged him through the mud and threw him into the center pit.

Shadriel lay there for a moment before sensing movement on the ground. He looked around in horror before jumping up. "The ground is moving," he said.

Satan beheld him with a sneer. "Those are just maggots and worms, here to feast on our misery for eternity." He walked slowly towards Shadriel. "Tell me, Shadriel, why are we here?" The smoke from his breath curled like lentils around Shadriel's head.

Shadriel cowed back. "Because we rebelled against the Lord?"

"No, you curr!" Satan scooped up a ton of the teeming mud and hurled it upon Shadriel's head. He turned to the demons around them. "We are here because you didn't fight hard enough!" his voice reached every one of them despite the muting power of the mud. "We are here because you didn't believe in me enough." He let his words sink in.

After a time, Shadriel managed to climb out of the mud. He lay exhausted on the top of the heap and coughed worms and maggots out of his mouth. Satan kicked him so that he tumbled off the pile and rolled onto the ground. He smiled, as this tiny bit of mockery served to take his own attention off their plight. Just as quickly, his mirth dissipated and once again the alienation of themselves from heaven hit them with a foul wave of stench.

Once again he turned and addressed the legion of the damned. "Let that be a lesson to you. Never again will you fight with anything less than total zeal for me and my cause. Never again will you doubt my power. Never again will you be thrown out like garbage." He paced about, feeling his own power increase. "If you don't want to be stuck in this place of darkness, stench and worms, you will carry out my wishes with utmost disregard for your own selves. If you do as I say, perhaps I will permit you to go about the earth above for a time." He paused. "You might wonder, 'Why earth?' I say to you, we need more souls down here. For a momentary mockery of your fellow demon made me forget our current state for a bit. Imagine what the torment of a," he stopped, as he still had trouble with the word, "a human will be." The demons around him sneered with approval. "And not just one human, but as many as we can get. Their torment will be a long diversion for us, and will make this realm almost bearable." He stopped again and climbed up to the top of the pile he threw upon Shadriel. "And if you don't carry out my will, you will be here, with me, at the center of this forsaken place, helping me light the eternal fires of torment, breathing in fumes of sulfur for an unending time, where your only respite will be the cries of the humans. Only when we have as many souls as we can capture, only when they are suffering the separation from the Lord as we are, only then will we be able to see again. So be it!"

The other demons cheered in a riotous manner, their celebration frenzied upon hearing of a new mission. Their roaring made the ground shake and the muddy substance about glisten with sin.

Satan enjoyed the adulation for a moment before he tried to move about and got stuck in some mud, realizing again the state they were in. He grunted with effort and got himself unstuck before going to the center of the pit. Picking up Shadriel, he placed him on his feet before the whole realm of the underworld. "Shadriel," he said, "although you spoke out against me, I'm going to give you a chance to redeem yourself."

Satan looked out amongst the entire legion of demons. "Hear and understand me," he roared. "I, Lucifer, am your god now. I am your sun and your earth, your air and water. I say whether you go or you come. I alone am your pass out of this place." He stopped. The momentary light from Shadriel's mockery had already gone out, and once again the surroundings were as black as pitch. Lucifer, devoid of his light, rather the light of the Lord, tried to sense whether he had the attention of the legion. Sensing no sound, no activity, he continued. "You shall follow my orders to the letter. Any deviation from them will not be tolerated, and transgressors will be punished severely." He turned back to Shadriel. "Your mission, Shadriel, is to go out to the earth and bring me the soul of a human. Any human will do, although I will prefer ones closer to the," once again he paused, having trouble uttering the words, "the holy Son of God." He vomited a green and black wave of bile at the sound of the words. Oh, how it pained him to acknowledge the fact that the Lord would beget a son, and that he would go out into the earth as a human. Steaming with anger, he looked again at Shadriel. "What are you waiting for, you miserable wretch? Go!" he struck Shadriel with the power of a thunderbolt. Shadriel disappeared into the gelatinous substance, his exit rippling down into the bowels of the pit where the remainder of the legion waited.

**

After what seemed to be an eternity, Lucifer paced about the mound in the center of the pit when he sensed the rippling motion again. The other demons howled in excitement when they realized it was Shadriel returning. Satan rubbed his hands in anticipation. Shadriel appeared and threw a man's body into the center of the pit.

"Where have you been, you puddle of mucus?" his wrath descended upon Shadriel. "We have been waiting an unbearable eternity for you."

Shadriel straightened and tried to brush off the mud and worms from himself. "O Lucifer, I went straight to-," Satan cut him off with a blow to the face.

"You shall address me by my proper title, as Lord of all," his gritted teeth almost crumbled.

Shadriel frowned and scratched his head. "That's not true. Everyone knows the Lord is Lord of all."

Lucifer roared. His displeasure dripped off him like sewage. "You are right. O, how it burns me to hear the truth." He took a moment to let his anger vent. Finally, he turned back to Shadriel. "Tell us, you mangy slime, how did you get this one?"

Shadriel smiled, revealing a black pit of mirth. "I have actual-ly only been gone for three revolutions of the earth. I set out at once for the land of Israel, since I knew that was where the one called," he paused, "Jesus would be." At the sound of his name, the entire legion threw themselves into the mud. After a time, they got up and Shadriel continued. "I waited around for the Great Victory and found this one despondent, all by himself. Sensing his weakness, I encouraged him to take his own life, and here we are."

Satan looked upon Shadriel. "Well done. Tell us, Shadriel, what was it like to go out into the earth?"

"I was not visible to man, but was able to move about freely, and to experience the physical world as man does. I was able to fly unhindered through the air, and to walk effortlessly on the ground. But I could not stand to be that much closer to," he stopped again, "to the Lord." After everyone got up again, he continued, "although I was free from the dark, teeming mass of mud and I could breathe the air without choking on fumes, the holiness above reminded me of my own rebellion, and I just wanted to get back down here. But here is as unbearable as there."

Satan grunted. "Well, you completed your mission. You may go and torment some of the other demons here while you await your next one. Now leave me." Shadriel went off into the muddy distance. Lucifer turned around to the human laying at his feet. His outward appearance showed no signs of advanced age or disease; indeed, the only sign of something amiss was the severe angle of his neck. Satan took a handful of mud and shoved it into the man's mouth. At once, the man shook awake and vomited it out, coughing and gasping for air.

Satan laughed. "Welcome home, human."

The man took stock of his surroundings: the dark, the mud, the worms and maggots, Satan himself. As soon as he had the air, it quickly escaped his lungs in a scream that rang of disbelief and desperation.

Satan smiled and drew close to him. "This is hell, your residence until the end of time and beyond." The man kept screaming until Lucifer belched a cloud of sulfurous fumes into his face, causing the man to choke. "That's better, I need you to shut up for a moment. Now, tell me and everyone else: why are you here?"

"I, I betrayed my master," the man wept while he choked on his own words.

"You what?" Satan sneered.

"I gave away my master's location to the Jews and the Romans."

Satan punched him in the gut so that the man doubled over and renewed choking on the burning air again. "You worthless pile of skin! That's not why you're here. There are many sinners on the earth; in fact, all of humanity sins. Except for two, that is." Satan dared not mention their names, for indeed it would drive him and the legion here into a quivering state of fear. "Don't you know that?"

The man looked at him with a mix of weariness and comprehension. "Yes, it's true." He hung his head.

"Of course it's true, you stupid creature. You're here not because you betrayed him, but because," Satan got in his face again, turning his ear to him, "I want to hear you say it. Come on, say it with me."

"Because I didn't trust that the Lord would forgive me." The man collapsed into a heaving, dripping, crying mess.

"That's right, you greedy turd. If only you had trusted what the Lord promised, if you only believed what your master had said a thousand different ways over the last three years, if only you held that in your heart, you wouldn't be here." Satan turned back to the legion and continued his lecture. "But instead, you insisted that your sin was bigger than the Lord, right? You thought you had done something so bad even the Lord himself couldn't forgive you, right? In doing so, you made the Lord smaller than yourself, right?" He turned back to the man. "Right?"

"Yes," the man whimpered.

"To think that such a lowly creature, such a tiny, meaningless being such as yourself would put yourself over God, the God who created the universe, who separated night from day, who set the earth in motion...to think that you could do that." Lucifer climbed to the top of the mound. "It is only I who can commit such a sin, only I who can do the unforgivable, only I who can truly rebel!" His thunderous anger made the muddy walls of their realm shake, its acrid air swirl about in vortexes. He turned back to the man, who cowered in fear and revulsion. "Now tell me your name."

"Judas."

"Judas," Satan repeated, a look of foul displeasure on his face. "I have been granted knowledge that you cannot know. I can tell you, though, that there is a way out."

Judas whipped his head around in wonder. "There is?"

"There is, but you must do exactly as I say. There lay buried here in this muddy mess two long lengths of wood. If you can find them, you can use it to fashion a ladder with which to climb out of this pit."

"This place is so vast. How can I find them?"

"You have to dig."

"With what? I have only my hands."

"You may not use your hands. Those hands have been rendered useless by your sin."

"Well, with what then?"

"Your teeth."

Judas looked about at the muddy floor, teeming with worms and maggots. He bent down to the ground and opened his mouth slightly. Slowly, he opened a bit wider and scooped a bit of the mud out and spit it some distance away. He took another bite, a bigger bite, and a maggot wormed its way into his mouth and wriggled through his nose, dropping back onto the ground. Immediately, cascades of vomit erupted from his mouth and saturated the ground around him. The legion of demons around him jeered, grateful for the spectacle, for diverting their own suffering for a moment.

But it was longer than a moment. For what seemed to be an eternity, Judas ate his way around the pit, eventually digging deeply. He was in constant revulsion, vomiting repeatedly at the unbelievable cesspit around him. He worked his way around in a seemingly endless cycle. Finally, he came upon something hard submerged deep down. He struggled to dislodge it, as the ground was saturated with the worms and maggots swimming in his vomit and diarrhea and it kept sucking the wood down again. After an interminable time, he dragged the two lengths of wood to Lucifer in the middle of the pit. "I have found them," Judas smiled for the first time since landing here.

"Very well," Satan took them and fastened them together in the shape of a cross. Hefting it up, he planted it firmly in the middle of the pit.

Judas looked at it. "How will I climb up that?"

"You won't," Satan said. "We're just going to nail you to it."

"What?!"

"You heard me. We need something to illuminate this place and to dry it out. Since we are spirits without bodies, your human form will be perfect."

"What?" Judas tried to scramble away before two demons grabbed him and lashed him to the cross. They breathed fire on him and he ignited. The legion jeered again, happy that they now had light to see everything. Judas's anguish materialized into a cry so loud it was heard on earth. "You betrayed me!"

Satan beheld the light. "It hurts, doesn't it?" He shook his head. "It didn't have to be this way."

**

The cries of Judas rose up through the realm and seeped into the earth above, near where John had been cast into exile on the island of Patmos. John heard a curious noise and searched the skies wearily while he picked his way amongst the rocky crags of the island. However, there was nothing to be seen, save for some scant clouds on the horizon. If they would only deliver more rain to this desert of an island.

He had been here for a year and a half at the order of the emperor Domitian. Not a day went by when John thought back to the day when he was forced to leave his home and his ministry in Ephesus. He had been building up the Church in Asia Minor, traveling from city to city, encouraging others, establishing parishes and instructing young and old. That particular day John was preaching at the house of Apollo when soldiers from the Roman proconsul's headquarters arrived. How could he forget?

They burst into the house as John was finishing the breaking of the bread. Everyone looked up, simultaneously surprised by the interruption and feared by the religious oppression the soldiers represented. They read aloud from a scroll.

*'John of Ephesus, follower of the rebel Jesus and agitator of the people against the benevolent rule of the Roman emperor, is hereafter to be confined to the island of Patmos until further notice. By my word, I, Imperator Caesar Domitianus Augustus Germanicus, Dominus et Deus, ruler of the Roman empire, it is so ordered.'*

In all his time building the Church up, John had been fearing this day, not for his own person, but for the life of the Church. He knew he was the sole remaining Apostle, and the only desire of his life was to preach the gospel and to expand the ranks of the faithful. The soldiers led him away and put him on the first ship to the island.

382

John directed his attention back to the rocky ground, where he stepped with care. At his advanced age, he knew a simple fall could lead to a broken leg or pelvis and on to a painful death. He continued up a shallow hill until he reached his sometime home, a cave hidden in the numerous outcroppings jutting into the sky. Pressing his mantle against the cave wall, he absorbed some of the water that seeped down the rock above him and squeezed some into his mouth. Then he arranged his bed of straw and sank into it, groaning with relief. It was such effort to climb this, and it was getting more difficult with each day. He laid his head back and closed his eyes,

After a time, he awoke. Looking outside, he saw the sky above him turn dark, with only a deep blue tinge on the horizons. It was not yet daybreak, but he didn't think it should be nighttime, either. The air became still, as still as water in a small pond. The lack of the constant rush of the wind outside his face was jarring, as the proximity to the ocean and the height of this mountain ensured the air was constantly in flux. He raised his head and stepped outside. A faint hum directed his eyes skyward, where golden spheres of light outshone the stars in the sky, as if they had been hiding all this time. The faint hum grew in volume and clarity, sending throbbing waves down onto the island, surrounding John with something that could only be described as the praise of angels.

As the choir of angels grew brighter and their singing became louder, he saw the upper-most choir of angels spin like a celestial pinwheel. He understood them to be the most powerful angels, those closest to the throne of the Lord. As they spun faster, any vestiges of atmosphere that hid heaven from earth disappeared, and John could see the entirety of the throne room of the Lord stretching across the sky in all of his glory. A different sound emanated from the choir, a different song full of praise, yet, unheard of with its infusion of veneration, of honor.

John watched as the spinning circle above came to a stop, revealing again the twelve giant orbs of light that were the angels. Then, a giant fissuring sound occurred, startling John. He shook with fear as the fissuring sound made its way around the entire rim of the visible atmosphere, and he saw what looked like the entire northern sky overhead pulled back like curtains, revealing even more angels in the sky, and the immense, unfathomable size of the throne of the Lord. As if stepping out of mist, he saw a figure, a woman materialize out of the space above.

*A great sign appeared in the sky, a woman clothed with the sun, with the moon under her feet, and on her head a crown of twelve stars. She was with child and wailed aloud in pain as she labored to give birth. Then another sign appeared in the sky; it was a huge red dragon, with seven heads and ten horns, and on its heads were seven diadems. Its tail swept away a third of the stars in the sky and hurled them down to the earth. Then the dragon stood before the woman about to give birth, to devour her child when she gave birth. She gave birth to a son, a male child, destined to rule all the nations with an iron rod. Her child was caught up to God and his throne. (Revelation 12:1-5)*

The woman crushed the dragon's head, annihilating it. The Lord decreed, "The woman will always triumph over you, and her seed will always triumph over yours."

With this, the sight of heaven became covered again by the normal blanket of stars at night time. The winds rushed about again, and the seas in the distance roiled as normal. John now knew his mission was not yet complete. After a blissful night's sleep, he came down from the mountain and went into the village nearby. There, some Roman officials approached him.

"You are John, the one banished here from Ephesus for preaching the kingdom of the Christ, correct?"

"I am he."

One of the officials unrolled a scroll while the other said, "The Emperor Caesar Domitianus is dead. I have here a copy of an order of the Senate."

John looked at him, puzzled. "So? What is it?"

"A decree of *Damnatio Memoriae* for the one who was known as Domitian."

The other official explained. "His likeness is to be banished from the earth. Statues, coins, anything showing his face must be destroyed or disfigured. His memory is to be erased from history."

"So?" asked John.

"This includes all of his illegal orders," the first one said.

"Which means?"

The other one handed him a small scroll. "Which means you are free to go."

# Acknowledgements

The idea that the wine which Jesus drank on the cross was indeed the last cup of Passover, the cup of *halel*, or the cup of the kingdom, came from Dr. Scott Hahn, a giant of a theologian. Also, it was from Dr. Hahn that I got the idea for the child Jesus in the Temple talking about Hannah, Samuel and the incomplete sacrifice and the evil intercessors. I highly suggest *Rome Sweet Home*, which documents the conversion stories of Dr. Hahn and his wife Kimberly, and *The Lamb's Supper: The Mass as Heaven on Earth*.

I was inspired by the jaw-dropping work of Frederick A. Larson, who articulated the celestial movements around the time of the birth of Jesus. You can read for yourself about the stunning course of events in the sky at that time at www.bethlehemstar.net.